THE DEAD ROOM

Robert Ellis

PINNACLE BOOKS

Kensington Publishing Corp.

http://www.kensingtonbooks.com

PINNACLE BOOKS are published by

Kensington Publishing Corp.
850 Third Avenue
New York, NY 10022

All Kensington Titles, Imprints, and Distributed Lines are available at special quantity discounts for bulk purchases for sales promotions, premiums, fund-raising, and educational or institutional use. Special book excerpts or customized printings can also be created to fit specific needs. For details, write or phone the office of the Kensington special sales manager: Kensington Publishing Corp., 850 Third Avenue, New York, NY 10022, attn: Special Sales Department, Phone: 1-800-221-2647.

Pinnacle and the P logo Reg. U.S. Pat. & TM Off.

First Printing: August 2002
10 9 8 7 6 5 4 3 2 1

Printed in the United States of America

ALMOST DONE

Eddie heard something hit the concrete floor and peeked around his canvas as he tightened the straps on the gas mask over his head.

It was Rosemary. She'd fallen on her face, hit her chin, and wasn't moving. Her eyes were cracked open, and she was drooling. It looked as if she might have chipped a tooth. With her smile gone, she reminded him of a stupid whore girl again.

Eddie ignored the interruption and returned to his canvas. He'd been experimenting with various shellacs and thought he'd finally found one that would do. The work was coming together, he decided. It hadn't been a waste of time after all. He could feel the excitement in his chest as he took another step back, then another. The painting's perspective was changing. He liked the way the shellac drew out the color of the oils and gave the work added depth.

He sat down and peered at the painting through the mask. He couldn't take his eyes off it. His work even looked good in a fog. After a few moments, he got a grip on himself and noticed a gurgling sound coming from somewhere in the room.

It was his model, Rosemary—interfering again.

He rolled her over with his foot as if he'd come upon a casualty from a great war that couldn't be helped. Her eyes were open but lost somewhere in the battle. Sweat streamed from her body as if she'd been caught in the rain. He felt her forehead. She was warm, but not piping hot.

It was time, he decided.

BOOK YOUR PLACE ON OUR WEBSITE AND MAKE THE READING CONNECTION!

We've created a customized website just for our very special readers, where you can get the inside scoop on everything that's going on with Zebra, Pinnacle and Kensington books.

When you come online, you'll have the exciting opportunity to:

- View covers of upcoming books
- Read sample chapters
- Learn about our future publishing schedule (listed by publication month *and author*)
- Find out when your favorite authors will be visiting a city near you
- Search for and order backlist books from our online catalog
- Check out author bios and background information
- Send e-mail to your favorite authors
- Meet the Kensington staff online
- Join us in weekly chats with authors, readers and other guests
- Get writing guidelines
- AND MUCH MORE!

**Visit our website at
http://www.kensingtonbooks.com**

*In memory of my father
Francis J. Ellis
1926–1999*

ACKNOWLEDGMENTS

Without the help and effort of many friends, this book wouldn't exist. . . .

The novel was refined with the assistance of my editor, Kate Duffy, and my friends, John Truby and Michael Conway. Further creative distillations occurred with the help of Charlotte Conway and Meghan Sadler-Conway. I can't thank you all enough. I'm also grateful to John Diliberto and Kimberly Haas, who assisted with background information resulting in one of my favorite chapters in the book.

Special thanks go to Detective Rick Jackson, LAPD, Robbery-Homicide Division; Art Belanger, Pathologist Assistant, Yale University School of Medicine; and Don Widdoes; for their valuable knowledge, experience, and attention to detail. Any technical deviation in the book is my responsibility alone.

Further thanks go to Neil Oxman, for his good advice; Sharon Pinkenson and Peter Leokum, who opened the gates to the city; and all those who helped out at the district attorney's office, the Philadelphia Police Department, the Philadelphia Prison System, and the Philadelphia Museum of Art.

Thanks also go to my agent, Frank Weimann; my publisher, Laurie Parkin; my copy editor, Dan Larsen; and everyone who makes up the team at Kensington. Thanks for your enthusiasm and guidance and for giving me this special opportunity.

I'd also like to thank the booksellers I've met over the past year with the publication of my first novel, ACCESS TO POWER. Words can't describe how grateful I am for not only your effort and support, but also your great feedback and introducing me to readers.

Last but not least, I'd like to thank Mark Moskowitz; Clare Quinn; Thomas "Doc" Sweitzer; Karim Olaechea; David Marks; John W. Nelson; Ray Noll; Adrianne Carageorge; Lisa Cabanel; Bill Wachob; Deborah Conway; Olivia and Louie; my mother, Constance; my brother, Peter; Sharon and Nelson Rising; and Christopher, Cori, and Matthew Rising; for their unyielding support and goodwill.

AUTHOR'S NOTE

The events in this story are real and in some places happen every day. Still, this is a mystery/thriller, not a manual. Given the choice between fact or fiction, the story always won out. That's why the word *fiction* is printed on the spine of this book. If you've done any research, then you know that this is particularly true of the setting. Of all the cities that could have been chosen, Philadelphia is perhaps the least likely place this story could have occurred. Yet the style of the city, its relationship with art and history, and its European feel made it the only place I considered. When the story jumped out at me, I thought we could have some fun with it, get scared, check beneath our beds at night, and be happy together the next day. I hope you agree.

Sleep loose,
Robert Ellis
http://www.robertellis.net

A snake coiled in its wisdom strikes
spitting on my skin a third eye
showering my body with sparks
I listen to the silence between breaths
I speak to the silence after the breath
I am the silence before the breath
and then we move together
in jeweled conversation. . . .

One

She liked the way her hair looked. Her eyes. She crossed the room to the full-length mirror on the closet door and struck a pose. Shifting her weight, she turned. The nightgown was the color of falling snow and almost perfectly transparent. She liked the warm tone of her skin underneath. The way her breasts seemed to bob with the slightest move. It had been exactly the right choice.

Darlene had purchased the babydoll nightgown with matching G-string at the Victoria's Secret Web site on the Internet using her mother's credit card. She knew her mother would never notice. Christmas was less than ten days off. There would be a lot of gifts bought with that credit card. Some even from the same store.

She glanced at the clock. Lunchtime wouldn't be for another two hours, yet she was already hungry. She lifted her arms in the air, letting out a yawn as she stretched. Then she walked out of her bedroom leaving her clothes on the chair. She had the place to herself and didn't have to worry about privacy. Her parents were at their second home in the Poconos, on vacation until New Year's Day with her younger brother and sister. Darlene would be driving up to join them tomorrow afternoon, her skis waxed and ready. But there was a lot to do before then.

She was throwing a party tonight, and had to get the house ready.

Her boyfriend, Russ, had purchased a keg of beer with the help of his older brother who was home from college and of legal age. They had set it up earlier that morning on the rear terrace off the kitchen and dining room, packed in snow so the brew would be ice-cold. After the party, Russ said he would help clean up so her parents wouldn't notice, maybe even stay over the whole night. That's where the baby-doll nightgown came in. They'd been doing it since last summer, but had never spent an entire night together. She wanted to sleep with Russ and wake up with him. She wanted him in the morning.

Darlene walked downstairs, turned the foyer light on, and stepped into the kitchen. She poured a glass of cold spring water from the five-gallon dispenser in the pantry and crossed the room to sip it by the window. The sun had vanished and it was gray outside, the jittery movement of the black clouds overhead visible even at a glance. If it snowed again, the night might be a bust. She flipped the radio on, switched it to AM, and found KYW, hoping for a weather report on the news station. As she waited, she returned to the window and looked out at the terrace. There was a squirrel on the keg, sitting on his hind legs and eating nuts. From the pile of discarded shells littering the snow, it seemed as if the squirrel had been at it for some time. Darlene tapped on the window. The squirrel turned to look at her without much interest. She knocked on the windowpane again and made a face, but the stupid squirrel wouldn't budge. When she shook her fist, the squirrel began shredding through his pile of nuts at a faster clip, making the mess even bigger with his sharp teeth.

She turned away and shook her head. There was a story on the radio, a live simulcast from the district attorney's office in Philadelphia and the law school at the University of Pennsylvania. It didn't sound like they would be getting to the weather any time soon. The district attorney was in hot water with the press for something he'd done in the past. What else was new? Darlene found the story so boring, she couldn't take it anymore and switched the radio off.

That's when she heard it. The noise at the front door.

She looked at the clock, guessing it was the mailman. That weird geek who couldn't keep his eyes off her when she teased him. Although she found the man way past disgusting, for some reason Darlene couldn't explain, she loved teasing him. She liked the feeling she got when his eyes lingered over her body. Last summer he had walked a package to the back of the house while she was sunbathing by the pool. When he spotted her, he became shy and nervous and tried not to look at her as if he were a little boy again. He was fighting it but stealing peeks through his eyelids and losing the war. That's when she realized her power. Ever since, she noticed he no longer presorted her family's mail. Instead, he'd walk from his Jeep to the front steps, casually peeking through the lace curtains on the door as he went through the letters and magazines in his bag and carefully placed them in the letter box.

Darlene remembered what she was wearing and smiled as she gazed at her body through the sheer nightgown. Her smile widened as an idea formed. Why go through the effort of stuffing the mail in the letter box when he could simply hand it to her? Outrageous, maybe. Thrilling, yes. Besides, catalogs were still coming and there were all those Christmas cards. She'd be doing the big slob a favor.

She placed the glass in the sink and walked out of the kitchen, following the foyer around the corner until she could see the front door. It was made of heavy oak, the curtains her grandmother had sewn drawn loosely over the glass. Looking through the opaque cloth, Darlene could almost make out his figure. He seemed to be sorting through his bag, taking his time, not facing the mailbox but the door.

She smiled and moved closer, her bare feet feeling the chill of the hardwood floors until she reached the oriental carpet directly in front of the door. As she wrapped her fingers around the handle, she caught a glimpse of herself in the foyer mirror. She felt her heart pounding and tried to get rid of that naughty smile. She looked perfect, she decided, ready to give this guy a thrill he could take back to the post office and mail. Then she flipped the lock over and swung open the door. . . .

Two

Teddy Mack finished the first half of his chicken salad sandwich and took a sip of tea. The hot brew warmed his stomach, but wasn't doing much for his feet. He was sitting at the counter of a lunch stand set up like a diner—just one booth among fifty or so in the heart of Redding Terminal Market. At one time, the place had been a train station. Now it was a farmers market in the heart of Center City with fresh fruits and vegetables, butchers and bakers, and various lunch counters where you could taste the delicacies from almost any country in the world for not more than five bucks or so. Teddy loved the smell of the place, the ambient sounds of the people crowded into the long, narrow aisles moving from one booth to the next.

Today he'd picked the diner for a far more practical reason. Two months ago an ATM machine had been installed on the wall at the end of the counter. Teddy only had twenty minutes before he had to get back to City Hall. It wasn't more than a two-block walk, but the day had turned cold and dark, and the weather forecasters were calling for more snow.

Teddy knew that his future at the law firm of Barnett &

Stokes could very well be determined by what happened after lunch at City Hall. In twenty minutes he would be meeting with Judge Roland Brey, along with the attorneys representing Capital Insurance Life. It was a small case, but it was also Teddy's first case handled entirely on his own. Teddy had graduated from Penn Law and passed the bar just three months ago. But what made the case important was that it had been handed to him by Jim Barnett himself, as a favor to one of the firm's biggest corporate clients. Teddy knew he had been given the assignment because expectations for success were low. For Teddy to win, Judge Brey would be required to break new ground. It didn't take experience to understand that judges rarely liked to break new ground. Teddy also knew that no one else in the firm wanted to get involved because it amounted to a personal injury case. Barnett & Stokes represented thirty-five of the fifty richest corporations in the tristate area. PI cases were held at arm's length. At best, they were quietly farmed out to one of three firms in the city who didn't advertise their services on the side of a bus.

But this one was different. A favor for the president of the Pennwell Oil Company, who walked into Jim Barnett's office and asked him to see what he could do.

Fifteen years ago the man's son had been driving west on I-70 en route to college when he was rear-ended by a tractor-trailer carrying parsley and basil for Golden Valley Spices & Co. The accident had been horrific, the kid's survival nothing short of miraculous. He'd been driving a Volkswagen bus and had stopped for road construction. The truck had plowed into the VW at full speed with the weight of the world behind it. The accident occurred in Washington, Pennsylvania, a small town about thirty miles south of Pittsburgh. When the ambulance arrived, the kid was taken to Washington Hospital, which was also under construction at the time and filled to capacity. After two hours, a doctor finally examined the young man and a series of X rays were taken. When it was determined that no bones were broken, the kid was released without supervision or a place to go.

The next few days in the kid's life were fairly complicated with most of the time spent in a local motel room. Unable to move because of a sprained neck and back, he was nursed by the motel staff until a college friend could make the five-hundred-mile drive to Washington. What was left of the kid's possessions were then packed into the friend's car, and together they set off for school. The kid had been in strong physical condition when the accident occurred, running five miles a day and an active swimmer, which was probably what saved his life. After two months, his neck and back were healed and he was more interested in his studies than initiating a lawsuit that would require him to return home. His father agreed, thankful that his son had survived and made what he thought was a full recovery. Settlement was reached with Capital Insurance Life for material damages, though the father remembered being surprised at the time by the insurance representative's tough attitude when it came down to negotiating the value of his son's damaged possessions. The insurance company was getting off easy on this one and everyone involved knew it. Their bullshit attitude didn't make sense.

Ten years passed, the accident forgotten. Then one day the son had to travel for business and got on a plane with a cold. When the plane landed, his right ear began ringing and wouldn't stop. After the trip, he went to see a doctor. Tests were conducted and it was determined that he'd lost thirty percent of his hearing in his right ear because of the concussion he'd received a decade ago. The spectrum of sound lost was very specific and could not have occurred from a sudden loud noise or even music. Five more years passed, and the young man's condition worsened. Now thirty-five years old, he was having difficulty maintaining his balance. Life had changed for the young man, and he was at his wits' end. At the time of the accident he'd done what he thought was the right thing. But now he realized that he'd been burned.

The boy's father had come to Jim Barnett with the problem knowing fifteen years had passed and there wasn't much a lawyer could do now. Barnett explained the difficulties frankly, then asked Teddy to have a look in order to appease their client. The family had kept all their records from the accident, and Teddy examined them carefully. Three weeks later, and to everyone's surprise, Teddy came through. That was a month ago, and Judge Brey had already agreed that the hospital released the boy prematurely. The proper care for a serious concussion required more than a simple X ray for skeletal fractures. They should have checked out his hearing. Given the weight of the accident, they should have checked everything, whether it was convenient for them at the time or not. Teddy couldn't help but notice that Judge Roland Brey wore a small hearing aid in his right ear.

But what Teddy really wanted was the insurance company. Capital Insurance Life, and their two well-fed legal representatives who wore thousand-dollar suits and drove matching Mercedeses. After studying letters sent to the family by the claims representative at the time of the accident, it was clear to Teddy that Capital Insurance Life was working the statute of limitations like a cat standing over a wounded bird. Even worse, several letters seemed to indicate the insurance company was limiting their responsibility in the matter. If he studied the letters carefully, got past what they said to what they intended to say and really meant, it seemed to Teddy that it amounted to fraud and that he may have found a way around the statute of limitations. Judge Brey would be making his decision after lunch. If he interpreted the evidence as Teddy had and ruled there was enough documentation to prove fraud, then the case would either go to trial or the insurance company would try to reach another quick settlement. Barnett was delighted, if not shocked, as was their client. Better yet, the lead attorney for Capital Insurance Life had called Teddy last night, trying to get a feel for what a second settlement might cost. Teddy's response had been simple. The insurance company had taken advantage of his client and now it was time to pay up. Teddy wanted everything. Not just a couple of Mercedeses, but their suits, their homes, a truckload of cash, and fifteen years' worth of interest.

His cell phone rang. As Teddy dug his hand into his pocket and pulled the phone out, he noticed the man staring at him in the next seat and stepped away from the counter to take the call. It was Brooke Jones, an attorney from his office. Jones had joined the firm one year ahead of Teddy and done everything she could to make his first three months difficult.

"Barnett wants you to come back to the office," she said. "Where are you?"

He checked his watch. His meeting with Judge Brey was in fifteen minutes. Jones's voice seemed particularly strained.

"I'm on my way to City Hall," he said. "What is it? What's wrong?"

Jones hesitated a moment, then cleared her throat. "I'll be taking your place in court with Judge Brey," she said. "Barnett wants to see you right away. He didn't get into details. He doesn't have to because he owns the firm. All he did is ask me to fill in for you and make this call. That's what I'm doing."

She hung up. Teddy couldn't believe it but she did.

He closed the phone, returning to his place at the counter and wondering what had happened. He waved at the waitress for his check. While she wrote it up, he worked on his sandwich, finishing it in three quick bites. Someone had turned on the TV mounted on the wall, probably a result of his cell phone conversation. Teddy didn't blame them. He hated people who used cell phones in public places, too.

He glanced at the TV. The local stations had interrupted their program schedule with a special report, confirming the rumors Teddy had been hearing all morning long. William S. Nash and his legal workshop at Penn Law had substantiated that someone District Attorney Alan Andrews prosecuted for murder and later died by lethal injection was actually innocent. Nash had the DNA results, the evidence of Andrews's blunder as indisputable as science. But just in case anyone still had doubts, Nash also presented DNA results and a confession from the man who really did commit the murder, a career criminal facing rape charges and a second murder rap now awaiting trial in a city jail. In spite of this, the district attorney's first response was to attack Nash and the students participating in the workshop. DA Andrews wasn't known for his mistakes, but for his high percentage of prosecutions. Teddy knew Andrews had career plans and watched the man sweating it out before the cameras. Alan Andrews was in line to become the city's next mayor. The election wouldn't be held for another year, but everyone knew Andrews was the front-runner. Even if he'd just skidded on the ice and slammed headfirst into a brick wall.

The waitress walked over with the check and handed it to him with a smile. Teddy left a tip nicer than he could afford, grabbed his briefcase, and stepped over to the cash register. Andrews could scream at the cameras all he wanted, but it would never work. William S. Nash had a national reputation for being one of the finest attorneys ever to step into a courtroom. He'd retired a half decade ago and begun teaching at Penn Law. The law school couldn't believe their good fortune, and Teddy knew that they would do everything they could to back him up.

Teddy glanced at the clock on the wall, buttoning his overcoat and bolting out of the diner. As he approached the doors to the market, a blast of ice-cold air hit him in the face and he stepped outside. Bracing himself in the wind, he started up Filbert Street at a pace just short of a run. The district attorney's problems seemed less important than his own right now and he was angry. Barnett had given him a throwaway case, yet Teddy had come through. The judge was about to make his decision. This was the moment. Teddy's first decision in his first solo case. What could Barnett be thinking?

It occurred to Teddy that Barnett didn't really want to see him at all. Brooke Jones had made the whole thing up out of spite. By the time he reached the office, found out it was a joke, and made it back to court, he would be ten minutes late. He knew Jones was capable of this sort of thing. That for some reason he didn't understand, she resented him. But as he passed the Criminal Justice Center, he caught a glimpse of Jones on the sidewalk outside City Hall. She was rushing toward the building entrance with her briefcase and lugging research files in a canvas tote bag that Teddy recognized as his own. Teddy had the motion papers in his briefcase. But the judge had already made his decision, so there was no real reason to bring any files at all. Unless you were Brooke Jones.

He crossed the street, zigzagging his way past City Hall to Market Street and picking up his pace again. Barnett & Stokes occupied the sixteenth and seventeenth floors at One Liberty Place, the tallest building in the city. Construction for One Liberty Place had been controversial because of the building's height and what it might do to Philadelphia's historic skyline. But when the developer had completed the job, no one said a word. One Liberty Place was a work of modern art that seemed to draw out the historic buildings so you could see them again. The skyline never looked better.

Teddy rushed through the building lobby, nodding at the guards and ignoring the Christmas carols over the PA system as he found his way to the elevators and made the quick ride up to the seventeenth floor. Racing past the receptionist, he pushed open the glass doors and legged it down the long hall to Barnett's corner office at the very end. Barnett's legal assistant, Jackie, was on the phone and looked worried. As Teddy approached her desk, she lowered her eyes and waved him through.

"Where the hell have you been?" Barnett said as he entered.

Barnett was standing before his desk, loading his briefcase with files, various prescriptions from his doctor, even a backup battery for his cell phone. He appeared upset, more worried than his assistant, maybe even sick.

"I was due in court," Teddy said. "What's happened?"

"Where's my fucking address book?"

Teddy moved closer and looked at the man's desk. He noticed a copy of the newspaper opened to the society page. Barnett and his wife, Sally, had hosted a charity scavenger hunt benefitting Children's Hospital last weekend, and the story, along with their photographs, had made the paper. Beneath the newspaper, Teddy could see a copy of *Philadelphia Magazine*'s *Power 100* issue. Barnett had risen from thirteenth to eleventh this year and no doubt would eventually make the top ten. He was in his midfifties and still grinding. The man had plenty of time to reach his goal.

"I'm supposed to be in court," Teddy said. "Brooke called. Now tell me why."

"It couldn't be helped. I should've called you myself, Teddy. I'll make it up to you, I swear." Before Teddy could respond, Barnett gave him a nervous look and added, "I need a big favor."

Barnett found his address book underneath the magazine and threw it into his briefcase. As he yanked open a desk drawer and fished out a bottle of Extra Strength Tylenol, Teddy noticed that Barnett's hands were trembling.

"Someone's been murdered," he said. "I need your help."

Teddy lowered his briefcase to the floor and leaned against the arm of the couch. It was a big office, luxuriously furnished, with a million-dollar view. For some reason, it appeared unusually small and insignificant just now.

"A girl," Barnett went on. "Darlene Lewis. She was only eighteen years old. Shit, Teddy, she was still in high school. I'm in a jam, and I need your help."

"Do they know who did it?" Teddy asked.

"Her mailman. A guy named Oscar Holmes. They've got the murder weapon. It sounds like they caught him in the act."

Barnett shuddered. Teddy had never seen him act this way before and looked him over carefully. At six-feet-one Barnett was the same height as Teddy but bulkier by about fifty pounds. In spite of the extra weight, Barnett appeared in good shape and carried himself well. The man's grooming was meticulous, his clothing handmade by a tailor Barnett visited once a year in Milan. His hair was a wiry mix of brown and gray, his eyes sky-blue and sparkling, even in the grim light of a conference room. But what struck Teddy most about the man was his face, usually overflowing with confidence and a measure of charm he could turn on and off at will. Jim Barnett was a master at litigation, his skills as a negotiator well known. Until now, Teddy thought. It looked as if the man had lost his self-control.

"What's the favor?" Teddy asked.

Barnett forced the bottle of Tylenol open and gave him a look. "We're representing Holmes," he said.

A moment passed. Then Barnett shook two caplets out and swallowed them with whatever was in his coffee mug.

"We don't do criminal law," Teddy said, trying to suppress his concern. "No one here has experience."

"We'll get help if we need it."

"Who is this guy? Why are we getting involved?"

"I'll explain later," Barnett said. "The girl lived in Chestnut Hill. She came from a good family. A nice, old-money family. The cops are still at the house, processing the crime scene under what they're calling *unusual circumstances*. I couldn't send Brooke because I don't know what that means. That's where you come in. I want you to go there and find out what they're up to. I need to know what it means."

Teddy wanted to say no, but didn't. He had a revulsion for criminal law and had done everything he could to avoid it in school. His interest in law centered entirely on real estate. He wanted to work with architects and developers and build a career on something he could feel and touch with his hands. When he'd received a job offer from Barnett & Stokes, he jumped on it. The firm's real estate department was the rival of every other firm in the city, accounting for almost a quarter of their business.

"Where are you going?" he asked Barnett.

"The roundhouse. Holmes is already there. The cops are probably trying to beat him into making a statement right now. I've gotta get there before he does."

Teddy thought it over. The *roundhouse* was a nickname for police headquarters at Eighth and Race Streets. It seemed strange hearing Barnett use the nickname with such ease.

"I don't understand why you're doing this," Teddy said. "If it's another favor for someone, why not put them in touch with a criminal attorney who handles this sort of thing every day? This isn't a personal injury case for the president of an oil company. This isn't about money."

"Listen to me, Teddy. I know what you're thinking. I don't like it either, for Christ's sake. But I can't be in two places at once. You're driving out to the crime scene, and I'm heading over to the roundhouse. If they won't let you in, and they probably won't, then do the best you can from the street. Once you get a bead on things, I want you to get back here and handle the preliminary arraignment. I've gotta get home at a decent hour. Sally's got something going on I can't get out of. We'll talk tonight—keep your cell phone on—then trade notes in the morning and figure out what the hell we're gonna do. You've been like a son to me, Teddy. I need your help now."

The door swung open and Jill Sykes walked in with a notepad. Jill had been a student at Penn Law one year behind Teddy and managed to get a job at the firm as a law clerk without knowing anyone while she prepared for her bar exams. She had a witty sense of humor and the ability to cut to the bottom line in an instant. Although Teddy had seen her on campus last year, even found her attractive, they hadn't met until she was hired by the firm. Over the past three months, they had become good friends.

"Thanks," Barnett said to her. "Did you get the address?"

She nodded, tearing a sheet of paper from her pad and handing it to Teddy with a look. It was Darlene Lewis's address in Chestnut Hill. The murder scene. Barnett slipped the bottle of Tylenol into his jacket pocket and turned to Teddy.

"Now get going," Barnett said. "And be careful. My guess is the district attorney will be there. The way I see it, we're gonna cop a plea and then play let's make a deal. I want to avoid headlines at all costs. Be polite, and don't believe what you're hearing around town. Alan Andrews is Adolf Hitler, Joseph Stalin, and Osama bin Laden rolled into one pint-sized motherfucking asshole. He's on the political fast track. We need to keep things friendly, you understand?''

Barnett's charm was back. Teddy nodded, grabbing his briefcase and heading out the door.

Three

The elevator dropped from the seventeenth floor, and Teddy felt his stomach break loose from his body and slam against the back of his throat. When the doors finally opened, he stepped into the garage letting the dread follow him to his car. He found his beat-up Corolla parked between a restored Jaguar and a BMW 740i, complete with sport package. His Corolla had a hundred and twenty-five thousand miles under its rusting body. Something about the sight of his old friend in these surroundings brought a smile to his face and the tension eased.

He backed the Corolla out of the space and pulled up the exit ramp into the light, noting the time and quickly considering his route. There was no easy way in or out of Chestnut Hill, but he was ahead of rush-hour traffic by almost an hour. Avoiding the expressway just in case, he turned up the Benjamin Franklin Parkway, hit the circle before the art museum, and shot down Kelly Drive.

The road followed the winding path of the Schuylkill River, and it looked as if a thick fog was settling in. He checked the trees and noticed the wind had died off. As he passed Boathouse Row, he saw the buildings buried in the fallen clouds and couldn't help but think of brighter days in the warm sunlight. Teddy loved sculling, and had been a varsity rower as an undergraduate at Penn. Now he was on his way to a crime scene. A young girl had been killed and he was representing the man who murdered her. He could feel his heart bouncing in his chest and knew he needed to get a grip on things. Take a step back, keep the details at bay, and let the rest of the day just blow.

He eased the car onto Lincoln Drive and started through the woods, following the narrow S curves two miles up the hill. Turning right, he raced down West Allens Lane and made a left at the light onto Germantown Avenue. The road was cobblestoned, the Corolla vibrating over the choppy surface as he pushed past the trolley station and entered the quaint old town twenty miles an hour over the speed limit. Many of the buildings lining the street were over two hundred years old. Antique shops and art galleries whizzed by, along with restaurants and fashionable boutiques that could afford the high rent. He could see people on the sidewalks carrying packages to their cars. Most likely they were gifts for the holidays—the kind you couldn't buy from a chain store at the mall.

Teddy glanced at the address Jill had written down, 931 Scottsboro Road. He made another left, leaving the shopping district behind and entering a neighborhood of homes that seemed to grow in stature with each passing block. When he hit a stop sign, he looked down the street to his right and caught the flashing lights atop a long row of police cars. This was it, he thought, making the turn onto Scottsboro Road and finding a place to park behind a news van five houses down.

A small crowd had formed in front of the death house. As Teddy walked up the wooded street, he could see people being held back by crime scene tape that looked as if it extended deep into the property. Cops in uniforms stood behind the tape, one with a clipboard who checked off names as various people were let through. Another cop, this one dressed in a suit, stood off to the side and spoke with the press. Teddy's eyes moved to the fence in the neighbor's yard. When his view cleared, he got his first look at the Lewis house. It was a three-story Tudor, probably built in the 1890s, set on a well-planted, two-acre lot. On any other day, he would have called it majestic. But not today. Not with the medical examiner's van parked on the snow-covered lawn and backed up to the front door with its rear gate open.

Teddy grimaced, but kept walking until he reached the cop with the clipboard. He gave the man his name and told him who he worked for. What seemed like a long, icy stare followed before the cop grabbed the radio mike clipped to his parka and spoke with someone inside. Ignoring the black vibes, Teddy turned back to the death house. If the medical examiner was still here, then so was the body. That meant there was a chance Teddy would have to look at it. His eyes fell away from the van. He noticed an attractive woman with blond hair standing in the doorway with a two-way radio in her hand. She was staring at him. After a moment, she nodded at the cop with the clipboard. The cop nodded back and shrugged, taking Teddy's full name down and letting him pass without another word.

Teddy walked up the driveway, then cut along the slate path that had been cleared of snow from the last storm. Curiously, every window on the first floor of the house was open and he couldn't help but wonder why. As he started up the steps, District Attorney Alan Andrews met him at the door.

"Where's the package, kid?"

Teddy stopped under the weight of the man's eyes. He realized that Andrews had looked him over, mistaking him for a messenger or law clerk.

"You're from Barnett's office, right?"

Teddy nodded, watching the district attorney size him up. Then the woman with blond hair reappeared, moving in behind Andrews. Teddy was nervous and knew it was showing. After a moment, their gazes eased up and Andrews came close to fighting off a smile. It didn't take much to guess what the district attorney was thinking. Teddy wasn't a messenger. He was a kid just out of law school with no experience. When the case got to court, Andrews would eat him for lunch.

Andrews's half smile evaporated, and as he shook Teddy's hand, he introduced the woman as Assistant District Attorney Carolyn Powell. Teddy shook ADA Powell's hand as well, but Andrews broke in before he could say anything to her.

"So here's the deal, Teddy Mack. Your client's the friendly neighborhood mailman. Six hours ago a neighbor saw him running away from the house with blood on his clothes. She got a good look at him. Blood was all over his fucking face and hair like he was swimming in it. She's the one who found the body and called nine-one-one. She knew her mailman by name. Oscar Holmes. Detectives looked for him at work, but he was absent without leave. Holmes rents a small apartment at Twenty-third and Pine. They spotted his mail truck out front and caught up with him there. When Holmes answered the door he was all revved up. The detectives noted the blood on his face and made the arrest. Once the warrants arrived, the guys went in and found his clothes hidden in the trash."

Teddy cleared his throat. "What about the murder weapon?"

Andrews paused a moment, then met his eyes. "It was a knife. A big one with enough blood on it to make the lab's ten best list. We found it buried in his mailbag with this year's Christmas cards."

Andrews glanced at the street, his jaw muscles flexing like a predatory animal savoring its kill. He was shorter than Teddy by half a foot, but lean and tight and built like a sledgehammer. The man had a definite edge going and was obviously pissed off. He had a right to be, Teddy thought.

"So here are the rules," Andrews said. "The house has been cleared. Every room but the dining room. You want to look around, be my guest, but nothing's gonna be happening for another hour or two. If you have any questions, ask ADA Powell. Where's Barnett?"

"At the roundhouse," Teddy said.

"Is he gonna farm the case out?"

"I'm not sure."

"How come you're not sure, Teddy Mack?"

Teddy didn't say anything but held the man's eyes. After a long moment, District Attorney Alan Andrews turned his back on him and disappeared into the house. When ADA Powell started for the door, Teddy took a deep breath of fresh air and followed her inside.

The smell hit him as he passed the threshold. It was a chemical smell, almost like an acid that burned the nostrils and irritated his eyes.

"They're gassing the body," Powell said. "Superglue. It won't be ready for a while."

He nodded at her even though he didn't know what she was talking about. Still, the intense fumes were enough to explain why the windows were open and it felt like the heat was switched off. Powell pulled her jacket tighter in the mid-December air. Something about seeing a beautiful woman in this setting didn't compute. Her eyes were blue gray and gentle, her face refined and made all the softer by her shoulder-length hair. Teddy guessed she was in her late thirties, and had seen things most people, including himself, would never see or even hear about because those were the details newspapers always left out.

"Who's the lead detective?" he asked.

"Dennis Vega," she said. "I'll show you where everyone is. Then you can have a look at the rest of the house on your own. The place has been cleared, but I'd still be careful about what you touch. There's a lot of fingerprint powder around, and it's hard to wash off."

"Where's the family?"

"They've got a place in the mountains. They're on their way home." Powell turned away, leading him through the foyer and around the stairs. Then she added in a lower voice, "Given the unusual circumstances, I think it's good that you're here."

There were those words again. *Unusual circumstances.*

Teddy looked at the floor and noted the drop cloths. When

they reached the living room, fifteen people turned from their seats. They looked at him a moment, then lowered their eyes to the floor as if deep in thought or even prayer. Teddy knew the three people waiting on the couch were from the medical examiner's office because of their jackets. The men in suits looked like detectives or city officials and had taken the chairs. The rest appeared to be crime scene techs, sitting on long cases that had been unlatched but remained closed. No one was talking, but Teddy could hear voices from the next room.

He followed Powell farther into the living room and saw a man in the doorway straddling a dining room chair backward and balancing his weight on the rear two legs.

"It's gonna work," the man was saying to someone. "The conditions are perfect. You'll see."

Teddy guessed the man was Dennis Vega, the lead detective. In spite of the cool air, Vega was sweating. And from the tone of his voice, he appeared more than anxious.

Teddy moved closer, then flinched as he spotted the body stretched out on the dining room table. It was underneath a milky layer of plastic that had been formed into a tent enclosing the entire table. Teddy couldn't exactly see the girl's body, just its hazy form. A man wearing a gas mask was at the head of the table, lifting the plastic open. It looked as if a lamp had been rigged inside the tent, the lightbulb fitted with an aluminum dish. Teddy watched the man squeeze something from a small tube into the hot dish, eye the body, then repeat the process. Several discarded tubes were laid out on a sheet of newspaper on the floor. Reading the labels, Teddy realized Powell hadn't been kidding. The man was shooting superglue into the dish and watching it vaporize from the heat of the lightbulb. The plastic was actually clear, the young girl's body entombed in a dense cloud of noxious fumes.

The man gave the body another look. Then he lowered the plastic, sealing it to the table with a pair of spring clips.

"Not yet," he said, his voice muffled by the gas mask.

The man dropped the empty tube onto the newspaper and

opened a new one. As he straightened the drop clothes with his feet, Teddy noticed the blood pool on the floor underneath. He looked up and saw more blood sprayed all over the walls. Whatever happened to Darlene Lewis had been brutal. He took a step back, suddenly feeling nauseated.

"Are you okay?" Powell asked.

"It's the fumes," he said, lying. "I think I'll have a look around."

Teddy backed out of the living room, passing through the foyer into the kitchen. He'd been hoping for a glass of water, but someone had torn the sink apart, removing the pipes and garbage disposal. When he spotted the pantry, he swung the door open and found a canister of bottled water. The dispenser was an industrial model with hot and cold taps and a paper cup holder. Teddy poured a cup and guzzled it down. Then he poured another and moved to the open window, sucking fresh air into his lungs between small sips of more cold water. He could see the district attorney on the rear terrace, pacing back and forth with a cigarette burning and his cell phone pressed to his ear. Against the far wall, he noticed a beer keg packed in the snow. A squirrel was sitting on the keg, taking a shit and eating nuts as it kept its nervous eyes on Andrews.

Teddy turned away, his gaze resting on the disassembled garbage disposal. The delay in clearing the house had to do with the girl's body and whatever they were doing with those tubes of superglue. That much was obvious. But tearing apart the sink seemed odd as well.

Tossing the paper cup in the trash, he returned to the foyer keeping in mind the house as he'd seen it from the street and trying to get a feel for the layout. The living room and dining room were on the other side of the stairs to his left. Behind a double set of doors to his right he found a study and stepped inside. Scanning the room quickly, it looked as though the Lewis family used it as an informal sitting room. The chairs were overstuffed and placed about a luxurious oriental carpet before the fireplace. Most of the furniture were antiques, and the room had a feeling of warmth and comfort. He noticed a painting above the mantel and crossed the room for a closer look. It was an N.C. Wyeth. Not a copy, but an original. Teddy knew the painting was worth a fortune. He turned, taking the room in with his back to the fireplace. On the opposite wall he noticed three more paintings that he recognized. Seurat, Gauguin, and Cezanne. He looked at the chairs again and realized one had been turned to face these magnificent works of art. No doubt the owner of these paintings spent a lot of time sitting in that chair staring at them. Clearly, robbery wasn't the motive in Darlene Lewis's horrible death.

It was beginning to get dark outside. Teddy checked the doors in the room, expecting a powder room but finding closets instead. To the left of the fireplace was an entryway to a library—a long, narrow room with books lining all four walls from floor to ceiling. Beyond the library was another sitting room, smaller than the first with a desk and computer, then a laundry room, a breakfast room, and back to the kitchen.

Teddy returned to the foyer, eyeing it closely. A door was cracked open in the wall beneath the stairs he'd missed the first time around. Swinging it out of the way, he found just what he expected. The toilet had been lifted from the floor. When he opened the cabinets beneath the sink, the pipes were missing here as well.

He backed out into the hall, glancing at the living room as he climbed the stairs. No one was sitting around any longer, the waiting over. The crime scene techs had opened their cases and were rigging flourescent light fixtures on stands and carrying them into the dining room. A man with a video camera was opening a fresh tape.

Teddy continued up the stairs and down the hall, passing the master bedroom until he found a common bath. He hurried inside, switching the lights on. The plumbing had been ripped apart here as well. The detectives had combed through the house for most of the day. The job had been thorough because they thought Oscar Holmes, the friendly neighborhood mailman, wanted to get rid of something.

It seemed obvious that whatever that something was had everything to do with making the circumstances *unusual* as well.

Teddy stepped into the hall, looking for the girl's bedroom. It was the third door down, and he stopped to take it in before entering. It was a teenager's room. A room in transition furnished with hopes and dreams and the lingering mementos of a childhood about to be left behind. The sadness was overwhelming because the evolution from girl to young woman had been destroyed.

His eyes came to rest on an old oak chest against the wall by the window. Spotting a series of photographs, he flipped the light switch and crossed the room. The pictures had been dusted for fingerprints, along with the brass handles on the drawers. One photo stood out, and Teddy picked the frame up by its edges, trying to avoid the dark gray powder that ADA Powell had warned him about. It was a family shot, taken while on vacation and probably recent. It could have been Rome, but Teddy suspected it was Paris. He looked at the faces, the smiles, guessing the eldest daughter had to be Darlene. She was pretty, even beautiful. By the way her father was holding on to her, Teddy could tell he thought so, too. Teddy's eyes moved back to Darlene in the picture and he studied her face. She was more worldly than he expected, almost too sophisticated to live in this room.

He set down the picture and looked around. He noticed her clothes on the chair, a pair of jeans and a T-shirt. Then he crossed the room to the closet, reviewing her clothing. He spotted a pair of panties rolled into a ball on the floor and picked them up. As he opened them and examined them in the light, someone tapped on the bedroom door.

It was ADA Carolyn Powell, staring at him with a lazy smile and those blue-gray eyes of hers.

"Are you enjoying yourself?" she asked.

Teddy froze, embarrassed. "She was sexually active," he said.

"How do you know that?"

"There's a discharge. She had sex with someone, then put these back on."

Powell's eyes went to the panties, then flipped back to his face. "She was eighteen, living in a modern world. We could discuss it more thoroughly if you'd like, but I think they're ready downstairs."

Teddy nodded and tossed the panties into the closet. Giving the room a last look, he switched the lights off and followed Powell out the door.

Four

The dining room had changed in the last hour. Darlene Lewis's body remained entombed in the smoke beneath the plastic, but an exhaust fan had been placed in the window and the fumes from the hot glue were much easier to handle now. Six flourescent fixtures mounted on light stands stood off to the side, plugged into the wall and ready to go.

Detective Vega traded looks with the district attorney. After a moment, Vega nodded at the man wearing the gas mask, who then removed the lamp from beneath the plastic and set it down on the floor careful not to spill any glue that might have remained in the dish attached to the lightbulb. The girl's form underneath the plastic went dark, and Teddy tried to get a grip on what he was about to see. Then the man with the gas mask began releasing the spring clamps that sealed the plastic to the wood of the dining room table. Everyone took a step closer, whether they were conscious of it or not. The fan whirled in the background. The haunting sound of the man's labored breathing through his gas mask was almost too much to take. Teddy glanced at Vega, the detective's chiseled face beneath his short dark hair filled with hope and expectation. Then at the district attorney, all wound up like a spring.

The man in the gas mask gathered the plastic and pulled it away.

Teddy felt his heart skip a beat. The noxious smoke rose from the corpse like the plume from a mushroom cloud, the shock wave smacking everyone in the gut. Darlene Lewis was lying on the table completely naked, her arms and legs tied down with rags, her mouth gagged. Her eyes were open and bulging beyond their sockets, and her neck appeared bruiscd. From the hideous expression on the girl's face, it looked as if she died screaming. But it was worse than that. Skin had been removed from her body, and when Teddy noticed, he shuddered in terror. A large patch of skin on her lower right calf, another just above her shaved vagina, and even more from the underside of her breasts. A thick, clear liquid was oozing from the breast wounds and collecting on the table. Teddy tried to look away, but couldn't.

Unusual circumstances. He knew what the words meant now.

"Bring in the lights," Vega whispered.

Teddy took a step back with the others as the crimc scene techs grabbed their lights and positioned them around the table.

"Close the curtains," the detective said. "And turn off the houselights."

The room went black. Teddy wasn't sure he could deal with the darkness, then felt Powell take his hand, give it a gentle squeeze, and let go as the flourescent lights were switched on. They were black lights, casting the body in a deep blue, dreamlike glow. The girl's skin darkened and white-hot marks appeared all over its surface.

Fingerprints. Bite marks. Impressions left from the killer's lips.

Vega moved closer, his eyes dancing over the dead body in amazement.

The superglue had somehow mixed with the moisture left behind from the murderer's skin. What he'd done to the girl

blossomed to the surface like flowers smoldering in the void.
For Teddy, it was a leap into the darkness, almost as if he
were watching the murderer at work before his eyes. The
crime was in motion, yet he couldn't stop it as he watched
it unfold. The madman's hands pawing at the girl's legs,
then moving up her body. Kissing her open thighs, feeling
her arms, and then grabbing at her chest until he finally
reached her neck. It was almost as if his hands and mouth
had been dipped in bright white paint, leaving a record of
what they'd done. Now Teddy understood why Vega hadn't
wanted the body disturbed—why the detective had taken
the chance and tented the body before it was handled or
moved. Teddy couldn't help but admire him. Even at a
glance, the brilliance in the man's dark eyes shined through.

"Bring in the cameras," Vega said. "Video first, then
stills. We'll do prints and take samples later."

The man Teddy had seen loading his camera with a fresh
tape brushed by him and approached the table. After he
recorded the body in wide shots, he moved in for a series
of closer views. Vega stood by his side, pointing out where
the killer had squeezed the girl's breasts, pressed his lips
into them, and then removed the skin with a knife that must
have been as sharp as a razor blade or scalpel.

Teddy felt his stomach turn and thought he might vomit.
He'd seen enough and slipped past Powell through the
entryway. Not sure that he could drive just yet, he found a
seat in the living room and sat down in the darkness. He
wondered what kind of person could do this. *We all share
the same world and even breathe the same air,* he thought,
*but what could be going through this person's twisted mind?
What brand of madness brought him to think it and desire
it, let alone carry it through?*

Someone entered the living room. Teddy looked up and
saw the district attorney take a chair on the other side of
the coffee table across from him. Andrews was a seasoned
veteran. But Teddy could tell that what happened to Darlene
Lewis was a mile or two beyond even the district attorney's
everyday tour.

"You okay, Teddy Mack?"

Teddy nodded. The district attorney's continual use of his full name irritated him, but not enough to say anything right now. He watched the man light a cigarette. Andrews must have sensed his need and offered him one. Teddy took it, leaning into the flame with a shaky hand as Andrews struck his lighter. Teddy didn't smoke very often—one or two at parties—but the nicotine seemed to help quiet him down.

"What was wrong with her breasts?" Teddy whispered. "That clear liquid oozing out."

"Implants," Andrews said.

Teddy took another drag on the cigarette, drawing the smoke in and wondering why an eighteen-year-old girl who looked as good as Darlene Lewis thought she needed breast implants. He thought about what Carolyn Powell had said in the girl's bedroom—Darlene Lewis in the modern world.

"We're glad you're here," Andrews said after a moment. "You can go back to Barnett and tell him what you've seen. Holmes will face his preliminary arraignment tonight. After that, he'll be transferred to one of the city's prisons. When I know which one, I'll let you know."

Teddy looked for an ashtray, but couldn't find one. Andrews slid his across the table.

"The reason I mention it," Andrews said, "is that I'd like you to be there when Holmes checks in. I want to make sure everything's done just right. I'm offering you a chance to observe the process so you're as sure as I am. If he's got a black eye, it's because he walked into a door on his own. If he should die tonight with a bump on the head, it's because he slipped on the floor and fell down. If you'd like to meet with your client after he's checked in, that's okay, too. I'll make the arrangements no matter what the hour."

Teddy nodded, crushing the cigarette out and ready to hit the road. He stood up. Andrews followed, shaking his hand. As Teddy started for the front door, he remembered the dismantled plumbing and turned back to Andrews.

''What was with the sinks and toilets?'' he asked. ''What were you guys looking for?''

''Her skin,'' Andrews said quietly. ''We tore everything apart. We did the same thing at his place downtown. We couldn't find it.''

''What do you think he did with it?''

Andrews repeated the question, then paused a moment, mulling it over as he stared back at him. ''Don't you get it, Teddy Mack? It's the reason we let you in this afternoon. The reason you're going to the prison tonight. Your client's from the planet Neptune. He cut the girl's skin away, and then he ate it.''

Five

Teddy drove back into the city with the windows open and the heat off. The digital temperature gauge on the dash pegged the night air at a crisp thirty-five degrees. It may have been cold, but Teddy couldn't feel it.

He found a space in the garage at One Liberty Place, turned the ignition off, and sat for a while taking in the view of the concrete wall through his windshield. He listened to the silence, the stillness, the sound of his breathing. After a moment, he glanced at his watch. It was after seven and he thought he'd skip dinner tonight. He was numb, but he was also angry.

This was more than a favor for Barnett. More than shit duty.

He checked his cell phone and realized it was dead. Digging through his briefcase, he found a fresh battery and snapped it in. When he checked his messages, there were only two. The first was from Jill Sykes, his friend at the firm, updating him on how Brooke Jones made out in court this afternoon. Judge Brey had been disappointed by Teddy's absence, but it sounded like they won the ruling. Capital Insurance Life hadn't made a decision to settle though, probably because of the change in attorneys, and the case was scheduled for trial in two weeks. At least for now. The second message was from Jim Barnett, recorded one hour ago. Barnett was on his way home and repeated that they should talk later tonight, then meet first thing in the morning. Barnett must have spoken with the district attorney at some point because he agreed that Teddy should follow Holmes to prison, though not for the same reasons as DA Andrews. Apparently Holmes wasn't cooperating with Barnett. Instead of talking about a possible deal with Andrews that might include avoiding the death penalty, Oscar Holmes wanted to plead not guilty and take his chances in court. Barnett said he wanted Teddy to meet with Holmes tonight and try to talk some sense into him. . . .

Teddy switched his cell phone off and slipped it into his pocket. He knew that if he returned Barnett's call right now and spoke his mind, he'd be fired.

"Talk some sense into him," he said aloud. "In what language?"

Teddy shook it off, climbing out of the car with his brief-case. He took the elevator up to street level, then stepped outside heading for the Wawa minimarket one block south. As he walked in the fresh air, he thought about Barnett's message and how ridiculous it sounded. There was no way District Attorney Alan Andrews would want to make a deal on this one. Andrews had taken a big hit in the press this morning. Someone he prosecuted for murder and later died by lethal injection had been proven innocent. The Holmes case would clear the table. The crime was horrific enough to change the headlines. And Alan Andrews needed a fresh set of headlines. As big and bold as he could get them, and for as long as he could sustain them.

Teddy entered the market and poured a large cup of coffee. At the register he hesitated a moment before buying a pack of cigarettes. Then he walked out, heading over to the Criminal Justice Center at Thirteenth and Filbert with a pack of Marl-boros in his pocket. The high-rise building was fairly new, and in the past, Teddy had always found it architecturally impressive. It didn't have the look or feel of a typical government building. Instead, there was a certain elegance about the place, almost as if it were the flagship for a major corporation or even a four-star hotel. Because civil cases had been relegated to City Hall, Teddy didn't have a chance to spend much time in the building. Still, he knew that preliminary arraignments were held in a high-tech courtroom somewhere downstairs.

He skipped the view tonight and crossed the lobby, stepping over to a window on the other side of the front desk. An old man dressed in a uniform sat on a stool exchanging tickets for cell phones as if checking hats or coats at a nightclub. Behind him were hundreds of numbered slots where each phone was kept. The man smiled with reassurance, taking Teddy's cell phone and handing him a ticket marked 407. Teddy glanced at the number, then slipped it into his pocket on his way around the corner to the metal detectors and X-ray machines. Once he was through security, he gathered his things and followed the signs down the wide staircase, surprised they hadn't noticed his coffee and more than grateful.

Preliminary arraignments were held twenty-four hours a day, seven days a week, and only stopped when the judges were due to make a shift change or in need of a break. The court worked like a deli. You took a number and waited your turn. Teddy guessed it would be some time before Holmes's number came up, but didn't mind. He wanted to watch the cases that preceded theirs while he figured out what he was supposed to do. Not in the legal sense. He knew a preliminary arraignment wasn't much more than a formality, particularly in a murder case because there could be no discussion of bail. Teddy's concerns were technological. Besides, he was still rattled, still shaky at the core, and he needed time to chill.

The courtroom was just down the hall. Teddy entered and sat on a bench in the back row. But he wasn't exactly seated in the courtroom. It was more like an observation room completely enclosed by glass. Speakers were built into the walls so that the public could hear the proceedings. Teddy had read about this courtroom in the newspaper when the building first opened. The court consisted of two tables for the attorneys and the judge's bench, each furnished with speakerphones. Beside the judge, a platform took the place of the witness chair and a thirty-six-inch Sony television monitor replaced the defendant. The entire proceedings occurred via TV and over a telephone conference call. The defendants spoke to the court from a holding cell in the basement of the roundhouse five safe blocks away—the cell rigged with a camera and telephone as well. Economic and safety concerns that went with the transportation of prisoners were no longer relevant issues for the taxpayers.

Teddy glanced about, realizing he was the only one in the observation room. He looked through the glass, watching the judge talk to a defendant and listening to their conversation over the speakers. While the judge relied on the speakerphone, Teddy noticed the attorneys held the handsets to their ears. The process seemed straightforward enough. When the prosecutor began speaking to the judge, Teddy opened his coffee, leaned below the view of the bench, and sipped through the steam. He was trying to suppress the memory of seeing Darlene Lewis's mangled body bound to the dining room table, but he couldn't make it. The look on her face as she was murdered remained crystal clear. And the shock was beginning to give way to fear. At some point tonight, he would have to face Oscar Holmes without the benefit or distance of television. He'd have to talk to him in person. Maybe even shake the madman's hand.

Someone entered the room behind his back and he turned. It was ADA Carolyn Powell.

"They've bumped us up," she said, taking a seat beside him. "Unless the judge takes a break, we're next. Andrews wants to fast-track Holmes out of the roundhouse and get him into a cell, for his safety as well as everyone else's."

"Where are they taking him?"

"Curran-Fromhold," she said. "They know you're coming. Everything's set."

Teddy nodded. "Has the house been cleared?"

"The body's out, but Vega thinks we should keep the place under seal. I agree. There may be a reason to go back once the science is in."

"What about the family?" Teddy asked.

"They're in no shape to spend their holiday at the house in Chestnut Hill. Besides, any funeral arrangements will be delayed because of the autopsy. After they make the ID, they're heading back to the mountains. It's not much more than an hour's drive."

The attorneys in the courtroom behind the glass were rising from their tables.

"Come on," Powell said, motioning him toward the doorway. "The entrance is at the other end of the hall."

Teddy gulped down what was left of his coffee, ditching the empty cup in the trash and following her out of the room.

By the time he was seated at the table in the courtroom, the jolt of hot caffeine hit him square in the eyes and Judge Vandergast had explained how to use the telephones. Teddy picked up his handset, pressed the appropriate button as directed, and turned toward the TV. The camera in the holding cell was locked on a shot of an empty steel chair. Over the phone, Teddy could hear the sound of chains rattling in the background. They were getting louder, moving closer. Then the backs of two cops in uniforms came into view, blocking the shot as they shackled their prisoner to the chair. After a moment, the cops backed out of the shot and everyone in court got their first look at Oscar Holmes. . . .

The lighting was poor, but Teddy could see the forty-year-old man twisting in the chair and pulling at the handcuffs and leg irons. Oscar Holmes was a giant—six-feet-five, two hundred and ninety pounds. His body was loose and round, his short-cropped hair a dull brown. The circles beneath his eyes appeared jet-black, his skin as unnaturally pale as Teddy had ever seen. No matter what the standard, Holmes was an odd-looking man. A nightcrawler out of central casting. The kind of man who tried to keep his appetites secret and spent too much time in the dark digging holes to bury them in.

Someone in the cell told Holmes to settle down and handed him a telephone. The restraints were too tightly drawn to bring the handset to his ear so the big man leaned forward. As he bent down, his forehead blocked the camera lights and his colorless eyes vanished in deep shadow. The effect was terrifying.

Judge Vandergast didn't even blink, explaining to Holmes what would be accomplished tonight and asking the man if he understood the rules.

Holmes nodded and groaned, tugging at the chains again.

Then the judge turned to Powell. The charges were read, and Holmes was cited with the tortured murder of Darlene Lewis, eighteen years of age, from Chestnut Hill. Although details of the arrest and crime scene were excluded for the most part in favor of a dry reading of the statutes involved, the horror and gore were substantial enough that they easily crept through the back door. Teddy was just thankful that any mention of the word *cannibalism* had been left out, knowing full well it would come up next week at the preliminary hearing. That would be the time when the district attorney's office would be asked to demonstrate that they had enough evidence to send the case to trial. Three weeks after that, if the judge agreed, and Teddy was certain that he would, Holmes would be formally arraigned.

Judge Vandergast turned back to the TV and once again asked Holmes if he understood.

Holmes nodded a second time. "Yes, I do," he said, his words blurred by a gravelly voice mixed with despair.

The judge paused as if the weight of the charges were sinking in. He leaned back in his chair and removed his reading glasses. Teddy could hear Holmes's breathing over the phone and thought his *client* might even be crying. No one said anything as the judge wiped his glasses off with a handkerchief, slipped them back on, and reached for his calender. This was the world Judge Vandergast lived in eight hours a day. Teddy tried to compute the number of cases

the man heard in a week. Probably hundreds, he thought,
working the room with grace and professionalism but thank
God for weekends and holidays and any day he could get
off.

"Bail isn't an issue," the judge said, paging through his
calender. "How about next Tuesday? We'll schedule the
preliminary hearing for ten o'clock. Judge Reis is available.
I think we'll give this one to him."

The judge turned to Teddy with a practiced calm; they
were in the eye of the storm tonight, not fighting the heavy
winds and swirling sea that lay beyond. Teddy couldn't help
but wonder what Judge Reis may have done to deserve this
one.

"Thank you, Your Honor," he said. "But I was hoping
for a delay of a week or two in order to evaluate my client's
mental competence. I've just come from the crime scene.
Given the circumstances, it would seem to be a relevant
issue in the case."

"Maybe so," the judge said with a twinkle in his eye.
"Only it's not an issue tonight."

Teddy cleared his throat. "Thank you, Your Honor."

He glanced over at Powell as she agreed on the date and
everyone wrote it down. It was obvious from the look on
her face that she hadn't expected him to say anything at all.
Because of the weight of the crime and his lack of experience,
she seemed surprised by his attempt to stall.

Powell got up from her chair, still eyeing Teddy as she
gathered her papers. Then Judge Vandergast switched the
TV off. Once the screen went blank, once the image of
Holmes vanished into the night and they were safe, only
then did the judge rise from the bench, claiming he and the
court would require a brief, thirty-minute break.

Six

The steel door swayed open. Teddy was escorted from the lobby into a small passageway by the assistant warden—a tall, surprisingly gentle-looking man by the name of J.S. Dean.

"Welcome to the Curran-Fromhold Correctional Facility," Dean said, slamming the heavy door shut with what Teddy considered an overly dramatic bang.

They waited a moment for the electronic lock to engage. Then a second door clicked open and they started down a wide corridor to the holding area. Prisoners roamed freely here, pushing carts and carrying boxes in both directions. Teddy guessed that privileges were granted for good behavior and that the inmates he saw were on work duty even at this hour.

Good behavior or not, Teddy kept his eyes on them.

He'd made the ten-mile drive up I-95 to Prison Row without needing directions. Curran-Fromhold was one of four city prisons set side by side on State Road just off the interstate. The site of the prisons with their high walls, bright lights, and watchtowers could be seen from two miles away. Before leaving the city, he'd returned to the Wawa minimarket for another large coffee to go. He'd even tried calling Jim Barnett's cell phone once he cleared the parking garage. The attempt had been unsuccessful, which struck Teddy as odd. Either Barnett needed to change batteries on his cell phone, or he'd deliberately switched it off. Given the circumstances, neither possibility made sense or did much for Teddy's frayed nerves.

The assistant warden pointed to the right and they started down a ramp into a second corridor. As they walked, J.S. Dean recanted the history of the prison and how the city chose its name.

"It happened twenty-nine years ago," Dean said, looking him over.

Teddy was twenty-seven. That would make it 1973.

"Not here, but at Holmesburg Prison," Dean said. "Holmesburg's closed now, but you can see it from the parking lot."

"Just on the other side of the interstate," Teddy said.

Dean nodded. "Two inmates had a grievance over religious services and scheduled a meeting with Deputy Warden Fromhold in his office. But when they showed up, it turned out they didn't really want to talk about religion at all. Instead, one of them grabbed Fromhold and held him down while the other stabbed him to death with a homemade knife. Unfortunately, Warden Curran just happened to be passing in the hall and heard the struggle. His lucky day, huh? When he walked in, they were ready for him and ended up stabbing him to death, too."

Dean waved at an inmate pushing a cart past them and said hello. Teddy didn't find reassurance in the story or its timing.

"That's how the place got its name," Dean went on. "Curran-Fromhold. It's funny, but I haven't told that story in a long time. Must be because of your client."

"How so?"

"His last name's Holmes," Dean said. "Makes me think of Holmesburg Prison, I guess."

Teddy nodded, feigning interest. Dean seemed like a good

guy, but listening to him talk about two more murders was a strain. Teddy had seen and heard enough for one day. All he wanted was to get this over with and point the car home.

By the time they reached the check-in area he'd pulled himself together and had a look around. Two guards manned the booth next to the garage, and Teddy could hear the assistant warden being told that Holmes had arrived ten minutes earlier and was ready to go. Teddy turned to the holding tank and looked through the bulletproof glass. Three prisoners he didn't recognize were huddled on the far bench, staring at something on the floor as if they were trying to keep their distance. When Teddy moved closer, he spotted Holmes lying on the concrete in chains with his eyes closed.

He took a step back as two more guards entered from the hall, one armed with a taser. On the assistant warden's nod, the two men opened the holding tank door and called out Holmes's name. Holmes opened his eyes, getting to his feet without assistance. Then he was led out of the tank and guided across the hall to the property desk. His handcuffs and leg irons were removed. As he rubbed his wrists, he turned and looked Teddy directly in the eye.

It was a long, dead stare. Teddy tried not to flinch, but thought maybe he did. Holmes was bigger in person, and far more powerful. If Darlene Lewis had put up a struggle, it couldn't have lasted very long.

One of the guards gave Holmes a nudge. Holmes finally looked away and began emptying his pockets. The assistant warden joined Teddy by the holding tank door.

"At this point he's only been searched for weapons," Dean said in a lower voice. "His cash is counted and goes into an electronic account. If he's carrying contraband, it's taken away and forgotten. But after this it's illegal. After he signs off on the inventory, possession of contraband is a crime. That includes cigarettes."

For one fleeting moment Teddy wondered what the penalty might be for possession of cigarettes. But in the end, he wasn't really listening. He was staring at Holmes's massive hands. He hadn't noticed before. Holmes had been wounded, his hands wrapped in gauze and tape.

The man behind the property desk printed out the inventory, and Holmes signed at the bottom without reviewing the list. Then one of the guards pointed to a pay phone mounted on the wall.

"You're allowed one call," the guard said. "Collect."

Holmes grunted, approaching the phone and dialing a number. He gave the operator his name. As he waited for the call to go through, he turned away, shielding the phone from the guards and staring at the concrete wall in search of some degree of privacy. After several moments, he began whimpering into the handset. Teddy could barely make out what he was saying, but it sounded like Holmes was pleading with someone other than the operator to accept the call.

"But I need to talk to her," Holmes said in a louder voice. "I really need to talk to her."

Holmes sighed and then hung up. They wouldn't accept the call. No one wanted to talk to him, his plea falling on deaf ears. When he finally turned around, he looked ten years older, like the hopelessness of what was ahead for him had begun to sink in.

He lowered his eyes. Then the guards led him down the hall and placed him into an empty holding cell. There were no bars on the door, just glass. Teddy waited with the assistant warden as Holmes showered and was issued an orange jumpsuit. When the prison doctor arrived, he was given a physical, questioned about his general health, and samples of his blood were taken. Once the doctor had completed his required tasks, he removed the tape wrapped around Holmes's hands and examined the wounds. Teddy approached the holding cell for a closer look. Holmes had been cut by the knife. Somehow his palms had been slashed in the struggle with the eighteen-year-old girl.

The doctor dressed the wounds, saying the cuts were deep but didn't require stitches. Still, Holmes never looked at him. Since that aborted phone call, Holmes's eyes never rose from the floor.

Teddy stepped back, following the assistant warden out of the holding area. He was on autopilot, observing the process and keeping everything as far away as he could.

"We'll screen his blood," Dean was saying. "For the next five days, Holmes will be in quarantine. After that, we'll determine the risks and he'll be transferred to another pod for permanent housing. He's on suicide watch tonight. We'll see how things go."

They stopped at a door. Dean glanced at the camera mounted on the wall and nodded. After a moment, the lock clicked and the door opened revealing a hallway flanked by conference rooms. There were fourteen of them, seven per side—each with a sign beside the door designating them as OFFICIAL VISITING ROOMS.

Dean pointed to room eleven. "You can wait in here," he said. "After you meet with Holmes, I'll show you the way back to the lobby. It's not far."

Teddy watched the assistant warden vanish down the hallway. After a moment, he entered room eleven. It was about the size of a cell, with windows and doors cut into the cinderblock walls on both sides of the room. A small table stood in the center of the space, along with three plastic chairs. Teddy had thought that if someone wanted to speak with an inmate, they'd be separated by thick plate glass and limited by the constraints of a telephone. The idea of sitting at a table like this, face-to-face with Holmes, never entered his mind.

As he considered meeting the man, he sat down and turned to the second door. On the other side of the glass was a large meeting room where inmates could visit with their families. The way the couches and chairs filled out the room reminded him of a hotel lobby minus the frills. Curiously, fifty oil paintings hung on the far wall as if the space doubled as an art gallery. The condition of the room matched what he'd seen throughout the prison. Teddy had read the sign by the entrance as he entered the lobby. He knew the building had been opened seven years ago, yet everything about the place still appeared waxed and polished and brand-new. The only graffiti he'd seen was on the inside wall of the holding tank.

He heard the door close. When he turned, he saw Oscar Holmes walk into the room and sit at the table less than a foot away. His eyes raced over the man's body—no handcuffs or leg irons, just the orange jumpsuit. Teddy looked through the glass for the guards who escorted him here and saw them down the hall, talking to another man seated at a desk with their backs turned. Then Darlene Lewis's dead body flashed into his head. He looked at the new bandages on Holmes's hands, but all he could see were the man's finger-prints on the girl's skin jumping out at him under the black lights. His lips and the cuts left behind from his teeth. He thought Holmes might be fixed on the same image because the man lifted his elbows to the table, covering his eyes with his oversize hands.

"Who'd you try to call?" Teddy heard himself saying in a calm voice. The question had come out of nowhere.

Holmes remained silent.

"The collect call you made an hour ago," Teddy said. "They wouldn't accept the charges. Who was it?"

A moment passed, Holmes still burying his face in his hands. "My sister," he said finally. "She wouldn't talk to me."

Holmes peeked through his fingers. His eyes were the color of a faded pair of jeans and looked just as ragged. Teddy pushed his chair back slightly and made a point of crossing his legs, trying to get some distance without Holmes noticing or becoming upset.

"No one will talk to me," Holmes said, closing his fingers and hiding in the dark again. "Everyone's afraid. Even you."

"What happened to your hands?"

"They got cut. You saw 'em. What kind of question is that? You trying to figure out if I really did it or not?"

Teddy grimaced. "How'd they get cut?"

"I don't remember," he said, jumping to his feet. "They're gonna kill me for this, aren't they? They're gonna stick the needle in and watch me go to sleep. All those people watching me sleep. They want to get rid of me. They always have.''

Teddy wasn't sure how to react. Holmes was working himself into a frenzy, pacing back and forth in the small room and slamming his fists into the cinder-block walls as he made the turns. Teddy checked his watch. Ten-thirty. It'd been a long day on shit duty, and he decided he'd finally had enough.

''Fuck you, Holmes.''

The man stopped pacing as if he'd been slapped in the face. Teddy lowered his leg, ready to spring for the door if he had to.

''That's right,'' Teddy said, staring at him. ''I'm not gonna sit here and listen to you feel sorry for yourself. The girl's dead. Her body's all fucked up. Her parents are probably at the morgue looking at it right now. Merry Christmas, Holmes. If you want to sit down and talk, I'll listen. But if you're gonna rant and rave and get all worked up, then I'm out of here.''

Holmes was staring back at him with those ragged eyes. ''What's your name?''

''Teddy Mack.''

''You work for Barnett, not the police?''

Teddy nodded.

Holmes took it in, then seemed to relax some and sat down. Teddy thought about what he'd just done and couldn't believe it. Scared shitless, he cleared his throat and moved on.

''Tell me what you remember,'' he said.

''I want a trial. Even dogs get their day in court. Doesn't matter what they've done. If you're a person, you get a trial and go to court.''

''Tell me what you remember.''

''I can't remember anything,'' Holmes shouted in frustration.

Teddy looked through the glass and saw the guards staring at them, then turn away.

"I must've blacked out," Holmes said. "I know I was there. I'm not saying I wasn't because I woke up and saw the blood. It was all over the place. All over me and my clothes. It was like I was sleepwalking or something. I remember running to my car. Next thing I know I'm in my own house, and I don't even know how I got there."

Holmes covered his face with his hands again and started weeping.

"What about Darlene Lewis? Did you know her very well?"

Holmes nodded behind his hands.

"How well did you know her?"

"I don't want to get her into any trouble. She's just a girl."

"Not anymore, Holmes. Now tell me how you knew her."

Holmes peeked through his fingers again. "She used to tease me," he said.

Teddy shuddered, getting his first glimpse at a possible motive. "How did she tease you?"

"Sometimes it really got to me," Holmes whispered. "In the summer when she was out at the pool with her friends, she'd make fun of me. I could hear them whispering and laughing at me. But when Darlene was alone, she treated me different."

"How did she treat you different?"

"She used to let me look at her."

Teddy sat up, trying not to show any emotion. "What do you mean look at her?"

"She'd stand there in her bathing suit and let me look at her. She'd say something like, 'Okay, you've got two minutes.' Then she'd just stand there and let me look at her."

"Was she always in her bathing suit?"

"A couple of times she was in her bra and panties."

Teddy thought about the pair of panties he'd found in Darlene's bedroom closet. They were almost transparent.

"Was she always wearing clothes?" he asked. "In her bathing suit or in her underwear?"

Holmes nodded.

"Did you ever touch her?"

Holmes hesitated, but eventually shook his head. "I used to think about doing things to her though. I couldn't help it. When I started thinking, sometimes I couldn't stop."

"What kind of things?"

". . . Just *things*."

"Did you tell any of this to the police?"

"I don't remember," Holmes said, lowering his hands. "I'm tired. I want you to go away now. I wanna go home."

Seven

He used to think about doing *things* to her. He couldn't help it and couldn't stop. . . .

Teddy walked out of the lobby into the parking lot, looking for his car in the freezing rain and wet snow.

Things . . .

The *things* Holmes had done to Darlene Lewis were so brutal, the slob blacked out and couldn't even remember driving home. What Holmes had said didn't amount to a confession, but the motive was clear enough.

Teddy checked his watch. It was after eleven. When the day started, he was about to win his first ruling in civil court. Now he was helping Jim Barnett shepherd a maniac through the system who insisted on a trial. It would be prolonged. Loud and painful for everyone.

He spotted his car ahead, keeping his eyes on the ground and pretending to check the wet asphalt for ice. He knew Holmesburg Prison was on the other side of I-95, and didn't want to look at it. He was afraid to look at it because he thought he might break. It had been a long day of keeping everything down. Turning off his memories, forgetting what was past—he hadn't told anyone that this was the stuff of nightmares for over half of his short life. Having to meet Holmes had only been the hideous icing on a poisoned cake.

When the assistant warden told him about the Curran-Fromhold murders, Teddy had acted as if he were hearing it for the first time, even though he wasn't. His father had told him the same story when he was just fourteen. Teddy had heard the rumors at school and asked him about it while making a Saturday visit to the prison with his mother. His father admitted they were true, while trying to reassure his worried son that this kind of thing didn't happen anymore.

Everything would be okay.

Teddy wiped the snow off the windshield. As he started the car his eyes went directly to the temperature gauge on the dash. Thirty-three degrees. The roads might be slippery, but they wouldn't have turned to ice yet. He switched on the heat. While he waited for the car to warm up, he dug his cell phone out and checked his messages. There were three.

The first was from Brooke Jones, requesting his original files on that personal injury case. She said she couldn't find them in the canvas tote bag she'd taken from his office, and tried to make it sound like what she was doing for him amounted to a big favor. She was a bitch from the word go, and he couldn't stand the affected tone of her voice. Jones was one of those people you see so often on the road these days. In a hurry going nowhere. Teddy deleted the message before she was through.

The second message was from Jill Sykes, warning him that Brooke Jones was going to call. He smiled at her timing, listening to her urgent whisper with the sounds of the office in the background. As she hung up, he couldn't help hoping that the firm would hire her once she got through her exams. He needed an ally. Someone who wasn't always keeping score.

The third message would be from Barnett. Teddy switched the interior light on and grabbed a pen in case he had to write something down. The phone beeped and the message started. Two seconds later, the phone beeped again. It had been a hang-up, probably from Jones. Barnett hadn't called, and Teddy found it incredible. He punched Barnett's cell number into his phone. When the message center kicked in, he swore. Obviously, Barnett had turned off his phone. Teddy flipped open his address book and found Barnett's home number. He punched it in, trying to keep cool. The phone rang four times and then Barnett's service picked up.

Teddy slipped his cell phone into his pocket, wondering what the hell was wrong with Barnett. After a moment, he switched the wipers on and backed out of the parking space. As he pulled past the gate and out of the lot, the car made a sudden shift and slid. He couldn't tell if the roads were slick or it was just his car. He knew all four tires needed to be replaced, but had been trying to put off the expense until after the holidays. His credit cards were maxed out, and when he applied for a new one last week, they turned him down. Either way, he could feel the Corolla slipping on the asphalt. Teddy backed off the gas, easing the car up to speed in short bursts. As he climbed the exit ramp onto I-95, the lights from an approaching truck hit the rearview mirror and Teddy looked away from the glare. His eyes swept through the darkness and stopped on the abandoned building hidden in the falling snow.

Holmesburg Prison.

The building was completely dark, the ancient prison silhouetted against the wrecked cityscape of North Philadelphia. He hadn't wanted to look at it. He hadn't wanted to see it, but there it was—rising out of the muck after being buried in his mind for so long.

His father had said it would be okay, but it really wasn't.

Teddy tightened his grip on the wheel, knowing he was losing it. He checked the temperature gauge and watched the cold air drop six degrees below freezing as he reached the city, then left it behind, heading west on the expressway. The roads were covered in a black glaze, and the freezing rain had given way to heavy snow. Digging into his pocket, he fished the pack of Marlboros out and lit one. Then he cracked the window open and flipped the radio on, hoping that if he concentrated on the chatter, his mind wouldn't slip from the surface the way his car was skidding down the road.

It would be okay. His father said it would. Teddy had been so young at the time, he believed him. Two weeks later, the phone rang and his mother got the big call. . . .

Jonathan Mack had been an architect and builder of moderately priced homes in the suburbs fifteen miles west of the city known as the Main Line. He'd formed the business with a high school friend upon graduation from the School of Architecture at Yale, and after ten years of struggling, people began to notice their innovative designs. A few years after that, they couldn't build houses fast enough. But Teddy's father had been a visionary. He could see the sprawl eating up the countryside and had an idea that he thought could save it. Instead of building one development of single-lot homes after the next, he'd been playing with the idea of designing a self-contained community. People needed a place to live, and the government wasn't up to doing anything about the population, which was out of control. The choice seemed clear. Either you compacted the living space or you cut every tree down. Jonathan Mack's goal was to save the land.

A site was found for the project and a team of architects were commissioned to assist with his father's design. Teddy could remember watching his father go over the drawings every night at the game table in his study. His father seemed so happy, and Teddy would sneak peeks at him, hiding behind the rail of the staircase in the living room. There were lots for hundreds of town houses, a space for a shopping center so no one would have to drive very far and waste gas, and then just as much space for three corporate parks. It was as if his dad were designing an entire city.

The amount of money required to develop the project was enormous. Yet his father secured the financing easier than anyone anticipated. It was in the genius of his plan. It made sense and it was by Jonathan Mack. Everyone wanted to be in on it, Teddy remembered—except for the environmentalists.

One night he'd been allowed to attend a town meeting with his mother and younger sister. They sat in the back row and watched the presentation and the questions that followed. Some of the people seemed mean, Teddy thought at the time, and many of them were angry at his father. But Jonathan Mack never batted an eye. Instead, he told the environmentalists that he agreed with them. Then he turned the slide projector back on and showed them aerial photographs of what the area would look like in twenty years if it were developed as single-lot homes. They were caught up in the short-term view, he said, just as he had been less than two years ago. In spite of all the construction, his father pointed out that they were only using forty-five percent of the land. The rest of the property would remain untouched forever. By the time his father was done, the mood in the room changed and even the key environmentalists were on board.

Six months later, they broke ground. Everything seemed to be going according to schedule. Then one Saturday, Jonathan Mack's friend and partner was found dead in the office by the cleaning staff. Teddy was too young to get details, but he heard his parents whispering and knew the man had been shot to death with a gun. Several weeks passed with his parents going into the den every night after dinner and talking behind closed doors. The joy was gone, the house filled with a new kind of tension Teddy had never experienced before. He tried to compensate for the change by taking better care of his little sister, doing his chores before he was asked, and keeping his room neat—things he'd never been able to manage very well in the past. At night he went to sleep wishing everything would change back to the way things were. Who needed big building projects when a single house would do? Then one afternoon he was in the kitchen helping his mother get dinner ready when the doorbell rang. Teddy ran to answer it and saw four cops standing on the other side of the storm door.

They said all they wanted to do was talk, but as Teddy climbed the stairs with his sister, he knew they were lying. He watched from his bedroom window as his father was led out of the house in handcuffs. His mother was crying and he could see that his father was, too. She kept trying to touch him before he got into the car, hug him and give him a last kiss. But one of the cops grabbed her and pulled her away, yelling at her to stop.

Teddy raced downstairs and bolted out the front door. Before he knew it, he was hitting the cop, punching him, giving it everything he had. His body was still small, still a boy's, but he'd spent most of his life lifting rocks out of streambeds in search of salamanders and climbing trees until he reached the highest branches. He was strong for his size and didn't stop until one of the other cops pulled him off and threw him onto the ground. The cop held him down, asking him if he wanted to go to jail like his old man. Teddy looked him in the eye and told him that if his friend didn't stop touching his mother, he'd kill him. The cop looked at him a moment without saying anything. Then he let go and got in the car, taking Teddy's father away with his motherfucking cop friends. . . .

Teddy's idyllic childhood was over.

He lit another cigarette, thinking about how much he hated criminal law and the world that went with it. It hit hard and ran all the way to the bottom.

A report on road conditions came over the radio, jogging him back to the surface. The news was as good as his day had been. Apparently the snow was falling faster than it could be plowed. People were being warned to stay home. By the time he reached King of Prussia and exited onto Route 202, the snow was a foot deep and the four-lane road looked deserted. All except for one car a quarter mile up. Teddy kept his eyes on the car's taillights, riding the tracks left behind as if a train. When he hit the Devon exit, the car ahead continued along the four-lane vanishing into the night, and Teddy was on his own.

It took three tries to make it up the mile-long hill on Devon State Road—the third attempt a nail-biter at fifty miles an hour. The car slipped and skidded, requiring both sides of the two-lane road, but he made it over the hill with enough momentum and didn't veer off into the trees. Once he glided over the other side, he crossed Lancaster Pike and headed south on Waterloo Road. Two miles down, he pulled into the driveway noting Quint Adler's car beside his mother's as he parked. The lights were on in the barn out back. Even with the doors closed he could smell the oak burning from the woodstove and knew they were still working.

Teddy was grateful that Quint was here. He was grateful to Quint for a lot of things, but tonight it was just because he wanted to be alone.

He got out and looked at the house in the snow. It was an elegant colonial farmhouse built in 1820 and set on four acres of wooded land. A long way off from Holmesburg Prison. His father had bought the property before Teddy could remember, remodeling the stone house and building a greenhouse off the den for his mother. Once the renovations were complete, his father got started on the barn, converting the space into an art studio for her as well.

A car ambled down the road. Teddy watched it pass the house, listening to its engine tick and marveling at the way snow muffled the sound. He looked across the street where the open fields had been eaten up by one housing development after the next just as his father said they would. The big houses were set down in haphazard clusters as if the result of a tornado, the architecture cheap and grotesque. Even worse, none of the people who lived in these homes believed in planting trees. Instead they preferred the open look, marring the once pastoral setting with a show of money and turning the rolling hills into a garish eyesore. To Teddy, the layout reminded him of a graveyard.

Teddy flicked his cigarette into the street, grabbed his briefcase from the car, and walked around back to the kitchen door. Kicking the snow off his shoes, he stepped inside and got out of his jacket. He needed a drink. Not his usual beer, but something stronger. He decided on vodka, pulling the blue bottle out of the freezer and filling a large glass loaded with ice to the brim. He took a first sip, letting the smooth liquid coat his throat and warm his stomach. Then he headed up the back staircase to his room, hoping the medicine would quiet him down.

He switched the light on and closed the door, taking another sip of vodka before setting the glass on the table beside the bed. Opening his cell phone, he thought he'd give Barnett another try and punched in his number at home. After two rings, Barnett's service picked up again.

Teddy was trapped and he knew it. He couldn't leave the firm because his debt after four years of college and three more years at law school amounted to one hundred and ninety thousand dollars. The interest on his loans was costing him another eighteen thousand a year. After he made loan and credit card payments each month, his check barely covered food and clothes. He needed this job, but he couldn't continue helping Barnett either. Not with Oscar Holmes.

He grabbed the remote and turned the TV on. It was after midnight. A football game or movie must have delayed the schedule because the local news was still on. Teddy sat on the bed, watching the broadcast as he sipped his drink. The news readers had cut to a live shot of Darlene Lewis's house in the storm. The reporter was a woman who looked more like a model. She had big hair and capped teeth, wore too much makeup and jewelry, and in spite of the weather, left her jacket open so everyone could see her Armani suit underneath. The death house was dark and haunting and provided just the right backdrop for the story, the police long gone. The model stood on the front steps, explaining what happened that day in broad strokes and pretending that she was afraid. But she wasn't a very good actress, and her half smile seemed out of place. Teddy wondered if she wasn't really happy about what had happened to Darlene Lewis this morning. Ratings would be up. Murder paid for the Armani suit and the car and house and mutual funds that went with it. The model had a big story and everyone would be watching her tonight in spite of the hour.

Mirror, mirror on the wall . . .

The live shot cut to footage recorded earlier in the night, but it wasn't much of a relief. Teddy watched as the people from the medical examiner's office wheeled Darlene Lewis's corpse out the front door on a gurney and rolled it into their van. The sight of the body bag brought it all back, and Teddy could see the girl still tied down to the dining room table, screaming through her gag. The friendly neighborhood mail-man was standing over her. Holmes had been teased once too often, he imagined. Pulling out his knife, he'd cut her flesh away and eaten it.

Teddy switched the TV off and killed the lights, lying back on the bed and considering his options as he gulped down more medicine. There weren't any, he decided. His eyes moved through the darkness to the twelve-gauge shot-gun mounted on the wall beside the window. He'd inherited the gun after his father's death. A long time ago, when the world was a different place and the fields on the other side of the street were just fields and not graveyards. They used to shoot skeet together, just the two of them. Sometimes they'd leave the gun behind and just walk, spooking the pheasants hidden in the tall grass. He could see the gleam in his dad's eyes as the colorful birds took flight. He could still smell the scent of his aftershave mixed with sweat when he hugged his father and kissed him on the cheek. Teddy hadn't fired the gun since it came into his possession thirteen years ago. Instead, he preferred to look at it and dream about the way things were before they took his father away, accusing him of murder, and not protecting him from his own cellmate. Strung out and crazed, the man had beaten his father to death because he couldn't get his hands on enough money to buy drugs. The man needed another hot load and would've done anything to get it.

Holmesburg Prison . . .

Teddy finished off the glass of vodka. The room was spinning. As he laid his head on the pillow and gazed out the window at the falling snow, he hoped he wouldn't dream tonight.

Eight

Teddy poured a cup of coffee and walked down the hall to his office. Before he could get to his desk, Brooke Jones had picked up his scent and was in his face full-blown.

"Why didn't you call me back last night?" she said. "This is a professional office. When someone leaves a message, you're supposed to return the call. And don't tell me you didn't get it."

He sat down, taking in her attitude as he sipped the hot coffee and gazed out the window. It was eight-thirty, and he was already working on his third cup. The vodka hadn't worked. It had been a night of tossing and turning, fighting off his demons and nightmares, and waking up every hour or so in a cold sweat. By five A.M. the bedsheets were soaked through to the mattress and he'd had enough. Deciding to get an early start on the day, he got dressed and drove into town. It was a warm, sunny day—the weather as crazy as Brooke Jones.

"You're not hearing me," she said. "We're going to trial in two weeks and you still have the motion papers. I want your files. I want all of them right now."

He turned away from the window and finally looked at

her. She was in a hurry again. All worked up over nothing and shouting orders at him.

"Who says it's your case, Brooke?" he asked calmly.

"I was in court yesterday," she shot back. "It's my case. Barnett said so."

"That was yesterday, and I appreciate what you did for me."

"What are you talking about? I spoke with Barnett last night. He said it's my case until you're finished with whatever you're doing for him. He's pulling all your cases."

Teddy had been in the office waiting for Barnett for more than an hour. When he tried reaching him by phone, he hit his voice mail just as he did last night. Teddy's anger had subsided, and he was beginning to worry about the man. But now the anger was back. The feeling that he was being used.

"What time did you talk to him last night?" he said.

"After eleven. After you didn't call me back. Now where are the files?"

She pushed his mail aside and started going through his desk as if it were her own.

"Please don't do that," he said.

She picked up another file and opened it. She must not have heard him. Teddy stood up, stepping between her and the desk.

"Get out," he said.

She stopped and gave him a look. Her eyes narrowed.

"This is a favor," she said. "Who wants a personal injury case anyway? I could care less."

"If you don't care, then stop whining and get out."

"I've been here longer than you have. I've got more experience. Why is Barnett always asking you for help instead of coming to me?"

"I don't know, Brooke. I'm not a mind reader. I'm just asking you to leave."

He held her gaze, knowing she was seething. When she finally turned and stomped out, he sat back down and sighed in her wake. His head was throbbing, behind his eyes and just below the left temple. He opened his briefcase, grabbed the bottle of aspirin, and popped the cap. As he chased the pills down with more hot coffee, he turned away from the door and looked at his office. Even though it was half the size of a partner's office, he was grateful for the window and at least a partial view of the city. He slipped the bottle of aspirin into his jacket pocket and leaned back in the chair, gazing at the building across the street. He'd give Jones the files, he decided, but only if he had to. Only after he spoke with Barnett. There was still a chance Barnett could handle Oscar Holmes on his own from here on out. Still a chance Teddy could find his way back to the life he had before he stepped into the death house on Scottsboro Road.

Jill Sykes tapped on the door and gave him an anxious look.

"He's here," she said. "He wants to see you."

Teddy followed her into the hall, ignoring his natural attraction for her the way he always did. But as he swept past her, he could smell the shampoo in her light brown hair, the faint scent of her perfume. He caught the spark in her eyes, and glanced at her angular face. She looked fresh, as if she'd slept the whole night through.

She smiled at him, then wished him luck. He nodded back, starting down the hall to the other side of the floor. When he turned the corner, he saw Brooke Jones exiting Barnett's office with her tail down. Teddy filed the dirty look away as they passed each other and kept walking.

He found Barnett seated at his desk going through a three-ring binder. Teddy moved closer, but didn't sit down.

"I thought we were gonna talk last night," he said in an even tone.

Barnett kept his eyes on the binder, scanning a page quickly, then turning to the next. "Sorry, Teddy. I had my hands full. How bad was it?"

"About what you'd expect," he said, "for a cannibal. You want to tell me what's going on, or would you like me to guess?"

Barnett finally looked up. Not at Teddy, but at Larry Stokes, cofounder of the firm, peeking in the doorway with obvious concern. Stokes was ten years older than Barnett, his hair already as white as the clouds. And he was socially connected, which meant he spent more time acquiring clients and maintaining the firm's political contacts than actually practicing law. Larry Stokes had never been much of an attorney, but he played the role well and the arrangement had proven successful for over twenty-five years. Stokes brought the clients in. Barnett handled the legal work once they signed an agreement and the firm's accounting department received their retainer.

"I didn't mean to be eavesdropping," Stokes said to Barnett. "Is there a problem?"

"No, Larry. Everything's fine. We still on for lunch?"

"I hope so."

"Good. I'll see you then."

Barnett faked a smile, then closed the door and returned to his desk. Teddy kept his eyes on him. Barnett looked pale and washed out, and Teddy guessed the man had been up all night just as he had.

"I haven't broken the news to Larry yet," Barnett said. "Holmes has a history of mental illness. He should have been put away before it came to this. Before he hurt anyone."

Teddy glanced at the binder Barnett held against his chest.

"It's a copy of the murder book," Barnett said, closing the binder and handing it over. "At least the start of one. It's all yours. I want you to call the district attorney's office this afternoon and make sure it's kept up to date."

There were two chairs before Barnett's desk. Teddy slid one out and sat down without opening the binder.

"They're working fast," Barnett was saying. "They've got a witness, and the fingerprints match on both the body and the murder weapon. Same with the lip prints. If there was any question about Oscar Holmes, we're past that now. I was with his family last night. All they want is to make sure he gets the help he needs. An institution rather than prison. Life without parole instead of a shot in the arm.''

"There's no way the district attorney is gonna make a deal," Teddy said. "Not with the hit he took yesterday. Not if he wants to become the city's next mayor."

"You don't think so?"

It had been a question, but it was clear to Teddy that Barnett understood the situation as well as he did. District Attorney Alan Andrews had no reason to want to make a deal.

"We need to do the right thing," Teddy said. "We need to pass this on to a criminal attorney. Someone who has more experience than we do."

"I wish we could, believe me."

"Why can't we?"

Barnett sighed, loosening his tie and unbuttoning his collar. "It's not a favor for a client, Teddy. It's a friend. One of my oldest friends. I've known the family since I was your age. Even younger than you. If their name were to get out, it would make the papers. TV cameras would be all over their front lawn. Their reputation would be destroyed. I don't want to see them go through that. It's hard enough on them that it's Holmes."

"If they're trying to avoid headlines, tell them to forget it. I saw what the girl looked like. What he did to her. Forget about the newspapers. Forget about TV news. This is what's next on cable."

He saw Barnett tense up. He saw the fear rush into his eyes.

"You really think so?" Barnett asked.

Teddy nodded, hoping he hadn't hurt the man. Still, the reality seemed obvious. Darlene Lewis had been a beautiful young girl at an age when her hormones were on fire. She'd been taunting Holmes for at least six months with her body, maybe even longer. Holmes held on until his engines blew, then lashed out like an animal from another planet. The story had color and sex appeal. When the details got out, any hope of keeping the press away would be ludicrous.

"Well, we're stuck with it," Barnett said. "We'll do the best we can."

Teddy settled back in the chair, thinking that he was stuck with it, too, whether he wanted to be or not.

Barnett leaned over his desk. "When you met Holmes last night, was he still insisting on a trial?"

Teddy nodded.

Barnett frowned, thinking it over. "We've got plenty of time to talk to him before we make any decisions," he said. "If we need help, we'll get it."

"Who?"

"I spoke with William Nash last night, but he refused. I was hoping you'd give it another shot this morning. You went to Penn. He may not be practicing law anymore, but he's still the best defense attorney in the city. I think it's worth a try."

Teddy thought it over. William S. Nash and his legal workshop at Penn Law had been responsible for proving that District Attorney Alan Andrews prosecuted an innocent man and sent him to his death. It was a good bet that Andrews hated Nash for it. If Nash agreed to help, there was a chance the DA might want to make a deal in order to get rid of Nash. The DA would hold out for a week or two, working the Darlene Lewis murder until the headlines changed in his favor and his mistake was old news, but then he might give in to the pressure. He might be willing to deal. Andrews could take credit for Holmes's quick arrest and putting the man away forever. And Holmes would avoid the death penalty and get the psychiatric care his family was hoping for. Barnett's idea to bring Nash in was actually brilliant, and probably the result of a night spent mulling over the case in every detail. Quietly, Teddy imagined, with the phones switched off and a drink in his hand.

Teddy looked up and caught Barnett staring at him. He'd been watching him think it through as if seated at a poker table with a winning hand.

"You see how we're gonna play it," Barnett said.

Teddy nodded, even smiled. Barnett had found a quick

way out for everyone concerned. Once Nash was in, he guessed the only player in the mix who wouldn't be willing was Oscar Holmes. But Barnett was probably right about that, too. They had plenty of time to work on Holmes. The longer he sat in a cell, the more pliable he'd be.

Nine

Teddy set the murder book down on his desk and looked at Jill sitting before the computer at the worktable by the window. She had a desk of her own with the rest of the clerks in an open room off the library. Although there were times after hours when they were both working late and she used the computer in Teddy's office to study, this wasn't one of them. He knew she'd been waiting for him to finish with Barnett and wanted to know what happened.

"You're defending him, aren't you?" she said. "Oscar Holmes."

He nodded and took a deep breath, then sat down and opened the binder. The murder had occurred twenty-four hours ago, yet the paper on the homicide was already half an inch thick. Teddy thumbed through the pages and realized they were in chronological order. Half the reports were filed by Detective Vega. But the other half were written by a Detective Nathan Ellwood. Teddy hadn't met the second detective, but assumed he was Vega's partner. Barnett had told him the investigation was on the fast track, and Teddy checked the time and dates at the top of the detectives' preliminary reports. They'd begun writing at four in the morning. Both detectives had worked through the night.

Jill gently cleared her throat. "How could you defend someone who did the kind of things they're saying Holmes did on TV?"

"What are they saying on TV?"

"That he cut her up. That maybe he tortured her."

"I don't know," he said quietly. "I've never done this kind of thing before."

She looked at him a moment, her light brown eyes searching his face. When she turned back to the computer, he checked the time and returned to the binder. He needed to get through the murder book before he faced William Nash. And he wanted to be on campus within the hour.

The early reports mirrored what the district attorney had told him yesterday. An elderly neighbor, Beatrice McGee, had seen Holmes running from the house covered in blood. When he raced off in his mail truck, she noticed that the front door was open and walked inside the house. She found Darlene's body on the dining room table and called the police, then popped a nitroglycerin tablet because she had a bad heart. The officer who took her initial statement noted that she was upset, but appeared clear in mind and didn't require any medical assistance. She knew Holmes by name, and said he'd been her mailman for many years.

Once they had a name, Ellwood left Vega in Chestnut Hill and took off for the city. Holmes hadn't completed his mail route or returned his truck to the post office. Ellwood caught up with the man at his apartment at Twenty-third and Pine, where he made the arrest. Holmes was driven downtown to the homicide division at police headquarters. Ellwood stayed at the apartment, supervising the investigation. They found Holmes's clothing buried in the trash, the murder weapon stuffed in his mailbag on the front seat of his truck. After the crime scene was processed, Ellwood returned to headquarters and the interview began.

Teddy read Holmes's statement carefully. There was no mention of his prior relationship with Darlene Lewis. None of the sexual taunting and teasing. But Holmes seemed as confused as he'd been last night, admitting to Ellwood that he was there but saying he couldn't remember what happened and wanted to talk to his lawyer. He gave the detective Jim Barnett's name. Because he was so distraught, Ellwood made the call for him. Once Barnett arrived and they had a chance to speak, Holmes was photographed and finger-printed. Blood and hair samples were taken with Barnett's consent, along with two prints of Holmes's lips.

Although the results from the rape kit weren't in yet, the finger and lip prints were conclusive. Every print Teddy had seen on the girl's body under the black lights belonged to Oscar Holmes. Additional prints had been found on the legs of the dining room table where the girl's arms and legs had been tied down with rags. These prints matched Holmes's as well.

Teddy flipped the page and felt a chill ripple up his spine. He was staring at a photograph of Holmes that must have been taken in his apartment at the time of his arrest. The face the police had seen when Holmes answered the door. Holmes may have had time to ditch his clothing in the trash, but he hadn't washed up yet. And his face hadn't been sprayed with the girl's blood, but was entirely covered in it as if hit by a mud pie. The blood looked like it had dried and thickened, and Teddy could see it caked in the man's hair and between his teeth. Behind the hideous blood mask, the look of insanity in Holmes's wild eyes was something Teddy knew he would never forget. The man hadn't just killed the girl. He'd burrowed his face in her wounds and gobbled up her skin.

He threw the binder on the desk and gasped. Jill turned from the computer, saw the murder book opened to Holmes's picture, and jumped to her feet.

"Jesus Christ," she shouted.

Teddy grabbed the binder and slammed it closed. He was carrying enough of the horror inside his head for both of them.

"What do you know about William Nash?" he asked.

He was trying to distract her by raising a simple question, but her eyes were locked on the binder. From the look on her face, Teddy hadn't closed the book fast enough.

"He teaches at Penn," she said slowly.

"You ever take any of his classes?"

She nodded. "One. But only because I had to."

"Are you okay, Jill?"

She nodded again, her eyes finally meeting his as she sat down. Teddy made a point of settling back in his chair.

"I've never met him," he said after a moment. "But everybody says he's good."

"He gets people off for murder. I'm not sure I'd call that good."

Jill was still preoccupied with the binder. Teddy threw it in his briefcase, then got up and moved over to the couch.

"That's what defense attorneys are supposed to do," he said.

"I don't mean the innocent ones," she said. "I mean the people where all the evidence is against them, and Nash finds a way to get them off on a technicality. The people who really did it. Remember in your first year when you had to take everything? Who'd you get for criminal law? Diliberto?"

"Yeah."

"Well, Nash was filling in for Diliberto, and I got stuck with him. He went through his past cases. The Hilltop Rapist. The Venice Beach Strangler. That man who killed seven women in Michigan and buried them in the sidewalk outside his house. Nash defended them and got them off. It was like he was happy about it. Proud of what he'd done."

Teddy wasn't sure about the first two cases, but thought he remembered reading something about the Sidewalk Murders in a news magazine. The man lived in a suburban neighborhood outside Detroit. He'd been retired for ten years and spent most of his days working on his lawn and various gardens. It was a quiet neighborhood, most of the middle-class homes owned by families with young children. The kind of place where kids still played in the street. And the little man who lived at the end of the block always seemed to take great pleasure in watching the children play on his section of the sidewalk. Then one day an underground water main burst open. When the utility company tore up the street and sidewalk, they found the bodies of seven women buried in the concrete.

"How'd Nash get the guy off?" Teddy asked.

"Everyone in the neighborhood liked the old man. No one could believe he did it. And he was a small man with a bad back. The police couldn't figure out how he tore up the concrete, put the bodies in, and then laid new concrete down. Neither could the jury. Nash got the man off and he was set free."

Teddy laughed. He couldn't help it. Jill seemed so intense.

"Maybe he didn't do it," he said.

She shrugged, brooding in silence.

"Then how'd he get the bodies in the concrete, Jill?"

"The bodies weren't *in* the sidewalk," she said. "They were under it. He could've dug the holes when he was gardening and slid them underneath."

"I thought he was an old man with a bad back."

"Maybe he had help. What does it matter? He did it, and Nash manipulated the jury and got him off."

Teddy stood up, rubbing the back of his neck. His headache was gone, but not the tightness above his shoulders.

"Then why do you think Nash is so popular on campus?" he asked.

Jill shook her head. "Are you trying to recruit him? Are you trying to make the world a better place by getting Oscar Holmes off?"

"I don't think there's much chance of that."

He packed up his briefcase and got into his coat. As he headed for the door, he turned and gave her a look.

"If Jones stops by," he said, "tell her the files she wants are right beside you on the windowsill."

Ten

He scanned the building directory, unable to find Nash's name among the list of faculty members. Although he'd graduated from the school, Teddy had been so absorbed in his own studies that he never had a reason to meet Nash or visit him in his office. It struck him that the legal workshop operated out of its own building on the edge of campus. Nash's office would probably be there.

He looked around for someone to ask, but the lobby was deserted. With the holidays less than two weeks off and exams under way, students wouldn't be in class. Teddy exited the building. Squinting at the bright sunlight reflecting off the snow, he turned down the path and headed for the library. He could have called Nash, of course, but the man had already refused Barnett. Giving him another easy chance to say no over the phone didn't seem to make much sense.

The librarian behind the checkout desk found Nash's address in the faculty directory, confirming that his office and workshop were in the same building. It was five blocks west. Rather than return to his car, Teddy buttoned his jacket and set out on foot. The truth was that he needed Nash as much as Barnett or even Holmes did. He needed the case to go away, needed his nightmares to sink back into the past so that his fresh wounds would have time to heal.

The light turned green and he started across the street. It was a small, two-story brick building set on the corner. Teddy guessed it had been built sometime in the early 1900s, but undergone a major renovation in the last few years. The mortar between the bricks looked fresh, and the windows on the second floor were too large and modern to fit the period.

He found the front door unlocked and entered a central hallway. There were three rows of unmarked doors on each side of the staircase. The smell of fresh plaster caught his attention. When he glanced inside one of the rooms, he saw sheets of blue board stacked on the floor and realized the building's renovation was still under way.

He climbed the staircase, greeted by the smells of fresh paint and polyurethane. Directly before him were a set of glass doors opening to a small library. Skylights had been installed in the ceiling, flooding the rows of books with overhead light. When he checked the doors he found them locked. On the other side of the hall were two classrooms. Then Teddy noticed a door to the right of the library and opened it. Construction was complete, but the walls remained unpainted and it looked as if the room was being used to store the construction workers' more expensive tools.

The door at the other end of the hall opened. Teddy turned, watching a middle-aged woman start for the stairs.

"I'm looking for Professor Nash," he said.

The woman smiled. "Are you a student?"

"I used to be. I've never been here before."

She pointed to the door she'd just exited through. "In there," she said. "The signs aren't up yet."

Teddy watched her vanish down the stairway. Then he swung what seemed like an unusually heavy door open and stepped across the threshold.

It was a lobby. No one was at the desk, and Teddy figured the woman he'd just met was Nash's assistant on her way to an early lunch. When he heard someone begin speaking, he looked through a second doorway into Nash's office. He was on the phone, staring back at Teddy from his desk at the far end of the long room. It was an odd look, piercing at first, followed by the slightest of smiles, as if the man recognized him and had been waiting for him.

Nash waved him in, motioning Teddy to take a seat beside his desk. Not wanting to invade the man's privacy, Teddy hesitated a moment before finally deciding to enter.

The walls were more red than orange, the wood-planked floors, a light beech. He spotted a set of open doors leading to the library on his right and realized the books belonged to Nash. To the left, oversize windows had been cut into the wall, offering a view of the campus on the other side of the street. He passed a long table set in the middle of the office, thinking it looked a lot like the kind found in a jury room. When he sat down, he counted the number of chairs and hid his smile. There were twelve. Nash worked at his desk each day facing a jury room.

Although the office had been newly renovated, the place had the look and feel of being used and broken in. Files were strewn across the jury table and piled against the walls. Teddy noticed the media center beside Nash's desk. The cabinet was open revealing a TV switched to a local station with the sound muted. Numerous videotapes were stacked on the floor, labeled by hand.

From what Teddy could tell, Nash's telephone call wasn't personal. It sounded more like an interview. Nash was talking about his press conference yesterday. District Attorney Alan Andrews had questioned the results of the students participating in his legal workshop, Nash was saying. Unfortunately for Andrews, the DNA results spoke for the themselves and the science couldn't be discounted. Andrews prosecuted the wrong man, pressed for the death penalty, and now an innocent man was dead. This wasn't the time for political posturing, but for someone to step up and do the right thing. If Andrews couldn't, then Nash told the reporter he'd be more than willing. And, yes, because of these results, Nash and his workshop would be reviewing any past cases the district attorney handled in order to rule out what he thought might be a trend.

Nash may have been in his late fifties, but his voice matched his overall appearance, remaining young and virile. He was dressed in a black turtleneck sweater and black slacks. His face was lean and angular, his blond hair mixed with gray sweeping straight back from his forehead. But it was his eyes that Teddy thought probably worked best in a courtroom. They were cobalt blue and had a definite reach about them, his pupils dilated slightly as if a cat's. Nash didn't *approach* hostile witnesses in trial, Teddy imagined. He saw through them and *sprang*.

Nash finally hung up the phone, lifting a cigar out of the ashtray and relighting it.

"Actually, there are five," he said, toking up. "Five more cases Mr. Andrews has to account for. There could be others, of course. But we're just getting started."

Teddy didn't say anything. He'd just noticed the poster-sized lithograph hanging on the wall by the door to the lobby. It was an empty prison cell with afternoon light feeding in through a small window. The cell door stood open, and a blanket had been left behind.

"Do you like it?" Nash asked. "It's called *Free at Last.*"

Teddy nodded, watching Nash gaze across the jury table at the image of the empty cell.

"It's by one of my former clients," Nash said. "He was a bank robber in Los Angeles. A safe cracker. Now he's an artist living in New York City. Who would've guessed the man had so many talents?"

Nash laughed and shook his head. From the dreamy smile he bore, Teddy knew that at least part of what Jill had said was true. The man loved his work, was morally complex, and could easily generate fear in others because of his enthusiasm and intelligence.

Nash checked his cigar and tapped the end in the ashtray, his eyes drifting across the desk and settling on Teddy with weight.

"Your boss is in over his head," he said. "But you already know that, don't you?"

Teddy wondered how the man knew who he was. Nash spoke up before he could ask.

"I often take long walks," he said. "I used to watch you row from the bike path by the river. Barnett mentioned your name last night on the phone."

He sat back in the chair, savoring the rich smoke.

Teddy opened his briefcase, pulled the murder book out, and passed it across the desk. "Then you know why I'm here."

Nash took the binder, but didn't open it. "Not really," he said.

"We're trying to take the death penalty off the table. We're trying to make sure Holmes gets the psychiatric treatment he needs."

"What did Oscar Holmes do to win over so many good friends?"

Teddy noted the cynical tone in Nash's voice. He reached for the murder book and thumbed through the pages until he found the picture of Holmes wearing Darlene Lewis's blood on his face. When he passed it back, Nash examined the photo without any visible reaction, then held the notebook closer noting the flecks of blood between the man's teeth.

"It's the help his family wants and thinks he needs," Teddy said.

Nash grimaced, setting the binder on his desk. "I'm not particularly interested in what his family may or may not think he needs."

"All we're doing is seeing Holmes through the system. I'm willing to do the legwork. It shouldn't take much of your time at all."

"That's exactly what I was afraid you'd say."

Their eyes met. He'd put Teddy down again and wanted him to know it. He settled back into his chair, appraising Teddy by the inch.

"You graduated at the top of your class," he said after

a moment. "I've often wondered why someone with your ability avoided criminal law. You should've been drawn to it, yet you stayed as far away from my classes as you possibly could. You look scared, Teddy. Why are you frightened if the case is as straightforward as you say? It must have something to do with your past."

Teddy flinched. Nash gave him a long look with those cobalt-blue eyes of his, then swiveled his chair around to the window behind his desk. He was staring outside at a view of West Philadelphia digging out of the snow. He was looking at the long line of row houses mixed with larger homes from the neighborhood's grander past. But Nash wasn't seeing them. Instead, he puffed on the cigar with his eyes turned inward as if the window had become a looking glass.

"Teddy Mack," he whispered. "Teddy Mack."

Teddy could see Nash's mind sifting through the smoky past. After a moment, a look of wonder bloomed on his face, and Teddy assumed that Nash had answered his own question—Teddy Mack, son of Grace and Jonathan Mack, a man who stood accused of murder. It had been a long time ago, with Teddy Mack on the run ever since.

The chair swiveled back.

"I'd like to show you something," Nash said.

He stood up and walked over to the jury table, sorting through a stack of files. When he found the one he was looking for, he motioned Teddy over and opened it on the table. It was background information on the murder case the district attorney had prosecuted and botched.

"Derek Campos is a classic example of being in the wrong place at the wrong time," Nash said.

There were a series of family snapshots included in the file, and Nash laid a photograph of Campos with his wife and young daughter on top. They were at a picnic, enjoying a summer afternoon in the park.

"An elderly woman had been raped and bludgeoned to death in Mount Airy," Nash said. "Campos was a land-scaper, working in the churchyard across the street. The police saw him weeding the flower beds and thought he might be a witness. But Derek Campos had grown up in North Philadelphia and had a natural fear of the police. He was a simple, uneducated man with a low IQ. After speaking with him, detectives asked for hair and blood samples. Campos was nervous. He didn't know any better and agreed. Within twenty-four hours, the lab claimed they had a match.''

Teddy only had a sense of the case from what he'd seen on television at lunch yesterday, and Nash's findings and a transcript from the press conference printed in the paper today. Campos had been executed before the use of DNA analysis became routine and could have saved him.

"It was the forensic scientist that clinched it for the jury," Nash said. "Vera Handover. Her testimony, her assurance, and confidence that Campos was guilty. Now we know that everything she said at the time was a result of bad science. Lousy detective work. A prosecutor without any talent working his way to the top. Derek Campos died for no other reason that on the day the body was found, someone looked out the window and saw him working in a flower bed.''

Teddy could hear the deep-seated anger in Nash's voice. The contempt for everyone involved. He guessed at that moment that there was no way Nash would agree to help. He gave the photograph of the Campos family a last look, the wife and daughter, and stepped away from the table. Nash closed the file and placed it on his desk.

"This is how I'm spending my time," Nash said. "The focus of my workshop. Looking for what's slipped through the cracks. Lending a hand to the forgotten. So what makes you think I'd have any interest in getting involved in the Holmes case?''

"Alan Andrews," Teddy said without hesitation or much hope. "It's a chance to keep your story in the papers. A chance to keep what he did to Derek Campos alive.''

Nash smiled. "You mean the use of my name gets you and Barnett off the hook. That's why you're really here, isn't it? You need to think about what you're offering, Teddy. It's not enough.''

Nash had seen through him as if he were wrapped in cellophane. Nash didn't have any interest in holding their hand, or prepping the ground for negotiations with the district attorney. He wasn't going to budge, and that piercing look in his eyes was back. Teddy felt like an animal caught in the headlights of an approaching car. As he glanced away, his eyes skidded off the lithograph of the empty prison cell, then dropped to the floor, his nightmare surfacing again. *Free at Last.* The cell was empty because his father was dead. He could see the guards grabbing his father's feet and dragging the body away. They'd left his blanket behind. Teddy tried to get a grip on himself.

''A few words of advice,'' Nash said.

Teddy leaned against the jury table, watching the man strike his lighter and toke on the cigar again.

''I don't think your plan to avoid a trial will work,'' Nash said. ''Andrews's motives are obvious. He's a political animal, and thus his motivations in life are transparent. In the end, you'll have just as much trouble with ADA Carolyn Powell. She'll be the brains behind the duo while Andrews takes all the credit. But make no mistake about it. The crime they allege Holmes committed is egregious. And the pressure on them to prosecute will be substantial, particularly because the girl came from a family of means. To put it more bluntly, Teddy, I believe they'll want your client's head on a stick and nothing less will suffice.''

Nash was beaming. Teddy didn't find the pep talk all that reassuring. He wondered how Barnett would take the news and hoped he had a *plan B* in mind.

''How much do you know about your client?'' Nash asked.

''He worked for the post office,'' he said. ''We're just getting started.''

''Did you know that five years before Oscar Holmes became a mailman he was a butcher?''

Teddy shook his head, his stomach beginning to churn.

"No, I didn't."

Nash flashed another smile and sat down on the corner of his desk.

"That's right," he said. "Holmes was a butcher, Teddy. He worked at a shop just off South Street for years. I saw it on the news before you arrived. He loved his job and was good at it. Apparently, he was handy with a knife."

Eleven

Burying the news of Holmes's life as a semiretired butcher in a mental file labeled *worst-case scenarios,* Teddy made it back to Center City in less than fifteen minutes. By the time he entered his office, all he could think about was Holmes's head on a stick. Nash was an obvious genius. But even Teddy had been able to foresee that the case would come down to a long trial, and getting the death penalty off the table just wasn't in the cards.

He picked up the phone and dialed Barnett's office. Jackie said he was at lunch with Stokes and that they'd be a while. Teddy knew what that meant. Barnett was filling Stokes in on their new client. After the shock dissipated, Stokes would worry about the firm's reputation. They were probably drawing up a public relations plan. It might take hours before Teddy could reach Barnett to tell him that Nash had refused and they were on their own.

Jill walked through the door with her lunch and sat down before the computer. Cottage cheese and a salad with low-cal dressing and slices of canned fruit. Lunch looked more healthy than appetizing today.

"What are you working on?" Teddy asked.

"I finished early," she said. "I'm hiding out and trying to get some studying in for the bar. Did you check your messages?"

Teddy found them on the desk, recognized Jill's handwriting, and picked them up. Of the three, two could wait but one was marked urgent.

"Who's Dawn Bingle?" he asked.

Jill shrugged. "She called a few minutes ago. It sounded like she knew you."

"What did she want?"

"I think it's got something to do with that personal injury case. I asked if she'd like to speak with Brooke, but she refused. She said it was important and that she'd only talk to you."

"Where's her number?"

"She didn't leave one. She said she'd call back later."

The woman's name didn't register. Teddy shrugged it off, pulling the murder book out of his briefcase and sitting down at his desk. There was no real need to take a second look, but he did it anyway, reading through the preliminary reports until he came to the photo of his client, Oscar Holmes. When the phone rang, he picked it up and could hear a woman's voice mixed with digital noise from a cell phone. The woman spoke through the breaks in the signal, introducing herself as Dawn Bingle and apologizing for her phone.

"I'm in my car," she said. "But we need to talk."

"Brooke Jones is handling the case now."

"She's a bitch," the woman said. "I saw her yesterday in court."

Teddy didn't recognize Bingle's voice through the breakup, but guessed that she was in her late thirties. "What's this about?"

"I work for Capital Insurance Life. I've got evidence that proves what my company did to your client is a matter of corporate policy."

Teddy closed the murder book and pushed it aside. "What kind of evidence?"

"A memo sent to every insurance rep in the company

detailing how to string out claims and avoid sizable payouts. When your client was hit by that truck, they knew he was injured all along. The memo is a how-to on how not to write checks and send them out.''

"Give me an example."

He heard paper rustling, then Dawn Bingle's voice. "I'll give you two," she said. "Paragraph three, using distraction to push a claim beyond the statute of limitations in order to win a zero payout. Paragraph four, recommending a physician from the following list because of their strong support and special relationship with the company."

Teddy couldn't believe what he was hearing. The story he'd pieced together with letters from the insurance company amounted to fraud but was still open to interpretation. It sounded like Dawn Bingle, an obvious disgruntled employee, was ready to hand him the goods in black and white. The case would mushroom beyond a single client. The firm could hunker down and go for the kill.

"How much do you want?" he asked.

"You mean money?"

"That's right. How much?"

She paused. The question had thrown her off, and Teddy took this as a good sign.

"I don't want any money," she said after a moment. "It's my company that's corrupt, not me."

"Then we need to meet," he said.

"I work out of our Center City office, but I can't take the chance of being seen with you. I don't want to lose my job."

"You name the place," he said. "I've got all afternoon."

"My husband's the treasurer at one of the boat clubs. Maybe we could meet there."

"Which one?"

"The Nautilus," she said. "See you in half an hour."

When he asked for her cell phone number, she gave it to him and hung up.

Twelve

Teddy marveled at the lack of traffic as he walked down the bike path along Kelly Drive. The sounds of the road were as faint as a country lane, the din of the city behind him. He could see the Schuylkill River through the trees to his left. Even though it looked frozen solid, he could hear water spilling over the Fairmount Dam below the hill.

It was almost as if he'd left his worries behind and stepped into an oasis, a place where he could see his former life and the dreams he had for his future, but not touch them. After all, the insurance case was no longer his. Whatever he received from Dawn Bingle would have to be handed over to Brooke Jones the moment he returned to the office.

Maybe the act of giving Jones such an amazing gift would do something to change her attitude. As he thought it over, he had his doubts and laughed. You could feed a mean dog tenderloin steak, but it probably wouldn't make the animal any more friendly.

He didn't care.

As the bike path straightened out, his view cleared and he caught his first glimpse of the nineteenth-century buildings that had become known as Boathouse Row. Constructed of stone and cedar siding, they looked more like large homes from the period than anything else. Steam was venting from the snow on the ground. All ten buildings were set directly on the river and shrouded in a fine mist that lingered in the eaves along their rooflines. When the afternoon sun popped out from behind a cloud, filling the moist air with rays of warm light, Teddy couldn't help but think that the boat clubs never seemed more peaceful or majestic.

He spotted the Nautilus ahead and glanced between the buildings as he continued down the path. It looked as if the river had risen over the brim of the retaining wall before last week's flash freeze. Beneath the ice, the sculling course lay hidden until spring.

He stopped in front of the club and checked his watch. He was ten minutes early. Reaching into his pocket for his cigarettes, he lit one and watched a snowplow work its way up the street. Piles of discarded snow four feet high filled in the parking spaces off to the side. If Dawn Bingle was looking for a place to park, she'd have as much luck as he had, and wouldn't find one until she reached the art museum.

He gazed up the path and noticed a woman walking toward him. She was wrapped up in a long wool coat and scarf with a navy-blue beret pulled over her red hair. From what Teddy could see of her face, she seemed about the right age. But as she reached the Nautilus, she passed him by without a word or even a look and kept walking.

Teddy followed the woman's course until he lost sight of her in the trees around the bend. He was beginning to feel cold and thought he might wait for Dawn Bingle inside. Although the boating season usually ended with the Frostbite Regatta in mid-November, he knew the clubs were open to some degree all winter long. There were rowing machines upstairs, weight lifting rooms and meeting rooms, and probably a kitchen where he could get a cup of hot coffee.

He flicked his cigarette into the snow and started down the walkway, unlatching the iron gate and crossing a small terrace to the front door. A note was taped to the inside of the glass. It had been left for a plumbing company, indicating that a key card would be waiting in the usual spot if they needed to gain access to the building after hours. Teddy guessed that the call to a plumber had everything to do with the river cresting the retaining wall. Floods were a cyclical event for all ten boat clubs along the row.

He glanced at the key card access box mounted on the wall, then reached for the door and pushed it open. Kicking the snow off his shoes, he wiped them on the mat and stepped into the entryway.

The air inside the club was moist, the dank scent of the river trapped within its walls, overwhelming. As he unbuttoned his coat, he glanced at the pictures on display. The Nautilus Rowing Club was founded in 1854, and many of the photographs of the club and various regattas dated back to the Civil War. On the table beside a lamp he saw a blank envelope that had been crumpled up along with a key card. When he noticed the faint sound of a pump working in the background, he guessed the plumber had already arrived.

He climbed a short set of steps, following the sound of the pump around the corner until he found himself standing in the entrance to the base of the building. The lights were out, and he wondered if anyone was here at all. As his eyes adjusted to the dim window light, he could see the racing shells set in racks and slung from the ceiling. He called out, but no one answered.

He entered the room and looked past the boats to the four bay doors cut into the far wall. The set of doors closest to him were pushed into the walls a quarter of the way and open to the river. It looked as if the water had advanced halfway into the room. Several hoses were tossed out onto the ice beyond, pumping water from the building as fast as it came in. The pool of water on top of the ice appeared substantial, and Teddy figured that the plumber must have rigged the pumps sometime during the night.

He checked his watch again. Dawn Bingle was running late. Moving to the front window, he peered through the glass and looked outside. No one was on the bike path, and the traffic on Kelly Drive remained unusually light.

He pulled his cell phone out, flipping it open and punching the woman's number in. The phone rang eight times without an answer. As he slipped the phone back into his pocket, he decided he'd put off worrying about her for fifteen minutes. The roads were bad, the temperature dropping. She could easily be caught in traffic.

He heard a sudden crack, and turned around. Crossing the room, he eyed the boats until he reached the edge of the river rising up over the floor.

It wasn't the water damaging the building. It was the ice, pushing its way into the bottom panels of the bay doors. He could hear the wood blistering and breaking up. It looked as if a tree caught in the ice jam had punched through the set of doors at the far end. Water was gushing through the hole and showering over the trunk into the room.

He looked at the roots and tried to focus, wishing he could find the lights because something about the image seemed wrong. After a moment, he felt a quick shot of adrenaline streaking through his chest and heard himself gasp.

Inside the roots of the tree was someone's arm.

Teddy bolted into the water, charging across the room. The doors were latched in the center. Flipping the lock open, he grabbed hold of the recessed door and heaved it into the wall. When he stepped outside, he shuddered.

Her body was naked but for a black tube top clinging about her ribs. She was stretched out on the ramp beneath two feet of water, her blond hair encrusted in a thin layer of murky ice and discolored snow.

Teddy kicked through the crust with his heel, grabbing her by the shoulders. With brute force, he yanked her body up through the ice and into his arms. As he rushed inside, he shook her as if he could somehow bring her back to life. Spotting dry concrete, he laid her down on her back and almost choked.

A rope was tied to her ankles, the loose end frayed. Her pale gray skin was extremely wrinkled and littered with dark splotches. And she'd been cut down the middle of her chest. Lifting the tube top, he followed the course of the wound all the way down and knew she'd been split open with a knife. He looked at her swollen face. Her eyes were open, but missing. That's when he screamed.

Thirteen

They wouldn't be tenting this one. They wouldn't be fumigating the corpse in a roaster bag with burned-up superglue. What the river water hadn't washed away from the girl's body, time and schools of fish had. . . .

Teddy sat on the floor of the boathouse, leaning against the wall and trying to compose himself. ADA Carolyn Powell was kneeling before him, overwrought with disbelief and suspicion, and holding a flyer that included the victim's picture in her hand. Apparently, the girl's name was Valerie Kram and she'd been missing since mid-October.

Powell narrowed her eyes and told him to say it again. Teddy had shown her where he found the body and recanted his story six or seven times over the last three hours. Every time Powell got off the phone, she wanted more.

"I don't know what happened," he said. "Until yesterday, I was working on a personal injury case. I had an appointment with someone. I came down here, but she didn't show."

"And what?" Powell shot back. "You walked into the boathouse and found another body. Valerie Kram. Just like that."

Teddy gave her a look, knowing his story sounded preposterous. "Just like that," he said.

The medical examiner was working on the body ten feet away and well within earshot. "We don't know who this is yet," he said.

Powell ignored him, her eyes still drilling Teddy. Everyone in the room seemed to know who it was.

"The missing persons unit has been looking for Valerie Kram for six weeks," Powell said. "You found her in what, a half hour?"

Teddy remained quiet, his eyes drifting back to the body. It struck him that Valerie Kram looked remarkably similar to Darlene Lewis. They were roughly the same age. They shared the same coloring and overall style. The implications seemed ominous.

Powell stood up, clipping her cell phone to her belt. "The treasurer of the boat club is Fred Bingle," she said. "But his wife doesn't work for an insurance company and he doesn't know what you're talking about. Her name's not Dawn, it's Doris, and she's a housewife. Capital Insurance Life has no record of an employee by that name either. The phone number you gave us isn't even part of a cellular network. It belongs to a dot com company that hit the skids two months ago."

He didn't say anything. He knew that he'd been set up the moment he found the body. He knew that he'd been led here to find it, and that the Holmes murder case was no longer what it seemed.

"This is bullshit," Powell said. "You're gonna need a better story, Teddy."

District Attorney Alan Andrews was standing with Detective Vega and his partner, Nathan Ellwood, watching the ME cut the tube top away from Valerie Kram's body with a pair of scissors. But the district attorney was shifting his weight and fidgeting. Once Teddy had pulled himself together, he'd made the call to Powell on his cell phone. She notified Vega and Ellwood, but a dispatcher had made the mistake of using the radio to reach the ME rather than a land line. The press had overheard the conversation, and were waiting for Andrews outside in force. Andrews was still angry about it and looked edgy enough to snap.

"Forget about the kid," he said to Powell. "He made a mistake. A big one. He's trying to cover his tracks and it's not working very well."

"What are you talking about?" she said.

Andrews turned. He had a smile going now and appeared mean as his eyes locked on Teddy's.

"There's only one way he could've found the body," Andrews said. "And that's if Holmes told him where he'd left it. Nice work, Teddy Mack. You want a job with the prosecution team, just say the word. Either way your client's a dead man."

Powell moved closer. "Is that what happened, Teddy? Did Oscar Holmes tell you where the body was?"

Teddy lowered his eyes, trying to hide his anger and surprise and the feeling that the situation had a life of its own he couldn't control. He hadn't thought about the next step. He hadn't considered what the scene might look like to others when he called for help. He heard Andrews snicker, then watched the man return to the corpse. The ME had removed the cloth and was examining the wound down the girl's chest. It was long and deep, all the way through but still somewhat frozen. Unlike Darlene Lewis, none of her skin appeared to be missing.

"One thing's certain," the ME said. "You guys need to adjust your time line."

"Why?" Andrews asked.

"If this is Valerie Kram, then she turned up missing in October."

"It's Valerie Kram," Andrews said. "Her face matches the picture. She was last seen jogging on the bike path. So what?"

"This girl hasn't been dead for more than a week or two."

Andrews snapped to attention, then knelt down for a closer look at the body.

"The water would've been relatively warm in October," the ME said to him. "Once she went into the river, she was part of the food chain. Fish. Turtles. You get the idea. And she's swollen, but not bloated. Most of her hair's intact. Her flesh is still clinging to her bones. If she'd been in the water for two months, she wouldn't resemble that picture anymore. Not by a long shot. What was left of her would look and feel like Jell-O."

The ME pinched the dead girl's skin, trying to make his point.

Teddy turned away, glancing at the crime scene techs roaming through the building as he thought it over. Not many women jogged in a tube top. And if he could trust what he just heard, then Valerie Kram probably hadn't been murdered here or anywhere near Boathouse Row. The murderer had picked her up somewhere along the bike path. He'd taken her away and kept her for more than a month, then dumped her in the river when he was through with her. If the rope holding the corpse to the bottom had held, no one would have ever found her. But that didn't seem very important right now. What stood out for Teddy was the time the murderer spent with the girl. The place he held her. The dread in his gut that Holmes might be responsible for a second young woman's death.

"I'm gonna schedule a double autopsy," the ME said. "Her and Darlene Lewis."

"When?" Andrews asked sarcastically. "Next week?"

"Tomorrow," the ME said, ignoring the spike and turning to his assistant. "Let's bag this up and get it out of here."

Teddy rose to his feet and stretched. Outside the window he could see the press crowding behind the crime scene tape that had been strung along the trees on Kelly Drive. He turned back to the room. When Powell broke away from Andrews, he pulled her aside.

"I want the keys to Holmes's apartment," he said.

She gave him a suspicious look. "Why?"

"Because he's my client."

"It's still under seal," she said, turning away as if she had something more important to do.

"I have a right," he said. "I want the keys."

She turned back, studying his face and thinking it over. Teddy held the glance.

"You'll need an escort," she said after a moment. "Someone from the office. The keys are in my desk. I'll give you a call in the morning."

"I want to go tonight," he said. "Now."

She was sizing him up again. "What are you up to, Teddy? What haven't you told us?"

"Nothing," he said. "I want to look at my client's apartment."

"I'll have someone meet you there in twenty minutes."

She walked off. Teddy spotted Andrews standing before a mirror in the hall. The man was whispering something to himself. After a moment, Andrews began experimenting with different smiles and various shades of compassion as if he were alone. When he found what seemed like the appropriate facial expression, the district attorney vanished through the lobby and out the door ready to meet the press. Teddy waited a beat before following him outside.

The night air had a bite to it. And the afternoon mist had thickened into a rich wet fog. He saw Andrews waving his hands as the press gathered around and camera lights were switched on. Teddy started up the bike path, then stopped once he reached the shadows and turned to watch. He noticed the boathouses were lit up. The small white lights outlining the buildings were part of the festive nature of the city and burned every night of the year. They looked like Christmas trees. Only tonight didn't seem particularly festive, and the holidays felt like maybe they ought to be postponed.

"I have a short statement to make," Andrews said. "Then I'll answer any questions I can." He paused a moment, waiting for everyone to settle, then remained silent a moment longer as if to underline the gravity of the situation and his importance to the cause. "At two-thirty this afternoon the body of a young woman was found on the banks of the

Schuylkill River along Boathouse Row. As yet, the victim remains unidentified. Detectives Dennis Vega and Nathan Ellwood of the homicide division are heading the investigation. An autopsy will be performed tomorrow to determine cause of death. I'm sorry, but those are the only details I have right now.''

"What about the time?'' a reporter called out. "How long has the body been in the water?''

Andrews glanced at a piece of paper and pretended to read a notation. "Our preliminary examination of the body indicates that the victim died some time ago.''

"Hours, days, or weeks?'' another reporter shouted.

"Weeks,'' Andrews said. "We'll know more after the autopsy.''

"Who found the body?''

"The body was found as a result of our expanding investigation into the Darlene Lewis murder. We're working the case twenty-four-seven.''

"Then they're related.''

"I can't say at this time,'' Andrews said.

"Two bodies in two days,'' a reporter said. "Is it true that Oscar Holmes was a former butcher?''

"Yes.''

"Was the body you found today cut?''

"Yes,'' Andrews said with just the right hint of a smile. "And let me reassure everyone here tonight or watching on television that Oscar Holmes was arrested yesterday and is safely behind bars.''

He'd done it, Teddy realized. Andrews had succeeded in linking the murders to Holmes while denying it.

Teddy glanced through the crowd and caught Carolyn Powell staring at him. She looked back at Andrews, but Teddy could tell from the expression on her face that she knew exactly what Andrews had done.

He listened to the district attorney answer a few more questions, taking credit for as much as he could. When no one asked about Nash's press conference yesterday and the role the DA played in sending an innocent man to his death,

Teddy started up the bike path to his car. In one day, Alan Andrews had cleaned the slate. It had taken the gruesome murders of two young women to pull it off, but it was done. The city had been attacked. Because Andrews was perceived as playing a key role, he was beyond criticism much like a president leading his country into war. Teddy thought it over as he spotted his car. It took a certain kind of person to become a politician these days. And Alan Andrews seemed particularly well suited for the job.

Fourteen

A late-model Cadillac DeVille idled in the darkness taking up two parking spaces on Pine Street. Teddy legged it down the sidewalk, keeping his eyes on the spooky-looking guy behind the wheel. The man was staring back at him while smoking a cigarette with the windows closed and listening to an old Frank Sinatra song. When Teddy stopped before Holmes's apartment and looked about the street for his escort, the man turned off the ignition and climbed out of the DeVille with a rough groan.

"You the lawyer?" the man said like he was pissed off.

Teddy nodded slowly.

"I'm Michael Jackson," the man said. "Not the dancer, but the detective assigned to the district attorney's office. I've worked with Andrews since he got rolling."

He jingled a second set of keys in the air, then lumbered up the steps to the building's entrance as if his stomach was full. Teddy hesitated, watching the sixty-year-old man make the climb. His eyes were hooded, his skin pockmarked, and he wore a cheap black rug that Teddy spotted even before he got out of the car.

Jackson unlocked the building door and turned back, flicking his cigarette at the sidewalk by Teddy's feet.

"You coming or what, kid?"

Teddy hurried up the steps, following the detective into the building.

"Next time you need to see somethin'," Jackson said, "do me a favor and pick a better fucking time." The man let out a sigh, then pointed to the stairs. "It's the penthouse on the third floor," he said. "They're always on the third floor."

As Jackson opened his coat and started up the steps, Teddy caught a glimpse of the gun clipped to the detective's belt. It was an old .38. Teddy had grown up with guns and was comfortable using them. Still, there was something about the worn-out look of this one that made him uneasy. Mulling it over, he wasn't sure if the darkness emanated from the gun or the man who carried it. Either way, both looked used and dangerous.

He shook it off, following Michael Jackson's tired legs up the stairs. On the drive over he'd had a chance to review his conversation with the mysterious Dawn Bingle. She'd known the body was at the boathouse and led him there. That much he was sure of. But she'd also taken the time to find out who Teddy was. She knew where he worked, and seemed to have an understanding of his cases. The bait she'd used to get him to the boathouse had been perfect. A nice touch that itched beneath his skin.

They finally reached the third-floor landing. Jackson struggled to catch his breath and started coughing. When the hacking stopped, the man lit another cigarette, got the door open, and switched on the overhead lights.

"This is it," Jackson said, waving the smoke out of his bloodshot eyes. "Paradise lost. You wanna touch something, that's okay with me. You wanna take it, that's no good at all. Now start looking, kid. I don't wanna make a night out of this. It's only our first date."

Teddy stepped inside the door. He wasn't searching for anything in particular. All he wanted to do was see the place and get a feel for it. What Holmes had done to Darlene Lewis was horrific. What happened to Valerie Kram seemed beyond the pale. Even though the evidence wasn't in and there was still a chance the two murders weren't related, that feeling in his stomach told him that they were. Teddy needed to understand the way Holmes lived. Was it an apartment or a prison? A refuge or a hiding place? If Holmes kept Valerie Kram here for more than a month, Teddy needed to see how it worked.

The first thing that jumped out at him was the overt neatness.

The living room was sparsely furnished with a coffee table set before a cheap couch. A chair with a slipcover sat in the corner facing the television. Teddy wasn't sure why the place seemed so odd until he looked at the side tables and realized there was nothing else in the room. No family snapshots, no bric-a-brac, not even a magazine or newspaper by the chair. He checked the walls, noting that they were blank. The room was devoid of any humanity, even what little Holmes might possess, and looked like a run-down sitting room in a spent motel.

He felt Jackson watching him from behind his back and stepped into the kitchen. The garbage disposal sat on the counter. Teddy remembered the plumbing had been pulled at the Lewis house in Chestnut Hill as well. The detectives had been searching for the girl's skin.

Moving to the refrigerator, he snapped it open and found it filled with food. Holmes obviously ate in, and this surprised him. Curiously, the bottom shelf was loaded with small containers of fruit drinks in tropical combinations Teddy thought were meant for kids. He felt Jackson's presence in the doorway again. Ignoring the man, Teddy started going through the cabinets. From what he could tell looking at the variety of spices, Holmes was something of a cook. All except for one cabinet that was well stocked with junk food. Teddy quickly checked the contents of the drawers, stopping when he reached the knives.

They were imported from Germany, and looked as if they

were more expensive than anything else he'd seen in the entire apartment. When he pulled one out to test the sharpness, Jackson gave him a funny look and winked.

"Blackjack," the detective said. "Butcher's tools. Sharp as a rabid dog's teeth. I checked 'em out yesterday, kid. The man's got a thing for knives. He likes to cut things."

Teddy felt the razor-sharp blade and returned it to the drawer. Jackson had obviously participated in the investigation of the apartment with Nathan Ellwood yesterday.

"Where'd you find his uniform?" Teddy asked. "The one with blood on it."

"In there," Jackson said, pointing to the cabinet below the sink.

Teddy popped the cabinet open and took a quick glance at the trash can. Then he walked out, heading down the hall for the bedroom. As he stepped inside, he was struck by the neatness and lack of personal possessions again. A lamp was set on the chest of drawers, a clock radio sat on the table by the bed. But that was it. He ran his finger across the table, checking the surface for dust and smelling the light scent of furniture polish. When Jackson entered the room and sat down on the bed, Teddy moved to the chest and sifted through the drawers. Holmes seemed to take great care in sorting his clothing by color and keeping everything neatly folded. The man was so meticulous, Teddy guessed he even ironed his boxer shorts. Something about it didn't compute with Holmes's hulking, even sloppy appearance last night.

Teddy thought it over as he opened the closet and saw the man's postal uniforms cleaned and pressed on hangers. Holmes didn't have a life. His possessions would've fit inside a couple of suitcases. Each day he delivered mail to some of the wealthiest people living in Chestnut Hill, then came back to the blank walls of his own drab world. From what Teddy had seen tonight, Holmes didn't have a hobby or any interests other than food. The only thing that stood out were his collection of imported cooking knives. Teddy imagined Darlene Lewis probably took one look at the man and thought he was ridiculous or even stupid. For some reason she got off on teasing Holmes and letting him look at her flowering body. There was no way she could have been aware of what it was doing to him. Not until yesterday when Holmes finally blew.

Teddy shut the closet door, looking back at the furniture. Holmes didn't own much, but seemed to take unusual care of what little he did.

"You missed one," Jackson said, lying out on the bed and yawning.

"Missed what?"

"A room. Between the living room and kitchen there's a door."

Teddy walked out, spotting it as he turned the corner. He'd thought the door opened to a rear entrance because of the dead bolt. As he turned the lock and grasped the handle, he found the door swollen in its frame. It took a measure of strength, but he gave it a hard yank and broke the seal. Swinging the door open, he could feel cooler air rushing past him from the darkness, the familiar scent of oils as he switched on the lights.

Holmes was an artist. A painter.

Teddy froze, his eyes taking in the converted sun porch in ravenous bites. There was a love seat, a worktable, canvases leaning facedown against the glass pane walls in stacks ten deep. He noticed a stereo in the corner and grabbed a handful of CDs. Beethoven and Mozart, Coltrane and Coryell. None of it was working, none of it making sense.

He moved to the easel, staring at the dust cloth draped over a work in progress. He lifted the cloth and looked at the canvas, expecting to catch a glimpse of Holmes's path through the darkness.

It was a landscape. And the violent man he'd met in a city jail last night was more than a weekend painter. Holmes had an eye and a talent. He had a life—all crammed into this one room.

Jackson tapped on the door. When Teddy turned, he saw the detective in the middle of the living room and looked down. A little girl stood in the doorway dressed in her pajamas and holding a stuffed bear. Her light brown hair was braided, her golden brown eyes staring up at him and sparkling as if in sunlight. She couldn't have been more than five or six years old.

"May I have my paintings, mister?" she asked. "They belong to me 'cause I did 'em."

Jackson shrugged like it was okay. Teddy nodded at her, unable to speak in the face of her innocence.

She flashed an excited smile. "Thanks," she said, scampering across the room.

He watched her knee her way onto a chair at the worktable. As she began to sort through the stacks of watercolors, Teddy tried to get a grip on his emotions.

"Do you spend much time here?" he asked in a hoarse voice.

"Mr. Holmes is teaching me paints," she said.

"Where's your mother and father?"

"I don't have a daddy, and Mommy's not back from work yet. Mr. Holmes used to pick me up from school and then we'd paint. When Mommy got home, he'd make us dinner. Mommy says Mr. Holmes is still our friend, and I shouldn't listen to anybody that calls him bad names. Sometimes even nice people like the police make mistakes. Mommy says sometimes good people are wrong."

It hit him in the center of his chest. Watching her. Seeing her trust. Taking it all in. Holmes's life had a wider reach than the sun porch.

The girl climbed back down to the floor, then tore across the studio with her paintings and the bear. As she zipped into the kitchen, Teddy heard the refrigerator door open. After a moment, she ran out with a fruit drink and flew through the front door. Now he knew why the drinks were on the bottom shelf. He heard the door across the hall open and slam shut. When the lock turned, he looked back at Jackson staring at him like the grim reaper from hell.

"Kids," the detective said. "She's lucky Holmes didn't eat her for lunch."

Teddy's legs felt weak, and his head started spinning. He sat down at the table, feeling something deep inside him begin tumbling forward. It was clawing at the surface, flailing at the shadows into the light.

Oscar Holmes was innocent.

Even the thought of it cut all the way down.

Innocent.

In spite of the evidence—the fingerprints, his lip prints, a strong motive, and an eyewitness—there it was in his gut. The possibility, however faint, that everyone had been consumed by the details and missed the whole. The chance that somewhere along the way, someone had been distracted by the obvious and made a horrible mistake. Just the way they'd been mistaken about his own father.

Teddy looked at his hand and noticed he was trembling.

He'd been a part of it, too. Part of the rabble. Part of the mob adding it all up as if it were a simple math exercise. Only it didn't add up because everyone involved had been disgusted by the crime and either wanted something out of it or, like Teddy, needed to move on.

Jackson stepped into the doorway. "You okay, kid? You look a little pale. You're not gonna faint on me, are ya?"

Teddy didn't respond. He couldn't. He pulled his cell phone out and punched in the number Barnett had given him for Nash. When he hit Nash's service, he cleared the call, checked his watch, and entered his own number at the office. It was already past seven. In spite of the hour, Jill picked up on the second ring.

"I need you to find Nash," he whispered. "Then call me back."

"What is it?" she asked. "What's wrong?"

He noted the panic in her voice. She must have picked up on his as well.

"I'll tell you later," he said under his breath. "I don't care what anyone has you doing. Just find Nash and give me a call."

"Done," she said.

Teddy stared at the phone. After a moment, he got up,

switched off the lights, and closed the door. Jackson seemed pleased that the night was over, locking the apartment up and leading the way downstairs. As they reached the sidewalk, Teddy thanked the detective for coming. He heard the Cadillac start up, the muffled sound of Frank Sinatra singing through glass, and turned to watch Jackson gun it down the street like a broken-down hot-dog cop who was still pissed off. He heard his cell phone ring, felt it vibrating in his pocket. As he brought it to his ear, he heard Jill's familiar voice in the cold night air.

"He's at the Skyline Club," she said excitedly. "It's a nightclub. Nash will be there all evening."

He could feel himself being reeled back in. She'd found him.

"I know where it is," he said. "It's private."

"That's right. What's wrong with your voice?"

He cleared his throat. "Nothing."

"Barnett's looking for you," she said. "He's lost your cell phone number."

"Don't give it to him, okay? Don't say anything."

"I didn't. I turned the TV on and saw the news. They found another body."

"Yeah," he said. "They did. Let's talk in the morning."

"Take care of yourself, Teddy."

He closed the phone and turned the corner, spotting his Corolla in the middle of the block. His dizziness had passed, and he started for the car. Slowly at first, then picking up speed.

Fifteen

It was an exclusive club on the top floor of a high-rise building just off Rittenhouse Square, and the man at the front desk seemed adamant about not letting him in. He kept looking down at Teddy's shoes and pants, still damp from the river. When reason didn't work, Teddy grabbed him by the collar and shoved him aside.

Hurrying down the hall, he found the dining room and spotted Nash at a corner table by the window. He was seated with a beautiful, exotic-looking woman. Her clear skin was a deep brown, her face refined and gentle.

The light in Nash's eyes glowed a little as Teddy approached the table. When Nash looked past him and nodded, Teddy turned and saw the man he just pushed straighten up his jacket and vanish down the hall with a shake of the head the way little men do.

"Have a seat," Nash said. "We were just enjoying a little wine. Would you like a glass?"

Teddy nodded even though he didn't want any wine. A waiter appeared with a third glass and a bottle of Williams & Selyem Pinot Noir. As the glass was partially filled, Nash introduced Teddy to his friend, Lynn Guzmon. She smiled warmly and offered her hand. Teddy shook it gently, noting her British accent, and was happily surprised when she excused herself to make a phone call. It was an act, of course, an elegant gesture made by someone who understood something was up without being told.

"Let's go outside," Nash said. "Better bring your glass."

He followed Nash onto the terrace. Gas burners kept the space warm with benches and chairs arranged in small groupings along the entire side of the building. Nash stopped at the rail, gazing at the city. Teddy joined him, thinking that the name of the club was a perfect fit with its setting. The view from the terrace of the Skyline Club was tremendous. He could see the entire city, from the Museum of Art all the way down to the blue lights framing the Benjamin Franklin Bridge.

"It would seem you've had a long day," Nash said in a quiet voice, even though they were alone.

Teddy gave him a look. "You know, don't you? You know about the second body."

"We were listening to the radio on the drive over. I expected you might make a return visit in the morning."

"There's a chance he's innocent," Teddy said.

Nash sipped his wine without saying anything. But Teddy could tell that he'd struck a nerve and the man's wheels were turning.

"You know that, too, don't you?" Teddy said. "That's the real reason why you told me the story behind Derek Campos's arrest and execution. That's why you refused to help. In spite of the evidence, you knew there was a chance that Holmes might be innocent, too."

"You're reading meaning into things where it was never intended. I didn't have Holmes in mind when I told you that story. I was thinking about your father. He was innocent, wasn't he?"

Nash was staring at him now. From the look on the man's face, it seemed as if he'd spent the afternoon in his library reading up on the subject. But Teddy wasn't ready for the question. He reached into his pocket for his cigarettes and lit one. He'd never spoken about what happened to his father with anyone and was surprised when he heard himself say yes.

"It was the accountant," Nash said. "He's the one who murdered your father's partner. The three of them had been friends."

The skyline view fell away, and Teddy found himself staring into the abyss and nodding at it. "They were working on a project," he whispered. "A lot of money was involved. My father's partner caught their accountant embezzling money and confronted him."

"The accountant murdered your father's partner and made it look like something else."

Teddy drew on the cigarette. "It was a small police department in the suburbs. They lacked experience and made a lot of mistakes. After my father died in prison, the accountant had a nervous breakdown and came forward. A week later, he tried to deny his confession, but it was too late. He knew things only the murderer could've known. They had him."

"You were just a boy at the time. How did you feel when the police took your father away?"

Teddy shook his head at the memory. "Why do we have to talk about this?"

"Because it's important. How did you feel?"

"I wanted to kill them," he whispered.

"As time passed, did the rage go away?"

"Not really."

Nash paused a moment to take it in. "When you got involved in the Darlene Lewis murder case, did new memories of your father surface?"

Teddy nodded. "In living color."

"It got worse?"

"Yes."

"When you first saw her corpse, what were you thinking?"

"That I might be sick. Then all I could think about was the man who did it."

"And when you first met Holmes, could you still see her

corpse? Could you still see Darlene Lewis's mangled body lying before your eyes?''

"I couldn't get it out of my head."

"It made you angry," Nash said.

"After the shock it did."

"When you spoke to Holmes, when you were alone with him in the same room, did he seem like a killer? Did he look like one? Did he act the part?"

Teddy nodded, unable to speak and keenly aware that he'd almost repeated what had been done to his father. The idea had been haunting him since the little girl from across the hall entered Holmes's art studio.

He picked up his glass and finished it off in two quick gulps. The barrage of questions didn't feel like an interrogation. Instead, there was some degree of kindness in Nash's voice. Even understanding and compassion as he pushed Teddy on. Nash was peeling back the layers and pointing out his prejudices. Tossing a line into the black hole of his past, and giving Teddy his first glimpse at the way out. When Nash asked how the second body was found, Teddy filled him in on the events of this afternoon. Nash seemed particularly intrigued by the call from Dawn Bingle, agreeing with Teddy that he'd been led to the boathouse.

"It could be innocent, but it's not likely," Nash said. "There's the possibility that she found the body and didn't want to get involved with the police, but I don't think so. In the end, we don't have enough information to even make a guess."

Nash turned back to the view, his cobalt-blue eyes taking in the lights thoughtfully. Several moments passed before he broke the silence, his voice remaining quiet even though they were still alone.

"So now there's a second body," Nash said. "A second murder. But I'm guessing you haven't told me what caused the change in your point of view."

"Valerie Kram was kidnapped in October but only murdered a few weeks ago. I've just come from Holmes's apartment. It wouldn't have been possible to keep her there.

Holmes has a life. He's got friends. Neighbors. A schedule and a full-time job. If the murders are related, then there's the chance that Holmes is innocent. The chance the district attorney and everybody else are looking at the physical evidence, and for some inexplicable reason, they're wrong.''

Nash took another sip of wine. ''It seems odd, doesn't it?''

Teddy remained quiet, watching Nash think out loud.

''If Holmes has killed before,'' Nash was saying. ''If Darlene Lewis wasn't his first. How many times have you heard of a killer like that fleeing a crime scene in broad daylight wearing bloody clothes? They're usually more subtle about it, their indiscretions better planned.''

It hung there. Both of them staring at it. The one sign left behind at the crime scene that pointed away from Holmes.

''Then you agree that it's possible,'' Teddy said.

Nash turned and gave him a long look. ''What's significant is that you do. But none of this means Holmes didn't do it, Teddy. We're just talking over a glass of good wine.''

Teddy looked into the dining room and saw Nash's friend returning to the table. Nash followed his gaze and turned back.

''He didn't take Darlene Lewis,'' Teddy said.

''No, he didn't.''

''He didn't do the same things to her.''

Nash lowered his glass. ''Tell me what you think the next step is,'' he said.

''They need time to process the evidence. The autopsy's scheduled for tomorrow. While they're at it, I need to find out if there's any connection between Holmes and Valerie Kram.''

''It's important that you attend the autopsy as well. Bring the murder book over in the morning so I can take a closer look. And you better call Barnett tonight and let him know that I'm in.''

He was *in*. Teddy felt a sense of relief hearing Nash say

it. But so was Teddy now. He remembered that personal injury case he'd been working on yesterday, even this afternoon. It seemed so important then. Now it was meaningless. A million miles away.

"I'll give him a call on the way home," he said. "But I fucked up tonight. They think Holmes told me where the body was. They think that's how I found it."

Nash let out a faint smile. "If I'd been in their shoes, Teddy, I'm not sure I would've believed your story either. Let them think anything they want for now. We're just getting started."

Nash opened the door and they walked back into the dining room. When Nash offered Teddy another glass of wine, he declined. He wanted to keep his mind clear. The night had been filled with the back and forth of the past and present. It had been a strain to keep up with, and he was glad he'd pocketed that bottle of aspirin in the afternoon. Still, he felt more at ease about things and even nodded at the little man behind the front desk on his way out.

As he got into his car and pulled away from the curb, he tried reaching Barnett but hit his voice mail again. Guessing that Barnett had heard the news about the second murder and was consoling Holmes's family, Teddy left a long message, filling him in on what happened and letting him know that it had taken all day, but William S. Nash was finally on board. Teddy hated long messages, but he didn't want Barnett to be left hanging. He wanted to give him some degree of hope. Everything had changed. They wouldn't be walking Holmes through the system so that he could spend the rest of his life in an institution for the criminally insane. They wouldn't be trying to make a quick deal with Alan Andrews. Not yet anyway.

He made a right at Thirtieth Street Station and started down the ramp to the expressway. The fog had tapered off some and he could make out the string of lights outlining the buildings along Boathouse Row on the other side of the river. Checking his rearview mirror, he saw the city in the clouds and let his mind drift. He wasn't sure he'd be able to sleep tonight. If Holmes wasn't the murderer, if he'd walked in on the crime and interrupted it; then that meant the real killer was still out there. Somewhere in one of the buildings all lit up behind him in the smoky mist.

Sixteen

Eddie Trisco stood in the middle of the room at Benny's Cafe Blue sipping his second caffe latte for the night and knowing he looked like an idiot. He could hear the giggles in the background as he just stood there. The people laughing at him as he tried to blend. Even worse, the high dosage of caffeine had brought the voices back, and he could hear them over all the others as they crept into his head.

He didn't care. Not tonight.

Besides, everyone was always watching him, and he'd prepared himself for the painful ordeal before he even walked out of his house. Appearing in public went with the job, the life, the edge. He needed to get used to it. Everyone about to become famous did.

He had his eyes on the two students seated at the corner table by the window. College students, holding hands and talking the way kids do who live trouble-free lives. He found their naivete striking. They'd finished their drinks fifteen minutes ago, yet they remained at the table without any consideration for him or anyone else in the café who wanted to sit down. They were soft and round, the victims of the information age. They were of little interest to him. All he wanted was their table.

Eddie checked his watch. It was almost nine-thirty. The sports club across the street would be closing in another half hour. He needed a seat at that table and he needed it now.

He looked back at the students and could tell they knew he was staring at them. He crossed the room, watching them avert their eyes as he approached them. Then he stopped, standing over the table and looking straight down. At first they giggled like he was crazy. But after a few moments, the giggling stopped and they finally decided to leave. He heard the boy mutter the word *weird* as they collected their backpacks and walked toward the door in slow motion.

Eddie didn't care. He finally had command of the table and sat down facing the window. The seat remained warm and this bothered him a little. It felt like contact, and he tried to ignore it. Glancing at the table, he noted the empty cups left behind, sugar strewn across the Formica, droplets of cappuccino splashed here and there. He would ignore this, too, he decided. He wouldn't touch the table. He'd only sit before it so that he could gaze out the window.

She was working out on the Stair Master.

He could see her in the sports club across the street from his seat at the window. Up and down, up and down she strode. Proud, perhaps strong willed, perfect in every detail.

He'd first noticed her two months ago, but had been saving her for an evening just like this one. She worked out three nights a week and looked like she took good care of herself. Her blond hair was tied back at the moment, but he'd seen it down and knew it to be the right length. Her breasts were a little big, but she was only twenty and he guessed it would be a few more years before they broke loose from their moorings and swayed toward the ground. Still, it was her face, of course, that singled her out from all the rest. Her mouth and cheekbones. The way her eyes were set beside her nose—not too narrow and not too far apart. Perfect in every detail, he repeated inside his head. He didn't know her name yet, but he would.

She got off the Stair Master and appeared to be panting. He watched as she wiped the sweat away from her skin with a towel. Then she stepped away from the machine, heading toward the locker rooms.

Eddie sipped his caffe latte and waited. He'd been keeping an eye on her long enough to know she usually took about twenty minutes to shower and change. After her workout, nine times out of ten she crossed the street and ordered a caffe mocha on ice at Benny's Cafe Blue.

He switched seats so that he had a view of the entrance. Then he checked his watch and started counting. Twenty minutes could last forever when you were having this much fun. To pass the time, he played tonight's scenario in his head. Every detail, every beat. He'd been over it before and didn't really need any more practice. But he did it anyway, again and again, until he looked up and saw her walk through the door.

He glanced about the room and noticed the men looking at her. All of them, even the one behind the counter with that stupid grin on his face. She smiled back at the man, ordering her drink and trying to manage her purse and gym bag. She had her hands full. But that was part of the plan as well. One of the details. One of the beats.

Eddie felt his heart patter as he watched. It seemed as if her caffe mocha was taking forever to make, and he figured the guy behind the counter was taking his time on purpose so that he could flirt with her. She didn't look like she minded. In fact, it seemed pretty clear she was flirting back.

Eddie finished off his coffee, poised for his role in the scenario to begin. As she took her drink in hand and turned away from the counter, he heard the voice inside his head cue him and so he stood. He met her at the door and opened it for her, his timing perfect. Then he followed her outside, skipping the line he'd planned because he felt nervous all of a sudden. Instead, he ad-libbed a simple nod.

She'd given him a funny look, which he didn't understand. She may have been twenty, but he was only thirty. As he analyzed the moment, he thought he'd been polite and that they were ready to become friends.

She hurried off without saying anything. Eddie concentrated on the sweet scent of her body lotion riding her wake as he began following her. He popped a Hershey's Kiss into his mouth, savoring the chocolaty taste and smoothing it around his tongue. When she turned the corner and started up the alley, she still thought she was alone. Eddie looked around, trying not to laugh. Although the streets were clear of last night's snow, it had gotten cold again and not many people ventured out.

He turned back as she headed toward her car. Her pace quickened a little, then even more. He noticed her head cocked back, the corner of her eye watching him. She was digging into her purse for her keys. Digging deep and fast. She reached her car just as he did. Then she dropped her caffe mocha into the snow and turned, spraying Eddie with a canister of mace that she kept attached to her key ring.

Eddie took it in the face, the mace streaming down his cheeks like rain. He could hear her grunt and groan, and imagined she made the same animal noises toward the end of all her workouts. Mace had never bothered Eddie particularly. For the life of him, he didn't know why.

"Say," he said through the spray, "you don't have any tattoos, do ya?"

She seemed horrified by the question, too afraid to scream. This threw him because the question seemed so reasonable. It had been part of the script, part of the play. When she didn't answer, he struck her on the side of her head with a closed fist. The mace stopped and he heard her keys drop onto the street. He couldn't tell if he'd knocked her out, or maybe she just fainted. Pressing her limp body against the car so that she wouldn't fall and possibly bruise her clear skin, he glanced about for the keys and grabbed them. Then he shoved her into the backseat, tossed the gym bag in, and slammed the door closed.

He checked the alley again, the street. No one had seen him. Sliding in behind the wheel, he felt for the lever on the floor and pushed the seat back. The script had been well written, he decided, the scenario thoughtfully done.

Eddie settled into the driver's seat, wiping his face off with a handkerchief as he adjusted the mirrors and reviewed the dash. The car started on the first try. Then he switched the heat on, idling down the alley and turning at the corner. As he passed Benny's Cafe Blue, he glanced in the window and saw everyone laughing again. He knew they were laughing at him, but ignored it as he always did. They could laugh all they wanted, but he had the goods.

He popped another piece of chocolate into his mouth as a reward. At the light, he made another turn. When he checked the rearview mirror, he saw the girl lying against the backseat with her eyes closed. She looked like she was sleeping. By the time she woke up, they'd already be home.

Seventeen

Teddy opened the letter and began reading. The words were printed on the page by hand in cumbersome letters blocked out with a felt-tip pen.

Dear Asshole:
You motherfucking piece of shit lawyers are all alike.
Fuck you for defending that mailman killer. He deserves to die just like what he did to those pretty girls. You do, too, you dirty creep. I'm watching you. I'm staying close. I know where you are.

Locked and loaded and truly yours,
Colt 45

Teddy dropped the letter on his desk, wishing he hadn't touched it. Grabbing a pen, he flipped the envelope over and examined the return address: *45 Somebody Street*. He didn't need to check, but he did. His street guide was on the credenza beside his dictionary and almanac. Paging through the index, he searched for *Somebody Street,* but couldn't find it because it didn't exist.

It was only seven-thirty, and the new day was off to a good start.

He leaned back in his chair, watching one of the kids from the mail room push the cart down the hall and wondering if the death threat he'd just received had anything to do with being led to the boathouse. His first thought was that the note had been written by an angry crank, but the words *I'm watching you* stood out. It seemed like a lot of people he didn't know were watching him.

Jill walked through the door, wrapped up in a ski jacket with her face still glazed from the cold. Her briefcase was slung over her shoulder, and she held a cup of take-out coffee in her gloved hands.

"You're in early," she said.

Teddy nodded, even tried to smile. "I've got to leave in a half hour, but I'll be back."

He didn't want to worry her by showing her the note or envelope. As she got out of her jacket, he slid them into the murder book with his pen, closed the binder, and placed it in his briefcase.

"You got ten minutes?" he asked.

She nodded, prying the lid off the coffee and taking a tentative first sip.

"Valerie Kram," he said. "I need to go up on the Web and see what's out there."

"The woman they found in the river?"

He nodded. She paused a moment, taking it in like her day was off to a good start, too. Then she lowered her coffee to the table and sat down before the computer, ready and willing. As she typed her password in, Teddy rolled his desk chair over and took a seat beside her.

"Do you want a global search," she asked, "or should we just check the newspaper's archives?"

"I want everything," he said.

Jill typed Valerie Kram's name into the search window and hit ENTER. After a moment, thirty or more listings appeared on the screen. Jill scrolled down the page, weeding out entries about another woman with the same name working as an environmentalist in Oregon. When she was done, only five listings remained. The first three links sent them to missing persons organizations, offering help and guidance to families trying to cope with their loss. But the fourth link led to a newspaper article from the *Philadelphia Inquirer*, dated October 29, three days after Valerie Kram's disappearance. Teddy gazed at the girl's picture, then read the story. Valerie Kram of Manayunk, twenty years old and a student at the Philadelphia College of Art, was officially missing. Kram shared an apartment with a roommate, who became alarmed when Kram didn't return from her daily jog on the bike path along the Schuylkill River. The roommate called Kram's parents, and the police were notified. End of story.

Jill printed the article, then clicked back to the search list. Teddy didn't recognize the remaining entry and asked about it.

"It looks like a newsgroup," Jill said. "Someone probably set it up under Valerie Kram's name."

"Let's take a look," he said.

Jill clicked on the link and several hundred entries appeared. Fifteen minutes later, they'd read them all. The entries amounted to notes sent back and forth between Kram's mother and her daughter's friends over the course of the past six weeks. As time passed, Teddy could sense the level of panic rising in the mother's tone until just two weeks ago when the notes dwindled off and hopelessness set in.

Teddy found the whole thing disturbing as he mulled it over. Haunting and perhaps even ghoulish. The notes had been posted in the newsgroup before anyone knew the outcome. Before anyone knew that Valerie Kram was dead. From what he'd just read, it was apparent that she'd come from a tight-knit family and had no reason to run away. The money in her savings account hadn't been touched, and her car was found in the lot where she parked to go jogging. According to her roommate, Kram hadn't discussed any personal problems with friends or given any indication she wanted to leave home. Although the police considered her missing and registered her name and photograph on the FBI's National Crime Information Center database, they hadn't been investigating her disappearance as a possible kidnapping or murder. Friends and family had been interviewed, the bike path scoured with the aid of cadaver dogs. A witness who saw her jogging had been located, but no evidence was found indicating foul play.

Teddy got out of the chair and into his coat. Jill turned toward him, her brown eyes gently searching his face.

"They stopped looking for her," she said.

He shook it off and grabbed his briefcase, the frustration welling up into his chest. It came down to man power, he thought. And the lack of a single tangible lead, made all the worse by the fact that adults turn up missing every day. In Valerie Kram's case, they'd found her after the war was over. They'd been too late.

Eighteen

Teddy walked in on Nash's assistant. She was seated at her computer and concentrating on the screen, but didn't seem to mind the interruption. They'd met in the hall yesterday, and when she recognized him, she flashed a genuine smile and shook his hand, introducing herself as Gail Emerson. Teddy thought she might be about fifty, but couldn't really tell because her attractive appearance remained so youthful. Her hair was a mix of different shades of blond. Her eyes were blue and smart, but somehow easy and warm.

"He's expecting you," she said, glancing at the door. "Would you like a cup of coffee?"

Teddy looked at the fresh pot sitting on the table by the window, thanked her, but shook his head. He didn't need any more caffeine right now. On the drive over, he'd stopped at the post office and bullied his way into an early morning meeting with Holmes's supervisor. The clock was ticking. And Teddy was trying to determine what Holmes had been doing on the day Valerie Kram disappeared. October 26 had been a Wednesday. The supervisor could barely speak English but seemed to be able to read. Although the man wasn't pleased with Teddy's visit, he went through the

employment records and verified that Holmes checked in at
six A.M., worked his usual nine-hour shift, and punched out
at three that afternoon without incident. According to what
Teddy had read, Valerie Kram vanished at dusk. Nothing
he learned from Holmes's supervisor even hinted at a possible alibi.

He stepped into the office. Nash was standing over the
jury table puffing on an early morning cigar. When he looked
up, his face seemed a little pale.

"It's worse than we thought," he said.

Teddy noted the concern in Nash's voice. As he moved
closer, Nash handed him a sheet of paper. It was a missing
persons bulletin pulled off the national computer database.
The same flyer on Valerie Kram that ADA Carolyn Powell
had shown him yesterday at the boathouse. Below Kram's
picture was a complete physical description along with the
date and place she was last seen. Teddy didn't understand
Nash's concern until he glanced down at the jury table.
There were two more flyers. The dates were different, and
so were the names.

"After I pulled Kram's sheet," Nash said, "I broke down
her physical description and went back a month. Then two
months. This is what came up."

Teddy set the flyer down beside the others, struck by the
similarity of their faces. Though their individual features
varied to some degree, there could be no doubt that they
shared the same overall appearance and style. It was a certain
kind of beauty, but not the brand manufactured on a model's
face in a fashion magazine. Instead, their radiance emanated
from beneath their skin. Each one of them looked like they
had something more to do in life than primp before a mirror
or plan their next visit to a plastic surgeon. The word *soul*
came to mind.

Teddy noticed a calender on the table. "What are you
doing with that?"

"Checking lunar cycles," Nash said. "There aren't any.
The kidnappings are occurring at random. Four weeks apart,

then two weeks. Darlene Lewis was murdered six weeks after that. It started last September.''

"Did you call the police?"

"Not yet," Nash said. "I think we need to consider what's in Oscar Holmes's best interest. We need time to begin a profile of the killer and think this through."

Teddy's eyes moved back to the flyers on the table. He reached into his pocket and fished out his cigarettes. As he lit one, he tried not to let the shock he was feeling show. The victims were adding up. The horror.

"They could be twins," Teddy said. "You mean to tell me that the police aren't already aware that something's wrong?"

"If I had to guess, I'd say they were, Teddy. But you need evidence that a crime's been committed. You need something to go on. Darlene Lewis's murder set this in motion. Until two days ago there was no sign of foul play or we would've heard about it. Finding Valerie Kram's body indicates a trend and gives the investigation speed."

"I want you to see something," Teddy said.

He pulled the murder book from his briefcase and opened it on the table, pointing to the letter he received in the mail without touching it. Nash leaned closer and began reading. When he was finished, he examined the envelope and smiled at the return address, 45 *Somebody Street*.

"I'm afraid you'll have to get used to these," Nash said. "We both will."

"What about fingerprints?"

"If it'd make you feel any better, you should turn it over to the detectives working the case. Did you touch it?"

"I didn't know what it was at first."

"Send it in anyway. I've received hundreds over the years, but it's never gone anywhere. Some have prints and others don't. The trouble comes in matching the ones that do to a name and a face. John Q. Public, or should I say Colt Forty-five? I keep mine in a file in the drawer."

Nash was trying to make him feel better, but it wasn't working. As he watched Nash open a cabinet, he stubbed out his cigarette in the ashtray. Then Nash handed him a plastic bag along with a pair of tweezers from the top drawer of his desk. In a way he felt he might be overreacting. Nash had made it sound like death threats went with the job and that there would be more to come. At the same time, he felt a certain degree of terror as he pinched the note with the tweezers and read the words *I'm watching you* for the second time that morning. He dropped the note into the bag, then the envelope. As he placed them in his briefcase, Gail walked into the room with a sheaf of papers. Nash's eyes went glassy as he looked at her.

"I'm sorry," she said, passing them over. "They started last January. I went back two years. This is all there is."

She left the room, closing the door behind her. Nash laid the sheets of paper out on the jury table, one after the next. It was another series of missing persons bulletins off the NCIC database. Teddy flinched as he saw the faces, counting them while Nash arranged them by date. There were eleven. Darlene Lewis's murder made it twelve. Every one of them looked as if they'd been born of the same mother and father. As Teddy stared at them, it felt as though they were staring back.

He shivered, pulling a chair away from the table and sitting down before them. He tried to look away, but couldn't.

"At least we know what we're dealing with," Nash whispered in a gravelly voice. "It's a serial killer, Teddy. Holmes or somebody else. Either way, he's been working the city without detection for the past year."

Nineteen

Teddy entered visiting room three, resting his briefcase on the floor and taking a seat at the small table. His escort told him Holmes was on his way down, then closed the door and walked off.

He checked his watch. It was just after nine A.M. He would have liked to use the free time to check in with the office, but his phone had been taken at the front desk when they searched his briefcase. The door opened, and he turned to watch Holmes enter from the hall in his orange jumpsuit and sneakers.

Holmes's appearance seemed even worse than two nights ago. There was a certain edge to his face, as if the panic had taken root and wouldn't let go. And he looked worn out and ragged like he hadn't been sleeping. Teddy slid a chair away from the table, but Holmes shook his head and grunted without looking at it. He seemed fixated on the larger meeting room on the other side of the second door where inmates were beginning to visit with their families.

"Not in here," he said. "I wanna be out there with them."

Holmes stepped through the doorway. Teddy grabbed his briefcase and followed his client into the meeting room.

When Holmes passed an empty couch heading straight for the far wall, he knew Holmes wanted to look at the paintings. Teddy had wondered why fifty works of art were on display in the main meeting room at Curran-Fromhold Prison and asked the assistant warden about it on his way out the other night. They were part of the one percent rule maintained by the city. Teddy was already familiar with the requirement because of his interest in real estate, but hadn't expected it to filter down to a prison. If you were planning to build within the city limits, then one percent of your construction budget had to be designated for public art no matter what the amount. The one percent rule had transformed the city. Apparently, there weren't any exceptions.

Teddy kept his eyes on Holmes as the big man carefully examined the first canvas, then moved on to the next. Although the paintings were of varying quality, Holmes seemed to linger over them without distinction.

"How you holding up?" Teddy asked.

"Nightmares," Holmes said in a voice that wouldn't carry. "Bad dreams. There's a man in the cell block who cries all night. I think he's only a boy."

"You want to talk about it?"

Holmes shook his head without saying anything, his eyes moving to the next painting.

"What about your sister? You talk to her yet?"

Holmes stirred a little and shook his head again. Teddy was surprised.

"You haven't had any visitors?"

"No," he said. "Just you."

"What about your neighbors?"

Holmes paused a moment as if the question hurt. "Just you," he repeated more quietly.

Teddy stepped back as Holmes moved down the row. He guessed it would take fifteen minutes before Holmes was through. He didn't mind because it gave him a chance to review his first impression of the man. A lot had happened since the night Teddy met Holmes. His client had been a bona fide murderer then, fitting the part to a tee. He still looked menacing, his hands remained heavily bandaged from the knife wounds he'd received on the day of Darlene Lewis's murder, and the fingerprints Teddy had seen with his own eyes on the girl's body matched conclusively. As Teddy tried to imagine Holmes teaching the little girl who lived across the hall how to paint—picking her up from school and making her dinner the way a father would—he was struck by the same feeling he'd had last night. The idea that he was missing something and not seeing the whole. The possibility that even though the physical evidence added up to Holmes, somehow there might be another explanation.

Holmes finally reached the last canvas. When he turned away, they found a place to sit down where Holmes could keep an eye on the paintings. He was staring at them like he needed them, like he was trying to hang on to something meaningful from his former life.

"We need to talk about the other day," Teddy said.

Holmes remained silent and appeared frightened by the prospect.

"Darlene Lewis," Teddy continued steadily. "You said you couldn't remember anything. You ran away and the next thing you knew you were home."

"I'm having nightmares. I already told you that. I wake up screaming and then I hear that kid crying in his cell. It feels like the place is haunted."

Teddy nodded, beckoning the man on.

"I can almost see her face, if that's what you're asking. I can almost see it even though I'd do anything not to see it. It's like it's coming at me just before I wake up. Only she's not beautiful anymore. She's not even a she. It's chasing me like a ghost and laughing at me. It's a real bad dream. I'm glad I wake up."

Holmes shuddered, trying to shed himself of the vision.

"What about your hands? If you can't remember how you got cut, then how do you think it happened?"

Holmes shook his head in frustration, unable to find the words.

"It's important, Holmes."

"Why?" he asked. "What if it's more important that I don't remember? That I never remember?"

Holmes was getting loud. A guard looked over. Teddy turned back to his client and saw fear welling up in his eyes. Deciding he'd let it pass for now, Teddy pulled a file out of his briefcase containing the newspaper article on Valerie Kram's disappearance. Holmes took the sheet of paper, wincing as he gazed at the photo of the Darlene Lewis look-alike, Valerie Kram. Teddy watched him carefully, searching for any indication that he recognized the girl. But as Holmes began reading the article, the man's face remained blank, even numb. When he was finished, his eyes rose to the date and stayed there.

"Is she dead, too?" Holmes asked.

Teddy nodded.

Holmes's eyes rolled back to the picture of Kram. "Are they gonna say I did it?"

"I don't know. It's early. The evidence isn't in yet."

Holmes passed the article back, unable to settle in his chair. "They look the same, but they're not," he said.

"How so?"

"I don't know. They're just different. That piece of paper said this one wanted to be an artist."

"What about the date? I went through your place last night and didn't notice a calendar. Do you keep a date book?"

"No."

"It was a Wednesday. October twenty-sixth."

Holmes shrugged helplessly. "Then I must've been at work."

"It happened after work. Where's your checkbook? Maybe that would help you remember."

"I keep it on the kitchen counter with my bills."

Teddy didn't recall seeing his checkbook in the kitchen. The police either moved it when they tore up the plumbing or took it for some reason. He made a mental note to call ADA Carolyn Powell when he got out of here. A check written to a dentist or doctor or even for groceries or art supplies would do more than jog the man's memory.

"What about credit cards?" Teddy asked.

"I've only got one, but I've never used it. I got it just in case of emergencies."

"What about the little girl who lives across the hall? She says you pick her up at school."

"Not on Wednesdays. She takes music lessons. She plays the drums. Her mother picks her up on her own."

Teddy stood up, glancing at the picture of Valerie Kram as he grabbed his briefcase. Expecting Holmes to remember what he was doing almost two months ago seemed hopeless. As an exercise, Teddy had returned home last night and tried to piece together his own day on October 26. He'd started at the firm in September and kept a weekly planner. Even so, all he came up with was that he'd spent the morning in the library researching past cases and had lunch with Barnett. The afternoon and evening remained blank. How could he expect anything more from Holmes?

Holmes rose to his feet slowly. Teddy could tell the man didn't want his only visitor to leave, didn't want to return to his cell.

"How did the second one die?" Holmes whispered.

"It's a different case."

"How'd it happen?"

"The autopsy's this afternoon," Teddy said. "But she was cut."

Holmes seemed shaky as he took it in. After a moment, they started walking back to visiting room three.

"Would you agree to hypnosis?" Teddy asked.

"What are you talking about?"

"The day Darlene Lewis died. We'd bring a doctor in. We'd put you under hypnosis. Then maybe you could relax enough to remember what happened."

Holmes stopped in his tracks and that wild look was back. The fear and panic. Teddy noted the guard walking toward them who would escort Holmes to his cellblock. Holmes saw him coming, too, his voice pleading.

"No," Holmes said. "Please. She was just a girl. I don't want to remember what happened. I don't want to know what I've done."

It hung there, with Teddy staring into Holmes's dead eyes. The nightmares were winning.

He pulled Holmes away by the arm. Tears were streaming down the man's cheeks and his head was down. Teddy moved closer, whispering into his client's ear.

"Listen to me," he said. "You need to pull yourself together and figure a way to sort this out. There's the chance someone else was there. Do you hear me, Holmes? That's why we need you to remember. We need your help. There's a chance someone else was there."

Holmes didn't react. He was staring at the picture of Valerie Kram in Teddy's hand. When he finally raised his head, his face was blank, distant, in the zone. The guard led Holmes away. As Teddy watched them walk off, he doubted Holmes had heard him. Doubted that what he'd said got through. The man believed he'd murdered Darlene Lewis, maybe even Valerie Kram. His mind was a jumbled mess.

Twenty

Barnett slammed a copy of the *Daily News* down on his desk, shaking in anger.

"This is bullshit," he shouted. "This is exactly what I didn't want. Look at it. It's not a fucking headline, it's as big as a sign."

Teddy read the three-inch headline, THE POSTMAN ALWAYS RINGS TWICE, then glanced at the photo of Holmes in his postal uniform behind the bold text. The picture had been enlarged from Holmes's photo ID to fill out the page, the blowup so distorted anyone looking at it would think him a monster. In a three-box set below the monster's chin, pictures were included of Darlene Lewis and Valerie Kram, along with a shot of the boathouse and an arrow indicating the spot where Kram's body had been found in the river.

Barnett yanked his desk drawer open. When he found the pill bottle he was looking for, Teddy noted that it wasn't Tylenol anymore, but a prescription.

"I gave you a simple task," Barnett was saying as he threw a pill into his mouth and gulped it down. "You knew how we were gonna play this thing. Bring Nash in to scare the district attorney, then do the deal. That's all I asked of you. That's all you were supposed to do."

Teddy closed the door. "Things have changed."

"What change?" Barnett said, spitting out the words.

"It's possible that Holmes is innocent."

Barnett spun around, staring at him as if Teddy were insane. "Innocent? Yesterday Oscar Holmes was a guy with a history of mental illness who went off his rocker and was charged with a single count of murder. Today he's a serial killer and the whole fucking city's up in arms. Don't you get it? Don't you see what's going on?"

Teddy grabbed the newspaper and sat down on the couch, stunned by Barnett's attitude but keeping it to himself. As he thumbed through the first three pages, he realized that the headline may have been tongue-in-cheek, but what the articles implied were anything but. Holmes's connection to the two murders was now in print. He glanced at Barnett slumped in his desk chair, then got started reading.

The connection hadn't been made by new evidence or even a leak. It had been made by Andrews at his press conference last night just as Teddy feared it would. Both women had been cut. That, along with their age and appearance, was enough to bind the two cases together. Getting to Holmes without confirming anything alleged was even easier. While one reporter detailed the events leading to Holmes's arrest for the murder of Darlene Lewis, another writer spent yesterday afternoon at Holmes's former butcher shop, interviewing old ladies from the neighborhood who remembered Holmes, and getting photographs of them buying flank steak and pork sausages. The women recounted stories of Holmes's talent with a knife, mixed with excited laughter and occasional squeals over what he'd done. Most of the women seemed to be saying that, for the love of God, they could've been next. Teddy glanced back at their photos, fighting off an urge to smile as he noted their age and weighty figures. None of them looked quite like Darlene Lewis or Valerie Kram, and he imagined they were safe for now.

He closed the paper, concluding none of it was real. The

district attorney may have gotten the headlines he wanted. Oscar Holmes was tagged a serial killer without really saying it, and the case was the talk of the town. But the ground had been fertilized by innuendo. Not a single fact had been leaked and the word *cannibalism* hadn't appeared in print. They'd gotten off lucky, Teddy thought. When the details were brought out in court, the headlines would be far worse.

Barnett swiveled his chair around from the window. The pill must have kicked in because his anger had subsided and an almost eerie state of calm had set in.

"Do you understand why headlines are never going to work in our favor?" he said in an unusually quiet voice.

Teddy nodded. "They'll spoil the jury pool."

Barnett grimaced and blinked, trying to rein his emotions back in. "No, goddamnit. Because every new headline makes Andrews stronger and moves him further away from making a deal. I've spoken with Nash, and he agrees."

"When did you talk to him?"

"I hung up the phone when you walked in."

"What did you say?"

"Just what I'm saying to you. This case is about avoiding the press and getting Holmes to plead guilty. This case is about making sure someone who needs medical attention gets the psychiatric care he so obviously needs."

While Barnett may have spoken with Nash, Teddy didn't believe that Nash agreed to capitulate. Particularly now, when they'd just isolated ten more victims, and Holmes's guilt remained up in the air. It didn't make sense.

"What did Nash say?" Teddy asked.

"At first he didn't see it that way. When I brought him back to reality, he did."

"What's the reality?"

Barnett gave him a look. "That in a civilized world, we don't execute the mentally impaired."

Teddy had to hand it to Barnett. The man had an uncanny ability to dig up a bottom line and make it sound good even if it might be the wrong one.

Holmes stood out. There was no question that he was

different, maybe even odd. And he was distraught, confused, teetering on the edge. But he had a right to be, Teddy thought. For two days he'd been told he murdered someone, and like everyone else, he didn't appear to know what actually happened. He was alone. All he had were glimpses of the murder scene, the dead body, a young girl's blood on his clothes. Who wouldn't be having nightmares? Given the circumstances, the gore, who wouldn't lose faith in themselves? The man needed help, but nothing Teddy had seen in his two visits indicated he was mentally ill.

"How'd you leave it with Nash?" Teddy asked.

"What's with the twenty questions?"

"How did you leave it?" he repeated.

Barnett adjusted his cuff link, his eyes glazed. "The way you did last night. He's still on board. What's with you?"

Teddy didn't say anything. As he looked at Barnett, he became overwhelmed with worry for him. He liked Barnett and admired him, but didn't understand his reasoning. It was obvious enough that Barnett still wanted to sweep Holmes under the rug and make the case go away as quickly as possible. How the truth might play out seemed lost in Barnett's frayed emotional state. Maybe it was to protect Holmes's family. Barnett had mentioned that they'd been friends for a long time. Perhaps Barnett looked at what happened to Darlene Lewis and guessed that no crime so horrible could be a killer's first step into the gloom. Given the circumstances, there had to be more. Teddy wished he could help Barnett. He wished he could understand and do something for him.

"What time's the autopsy?" Barnett asked.

"In another hour."

"You okay about going?"

In spite of his doubts, Teddy nodded.

It would be another afternoon spent with dead bodies. He was glad Powell was bringing Holmes's checkbook. He'd called her on the drive into town from prison. Although she still appeared distant, she confirmed that the police had the checkbook and agreed to bring it with her to the medical examiner's office. Any distraction would help him get through it.

"We need this to end," Barnett said quietly, "so that we can both get back to work. I'll make this up to you. I swear I will."

Teddy laid the newspaper on his desk. Barnett gazed at Holmes's photo, then turned the paper over and shook his head.

"In another week or two the evidence will be in," Barnett said. "By then Holmes will have gotten tired of living in a jail cell. We'll go out together, Teddy. We'll show him what they have and talk to him. I'm sure he'll agree that a plea is his only way out."

Teddy didn't say anything. Instead, he nodded like he thought Nash would and hoped Barnett would come to his senses. But as he left the office, he thought about what Holmes had admitted to him just an hour and a half ago. That he didn't want to know what happened because he thought he might be the one. If Barnett wanted the man to plead guilty, Oscar Holmes was just about there.

Twenty-one

Teddy hadn't prepared himself for the smell. . . .

It rolled toward him in waves, growing more oppressive as he moved deeper into the medical examiner's building and finally reached the examining rooms. The smell of death was so thick Teddy thought it might knock him down. As a boy, he'd once found a deer lying by the side of the road. As a student, he remembered opening a refrigerator that had been switched off for a week or two. But nothing he'd experienced in his past even came close to this.

They stopped before what looked like a prep room. Teddy followed Andrews, Powell, and Detective Vega inside. As two medical examiners passed out jumpsuits, Teddy caught Andrews staring at him. The man was laughing at him, and must have been waiting for Teddy's reaction to the foul odor.

"You get used to it," Detective Vega said.

"How long's it take?"

"A couple of years," Andrews shot back.

Teddy ignored Andrews, stepping into the jumpsuit carefully because it was made of paper. In the corner of the room he saw several jumpsuits in the trash and realized the protective clothing was meant to be thrown away once the autopsies were completed. He glanced at Powell, noticing her long legs as she slipped the paper suit over her short black skirt. She hadn't mentioned Holmes's checkbook. She hadn't said a word to him since they entered the building. He knew she was still angry with him, still didn't believe his story about how he'd found Valerie Kram's body at the boathouse. Even worse for her, it was over now. It had ended the moment Andrews took credit for finding the body. She looked frustrated—trying to balance her job in the face of Andrews's political career. As he watched the two of them interact, they seemed as different as night and day, and he wondered if they got along.

Teddy buttoned himself up. An ME handed him a shower cap and a pair of goggles, pointing to the face masks and box of latex gloves on the table while he warned him about the dangers of tuberculosis and HIV. When everyone was suited up, they entered the examining room.

The walls were tiled. The stainless steel gurneys tilted forward slightly with the naked bodies of Darlene Lewis and Valerie Kram lying side by side like dead twins.

Teddy shuddered at the hideous sight and looked away. When he caught Andrews staring at him again, even smiling behind his mask, he knew the man had been waiting for this moment, too.

The ME gave Teddy a nudge and pointed out the rails on the gurney. They looked more like gutters on the roof of a house. He saw the holes at the foot of the gurney and now understood why they were tilted forward slightly. In a few minutes, body fluids would be streaming down the rails venting through the holes like rain onto the floor.

"If you begin to feel faint," the ME said, "then leave the room. Believe me, you want to limit your contact with the floor."

Andrews was smiling again; Carolyn Powell and Detective Vega were gazing at him evenly. Teddy gritted his teeth behind his mask, determined to hang on. But it was tough. He glanced at Valerie Kram's body on the far table, her chest

already open like a jacket. Then back at Darlene Lewis's face
with her eyes bulging out of her head. As his gaze moved
down her body, taking in her bruised neck and the missing
patches of skin, the ME made his first cut.

It was a long, deep slice, as if Darlene Lewis were a piece
of meat. Even more horrific, the incision looked identical
to the wound the murderer had already inflicted on Valerie
Kram. The cut formed the letter Y, running from the girl's
shoulders across her upper chest, then straight down to the
missing skin just above her vagina. When the ME pulled
out the gardening shears and began clipping the girl's ribs
away, Teddy realized he'd seen enough and kept his eyes
on the ME's face the rest of the way.

They worked for hours, the ME showing no emotion, just
an ample supply of curiosity and professionalism. With each
step, he recorded his observations into a tape recorder and
often stopped to wipe his hands off and write something
down. Sometimes he would confer with the ME working
on Valerie Kram at the next gurney. Occasionally, Teddy's
eyes would wander down to one of the bodies. But as the
autopsies proceeded, the view became progressively worse
and his eyes popped back up again. Every time he glanced
at Andrews, he found the man staring at him. It was almost
as if the DA was using the horror of the autopsy as some
sort of initiation or dare. Almost as if Andrews was taunting
him and hoping he might faint.

But the gruesome ordeal bore fruit. It had been worth
it because they were learning something. When the ME
examined Darlene Lewis's neck, he found torn cartilage and
a broken bone, which indicated she died from strangulation.
And it had been quick, the ME noted, the murder performed
by someone with powerful hands. Teddy tried not to think
about the size of Holmes's massive hands, or his client's
fingerprints that glowed about the girl's neck like a string
of pearls under the black lights at the crime scene. As he
glanced about the room, it was obvious that everyone else
was thinking the same thing, but wouldn't be letting the
thought go.

Although the end came quickly for Darlene Lewis, the ME concluded she had been tortured by the murderer for perhaps as long as two hours before her death. The ME pointed to the missing skin. He likened it to foreplay, and said it had probably been removed while she was still alive. Detective Vega seemed to have already guessed as much, saying this would account for the amount of blood at the crime scene. The ME agreed, and told them the killer probably removed the skin and waited for her to bleed out. Then for some reason, he changed his mind and strangled her to death. Holmes's name was mentioned freely, as was a lengthy discussion on what he'd done with the skin. All conclusions were preliminary, and Teddy listened without saying anything. At some point he began to wonder if they'd forgotten he was in the room. But when the ME offered his own theory—that Holmes ate the girl's flesh before her eyes, then killed her when she passed out—the room suddenly quieted.

The silence underlined their theory. Holmes got off on the shock. The minute Darlene Lewis passed out, he'd lost his audience and the thrill was gone. This was the work of someone who was more than troubled and a long way past being sick. When she fainted, he strangled her—simple as that.

Valerie Kram's fate was much less conclusive because of the time she'd spent in the river. Still, the cold water had preserved her better than either ME would have guessed. Although she was an avid jogger and probably in good shape the day she vanished, her muscle tone had wasted away before her death. She'd been worn down, perhaps even starved. An examination of her neck revealed that Kram died in exactly the same manner as Darlene Lewis. It hadn't been the cut. The hyoid bone was broken, indicating that she'd died as a result of strangulation as well.

Andrews seemed to get off on the connection and threw an exalted fist in the air.

While the others ignored the DA's outburst, Teddy noticed that both MEs found Kram's open chest particulary intriguing. Inside her body things weren't necessarily where they were supposed to be. The tube top had held her together, her organs remarkably preserved. The word *cannibalism* came up again, in spite of Teddy's presence. The MEs discussed the length of time she'd been in the water again, and agreed they couldn't be sure what happened. What troubled both of them was the appearance that things were handled inside her body and deliberately moved around.

Teddy felt his head lighten and begin to spin. It had been a valiant effort. He'd fought the fight, lasting for hours, but knew he was done. As he excused himself from the examining room, Andrews cackled.

"What did I tell you?" the DA was saying in his wake. "He couldn't hack it. He's just a kid, and doesn't have the stuff."

Twenty-two

Teddy ripped the door open, bolting through the main entrance of the medical examiner's office in search of fresh cold air. He grabbed the handrail and held on. A noisy bus was lumbering up University Avenue loaded with people who looked like they were alive and on their way home. He realized it was night and wondered where the day had gone. When he turned toward the parking lot, he noticed the press assembling with their video cameras and microwave transmitters. No doubt the DA would be holding another press conference.

Teddy dug into his jacket pocket and found his cigarettes, then lit up trying to get rid of the rotten smell lingering about him. The sounds of garden shears and images of death that were seared into his mind, his memory. As he inhaled the nicotine-rich smoke and blew it out, he saw a man with long hair take his photograph, then fade into the crowd.

The front door opened and Powell walked out of the building. He turned away, needing a break from her, too.

"Alan Andrews is a world-class asshole," he said in a quiet voice.

Powell didn't respond. He thought she might have gone

back inside. But when he turned, he found her still there. He looked at her face, her wide-open blue-gray eyes staring at him. The distance was gone. She held Holmes's checkbook in her hand.

"You made it all the way through," she said gently.

"What do you mean?"

"They're taking fluid samples and sewing them back up. What's left will take time and be in the ME's report. You didn't miss anything at all."

She was trying to soften the blow. Teddy knew that he'd flamed out. This wasn't his world. He'd done the best he could to hang in and wasn't about to beat himself up for it.

She held the checkbook out and smiled. "If you want a look, you better do it now," she said. "It's gotta go back with Detective Vega tonight. If you're not feeling up to it, you can go down to the roundhouse in the morning and look at it there."

Teddy was up to it and got rid of his cigarette. As he took the checkbook, Andrews strode out of the building with Vega. The district attorney looked as if he might hit Teddy with another wisecrack, but the camera lights powered up as soon as he cleared the entrance and the man knew he was on. Andrews raised his arms in the air, fending off questions that hadn't come yet and hustling down the sidewalk to the news vans. As he greeted the press wearing the look of concern Teddy had seen him practicing at the boathouse the other night, Teddy couldn't help thinking of the flaw in Barnett's plan. He'd thought it before, but it was even more apparent now. Andrews loved what was going on. The two bodies they'd spent the afternoon ripping apart were a godsend to the man. A leap forward, not two steps back.

"There's a connection," Andrews said in a dramatic voice to the reporters huddling around him. "A definite connection between the murders of Darlene Lewis and Valerie Kram. The medical examiner's results won't be in for a while, but let me tell you what I've got. The cause of death in both cases wasn't from the wounds these two poor souls endured.

The cause of death was strangulation. If I haven't said it before, I'm saying it now. Our hearts go out to the families of both these young women.''

The man's tone of voice was over the top, his pretense abhorrent. All afternoon he'd been dancing on their graves.

Teddy stopped listening and opened the checkbook. Glancing at the register, he noted that Holmes wrote checks on the first and fifteenth of every month without much variation. Between rent, telephone, insurance, and utilities, it amounted to only seven checks a month. His balance averaged about ten grand. Once a quarter Holmes wrote a check to an investment firm for two thousand dollars.

Teddy paged back to October. Unfortunately, Holmes kept to his routine. There were no entries made on the day Valerie Kram had been kidnapped—no checks written between the fifteenth of the month and November 1. Oscar Holmes didn't have an alibi for the twenty-sixth, and trying to figure out what he was up to on that day seemed like a dead end.

He looked at Powell, hiding his disappointment. She was watching Andrews field questions, but he could tell she was thinking about something else. He wondered if she didn't have a husband, even children to go home to. He glanced at her left hand and didn't see a wedding ring. It had been a long day. Maybe she just needed a break, too.

"What about the ten others?" a reporter shouted, pushing his way toward the DA. "Families are worried. Our phones are ringing off the hook."

Teddy turned sharply. Powell must have noticed because he could feel her eyes on him. To Teddy's surprise, Andrews was ready for the question.

"We've isolated ten missing persons we think require a closer look," Andrews said. "I'm meeting with their families in the morning to give them a full briefing. There's no question that the investigation is widening out. But remember, Holmes is already confined to a cell. We're saddened by what these families have lost. There's no reason for anyone to jump to any conclusions. There's no reason for anyone else in the city to panic right now."

Teddy looked at the reporters' faces and realized they wanted to believe the district attorney but were still frightened. He turned away, thinking about the ME's initial conclusions.

Nothing he'd heard anyone say today discounted his own theory about what might have happened—the idea that in Darlene Lewis's case Holmes may have interrupted someone else. In some ways the observations made in the examination room actually bolstered his theory. Darlene Lewis had been cut, the murderer waiting for her to bleed out. Then, for some reason, he strangled her. It had been a sudden act, a quick and powerful move, the kind of response someone might have if they needed to end things in a heartbeat because they were interrupted. It didn't explain why the killer hadn't kept the girl alive for a month as he did with Valerie Kram. Teddy knew it didn't shed any light on why the murderer cut Lewis up at her home rather than stealing the girl away and wearing her down. Still, his theory had survived the autopsy, and he didn't think he was grabbing at straws. The possibility that everyone was caught up in the details and missing what really happened—the chance that Holmes might actually be innocent—still had legs.

His mind was rolling. Teddy was thinking clearly again. When he looked up, he found Powell appraising him. She took a step closer, staring at him as if maybe she'd been reading his mind. Teddy shrugged it off and handed her the checkbook. When he thanked her, she didn't step back.

"Let's go get a drink," she said.

Twenty-three

It had begun to snow. The restaurant was just off campus and nearly empty, and they were shown to a table by a window in the back. Powell ordered a Bombay martini, dry, with three olives. Under normal circumstances, Teddy would have asked for a beer. But with the weight of what he'd seen that day still with him, he told the waitress to make it two.

As they waited for their drinks, Powell gazed out the window watching the snowflakes float to the ground without saying anything. Teddy realized that what Detective Vega had told him before the autopsies wasn't necessarily true. Getting used to it was something a medical examiner might achieve, but for the rest of the world the prospect would take more than time. Even Powell, a seasoned prosecutor who'd probably attended a hundred autopsies, looked as if the afternoon was still preying on her mind.

The waitress arrived with their drinks. As she set them down on the table, Teddy couldn't help but notice something was wrong. She stepped away quickly, her banter forced.

"It's the smell," Powell said when they were alone. "That's why we got the window table in back."

Teddy wasn't sure what she was talking about until Powell sniffed her own blouse. On her cue he pulled his shirt to his nose and inhaled. It was the smell of death. The scent he thought he'd only been carrying around in his head. The odor had permeated their clothing.

"You'll have to get your suit dry-cleaned," she said. "It's the only way I know to get it out."

They sipped their drinks. The gin was smooth, rolling through him and sparking an immediate glow. He could feel his shoulders and neck loosening up and was glad he'd ordered the martini rather than a beer.

"There's a problem with your story," Powell said after a moment.

"What story is that?"

"The way you found Valerie Kram's body at the boat-house. The reason you were there."

She wasn't grilling him. Instead, she appeared relaxed, and he thought he detected a faint smile.

"What's the problem?" he asked.

"The assistant warden called and said you visited Holmes today. When he walked you out, he noticed you were carrying a picture of Valerie Kram. Obviously, you showed that picture to your client. You wouldn't have done that if he'd already told you where she was."

Nash had been right about her. She was smart. Even if she remained preoccupied by the physical evidence, she was still doing her job. Still searching and trying to understand. And she was also stunning. Teddy tried to ignore her looks, but the martini had a firm grip on him by now. His eyes kept drifting over her face.

"But that was never my story," he said. "When I saw her, I didn't know who she was. Andrews assumed that Holmes told me where to find her. I'm glad you agree that it couldn't be true."

That hidden smile of hers burgeoned and she leaned closer. "Come on, Teddy. I need to know why you were there for my own peace of mind. In a way it's embarrassing that you found the body. Like maybe everyone at my end dropped the ball.''

"Everything I told you yesterday happens to be true. I went to the boathouse because I had a meeting.''

"A date with Dawn Bingle.''

He caught the sarcasm in her voice, the glint in her eyes. She seemed to think the name was funny and that he'd made it up on the fly. She was leading him along, rooting the story out, having fun while she needled him. It was more like a tease, and the playfulness was as much a relief as the gin.

The waitress appeared, interrupting the moment and standing ten feet back as she checked on them. They turned to the window and weighed the progress of the snow. It was picking up, but the streets remained clear. They decided to order another round, and the waitress hurried off somewhat concerned.

"I saw your face tonight,'' Powell said. ''You knew about the ten others.''

"Not until this morning.''

"You're investigating the case. You went to the boathouse looking for Valerie Kram. You went because somehow you knew she'd be there.''

"I had a date with Dawn, remember?''

She sipped her drink. ''So now it's Dawn. I thought you said you never met. What's she look like?''

"Slim and pale,'' he said. ''Almost transparent, like she's not really there.''

Powell laughed. But for his own peace of mind, he wished he had the answers and could tell her what she wanted to know. He remembered the letter in his briefcase. The death threat. He looked at Powell's smile in the dim light and didn't want it to go away. This wasn't the time or place to show her what he'd received in the mail. When the waitress arrived with their second round, he watched Powell down what was left in her glass and pour the olives into her new one. Teddy did the same, and the waitress left.

"It doesn't make much difference now,'' he said. ''It's a matter of public record. Your boss found the body. The city's being terrorized, but everything's okay because Alan Andrews is on the job.''

She popped an olive into her mouth. ''You committed a burglary, you know.''

Teddy shrugged. ''At the boathouse?''

''I could probably get the charges reduced to trespassing, but you'd have to plead guilty.''

''You think the judge will go easy on me?''

She thought it over and shook her head and they laughed. By the time they'd finished their second martini, the question seemed forgotten and he found her appraising him again. He turned away and looked at the people sitting at tables ordering dinner. Somehow the restaurant had become full without them noticing. Two groups seated close by with menus in their hands were eyeing them carefully. Teddy understood why when he checked his shirt again. He'd almost forgotten about how he and Powell had spent their afternoon. Almost been able to let it go.

''I know a place that won't be so crowded,'' Powell said. ''Let's get out of here. We'll have one more before the storm hits and call it a night.''

Teddy agreed, and to the delight of the waitress, they paid their bill and left. As they walked to their cars laughing about it the way you would after two drinks, Powell got into a late-model BMW and told him to follow her. They drove east toward the Delaware River, the roads wet but clear of snow. When they reached the waterfront district, Powell made a left, heading north. Teddy was surprised, thinking she was leading him to a place on South Street. A few blocks later, she pulled to a stop beside a parking space on the street and tapped her horn. Then she idled ahead, letting Teddy have the space and turning into a private garage.

Teddy's curiosity was up. As Powell stepped out of the garage and met him on the sidewalk, she pointed at the building. The place wouldn't be crowded because it wouldn't be public. Powell had brought him to her home.

It was a large condo on the fifth floor, its open design

taking advantage of the Delaware River from every window. The construction had been high end, and Teddy noted the quality of craftsmanship at a glance. Powell's furniture was more casual, the feeling of warmth hitting him as she switched on a series of low-wattage lamps and made her apologies for not cleaning up.

Teddy noticed the wide staircase leading upstairs. He hadn't expected a second floor and turned to the fireplace as Powell stepped into the kitchen. Over the mantel he saw a painting by a local artist he recognized and knew had hit the big time. It was a simple landscape depicting the fields and forests meeting the Schuylkill River—a long way upstream from the city—with two figures standing in the foreground. But there was a dreamlike quality to the work, almost surreal in its use of color. Teddy thought of Diana Ong's painting, *Land of the Midnight Sun*. It was almost as if the artist wanted the viewer to take one last look at the valley before the sprawl took over and the image vanished for good. Even more intriguing, it felt as if the people were in motion, as if maybe they were disappearing, too.

"You like the painting?" Powell asked.

Teddy nodded, turning to watch her mix the martinis on the other side of the counter. That smile was back, and he noticed she'd slipped out of her shoes.

"I like the whole place," he said.

He was trying not to look at her long legs. Her tangled hair. The way her lips were parted. He was trying to remind himself that their relationship was nothing more than professional.

She passed a martini over the counter and lifted her own. They took quick sips so none of the gin would spill. The drink tasted stronger than the two he'd ordered at the restaurant and he noticed the glass was bigger. He'd have to be careful, have to keep cool.

"Follow me," she said, easing her way out of the kitchen.

They crossed the living room to a doorway. Powell entered first and sat down on the couch against the wall without turning on the lights. Teddy noticed the chair pressing against the couch and rested his drink on the coffee table as he sat down in the darkness. It was a small, narrow room. The wall facing the river rose three feet from the floor giving way to a single sheet of plate glass. He looked outside and saw two tugboats dragging a container ship up the river as the snow fell from the sky. The view was incredible and spanned from the Benjamin Franklin Bridge all the way down to the Walt Whitman.

"I bought the place because of this room," she said in a quiet voice. "It's peaceful. I like to sit here for a little while before I go to sleep."

"Who wouldn't?" Teddy said.

They sipped their drinks and settled back in their seats.

"When did you start at Barnett and Stokes?" she asked after a while.

"Three months ago."

"So this is all new."

He nodded. "I joined the firm because of their real estate department. Then this happened. Who knew?"

She smiled. "How big's your debt from school?"

"Huge and scary. What about yours?"

"I finally got it paid off two years ago."

There was an antique cabinet between the couch and chair. Powell opened the door and switched on a receiver, scanning the dial until she found some soft jazz. When she turned back, she sipped her drink and rested her legs on the coffee table.

"Are you seeing anyone?" she asked.

It was the sort of question that seemed innocent enough. Still, the sexual tension in the room felt as if it had just gone nuclear. Teddy felt the rush, the burn, his eyes moving up her legs and across her body until they reached her face. She'd been watching him. Even in the darkness, her eyes had a certain reach.

"I haven't really had time," he said. "Between the bar exam and a new job, I haven't been getting out much."

"Me either," she said. "And the people I work with are so damn depressing."

They laughed. It was a nervous laugh. The kind of laugh you make when your entire body hits the afterglow.

"Do you think you could keep a secret?" she said after a moment. "Break the rules for one night and then never do it again?"

He thought it over. "You mean forget that it ever happened?"

"Something like that."

He leaned forward and kissed her.

It was a gentle kiss, their mouths just opening, their tongues swirling back and forth and finding their way to the middle. They kissed again and again, smoother and deeper. As Teddy lowered himself onto the couch beside her, she reached around his shoulders and gathered him in. The smell of death was lingering in their clothing, but the scent of her skin as he kissed her neck was even stronger.

Teddy watched as she unbuttoned her blouse and opened her bra. When her breasts bounced out, he touched them with his fingers. They were soft and smooth and felt like something one might find in paradise. Lowering his lips to them, he caught her smile and heard a light moan. He could feel her slipping out of her skirt, unzipping his pants and reaching inside. She sank to the floor and in between his legs. She was pulling his pants away, squeezing him and stroking him. Death had vanished, finally and completely, overtaken by the scent of her sex in the air. He found it intoxicating, better than any dream. When he looked at her blond hair falling off her shoulders, her swollen breasts and gorgeous face, their eyes met for a moment. Then she smiled again and went down on him.

Twenty-four

Jim Barnett hung up the phone, reviewing the changes he'd penciled in that Nash had asked for. Before their conversation, he'd thought the press release was perfect. But now, as he read it a second time, the copy seemed even more perfect. Nash's suggestions were subtle but necessary, he realized. A word here and another one there. They were the observations of a true legal genius, and Barnett laughed. He admired Nash and looked forward to working with him. As he thought it over, he shook his head and rose from his desk. He was more than grateful that Teddy had come through.

It was after eight. His assistant, Jackie, had gone home two hours ago, but she'd prepared her computer for the press release and left the monitor on. All Barnett had to do was type in the changes and hit SEND. Jackie's computer would take care of the rest.

He sat down at her desk and switched on the desk light. Because of the energy crisis, the overhead lights in the hall were turned off at seven. Barnett was a skilled typist and the whole thing only took ten minutes. He checked the screen carefully for any mistakes. Grabbing the mouse, he moved the curser to the icon marked SEND and gave the button a heavy click. When the modem began screeching, he walked into his office for his coat and briefcase, downed another pill, and killed the lights.

It was late and he wanted to get home. The weather forecasters had been calling for another storm since last night. He wasn't worried. He'd left his Mercedes in the garage, deciding on the Grand Cherokee just in case.

As he pulled out of the garage, he noticed the snow covering the streets and switched to four-wheel-drive. Adjusting the heat, he flipped on the wipers and set out for home. There wasn't much traffic. In spite of the storm, he estimated the trip from the city to Villinova wouldn't take more than thirty minutes.

He slipped a CD into the player, a new movie score his wife Sally had given him at breakfast, and turned up the volume. As he cruised down the expressway, he tried to sort through what he'd accomplished today. Not much, he realized. Most of the morning and afternoon had been spent in a jumbled blur. He'd been eating tranquilizers as if they were Good 'N Plenty all week. He needed to get a grip on things, take control of himself, but there was so much at stake. Everything he'd worked for.

The thought of losing what he had sent a dead chill up his spine and he broke out in a cold sweat. Nash had warned him that given the mood of the city, their press release might fall on deaf ears. His plan to force Andrews's hand might not work out. The body count was rising, the case against Holmes on the verge of spinning out of control.

He looked back at the road, trying to find his lane through all the fucking snow. When he spotted a car ahead, he backed off the gas and moved over to the right lane. He'd follow the bastard, keep his eyes on the taillights, and let him do the hard work.

His mind began to wander again. By now Jackie's computer would have sent his edited press release to every newspaper and TV news department in the city. He'd even asked

Jackie to include Andrews's personal fax number, knowing it would really piss the guy off. This was more than just a press release announcing that William S. Nash had joined the legal team that would defend Oscar Holmes for the murder of Darlene Lewis. It was a warning shot sent across the bow of the district attorney's office.

So why was he suddenly overcome with doubt? Why was he still sweating?

Barnett turned the music down, trying to pull the upside out of the haze. He'd watched Alan Andrews's press conference on TV tonight from his office. Andrews coming off as if he were some kind of conquering hero from the parking lot at the morgue. Andrews thinking he'd gotten off scot-free after sending some poor asshole to his grave. Well, all that was in the press release and would be dredged up again. That's what Nash's name was about. His standing and reputation would work like a vice. Barnett wondered how Andrews would react, wishing he could see his face when he read the press release. Andrews might be playing the city's next savior tonight, but tomorrow would be another day. If he wanted a career in politics, Andrews would be forced to play ball. If not, then all he'd be is another prick.

If it worked, Barnett reminded himself. Only if it worked.

He hit the brakes and swerved, almost missing the Gulf Mills exit. As he glided down the ramp, he made a short left, then another at the light onto Route 320. He was close now. Almost home.

The snow was deeper here, the road not yet plowed. Still, the Grand Cherokee climbed the winding hill without much effort. Marveling at the smooth ride, he made a left, then a right onto Berkley Lane and eased down the drive.

He'd made it. He could see the lights on in the kitchen. Sally busy putting together a late dinner. He stopped before the garage and looked out the driver's-side window at the snow on the ground. Better than six inches. Reaching behind his seat, he pulled his rubbers out of the cargo bag and slipped them over his shoes. He kept the engine running, the lights on, then hit the locks and got out to open the garage door.

As he trudged through the snow he thought about how nice it would've been to have a remote. But their house was a Victorian that he and Sally had spent years restoring down to the most infinitesimal detail. The garage was a converted stable. Even though the two-acre lot was wooded, the stable could be seen from the road. Changing the style of the doors to accommodate an electric door opener wasn't an option and never would've worked out.

Barnett waved the snow away from his face, giving the heavy wooden door a hard push to the side and hoping Sally had thought to light a fire in the den. But as he stepped off the concrete pad into the snow, he lost his footing on the ice and slipped.

It was a hard fall—the glare of the headlights in his eyes as he lay flat on his back and tried to get his bearings. He'd hit his head, but didn't think he was hurt. Didn't think he'd broken any bones. He looked back at the car and noticed that the driver's-side door was open. He thought he'd closed it. Given the snow, he normally would. As he lifted his right leg and slipped onto his back again, he wondered if that last tranquilizer had been one too many, or maybe he was just getting old. Either way, he was glad Sally hadn't seen him fall because he felt embarrassed.

That's when he heard the car start forward.

He turned and squinted at the approaching lights. At first he watched in disbelief, even confusion. Then his heart started pounding and it suddenly occurred to him that what was happening was real. His eyes jerked down to the heavy wheels moving toward him. He heard the squeaky packing sound rubber tires make when they press down snow. He tried to scream but couldn't. Digging through the snow with his fingers, he pushed at the ice, clawed at it. When the oversize wheels rolled over his legs and his own blood splashed him in the face, he peered up from beneath the car and saw someone running from the house. It was Sally. Waving her hands in the air and screaming as he looked back at his crushed legs. His arteries must have been severed. Blood was shooting onto the snow as if from a garden hose. He tried to keep his eye on it, reaching down to cover the wounds, but everything went black.

Twenty-five

Teddy ran down the hallway at Bryn Mawr Hospital, trying not to think about the woman he'd left behind because he knew he couldn't right now.

It was after midnight. He found Sally Barnett huddled in a chair in the waiting room all alone. When she saw him enter, she stood up and rushed toward him, laying her head against his chest. She was sobbing, and he could feel her body shaking in his arms.

"How is he?" Teddy asked.

She gazed up at him with tears streaming down her cheeks and shook her head.

Sally was ten to fifteen years younger than Barnett. Teddy had liked her the moment they first met. She was easy to talk to and had a cheery spirit. She was one of those kind of people who could calm any situation down by her mere presence. When Teddy joined the firm, Barnett invited him over to the house for dinner. Sally gave him the tour, showing him photographs of the restoration. She'd documented the entire process, and he realized they shared an interest in architecture.

"They're trying to save his legs," she said. "But it doesn't look good."

"Is he still in the operating room?"

"No," she said, pointing to a set of doors. "It lasted three hours. He's in the critical care unit now."

Teddy glanced at the doors and turned back. "Is he conscious? Can we see him?"

She nodded slowly, the agony in her face clear. "He's lost a lot of blood though. He's very weak."

Teddy pressed the button on the wall and the doors swung open. As they entered the unit, Sally led the way down the hall to the nurses' station. Although the lighting was subdued, he spotted Barnett in the first alcove and moved toward him hesitantly. He was lying on the bed, his entire body trembling. His eyes were pointed at the ceiling and fluttering. Teddy looked at his legs wrapped in bandages and held in place by a series of metal pins and hardware. IVs couldn't handle the drug load. Four bags of medication hung from two racks over the bed, feeding his system through the ports of a central line injected into his neck.

Teddy had picked up the call less than an hour ago. He'd been in Carolyn Powell's bed—in her arms—when his cell phone rang. All Sally could manage to say was that Barnett had run himself over with his own car. Teddy threw his clothes on, the drive to the hospital manic. Even though the snow had stopped, the roads were a mess.

"How could this happen?" he said.

"He was working on something at the office and got home late. When he opened the garage, he slipped on the ice. I saw it happening from the window. I couldn't get there in time."

Barnett grabbed Teddy's arm. He looked at Barnett and saw the man's face turned toward him, his eyes still blinking uncontrollably. He could feel Barnett pulling him closer. In spite of the tube in his mouth, the man was trying to speak. Teddy leaned closer, concentrating on the sounds, but the words were unintelligible. The sight of Barnett twisting on the mattress and straining to be heard was harrowing. Whatever he was trying to say appeared more than important.

A nurse hurried over from the counter, pulling Barnett's hand away and checking his vital signs on the monitor.

"This patient is in critical condition," she said in a harsh voice. "His heart rate's up. You can't do this. I'm sorry, but you'll have to wait outside."

Teddy looked back at Barnett. The man's eyes were tacked to the ceiling again. As he walked Sally into the waiting room, he noticed she didn't have a coat or even her purse.

"Where are your things?" he asked.

She looked back at him helplessly, shaking her head and unable to speak.

"Tell me what you need," he said. "I'll drive over and bring them back."

Twenty-six

Teddy skidded to a stop at the curb, thinking he'd better do something about his tires and still trying to decipher what Barnett had been struggling to say with a half-inch hose stuffed down his throat and a central line piercing the artery in his neck.

He climbed out of the car, looking at Barnett's house and the lighted windows through the trees. Given the hour, every other house on the street was dark. As he walked down the driveway, he spotted the Grand Cherokee smashed into the side of the garage at an odd angle. Moving closer, he saw Barnett's blood splashed all over the white snow. The deep red stain covered a fifteen-foot square of ground, and Teddy wondered how the man had survived long enough to make it to the hospital.

Sally had ridden in the ambulance with Barnett, and not wasted time running back into the house for her things. She'd asked Teddy to bring her a coat and sweater. In the den he'd find her purse and knitting bag. Keeping her hands busy would calm her down, she said.

The snow was almost a foot deep. Ignoring it, he stepped around the blood and kept to the shoulder of the drive. As he reached the Grand Cherokee, he moved to the front and examined the hood. The car had rolled over Barnett's legs and turned slightly until it crashed into the wall beside the open garage door. The entire front end on the left side was crinkled like an accordion. He looked back at the driveway, noting the rise in elevation. He could see Barnett's footprints in the snow and followed them with his eyes until he found the spot where Barnett parked to get out of the car.

Teddy opened the driver's-side door, checking the automatic shift and finding it set in DRIVE. Piecing it together, he realized Barnett got out to open the garage with the car still in gear. Grand Cherokees were built like tanks. The heavy car must have picked up speed as it rolled down the hill.

He shook his head, picturing Barnett on the ground trying to get out of the way and knowing he wasn't going to make it. For some reason, he thought about the tires that needed to be replaced on his Corolla again.

Teddy spotted Barnett's keys still in the ignition. Pocketing them, he swung the door closed and moved back down the drive along the shoulder. *People make mistakes,* he thought. *Accidents happen every day.* But Barnett had just driven home in a storm. Teddy couldn't believe that the man wouldn't have been more cautious, particularly with the car that had just brought him home.

He turned and took another look at the blood in the snow. When he noticed the footprints leading across the yard into the trees, he became very still.

They shouldn't have been there. There was no reason for them to be there.

He lit a cigarette, staring at the tracks in the snow and considering the possibility that he was imagining things. He wasn't, he decided. The tracks came and went from the exact spot Teddy calculated Barnett had parked when he first got out of his car.

He looked back at the driveway, trying to account for all the different sets of prints in the snow. There weren't that many, the snow fresh, and his mind was clear. He saw the

Grand Cherokee's tracks intermingled with a double set of tire tracks that could only have been made when the ambulance arrived. That covered the vehicles, and he stepped back to take in the different sets of footprints. He saw Sally's moving from the house to the bloodstained area where the car ran over Barnett's legs. Turning back to the spot where the ambulance had stopped, he noted two sets of different prints left behind by the medics. The space between the footprints was spread out, and Teddy could tell the medics had been running.

But the set of footprints leading into the trees was spread out as well. As he moved closer, he realized that whoever left them behind had also been running. What happened to Barnett hadn't been an accident. Someone had shifted the car into DRIVE, goosed the accelerator, and fled.

He felt a sudden burst of fear rise between his shoulders and touch the back of his neck. There was a light breeze moving through the yard, the leafless branches knocking into one another and rattling all around him. As he turned and checked his back, he gazed at the dark houses lining the street and couldn't help being struck by the eeriness. A neighborhood dog started barking from somewhere in the distance.

He took a last drag and flicked his cigarette into the snow. As he picked up the tracks and started following them out of the yard, he examined each footprint with great care before moving on to the next. Although the impressions had been made on the run and weren't perfect, he knew he was looking at a man's hiking shoe. Measuring them against his own size-twelve dress shoe, he estimated they were a size or two smaller.

The tracks moved off the yard, and he found himself standing behind a tree. The snow was well packed, and it looked as if the man had spent some time here. He noticed a row of pine trees blocking his view of the street, and realized the man could've waited for Barnett without being caught in the stray headlights from a passing car. When he turned back to the house, the view of the driveway was striking and only twenty-five yards away.

Teddy stepped out from beneath the tree, following the tracks farther away from the house. They seemed to move from tree to tree in the shape of an arc. As he looked ahead, the footprints cut back to the street before an empty lot.

He could feel the blood coursing through his body. It hadn't been an accident. He knew it now.

Something in the snow caught his eye and he stopped. Something shiny.

He knelt down, brushing the snow away from the spot until he found what looked like a small shot glass. Pulling the scarf away from his neck, he picked it up, careful not to touch it with his own fingers. It was a small shot glass made of Sterling silver. He held it to his nose, thinking the man had brought a flask to keep warm as he waited for Barnett to come home. Maybe he even needed a drink for courage. But as he took a whiff, he found the shot glass odorless and picked up the scent of Carolyn Powell's sex still on his fingers. He drew in a deep breath, her image flashing through him and dissipating. For one night, they'd broken the rules and it had been wonderful. When he'd taken Sally's call and had to leave, they'd scheduled a breakfast meeting before work tomorrow. The thought of being with Powell in any setting stirred the night up all over again. It had been worth it. Even if it would have to remain secret.

Teddy got to his feet, gazing at the silver shot glass as it glistened in the reflected light of the snow. He noticed three rivets in the side, holding the seam together. It looked old and valuable, the design ornate. There were pictures etched into the precious metal, and he turned it in the scarf noting the depictions of tall ships and whales. The man who ran over Barnett had left something behind that told a story. A piece of evidence that looked as if it led somewhere.

Teddy heard a sudden whooshing sound from behind his back and turned. Something cracked over his head. He was stunned at first, the blow crushing him. He took a half step forward, but knew his rubbery legs were giving way. As he tumbled forward and hit the snow, he thought he saw the shape of a man standing in the darkness with his arms raised. The figure held something in his hands, ready to swing it down again. But it was only a glimpse made in a split second. A glimpse at something before the world started spinning and the lights went out.

Twenty-seven

Through the haze he could see his father picking him up out of the snow and carrying him away in his arms. His teeth were chattering from the cold, his bones shaking like sticks rubbing together in search of heat, fire. As Teddy considered the image, he thought maybe he'd punched his ticket out, and this was the view from the slow train ridden by the dead.

His father lowered him onto his bed, touched the wound on his forehead, and left the room. Time was rushing back and forth, and Teddy found himself caught in the wind. He was twenty-seven, then twenty. When he jumped off the bed and ran to the window, he could see the cops taking his father away and knew he was fourteen again.

They never found the money.

The accountant had murdered his father's business partner when he was caught embezzling huge sums of money from the company. After Teddy's father was arrested for the murder and later died in prison, the accountant finally came forward overcome with guilt. Still, he never told anyone what he did with the money. Facing a guilty verdict for murder and a life behind bars, he knew he didn't have to.

Money had been a major issue in Teddy's life ever since his father's arrest. Every time he picked up the phone, it was another rude stranger with a harsh voice asking to speak to his mom. He could hear her answering questions with a worried expression on her face. Her answers were usually the same, even when she started working. "Next week," she would say. "Next month." Or even, "I don't have it right now. Feeding my family comes first. You'll just have to wait."

She was a remarkable woman. It would take a few minutes after each call, but she always had a warm smile lying around. Always a good hug for Teddy and his little sister after one of those phone calls. Sometimes her hugs were too good, like maybe she was hanging on. He didn't really mind though. Her cheeks were soft and he loved her long brown hair and the light, clean smell of her perfume.

They seemed to be eating spaghetti more often, Teddy noticed. And when he or his sister's clothes wore out, his mom sewed them back together or ironed on patches instead of buying something new. At night, Teddy would often sneak out to the barn and watch her paint through the window. She could only paint at night and on weekends because of her new job. He knew painting was her favorite thing in the world, the thing she called her *mission*. But she looked tired, and oftentimes when he peeked through the window he found her crying. He knew she was lonely, the whole thing getting to her.

Still, everything at home was a lot better than school. Teddy was no longer the son of a man who built worlds. According to his classmates, Teddy was the son of a murderer and would probably grow up to be one, too. The wrath started out as teasing and occasional wisecracks. After a few weeks, he was no longer allowed to play with certain friends. Their parents wouldn't have it. When he caught his best friend taunting his little sister at recess, calling her a stupid cunt and a convict in waiting, Teddy knocked four teeth out of the kid's mouth before a teacher could pull him off.

His suspension lasted three days—without a lecture or

an admonishment from his mother, he remembered. After that, everyone pretty much left him and his sister alone. His friend's face was the reminder. The false teeth and the hook in his lip had come from Teddy's fist, and both remained even as they had their pictures taken for the yearbook as seniors.

Curiously, the accountant had two kids in the same school who never seemed to suffer anything at all. Even when their father was convicted of the murder and carted off to jail, everyone still seemed to think Teddy's father was the one. Teddy couldn't figure it out. After a few months, he thought maybe it was because they were girls. He shared three classes with one of them. Janice Sawyer acted as if nothing happened or ever would. Teddy knew it was an act because she never once looked at him after her father went to jail. Still, with everything that had gone down, he was fascinated by her performance and found it hard to keep his eyes off her.

She had natural blond hair and a certain sophistication beyond her years. She'd also matured more quickly than most of the other girls. He could remember seeing her on the first day of class in ninth grade. It looked like she'd spent the summer growing huge breasts and turning herself into a woman. Teddy found his attraction for her confusing because deep inside he hated her. Even more troubling, he noticed she wore something new every day and her clothes looked expensive. When he asked around and found out the girl's mother didn't have to work, it got underneath his skin.

Teddy thought about the money her father had stolen a lot. The money that had ruined all their lives. Sometimes it worked him over so hard he couldn't even get to sleep at night. He had his theories—the most likely being that the Sawyers had buried the cash in their backyard. He often fantasized about digging it up and stealing it while they were asleep. Giving it to his mom and watching the Sawyers suffer the way his family had. One Saturday he walked over to their house and saw Janice's mother gardening in the backyard. Teddy hid in the bushes behind a tree for two hours keeping an eye on her, but it turned out all she was doing was planting flowers.

When he came home, he found his mother in the kitchen rooting through some of his father's old papers. She'd spent the afternoon cleaning out closets, not spying on people, and found a life insurance policy his dad had never talked about. Things changed after that and became easier. Not at first, because the insurance company tried to deny that the policy was valid. Teddy was sixteen at the time and guessed the insurance company was hoping that after two years no one would bother to call and they could keep the money for themselves. But his mom called and kept calling. And when that didn't work, she asked a friend she often painted with, Quint Adler, to see what he could do. Quint had been a family friend and owned a farm just up Sanctuary Road. His brother worked for their congressman, and Teddy guessed the call from Washington had been the real breakthrough. Still, Teddy always looked at Quint as the one person in their lives who tried to right at least part of the big wrong. Teddy was forever grateful to the man. Years later, when Quint started seeing his mother more often, Teddy was delighted. He hadn't replaced his dad. He'd just become another member of the family.

The money hadn't been enough to make them rich, Teddy remembered. There wasn't enough to pay for either his or his sister's college tuition. It wasn't even enough so that his mother could paint during the day—she couldn't give up her job. But it ended the rude phone calls from all those bill collectors. No one with a harsh voice ever called asking for his mother again. And if they did, Teddy had permission to hang up.

Of course, Teddy had thought the money would do more than that at the time. He'd hoped it would. But at night, sneaking out to the barn and watching his mom paint through the window, there were times when he still found her crying.

The money didn't change that. It couldn't raise the dead or rebuild a dream that had been chopped down by the greedy. It couldn't bring back a husband or even a father. It was just money.

Twenty-eight

He could hear her crying. The sound of his mother moved from the barn, across the snow, and into the house until it reached the other side of her bedroom door. The hour seemed so late. When he opened his eyes, he saw Sally Barnett's face moving away from his and realized she'd just kissed him on the cheek.

He was lying beneath a heavy blanket on the couch in the Barnett's den. His shoes were off, his collar and tie loosened. Sally held a washcloth in her hand, rinsing it in a bowl of warm water and returning it to his forehead. He looked at the fire burning in the hearth, then back at her face. It had been Sally's sobs he'd heard, not his mother's, and she looked more than just upset.

"What happened?" he whispered.

"I found you in the snow."

He took in the news as he tried to collect himself. His arms and legs felt weighted down. He didn't know how he got here or why, and couldn't think through the pain eating at him from just above his brow.

"I've got a headache," he said, propping himself up.

She left the warm washcloth against his forehead and

rose. The kitchen was to his back, and he couldn't see what she was doing. As he listened to several cabinets open and close, his eyes returned to the fire. The oak logs were dry, the heat reaching him with its soothing touch from across the room.

Sally sat down on the couch, passing him two Tylenol caplets and a glass of cold tap water.

"What time is it?" he asked.

"Three in the morning. When you didn't come back to the hospital, I got worried and called a cab. You were lying beneath a tree by the front door."

Her words were barely audible, her eyes swollen with worry. Teddy swallowed the pills and noted that she was trembling. Barnett had been in an accident, he recalled. He'd come to their house to pick up some things for Sally. He remembered seeing blood all over the snow in the driveway. What happened after that wasn't clear. It had been dark, and he wondered if he hadn't run into a tree.

Sally took the glass and set it down on the table. Then she picked up a tube of Neosporin and a large Band-Aid and set to mending the wound on Teddy's head.

"It just missed your temple," she said. "Do you think you need to see a doctor?"

"I'm okay," he said, even though he wasn't sure. His headache seemed way too big for a couple of pills. "How's Jim?"

"They won't know for a few days," she said, turning her face away. "But they think he'll make it." She covered her eyes with her hands. "The car crushed his legs. They won't tell me if he'll ever walk again. His recovery will take time, they said. A long time. I'm not very good at living on my own. . . ."

Teddy listened to her voice trail off and didn't know how to respond. The reality of what had happened to Barnett seemed so overwhelming. So horrible. She turned back to him, dabbing his wound with Neosporin and applying the large bandage. As she smoothed her hands over his forehead, he noticed the smell of fresh coffee brewing in the kitchen.

Sally got up and left the room. A few minutes later, she returned with two, piping-hot mugs.

"Jim's a fighter," Teddy said, trying to sound hopeful.

She didn't say anything. She couldn't.

"If the doctors are saying he's gonna make it, then he will," he said.

She listened to him and nodded, taking a seat at the other end of the couch and sipping her coffee. Barnett was strong willed and in good shape. Teddy had spent enough time with him to know that if the man had a chance, he'd take it and run with it. While it was true that he seemed to be dipping into an unknown variety of medications recently, Teddy had never seen him do it before they took the Holmes case.

"He's been upset lately, hasn't he?" Teddy asked.

She turned to the fire without responding, her expression blank as she stared at the flames.

"I've never seen him like this before," he said. "It's got something to do with Oscar Holmes."

"He wants it to end quickly," she whispered.

"That's the part I don't understand."

"He's lived a troubled life, Teddy."

"Holmes, you mean."

She nodded, still gazing at the fire. "His family's been worried about him for most of his life."

"How so?"

She paused, thinking it over. "He never seemed to fit in," she said after a moment. "He always had to do things his own way. There have been times as an adult when he couldn't take care of himself very well. He's had a problem with depression, but I think Jim already told you that. His family knew it would come to something like this one day and it has."

"Jim told me he's known the family for a long time," he said. "Who are they?"

She turned to him, the fire reflecting in her eyes. "Oscar Holmes is my brother, Teddy. My maiden name is Holmes."

It settled in with the subtlety of a death ray.

Oscar Holmes was Sally's brother. Holmes was Barnett's brother-in-law. It settled into the room like a deeply kept secret that had just been ripped open and exposed. As far as Sally knew, her own brother had brutally murdered two young girls. And now the DA was saying there might be ten more.

Another family tragedy was unfolding, Teddy realized. He thought about Barnett's desk drawer again—how it had become the pharmacy drawer in recent days. And Barnett's attitude from the beginning—how he couldn't be reached on the phone, and when he could, all he wanted was to end the case quickly and make sure Holmes got the care his family thought he needed. Barnett was the family, not a mysterious friend from childhood or a client with the firm. The murders weren't something to be read about from the safe distance of words printed in a newspaper. Jim and Sally Barnett were part of the story, the crime, intimately connected to it by family. No wonder Barnett wasn't seeing things clearly.

Teddy set down his coffee mug. It occurred to him that the night Holmes checked into prison he'd tried to make a collect call to his sister but she wouldn't accept the charges. That sister was Sally Barnett. He looked at her at the other end of the couch, her head against a pillow and her eyes closed. Her breathing had quieted and it appeared as if she was sleeping. He wondered why she hadn't taken the call that night. It seemed odd, curious. She hadn't paid her brother a visit either.

Teddy lifted the blanket away and draped it over her. He slipped into his shoes and stood. His legs wobbled at first, and as he steadied himself and felt the ache deepen inside his head, he wondered if he shouldn't call a doctor after all. He saw his coat on the chair by the fire and pulled it on. As he walked to the front door and looked outside, he noticed it was snowing again. He could see the impression his body made in the snow right outside the door. Stepping out into the cold air, he buttoned up and looked at the marks he'd made crawling up from the driveway. The falling snow had almost filled them in. Curiously, there were a faint set of footprints running alongside the same path. He stared at them for a while, wondering what he was looking at. It didn't really seem like he'd crawled to the door. Instead, it looked more like his body had been dragged.

The fog lifted and burned away in a single moment. He remembered the Sterling silver shot glass with tall ships and whales etched into its side. He hadn't run into a tree. Nothing that occurred here tonight had been an accident. He glanced back at the snow falling to the ground, softening the impressions and wiping them out.

He bolted across the lawn to his car, ignoring the pain. Ripping open the glove box, he fished out his flashlight and switched it on. Then he hurried into the yard, picking up the footprints and following them across the drive into the trees. It was difficult to see them; the impressions had become vague—some of them already obliterated by the falling snow.

There was a man, he remembered. The shape of someone standing in the darkness right behind him. A dog had been barking from somewhere in the neighborhood, but Teddy hadn't understood it as a warning.

He moved to the spot where he remembered standing with the silver shot glass. The place he'd been knocked out and fallen to the ground. He didn't expect to still find it here, but knelt down anyway, sifting through the snow with his hands. After fifteen minutes, he'd covered the entire area and knew it was pointless. The man had obviously returned for the shot glass, seen Teddy holding it in his scarf, and struck him as he turned.

Teddy looked back at the house, watching the lights in the windows switch off one by one. The dark house looked like every other house in the neighborhood. When the breeze picked up again and he heard the branches rattling overhead, he pretended he wasn't afraid even though he really was. He turned his flashlight the other way and took a step into the vacant lot bordering Barnett's house, raking the beam of light across the snow. The tracks leading from tree to tree toward the street were gone now. Everything the man had left behind was either gone or erased, except for those impressions, however fleeting, Teddy kept locked in his head.

Twenty-nine

Jackie, Barnett's assistant, clicked open a window with her mouse and pointed at the monitor with a shaky finger. Teddy leaned in for a closer look. It was a press release announcing that Nash had joined the legal team defending Holmes.

"I told him not to send it to the DA," she said in a nervous voice. "I told him not to, but he did. And look what happened. Sally called and told me he may never walk again."

She printed a copy out and handed it to Teddy. She was upset, even frightened. What she was implying—that Alan Andrews might have had something to do with Barnett being run over—caught Teddy by surprise.

He sat down in the chair beside her desk and studied the copy. It was a press release, but it read more like a negative hit piece in a political campaign. Nash's name was mentioned, along with his biography. But the results of his legal workshop were detailed as well. An innocent man had been executed as a result of Andrews's mishandling of the case. Even worse, Andrews had suppressed evidence to win the conviction. Before his election as district attorney, he'd been branded an overzealous prosecutor by more than one judge. Nash believed there were other cases where the DA had been less than forthright and planned to continue his investigation of the man in his workshop after the holidays. Making sure Andrews got it right in the Holmes case would only be the beginning.

It was clear to Teddy that both Barnett and Nash wanted to drag Andrews's nose through the mud. It was a message. A first salvo. Do the deal or Andrews's name could become the issue, not Holmes. Take the death penalty off the table, or else.

Teddy actually admired it. Particularly now that he knew Holmes was Barnett's brother-in-law. It was ugly, even brutal, a small sample of what Barnett would do to Andrews's name and reputation in order to save Holmes's life.

"Do you think it had anything to do with what happened?" Jackie asked.

Teddy looked up and saw the fear still haunting her.

"No," he said, even though he wasn't sure. "What happened to Jim was an accident."

He didn't want to scare her. Didn't want to tell her what was really on his mind.

He'd been thinking it over since four in the morning. When he finally got home, he couldn't sleep. Instead, he stretched out on top of the bed watching the snow swirl in the breeze outside his window and letting his mind drift. He couldn't be sure, of course, but he didn't think the man who ran over Barnett last night was the same person who murdered Darlene Lewis and Valerie Kram. Whoever it was had left his silver shot glass behind and returned for it. When he saw Teddy had found it, he hit him over the head and knocked him out. But the man had done one more thing before leaving that would seem to rule him out as the killer. He'd dragged Teddy's unconscious body out of the darkness of the vacant lot and left him in front of the entrance to Barnett's house. The distance from the empty lot to the front door of the house was in excess of thirty yards and would have required considerable effort. Even risk with the house-lights on.

Why?

The only answer that seemed to make sense was that the man wanted Teddy to be found. He'd smashed Teddy in the head hard enough to knock him out, but he didn't want to kill him.

Now, in the face of what Jackie had shown him, it seemed to make some degree of sense. If not sense, it was a perversion worth considering. Barnett's *accident* meant Teddy was essentially alone in his defense of Oscar Holmes. While it was true he still had Nash, the pressure on the DA had been coming from Barnett. Andrews must have been livid when he read that fax—seen his future in politics in jeopardy again and gone ballistic.

He thought about Michael Jackson.

Not the dancer, but the detective who'd worked with Andrews from the beginning and came off like Dr. Gloom. The man who had given Teddy the tour of Holmes's apartment, following him around from room to room as he chained cigarettes and gagged on the smoke.

Teddy wasn't sure why the man popped into his head, but remembered that old gun he saw clipped to the detective's belt. The ominous feeling that hit him the moment they met. Jackson was another nightcrawler and looked like a real drinker. The kind of guy who walked into a bar, picked a seat away from the lights, and made sure he faced the door. Had he been the one, he probably would've brought a flask. Not for courage, but to keep warm.

Teddy checked his watch. It was seven-thirty, his breakfast meeting with Carolyn Powell just fifteen minutes away. Slipping the press release into his briefcase, he left Jackie at her desk and told her he'd be back soon.

Thirty

She was waiting for him at a table on the other side of the open dining room at the Marathon Grill. As he moved toward her, he caught her black suit. The material was tight fitting and carefully tailored, rolling with the smooth contours of her body instead of hiding them. She wasn't wearing a blouse beneath her jacket, just a thin gold necklace. When her blue-gray eyes popped over the menu, he saw them still reaching out at him and couldn't believe that they'd made love last night. She was gorgeous, the most striking woman he'd ever seen, let alone been with.

As he reached the table, her eyes rose to the cut just above his eyebrow. Teddy had removed the bandage deciding the wound needed air and light.

"What happened to you?" she asked.

"We can talk about it later."

He sat down across from her and picked up the menu. He could smell her skin, the faint scent of body lotion and shampoo. He was hungry, ravenous, though he probably could have skipped the food.

"Tell me what happened right now," she said.

"I ran into a tree."

She lowered her menu and gave him a look. She wasn't buying it.

"Do you often run into trees?" she asked.

"Okay," he said, deciding to spill it out. "I went over to Barnett's last night to bring some things back to the hospital for his wife. When I got there, I realized it hadn't been an accident. Someone deliberately ran over him. I even found an antique shot glass made of Sterling silver that someone left behind in the snow. But I didn't know the guy was still there. When I turned, he hit me over the head with something and knocked me out."

She started laughing.

She looked good when she laughed. And either it was contagious, or hearing himself say what happened aloud was so convoluted, Teddy began laughing, too.

"Every word of it's true," he said.

"And I suppose when you woke up, the antique shot glass had vanished."

He nodded slowly. She started laughing again.

He didn't want to say anything, but when you fall for someone, it doesn't really take a lot of work. You don't have much choice in the matter. It sort of just hits and then you *know*. He looked down at the menu, his mind reeling to the point where the entrées looked as if they'd been written in a foreign language.

"I'll bet this silver shot glass had something unique about it," he heard her saying. "Some sort of ornate design."

"As a matter of fact it did."

"I thought so. What was the design?"

"Tall ships and whales," he said.

When she finally stopped laughing, he looked at the warm smile on her face, took the hit, and just *knew*.

"Em," she said, "my advice would be to keep your eyes open in the future and stay away from the trees."

Had she not been the prosecutor in the Holmes case he would have yanked her out of the chair and pulled her into his arms. Had he not been the defense attorney, he would've stood up and kissed her on the spot. But they were professionals, keeping a secret Teddy knew anyone watching them could guess.

He closed the menu thinking he was dyslexic. He still knew what breakfast was, and when the waiter filled their cups with coffee and took their order, Teddy ordered from memory. Bacon and eggs, over easy with whole-wheat toast.

At this hour, more than half the tables were full, but it was a big room with a thirty-foot ceiling. They could talk freely without worrying much about being overheard through the din.

"So how's Barnett?" she asked.

"I called the hospital before I came in. They say he's gonna pull through. It'll take a while though."

He stirred a packet of sugar into his coffee and tasted it. It was strong and hot, and he began to relax. On the walk over he'd had a chance to think about Barnett's *accident,* and the possibility that Andrews may have played a role. He'd only touched on it before, and Powell laughed. Still, he felt the need to press the issue with her. Other than the murderer, the only one who gained anything by running over Barnett was Andrews. Teddy was fully aware that it could have been an attempt to just scare Barnett. An errand given to Michael Jackson that got out of hand when Barnett fell down on the ice and couldn't get out of the way. Andrews had proven himself an asshole at the autopsy yesterday. And Jackson seemed more than capable of carrying out anything that he might be asked to do.

"How well do you know Andrews?" he said.

"I've been a prosecutor for ten years. Why?"

Teddy leaned closer. "I guess what I'm asking is how far do you think he'd go to win a case?"

She set her cup down and looked at him without saying anything. She wasn't laughing anymore and he could see her wheels turning at high speed.

"A case like this," Teddy said. "Andrews has political ambitions. This case is a godsend. You saw the way he acted at the autopsy. What do you think he'd do to win?"

The reach had vanished from her eyes. Just distance now.

"It sounds like you're asking me if I think he's capable of running over Barnett. I hope that's not what you're asking, Teddy."

He cleared his throat and looked at her. "I guess I am," he said.

She sat up in the chair, straightening her back. She was upset but trying not to show it. Her voice was quiet, just above a whisper, but steady and strong.

"Listen to me," she said. "Andrews may be a phony. That goes with the territory. He may even have made one or two mistakes in his past. Who hasn't? But there's no way he had anything to do with what happened last night. He didn't run over Barnett, and he's not responsible for that bump on your head. I thought you were joking."

"But I wasn't, Carolyn. Someone was out there. When I found the shot glass, someone hit me."

She looked down at the table, her voice sarcastic. "Maybe it was Dawn Bingle."

Teddy pushed his coffee aside, ignoring her attitude. "This time it was a man," he said. "At least I think it was. I couldn't really see."

She shook her head without a response as if he were crazy. As Teddy thought it over, he realized that he couldn't be sure of what he'd seen last night. Not sure enough to testify under oath. It had been dark. As he lay in the snow, he saw a figure and assumed it was a man. But maybe it wasn't.

"Andrews needs this case," Teddy said. "With Barnett out of the way, it's just me against all the physical evidence. After last night, his chances went from one hundred percent to a sure thing."

She was speechless. When their breakfasts arrived, she looked away from her plate.

"I'm sorry we made love," she whispered after the waiter walked off. "You're not the person I thought you were."

"What are you talking about?"

Her briefcase was on the chair beside her. She pulled a file folder out and tossed it on the table.

"Our chances of winning this case became a sure thing a half hour ago when I picked up the DNA results at the roundhouse," she said. "Read the report while you're enjoying breakfast. That's your copy for the murder book. The knife found in Holmes's mailbag had blood on it matching both Darlene Lewis's and Valerie Kram's. Holmes's blood was found on it, too. It's a statistical lock, Teddy. Your client murdered both of them."

With that, she grabbed her things and marched for the door. She was in a hurry, too angry to get into her coat until she was outside. Teddy pushed his breakfast away, watching her through the window. When she vanished down the street, he asked the waiter for their bill.

Thirty-one

Nash sat back in his desk chair with the DNA report on his lap, listening to Teddy recant his story. Except for making love with Powell, Teddy didn't leave anything out, describing the tracks he found in the snow, the Sterling silver shot glass, and the events leading to the point where he was knocked unconscious. On occasion, Nash would interrupt and ask for more details. Once he was satisfied, he'd nod with a troubled look in his eyes and Teddy would move on. He seemed particularly intrigued by the knowledge that Holmes was Barnett's brother-in-law. He found the idea that Barnett and his wife were trying to keep it a secret fascinating, though naive. When Teddy got to this morning's breakfast meeting with Powell and his accusation that Andrews might be responsible for the attacks, crimes that amounted to attempted homicide by the district attorney, Nash let out a smile and shook his head.

"I'm not that cynical, Teddy. Andrews may be a lot of things, but I don't think he'd be that stupid. You're right when you say he's the primary beneficiary, and the idea's certainly worth considering. But there could be more than one explanation for what happened last night. A rogue cop like that detective you mentioned, working on his own, or even the man who murdered Darlene Lewis. And what about this woman who led you to the boathouse? There's a lot we don't understand yet, and it would seem we can't go to the police until we've reached certain conclusions. When Barnett's able to talk about it, we'll pay him a visit together. Let's just be grateful that he's going to survive, and you're okay, too.''

Teddy's eyes rose from the jury table. He noticed that Nash had tacked the missing persons bulletins to the wall, one after the next in a long row. As Teddy looked at their pictures, he pulled his cigarettes out of his pocket. It seemed early, but he lit up anyway. His problems with Carolyn Powell seemed minuscule in comparison to the job that lay before them.

''The DNA found on the knife connects the Lewis murder to Valerie Kram,'' he said.

''That's right,'' Nash said.

''And you still don't think Holmes did it.''

''His blood was found on the knife, but we already knew that it would be.''

''Because of the cuts on his hands,'' Teddy said.

Nash nodded. ''All the DNA report confirms is that the same murder weapon was used to kill two women. It doesn't tell us who the murderer is or who dropped the knife in Holmes's mailbag.'' Nash turned back to the report and began paging through it until he found what he was looking for. ''But there's something more interesting here. I count six additional samples. Six good reads that can't be identified.''

''Other victims.''

''I think so,'' Nash said. ''The murders are linked by the DNA. It's confirmed. Without question, we're talking about a serial killer now.''

Nash turned back to the report. Teddy stubbed his cigarette out and moved to the window. As he looked outside at a man buying a paper at the newsstand on the corner, he couldn't help thinking about the evidence. It was mounting up along with the body count, and every new piece pointed to Holmes. Although Nash didn't seem concerned with the DNA results, Teddy knew it wouldn't have the same effect on a jury. In Holmes's defense, all they had were best guesses, pure conjecture. A theory that it was possible Holmes stumbled onto the scene delivering mail as Darlene Lewis was murdered. A supposition that because of his seemingly close relationship with his neighbors, Holmes couldn't have kept Valerie Kram in his apartment for a month without someone noticing. The holes in each idea seemed overwhelming, and Teddy began to think that Barnett might be right. Holmes did it because each new fact said he did. It was in Holmes's best interest to do everything they could to force the DA to make a deal that would save the man's life.

Teddy moved to the jury table and sat down. "But what if we're wrong?" he said. "What if Darlene Lewis fought back? What if Holmes cut himself during the struggle?"

"It's possible but not likely. The science is starting to come in. The results are piling up against Holmes. I imagine that will continue. You better get used to it, Teddy. We're looking for someone who's taken great pains to cover his tracks."

"But even Holmes thinks he did it. How can you be so sure he didn't?"

Nash picked up his cigar and crossed the room. As he walked past the row of pictures tacked to the wall, the girl's faces seemed as if they were staring at him again. Nash stopped at the very last one, removing it from the wall and placing it on the table before Teddy.

Nash had posted the bulletins in chronological order. Teddy looked down at the flyer, expecting to see Valerie Kram's picture. Instead, he found himself gazing at someone new. Another missing persons bulletin off the FBI's national computer database.

"This only became official last night," Nash said. "Her name's Rosemary Gibb. Holmes has been in prison for four days. Rosemary's been missing for two."

Teddy stared at the photograph. Gibb was another obvious Darlene Lewis look-alike. Another missing twin.

"Powell didn't mention it," he said to Nash.

"She probably doesn't even know about it."

"But they're looking for the other victims."

Nash smiled. "Do you really think so? Let's assume they're not. You tell me why."

Teddy got up and started pacing. At first he wondered if Nash wasn't enjoying his role as a teacher and playing a mind game. But as he thought it over, he saw the man's point. Andrews had said at his press conference last night that they'd isolated ten missing persons and would be meeting with their families to brief them. It could've been a political move to buy time. He may have said it for show.

Teddy turned and found Nash studying him as he figured it out.

"It's because of the evidence," Teddy said. "Andrews will concentrate on the Darlene Lewis murder because he's got Holmes in a cell and that's where all the evidence is."

"Keep going," Nash said.

"Assuming Andrews thinks Holmes is guilty, if he gets him for one murder, then that's just as good as getting him for all twelve. Holmes is locked up and out of the way, and that would be the DA's only concern. Even if he could bring the others in during trial, he wouldn't because that might weaken his case against Holmes for the Darlene Lewis murder. He wouldn't take the chance. You wouldn't either. No one would. If someone in the jury didn't think Holmes murdered one or all of the victims, Holmes could be acquitted and walk."

"Then you're telling me Andrews was lying at his press conference," Nash said. "Andrews doesn't have any intention of looking for the others. They're still missing. Still forgotten."

Nash was pushing him as he did the night before last. Forcing Teddy to reject the apparent and see what lay on the other side.

"No," Teddy said, glancing back at the pictures tacked

to the wall. "Andrews wasn't lying, but that doesn't mean these victims still aren't forgotten. He'll work on them after he's finished with the Darlene Lewis case. Until then, he'll do enough to get by. He probably asked the families for DNA samples in order to match the six samples on the knife. But spreading out his resources by wasting staff time to look for them could jeopardize the Lewis case as well."

"You're doing great, Teddy. Now tell me why Rosemary Gibb will never even come up."

"Because everything we've talked about depends on Holmes's guilt. Like you said, Holmes has been locked up for four days. Rosemary Gibb's been missing for two."

Nash had known it all along, guiding Teddy through the maze until he saw it as well. Rosemary Gibb would slip through the cracks. The DA's office would have no interest in locating her because they had the killer and there was no reason for them to think otherwise. Andrews had followed the evidence to Holmes and was certain he had his man. Now the murders were connected by DNA, the scientific results indisputable. The likelihood that Andrews would look beyond the evidence and admit that he'd made another mistake was nil. Even more troubling, the FBI wouldn't be called in to assist because everyone involved thought the case was over. Why spend time and money on an investigation when the serial killer was already awaiting trial behind bars?

"Andrews is running out line," Nash said. "He hasn't caught his mistake, and he's in too deep to make a change now. The man's got blinders on. He always has."

Teddy wasn't thinking about Andrews anymore, or even ADA Powell for that matter. His mind was riveted on Rosemary Gibb. Without Nash and himself, she was in the weeds.

"The killer's doing something to the bodies for a reason," Teddy said. "Valerie Kram was taken away and worn down, then hidden in the water when he was through with her. Darlene Lewis was murdered on the spot. Maybe it was because Holmes interrupted him, but maybe it's more than that. It's almost as if he got to Darlene Lewis and rejected her for some reason.''

Nash turned to him and smiled like he hadn't thought of it before. It was a look of genuine surprise. Another step down the road.

"That's a good point," Nash said, lighting his cigar. "And with a decent profile of the man and a little luck, that's just how we'll find him."

Thirty-two

She was in the bathroom. It had been two days and she was still in there. But Eddie Trisco was patient. Tired of waiting maybe, but patient.

At least the screaming had stopped. All the crying. She'd quieted down at some point last night after he ran an important errand and ditched her car in the long-term parking lot at the airport. When he returned and checked the lock, he knew she was still alive because she kicked the door and moaned.

He could drag her out, of course. He could do it any time he wanted. But she had to be willing. That was the key to the whole thing. They had to *want* to come out. They had to *want* to be with him. And in the end, every one of them always did. Even if it took time and a little training from their master.

The truth was that he'd let her run into the bathroom the same way he'd done it with the others. It was part of the plan. Once he'd helped her down to the basement, he gave her the tour. And like the rest, she'd fled into the bathroom and slammed the door. There were no windows and the light switch was outside the door. Two or three days in solitary without light usually brought them around.

Eddie checked the water pipes, making certain the valve to the bathroom was shut off. He'd examined the valve five or six times in the last hour. A creature of habit, he told himself. When the toilet bowl was empty, they got thirsty and opened the fucking door.

The basement was as large as a two-bedroom apartment and offered just as many rooms, including a greenhouse off the main workroom just through the door. Eddie used the basement for his experiments, his work. Even though the house was large and there were plenty of rooms upstairs, he spent most of his time down here. It was safer in the basement. More comfortable. There were too many windows upstairs, and every time he looked outside he could feel his neighbors watching him.

Particularly that house on the corner. When the new people moved in six months ago, they looked like a regular family. But Eddie knew they weren't regular at all. They were only playing a family. They'd found him and staked his house out, and Eddie had been careful not to go outside during the day ever since. Once their fake kids went to school, the *watchers* would show up like clockwork. Men dressed like construction workers carrying boxes of tools. Trucks delivering construction supplies in containers with the words *Home Depot* printed in big letters so that Eddie could read them from across the street. In spite of the banging sounds the men made, Eddie Trisco wasn't fooled. They were fake sounds made by fake workmen. Eddie knew what was really in all those boxes. He knew what they were up to. It was all about eavesdropping. They were setting up their equipment—state-of-the-art equipment—so that they could keep an eye on him and listen in.

When a satellite dish went up on their roof last week, Eddie began to really worry. The device was pointed just over his house. He'd read a magazine article a few months back about mind reading and the government's secret experiments with dolphins. The article indicated there had been some sort of technological breakthrough, and IBM was involved. According to the writer, you could point the device at someone's head and what they were thinking would appear as text on the FBI's computer screen. If the subject they were following was Chinese, you could click a button and the words would be translated into English in an instant. If they were dolphins, you were still out of luck because no one could speak dolphin yet. The article said the government was hopeful that someday they'd have a button you could click for dolphin, too. It read like a joke, but Eddie wasn't sure. He didn't like jokes. He didn't like the sound of people laughing.

Still, that dish on the roof changed everything for Eddie because the kitchen was upstairs, and so was his bedroom. For the past week he couldn't just run up and grab something to eat. He had to prepare himself, write a scenario, and play it in his head just in case the watchers were reading his mind on their computer screen. Sometimes he would make lunch thinking the thoughts he guessed a chef would ponder. *I slice onions like this. I grate cheese like that.* Other times he played the scenario of a mathematician or professional athlete whipping up dinner on the run. *Two plus two equals four. Jesus, man, God bless Jesus. I want more money. Look at my fucking box score!* When Eddie got tired, he turned on the TV, letting his mind wash out in the rinse cycle and just go blank.

Eddie heard a noise and surfaced. She was moving around in the bathroom. Grabbing a stool, he sat down at the large worktable and waited. After a moment, she became quiet again. Not yet, he thought.

He looked at the newspapers spread out before him, the contents of her purse, and her driver's license. Rosemary Gibb, twenty years old, five-feet-seven, from the art museum district. The picture didn't do her justice. He'd spent enough time sipping caffe lattes and watching her work out from the window table at Benny's Cafe Blue to know the snapshot wasn't even close. He tossed the license aside and took another look at the newspapers he'd picked up last night on his way home from the suburbs and that errand. Her disappearance wasn't even mentioned. Just the story about that mailman. He'd been a butcher, and now he was a serial killer. The world could be a dark place.

He heard the noise again. The bathroom door cracked open an inch or two, and he could see Rosemary staring at him from the darkness. She was squinting at the light, her body shaking from head to toe.

"I'm thirsty," she said in a hoarse voice.

"I'll get you something in a minute," he said. "Close the door."

"But my mouth's dry."

"Close the door," he repeated.

She looked at him a moment, then shut the door. She was in the dark again, and Eddie smiled. It was a good plan because it always worked. Be a hard-ass, then come to her rescue by becoming nice. On TV they called it the good cop, bad cop scene. Eddie liked the idea, and realized he had the talent and gift to play both parts.

He walked out of the room, climbing the steps and pausing a moment before he entered the kitchen. He calculated it would take less than a minute to get everything he needed. The curtains were drawn, the view of the corner house concealed. The watchers would never even know he was there. He started counting. Rushing into the room, he grabbed two glasses, a container of orange juice, his mortar and pestle, and the stash of pills he kept hidden in the drawer behind his Sterling silver flatware. Before he even got to twenty-six-Mississippi in his head, he was safely in the basement again. Twenty-six seconds. No harm done at all.

Eddie set the glasses on the table, realizing he'd forgotten a spoon when he hit the drawer for his stash. The idea of going upstairs again didn't appeal to him. He was tired of counting numbers and too exhausted to play the role of a chef. He'd have to make do, he decided, and use his finger to stir the brew. He twisted off the cap on the spice jar marked *Hot Chili Peppers* and dropped two pills into the mortar. MDMA. Ecstasy. The magic potion had more than one name, but Eddie liked *Love Drug* best. Treats for the trainee and her trainer, he thought. They had to *want* to come out of the bathroom. They had to *want* to be with him before they could see his genius and fall in love.

Crushing the pills with the pestle, he poured one hit into each glass, careful not to spill any of the powder. Then he added the orange juice and gave both glasses a good stir. He licked his finger, tapping on the bathroom door and hoping he wouldn't startle Rosemary. After a moment, the door opened slightly. She still looked frightened, but that would go away soon.

"Something to drink," he said.

Her eyes were on the glass. "Why are you doing this?"

"It's orange juice," he said. "I thought you were thirsty."

She took the glass and closed the door. Eddie returned to the table, picked up his own glass, and gulped it down. It would take the better part of an hour before either one of them began to feel anything. After that, they'd be in love and could let go. Eddie believed in group therapy. He believed in the magic of the *Love Drug*.

He passed the time sitting in the green house with a Tootsie Pop in his mouth. Although he couldn't be bothered with keeping plants, he liked the humid air and bright light passing through the milky glass. It was almost like sitting in the backyard without having to take the risk of being seen. At the thirty-minute mark, he began to feel the rush. Glimpses of the first wave.

The doorbell rang.

Eddie wondered if it wasn't his imagination. When the bell rang a second time, he checked the bathroom door and raced upstairs. He kept his back to the walls, sidestepping his way through the rooms quickly and avoiding the windows until he reached the den. Kneeling down, he scurried across the carpet and peeked through the curtain.

It was Mrs. Yap, his landlady, standing on the front porch wondering why he wasn't answering the door. He looked at his car in the drive and saw her Mercedes. She rang the bell again, cupping her hands around her eyes and peering through the foyer window.

Eddie had grown tired of her frequent visits. If he answered the door, she'd undoubtedly want to come in. Mrs. Yap may have been older than him, but was within range, and he knew she liked him. She owned several rental properties, some of them large buildings. When she was in the neighborhood, she often stopped by for a cup of coffee. She talked about her business, but spent just as much time asking questions about his. Eddie endured the interrogations because he knew he had to. Still, he hated her curiosity. She always wanted to look at his things and often asked how much they cost. The price of his silver and where he picked up the oriental rugs or bought his antiques.

Mrs. Yap tapped on the foyer window again like a bird. She reminded him of a bird every time he saw her. She wore bright-colored clothing, had a beaklike nose, and seemed way too peppy to be human.

The room began to vibrate and he felt himself break into a sweat—the *Love Drug* rolling through him freely now. He bit through the Tootsie Pop, crushing the hard candy until he reached the soft, chocolaty center. He was in the flow. He was wading through it. And he hoped Mrs. Yap would get the message that he wasn't home and just leave. He parted the curtain slightly and took another look outside. Then he did a double take and blinked.

There was a giant canary on the porch pecking at the window, then marching over to the Mercedes on stick-thin legs. He blinked his eyes again, trying to see through the hallucination, but the canary got behind the wheel and drove away.

Was it the *Love Drug* or could it be his unique way of seeing the world? His vision. His genius. And what the fuck did it matter anyway?

Eddie Trisco laughed, rushing back downstairs and hoping Rosemary was finally ready to come out of the bathroom and join the party. They'd start with water and more Tootsie Pops. They'd listen to music and dance. Then maybe take a shower and spend the rest of the afternoon in bed getting to know each other while they sucked on teething rings and sniffed Vicks Vaporub. The people in the corner house could watch and listen all they wanted now. Eddie didn't even care if they were reading his mind. He could feel his wings again. He could feel the joy. He was stronger than all the watchers in all the world put together. He was invincible. Soon to be famous and thinking in another language. Maybe it was the language of dolphins.

He entered the basement filled with anticipation, his arms and legs feeling finlike. The bathroom door was open, the light on. He found Rosemary sitting at the worktable staring at the picture on her license and giggling. When he approached her, she looked up at him and smiled. He pulled the pop stick out of his mouth and smiled back. Ready, Eddie. . . .

Thirty-three

He legged it out of the Central Detective Division offices located in the art museum district, hustled to his car, and punched Carolyn Powell's number into his cell phone. When her assistant refused to put him through, Teddy realized Powell was still angry with him. He told her assistant that he wanted another look at the Lewis house in Chestnut Hill, expecting that Powell would make things difficult for him. But when her assistant came back on, she said an escort would be waiting for him at the house in an hour with the keys.

His trusted escort. Michael Jackson. Perhaps the man who'd beaten him over the head until he was unconscious.

Teddy slipped the phone into his pocket, mildly surprised and wondering why it had been so easy. Shrugging it off, he pulled down to the corner, hit the parkway, and set out for another look at the death house in Chestnut Hill.

He'd gotten nowhere with the detective assigned to Rosemary Gibb's disappearance. Maybe nowhere. Although Detective Ferarro wouldn't show him a copy of the missing persons report, claiming it was confidential, he seemed happy to answer any questions Teddy might have.

Originally from Baltimore, Rosemary Gibb had moved to the city only one year ago and was a student at Drexel University. She didn't have many friends, and called home to check in on a regular basis. Her mother had been reading the papers and was aware of the Darlene Lewis murder. When she couldn't reach her daughter, she panicked and called the police. Detective Ferarro seemed to have taken a special interest in finding Rosemary, perhaps because Valerie Kram's body had just been found. Rosemary lived within a mile of Boathouse Row and only four blocks from the Central Detective Division. An examination of her apartment revealed nothing out of the ordinary.

Everything except for her picture. Her likeness.

Ferarro admitted to Teddy that he spotted the similarities among Rosemary, Valerie Kram, and ten other young women he'd been trying to locate over the past year. He stepped up his investigation and, with the help of a partner and ten cops in uniform, scoured the neighborhood. Because Drexel and Penn were set side by side, they worked both campuses with the help of volunteers from the police academy. By day's end, they'd narrowed their search to a health club just off Walnut Street downtown. A classmate, another young woman who worked out at the gym, remembered seeing Rosemary on the Stair Master that night. They checked every business around the club, including a café located directly across the street, but turned up nothing. Rosemary's classmate had been the last person who remembered seeing her before she vanished.

The following day, Detective Ferarro was given an early heads-up on the DNA results linking Holmes to the murders of Darlene Lewis and Valerie Kram. Detectives Vega and Ellwood were asking him for his files on any related cases dated prior to Holmes's arrest. That left Rosemary out, as Nash said it would. Ferarro was looking for her just the same as he was looking for thirty other people from all walks of life. But he was out of leads, and Teddy knew Rosemary was in the wind.

Teddy made a right onto Scottsboro Road, didn't see any

cars or news vans outside the Lewis house, and pulled over
to the curb. Breaking open the flap on a cup of take-out
coffee, he took a sip and lit his second cigarette of the day
while he waited for his escort. When a neighbor drove by
in a Lincoln Navigator, a woman with two young children
in the backseat, he caught the look in her eyes, the fear and
suspicion. Darlene Lewis's murder—that ominous feeling
of death—pervaded more than just the Lewis house. It was
part of the neighborhood now.

Teddy turned back to the house. He wasn't interested in
the dining room or even the plumbing. Three days ago he'd
walked through the place thinking Holmes had been caught
in the act. He wanted to get a feel for the house without all
that baggage. He wanted a clean view.

A car hit its horn. Teddy watched the DeVille sweep by
and pull to a fast stop before him. Michael Jackson got out,
not the dancer but the detective with tired legs and an old
gun who'd worked with the DA since Andrews got rolling.
He had a manila envelope in his hand. As he approached,
Teddy tried to remember the shape of the figure standing
in the darkness who clubbed him over the head. His memory
wasn't clear enough to make a match, but Jackson had a
big smile going, and Teddy wondered if the detective wasn't
overcompensating for what he'd done.

"I come bearing gifts," Jackson said with a cigarette
hanging out of his mouth. "Just like Santy Klaus."

Teddy took the envelope, pried it open, and peered inside.
Photographs from the crimes scenes and autopsy.

"You're keeping an album, right?" Jackson said. "A
murder book? Powell asked me to give them to you. She
said she wants to keep you up to date."

"She say anything else?"

"Yeah, kid. You can't be trusted. We'll have to stay
close."

Teddy tossed the envelope on the front seat and they
walked to the house. As Jackson pulled out the keys, Teddy
glanced at the letter box on the wall, then turned to the door.
The curtain on the other side of the glass was opaque. He

heard the lock click and watched Jackson swing the door open.

"Wait a minute," Teddy said before the detective stepped inside. "I want to see something first."

"What do you want to see, kid?"

"Stand out here a minute."

Teddy walked inside and started to close the door.

"Hey, hey, hey," Jackson shouted. "You heard the lady. We're supposed to stay close."

"I'm not going anywhere. I just want a look through the curtain."

"Okay, but no tricks. I don't like tricks, kid. I never have."

Teddy closed the door. Taking a step back, he looked through the curtain. He could see Jackson's form, but any details were masked by the cloth. Darlene Lewis could've opened the door for the killer, thinking it was someone else. She could've let the man in.

"You're wearing me out, kid," the detective barked through the door. "You seen it yet, or what?"

Teddy swung the door open. Jackson gave him a look and stepped inside.

For the next hour, it worked the same way it had at Holmes's apartment. Teddy would go through a room with Jackson standing behind his back chaining cigarettes and hacking on the smoke. When he walked outside for a look at the pool in the backyard, Teddy noticed the spent beer keg. He walked over and gave it a shake in the snow. To his surprise, the keg wasn't empty, but full. Darlene Lewis had been planning a party before her death.

Teddy stepped back into the dining room. The place hadn't been cleaned up yet. He glanced at the blood spatter on the walls as he passed through the room and headed for the stairs. It still bothered him, but not like it had. He could hear Jackson behind him in the hall, staying close but trying to keep out of his way as well. Teddy walked into the girl's bedroom, and paused. His eyes went right to the computer. He noticed a photograph on the table of Darlene with someone he guessed was her boyfriend. He turned the computer on. As the machine booted up, he heard the words *"You've got mail."*

Teddy saw him walk out of the library with his head down. Long brown hair, medium height with a pack thrown over his shoulder, and skinny as a rail. Teddy glanced at the snapshot he'd lifted from Darlene Lewis's bedroom when Jackson opened a window and flicked his smoke outside. They were a match. The kid exiting the library was Russell Moss—Darlene Lewis's classmate at the Friends School and the boyfriend who'd sent her the e-mail.

He slipped the photo into his glove box, watching Moss stroll almost aimlessly away from the building. The campus had the feel of a small college, and Teddy guessed that tuition for the private school was just as steep. When Moss reached the sidewalk heading for Germantown Avenue, Teddy got out of the car and approached him.

Moss looked up from the ground. Teddy's suit threw him a little, but Moss was eighteen and there wasn't much difference in their age.

"I need to talk to you, Russell."

"What about?"

"Darlene Lewis."

The kid's eyes fell to the ground. "Who are you?"

"A lawyer. Someone trying to help."

The kid was nervous, shifting his weight and adjusting his book bag over his left shoulder, then switching it to his right.

"I'll miss my bus," the kid said.

"You're girlfriend's dead and you're worried about catching a bus?"

The kid looked him in the eye. His nervousness wasn't born of fear, but of sadness. Maybe even a measure of self-inflicted guilt.

"Drive me home," he said. "What you want is there."

They got in the car and made the short drive to the teenager's house. Russell Moss was a latchkey kid. When he came home from school, there was no one there. The modest house was set on a heavily wooded half-acre lot three blocks south of Germantown Avenue a mile or so west of the school. Once they were inside Teddy noted the fresh paint on the walls, the polished hardwood floors, the comfortable furnishings. He glanced at the bookcases in a small room by the stairs as they headed up to the kid's bedroom. Moss came from a family of readers.

"What do your parents do?" Teddy asked.

"My father's a lawyer and would probably have a shit fit if he knew you were here. My mother teaches at Temple University."

They entered the room, the kid clearing a joystick off his desk and flipping on his computer. Once the machine booted up, he logged onto the Web, clicked a bookmark, and sat down.

"I couldn't show you at school," Moss said. "But I can show you here."

Teddy leaned over the kid's shoulder for a closer look. He saw an image of Darlene Lewis appear. He caught the sleepy smile and looked at her body. It was a porno site. She didn't have any clothes on.

"We built the site together," Moss said. "I didn't think anything would happen. But then it did."

Moss gave up his seat, moving to the bed and sitting down before the window. Teddy grabbed the mouse, clicking through the images. Darlene Lewis posing in a bra and panties, on her knees cupping her breasts in her hands, on her back with her legs spread open. The shots were crude and didn't leave much to the imagination.

"She got a boob job," the kid said. "She liked to show them off."

Teddy wasn't really listening. He was too busy clicking through the images. Toward the end, the photos switched to hard core. Darlene giving a guy without a face a hand job, then blowing him and fucking him. Moss glanced at the monitor and seemed to shrink. There were fifty thumbnail shots, and Teddy looked at every one of them. He could feel his heart beating in his chest.

"Are they real?" he said to the kid.

"I just told you she got a boob job."

"Not her tits," he said. "The tattoos. They're in every shot. Are they real?"

The kid nodded, thrown by Teddy's intensity.

Teddy paged back to the early photos of Darlene, enlarging a shot of the girl masturbating on a couch with her legs spread open. The lazy look in her eyes and the slow smile on her face were haunting. The pose all the more disturbing because it brought back memories of her lying dead on the dining room table—his response to seeing her corpse laid out on the gurney at the morgue.

Teddy winced as he studied her naked body. The tattoos were on her calf, just above her vagina, and on the underside of her inflated breasts.

He tried to keep cool. Tried not to think about why a girl who came from a family of means would do something like this. It was all about the murder, he told himself. The man who murdered Darlene Lewis had cut her skin away. But his approach hadn't been haphazard. There was purpose in the act. Some horrific reason.

Thirty-four

Teddy slid a disk into Nash's computer, copied the jpeg file onto his hard drive, and clicked on the image of Darlene Lewis masturbating on the couch. Nash found the black and white print of the girl's corpse on the dining room table and held it up to the monitor. Teddy didn't need to compare the images to know what the killer had done.

The patches of missing skin found on her body matched the placement of her tattoos perfectly. The killer had removed her tattoos with his knife and taken them.

Nash gazed at the nude photo for a long time. "The tattoo artist wasn't very talented, was he?" he said. "I can't say much for the photographer either."

"Her boyfriend, Russell Moss."

"Has he spoken with the police?" Nash asked.

"No. Not about this anyway. They came to the house and asked about his relationship with Lewis. He answered their questions, but that's it."

"How's he doing?"

"When I left, he was tearing the Web site down."

"I'm always fascinated by how people spend their free

time," Nash said as he finally looked away from the monitor.
"What do you think this means?"

"That we're on the right track," Teddy said. "Darlene
Lewis heard someone at the door. She thought it was Holmes,
delivering the mail. But it was someone else. Someone who
saw the tattoos on her body and rejected her."

Nash swiveled his chair around to the window behind his
desk. It was dusk, and the windows in the houses and buildings that made up West Philadelphia were glowing a deep
yellow red in the blue of early night. But Teddy knew the
man wasn't really looking at the view outside his window.
The man's eyes were turned inward again, and he appeared
deep in thought.

"He came to her house," Nash said quietly. "He saw
the tattoos and took them away with him. It sounds to me
like he got something in return. Why do you say he rejected
her?"

"Because he didn't take her. Valerie Kram was in good
shape. When she went into the water and then washed up
on shore, she wasn't. The man kept her and did things to
her. She may have been cut down the middle, but her skin
was intact. I saw her body. She didn't have any tattoos. I'll
bet it's the same with those pictures on your wall. I'll bet
not one of them has a tattoo on their entire body. If they
did, the bulletins would've said so."

"Tell me about the wound you saw on Valerie Kram,"
Nash said.

"You saw a picture of it just a few minutes ago."

"Describe it for me anyway."

Teddy wondered what Nash was up to. The photos Carolyn Powell had sent over in the manila envelope were lying
on Nash's desk beside the murder book.

"It was a single cut," Teddy said. "The kind you'd make
if you were gutting an animal in the field."

"Have you gutted an animal in the field?"

"I'm not much of a hunter. I used to shoot though. I've
seen it done before. It was the same cut they made at the
autopsy."

"From the ME's initial report, it says Kram's internal organs were accounted for. But they looked as if they were handled, perhaps moved. Too much time had passed and the ME couldn't be sure."

"The time she spent in the water," Teddy said. "He couldn't make the call."

"Her neck was broken as well."

"Yes," Teddy said. "Just the same as Darlene Lewis."

"So if we know why the killer cut Lewis, that he wanted the tattoos, then what do you suppose he was thinking when he split Valerie Kram open?"

"That's the million-dollar question, isn't it?"

Nash swiveled his chair around. He looked tired. Spent. Like whatever was preying on his mind had cost him something.

"What two things does Philadelphia grow best?" he said.

Teddy shrugged. He wasn't sure where Nash was going with the riddle.

"I want you to read a book tonight," Nash said. "*The Agony and the Ecstasy,* by Irving Stone."

Teddy found the idea of wasting the night reading a book more than disturbing. He was thinking about their search for Rosemary Gibb. If Nash had something, why wasn't he just saying it so that they could move on? And what about the riddle? The two things the city grows best. What was that about?

"Time would seem to be of the essence," Teddy said.

"It is," Nash said, rising to his feet. "I hope you're a fast reader. I've got an idea, Teddy, but I want you to confirm it. Call me as soon as you're done."

Thirty-five

There was a bookstore two blocks from the office on Walnut Street. Teddy flipped open his cell phone, entering his office number and filling Jill in as he wove through traffic on his way downtown. She offered to help and agreed to pick up two copies of *The Agony and the Ecstasy*, along with a pizza. With two people reading the book, they could get through the copy in half the time.

Teddy cleared the call, pulled Detective Ferarro's card out of his pocket, and punched in his number at the missing persons unit. The detective picked up the call at his desk and recognized Teddy's voice from earlier that afternoon.

"I need to know if there are any marks on the bodies," Teddy said.

"What kind of marks on which bodies?" Ferarro asked.

"We can start with Rosemary Gibb, but I'm asking about the files on the ten girls you sent down to the homicide unit. The families gave you pictures and physical descriptions. I know you asked. Did Rosemary Gibb's mother describe any marks on her body that would distinguish her from anyone else? Birthmarks, moles, or tattoos?"

There was a long pause. Teddy thought that he might

have lost the connection. When the detective finally spoke up, Teddy recognized the concern in the detective's voice and knew he had his ear.

"Where you going with this, Teddy? It sounds like you've got a body."

"I'm on my way back to the office. I was just wondering about the marks. I noticed on the missing persons bulletins that nothing was mentioned."

"If they had any distinguishing marks," Ferarro said, "they would have been registered with the FBI and listed on the bulletin. Rosemary Gibb does not have a birthmark or a tattoo."

"You get that from her mother?" Teddy asked.

"Yeah, why?"

"Because there's the chance Rosemary might have a tattoo where it can't be seen."

"You're forgetting that we interviewed her friend at the gym. She's seen Rosemary in the shower. There aren't any tattoos."

"What about the others?"

"No one mentioned they had any either. You're right when you said we ask. We always do."

Teddy closed his phone. He knew that Ferarro didn't want to end the conversation, but he was losing the signal on his cell as he pulled into the garage. He could tell the detective was suspicious. But keeping Ferarro suspicious was a positive step and reason enough to make the call and keep it short. It was in Rosemary's best interest. It kept her file on top and might spark an idea in Ferarro's head. Maybe the detective would hit on something and be moved to work the streets again.

Teddy found a place to park and hurried to the elevator. He found Jill in his office with two paperback copies of the book and a large pizza. Teddy picked up a copy as he sat down. *The Agony and the Ecstasy* was the novelization of Michelangelo's life. This surprised him, and he could tell from the expression on Jill's face that she was equally dumbfounded. He'd expected a book on crime, something that might shed light on the man they were looking for. Instead, this was a novel about the life of an artist. Even worse, the book looked long and the print was small.

"What's going on?" Jill asked.

Teddy put the book down and reached for a slice of pizza. "Nash seems to think it's important."

"What's Michelangelo have to do with Oscar Holmes?"

Teddy shrugged. "He gave me a riddle. What two things does the city grow best?"

She thought it over as she bit into a slice. Nothing came to mind for her either.

"Nash is weird, Teddy. I told you that before."

She opened her briefcase, pulled out a paper she'd written in law school, and handed it to him. Teddy glanced at the title page. She'd written it for Nash in her first year when criminal law was mandatory.

"It's about his defense of the Venice Beach Strangler," she said.

"How'd Nash do?"

"It depends on who you ask. Do you know where Venice Beach is?"

"Sure," he said. "Just below Santa Monica in California."

"Right. It's not Italy, it's Southern California. There's a canal that winds through the city a few blocks from the beach. The homes along the canal are expensive. Beautiful."

Teddy tore a second slice of pizza away from the pie, wondering what Jill was getting at.

"Once a month for six months," she said, "the people who lived along the canal would wake up in the morning and find a body floating in the water outside their homes. They were always young women, raped and strangled to death. The police had a hard time identifying the bodies. There weren't any clues and everyone was in a panic. After six months the murders stopped."

"How'd they get the guy?" Teddy asked.

"The murders started again. Only this time the bodies were found in the hills along Mulholland Drive, just north

of Beverly Hills. A homicide detective working out of the
Hollywood division put it together. He was looking for
runaway kids that seemed to be disappearing from the streets.
He had a house in the hills that he'd rebuilt after the earthquake, and it bothered him that someone was dumping bodies
in his neighborhood. He worked the case on his own and
discovered that a family had moved from the canals in Venice to Mulholland Drive. The dates and places the bodies
were found matched the time of the move. It turned out the
murderer was a twenty-year-old kid who still lived at home.
He was psychotic. He hated his parents, and was dumping
the bodies near the house to shake them up.''

"You're saying Nash got the kid off?''

"The boy's father was an executive at one of the movie
studios. They had a lot of money. Nash didn't defend the
boy as much as he attacked the detective who caught him.
Nash went after the man's character. The detective had been
abandoned by his parents and grown up in poverty. Nash said
the detective wasn't following the evidence, but targeting the
boy out of a deep-rooted jealousy. He accused the detective
of mishandling what evidence there was, and said the rest
couldn't be trusted. Because of the riots and police scandals,
the jury bought it and came back with a not-guilty verdict.''

"What happened to the kid?'' Teddy asked.

"He was released. Three days later they found him floating in the canal. He'd been strangled to death.''

"It sounds like he deserved it. Who did it? The detective?''

Jill shook her head. "No. He was working a case in
Florida. He and his partner left Los Angeles before the trial
was over. They were three thousand miles away when it
happened. No one knows who murdered the kid. The case
is still open.''

"Who do you think murdered him?''

She lowered her slice of pizza, unable to eat. "I don't
know who committed the murder. Maybe it was the brother
or father of one of the victims, or some cop who couldn't
take it anymore. That's not the point. All I'm saying is that

Nash plays games, Teddy. I could tell he knew the boy was guilty. Everyone in class could. Nash didn't get him off because it was the right thing to do. He got him off because he's smarter than everybody else and he knew how to. Once he'd won the case, he couldn't have cared less what happened to the kid. His interest was in the game and it was over.''

Teddy checked his watch. It was after six, and Jill's paranoia wasn't getting them anywhere.

"We've got some reading to do," he said.

She looked at him and nodded, then let out a faint smile as if she knew her words had fallen by the wayside.

"I'll get the coffee," she said.

They made a fresh pot together. When they returned to the office, Jill took the couch and began reading from page one. Teddy sat behind his desk, opened *The Agony and the Ecstasy* to page 300, and got started. The read went quickly. Because Teddy had always been interested in art, he found the novelization of Michelangelo's life fascinating. Still, Jill's story about the murders in L.A. troubled him, and he often found his mind wandering. Teddy had tried to give her a fair shake and listen to her story because he liked her and admired her and they were friends. Yet as he gazed at her on the couch, he couldn't help thinking that she was a victim of sorts, a measure of how well the media had been able to color what was happening and point their invisible electric finger at Holmes. It was clear to Teddy that Jill thought Holmes was guilty. It was clear to him that she was afraid they might find a way to get him off. The press was another player in the mix, Teddy thought. They were shaping the story in people's heads, jetting their way in the wrong direction with the police. Jill's fears seemed so outlandish. But then so did reading this book at a time when he knew he should be looking for Rosemary Gibb.

Why had Nash insisted on it? What was the idea he said he needed confirmed? *What two things does the city grow best?*

"Page two-O-nine," Jill shouted.

Teddy looked up and saw the terror on her face.

"Two-O-nine," she said, catching her breath.

He found the page and started reading. It was the story of Michelangelo's struggle to carve Hercules as a young man. Day after day he stared at the blank stone, unable to find the magic. He felt inept, even unworthy of the subject. How could he approach the stone without first knowing what was inside the man? Any man? He considered the idea of stealing a body from the graveyard for his studies, but realized he couldn't pull it off without getting caught. Several days passed and a new idea came to mind. The morgue. A place called *the dead room*.

Teddy's eyes lit up. The writer likened it to a sign from God. Michelangelo sneaking into the dead room every night with his knife and candle. Ripping the bodies apart with a slice down their chest. Cutting their ribs away, examining their muscles and organs, and feeling the tissue in his hands until he understood what a human being was made of.

What two things does the city grow best?

Nash was working up a profile of the killer. He'd been right. He'd been right all along.

"Shit," Teddy said.

He threw the book down and grabbed the phone. Nash was still in his office and sounded tired, almost as if he'd been waiting for the call.

"Lawyers and artists," Teddy said. "That's what the city grows best. The killer is an artist. That's why the faces all look the same. He's working on a painting or sculpture."

He looked at Jill standing before the desk. The investigation was another step closer and he could tell she knew it as well.

"It would seem so," Nash said over the phone. "But I wanted your thoughts first. He rejected Darlene Lewis because of her tattoos, and he cut Valerie Kram open because he wanted to look inside."

"But Michelangelo did it because of his time in history," Teddy said. "He didn't have the materials available today. He was starting from scratch."

"That's true," Nash said. "And he was working on

cadavers, dissecting them as if a scientist, learning about anatomy for the first time. The man we're looking for isn't Michelangelo, although he may think he is. The man we're looking for is beyond the pale.''

Holmes's makeshift art studio flashed through Teddy's head. "Holmes is an artist," he blurted out.

"So you've said before."

"I didn't get a good look at his work."

"If it would ease your mind any, I think you should have another look," Nash said. "Just make sure you're here in my office tomorrow by one o'clock. I'm having a criminal psychiatrist over. He's coming up from Washington and works with the FBI. I want a rough semblance of a profile completed by the end of the day.''

Teddy hung up the phone. Something about the idea of an artist becoming a serial killer rattled his bones. The two might pass each other on the sidewalk, but they were headed in opposite directions.

Jill cleared her throat and seemed upset. "I'm sorry about what I said before. I didn't mean it was a game. I didn't understand.''

"Don't worry about it," he said, checking the time and dialing Carolyn Powell's number over at the DA's office.

A man picked up the phone. Michael Jackson, not the dancer but the detective with the old gun.

"I'm glad you're there," Teddy said. "I need to speak with Powell first.''

"She was just walking out, kid. Let me see if I can grab her.''

The phone went dead. Teddy waited a moment, noticing that Jill had returned to the couch with another slice of pizza and was reading the book again. He heard the phone click and Carolyn's voice come on.

"What is it, Teddy?"

"I need another look at Holmes's apartment."

"I got a call from Ferarro in missing persons," she said. "He thinks something's up."

"Good," he said. "Because something's up."

"What have you got?"

"Nothing that would change your mind. Not yet anyway. All I'll say is that you guys should be helping Ferarro, not the other way around."

There was a long pause.

Teddy remained undaunted. "Jackson answered the phone so I know he's there. Can I get into Holmes's apartment tonight or what?"

"He'll be there in fifteen minutes," she said. Then, without a good-bye, she hung up.

Thirty-six

Michael Jackson made it up the steps to Holmes's penthouse apartment on the third floor. Once the hacking stopped he lit another cigarette and unlocked the door. His jacket was open, and Teddy got another look at the gun clipped to the detective's belt. He could tell it had a history, and wondered if it wasn't a throw-down gun. Teddy had read that some cops, the dirty ones anyway, were known to carry two weapons. The first gun was registered with the department. The second couldn't be traced to anyone and had a far darker purpose.

Jackson spotted Teddy's eyes on the gun and smiled as he swung the door open. "Two times in one day," he said. "We've gotta stop meeting like this, kid. People might get the wrong idea."

"This won't take long," Teddy said.

"I hope not. I clocked out a half hour ago. I could charge them for this, but it's on the way to my favorite watering hole."

Teddy entered the apartment, heading straight for Holmes's studio. He knew he couldn't sleep tonight with the chance that they might be off track. He needed to see the man's work and get a feel for it. He needed to know whether or not Holmes had any reason to study human anatomy firsthand in a psychotic misinterpretation of Michelangelo's dead room.

He turned the lock and yanked the door open. Switching the lights on, he crossed the room to the easel and flipped the dust cloth over for a look at Holmes's work. It was a landscape without any people. But it wasn't complete either.

He looked around and spotted the canvases leaning against the wall. There were five stacks, ten to twelve paintings deep. Teddy flipped through the paintings as quickly as he could. It was difficult because he realized Holmes's talent was genuine. Holmes had a way of playing with color that drew out the viewer's emotions. A hill might be black, the sky red. It was a singular view of seeing the world. A unique vision. There was a certain violence in the work, but it seemed to be a part of Holmes's natural style. And there were people as well, but they lacked detail. They looked like shadows, silhouettes—almost as if you took an abstract photograph of a strange landscape with the sun behind your back, casting your shadow across the foreground in a field of deep blue grass.

The works of art were remarkable.

It suddenly occurred to him that there wasn't a single painting by Holmes hanging in his sister's house. Sally and Jim Barnett had shown him the renovation of their home in detail, and Teddy had walked through every room. He would have remembered the style if he'd seen it before. As he thought it over, he played in his head the words the Barnetts had used to describe Oscar Holmes. Odd. Different. Holmes never seemed to fit in and always had to do things his own way. Teddy looked back at the paintings. No wonder Holmes was having problems with depression. He wasn't a mailman who painted on the side. Holmes was an artist forced to deliver the mail in order to make a living. He wasn't odd, but special. While van Gogh had his brother Theo behind him, all Holmes had were Sally and Jim Barnett. Two people who could have helped him, but didn't get it and seemed obsessed with the idea of making him fit in. Two people who on the day of his arrest wouldn't even take his phone call. Teddy felt sorry for them, for everyone involved, whether Holmes was guilty of the murders or not.

He looked up and saw Jackson standing in the doorway with an open flask.

"We came here tonight for a look at paintings?" the detective said.

Teddy stood up, his eyes on the flask. "Do you drink on duty, Jackson?"

The detective smiled. "I already told you I punched out. It's been a long day, kid. You want a hit or what?"

The flask was fitted in a leather case. Inside the strap was a shot glass that covered the neck of the flask and the cap.

"No, thanks," Teddy said.

"Suit yourself. But a shot or two would keep you warm. It feels like they got the heat turned down in here. Like everybody but you knows the guy ain't coming back."

It wasn't made of Sterling silver. Teddy's eyes rose from the flask to the detective's face. His bad-boy smile. He wondered if Jackson wasn't toying with him. Taunting him.

Teddy moved to the worktable and quickly thumbed through a stack of sketchbooks. If Jackson had been the man who clubbed him on the head and ran over Barnett's legs, then he would've known Teddy got a good look at the shot glass he found in the snow. The tall ships and whales etched into the silver. Jackson was smart enough to switch flasks. The fact that he was drinking and talking about keeping warm on a cold night seemed like a play though. Some sort of warning without details that hung over the night like Holmes's shadow cast in a field of blue.

Thirty-seven

The strange looks and long stares began the moment Teddy stepped out of the elevator. The receptionist at the front desk skipped her usual banter and remained quiet. When he strode down the hall to the kitchenette, he could feel everyone turning away.

He poured a cup of coffee and walked down to his office wondering what was up. Dumping his briefcase on the couch, he glanced at the morning papers on his desk and sat down. The coffee tasted stale, yet it was only eight A.M. Still, the blast of hot caffeine felt soothing, and he sipped the brew trying to wake up. It had been another sleepless night. Between nightmares of a delusional artist dissecting his models with a razor-sharp knife and dreams of making love with Carolyn Powell, the idea of a decent night's rest seemed ludicrous.

Teddy tossed the *Inquirer* aside and flipped over his copy of the *Daily News*. When he unfolded the newspaper and caught his first glimpse of the front page, he felt his pulse rocket upward and set the mug down.

Someone in the district attorney's office had leaked details from the crime scenes to the press. Even worse, someone had gotten to Holmes.

Teddy's eyes worked over the picture of Holmes filling out the entire front page—another distorted and particularly grizzly shot of Holmes as a monster. Instead of a headline, the editors had gone with the quote I DON'T EVEN EAT MEAT!, attributing it to Holmes and tagging him as *the Veggie Butcher*.

It was done. Holmes was a serial killer with a nickname. The Veggie Butcher.

Teddy's heart almost stopped. He turned the page, trying to remain calm as his eyes took in the headlines. Holmes was branded a cannibal for all the world to see. There was an old snapshot of Holmes behind the counter at his butcher shop, sharpening a long knife in front of three old ladies with big, wide-open eyes. Another of Darlene Lewis in a bikini by the pool. Then a third photo of the girl's corpse inside a body bag as it was wheeled out the front door of her house.

Teddy began reading, the words zipping by at high speed. Holmes had cut Darlene Lewis up and eaten her, a source close to the investigation told the paper. When Valerie Kram's body was fished out of the icy water along Boathouse Row, the medical examiner found the girl's internal organs disturbed, another unnamed source said. In his own defense, Holmes confronted the charges with the apparent claim that he couldn't have eaten their flesh because he was a vegetarian.

Teddy flipped the page, so nervous his hand was trembling. The words THE SKIN GAME leaped out at him. Beneath the headline was a photo of Jim Barnett. It was the same photo printed in *Philadelphia Magazine*'s *Power 100* issue. A reporter had been digging into Holmes's past and discovered that Barnett and Holmes were brothers-in-law. The secret was no longer a secret. Barnett wouldn't achieve his dream of making the top ten list this year.

Teddy threw the newspaper in the trash, thinking he might be sick. He heard someone enter his office and turned as he stood. It was Larry Stokes, cofounder of the firm, glaring at him.

"What have you done?" Stokes shrieked.

Teddy froze, spotting Jill down the hall waving her hands in warning. He looked back at Stokes. The man was seething, his eyes filled with venom, but also a large measure of fear—Jill's warning a moment too late.

"You're blaming me for this?" Teddy said.

"You bet I am," Stokes said. "Building this firm's reputation has taken me a lifetime. Look what you've done in just three months. Barnett said we weren't putting up a defense. There wouldn't be any headlines. You're obviously not doing what you were told."

Teddy remained quiet, his anger rising. If he said what was on his mind, he knew the idiot would fire him on the spot.

"He wants to see you right away," Stokes said. "I just got off the phone with him."

Teddy sat down in his desk chair.

"Not later," Stokes shouted. "Right away. He's in room three-fourteen."

Teddy grabbed his briefcase and left the room. As he passed Jill, she took a step back and cringed. Before turning the corner at the end of the hall, he glanced back at his office and saw Stokes still glaring at him from the door.

"Get out," the man said, rocking on his heels.

He found Barnett's room at Bryn Mawr Hospital. The shades were drawn, the man cloaked in darkness with a copy of the *Daily News* beside him and three needles in his arm. Barnett's legs were still held in place by a maze of steel tubing, his face more white than pale. After a moment, Barnett sensed his presence and lowered his gaze from the ceiling. His eyes were hollow and sick. Teddy didn't feel any anger emanating from Barnett, just devastation and terror. When he checked the medications hanging beside the bed, he realized the man was on morphine.

"Jesus, Teddy," he whispered.

Teddy pulled a chair over to the bed and sat down. Barnett took his hand and gave it a squeeze, not wanting to let go. Teddy didn't feel uncomfortable holding Barnett's hand. The gesture was an act of friendship, the kind of thing a father and son would do.

"Have you ever felt like shit?" Barnett asked, slurring his words.

"Yes."

"Well, this is worse than that."

"The doctor says you're doing good."

"The doctor's full of shit."

Barnett smiled, releasing Teddy's hand to adjust the hose feeding oxygen into his nostrils. As he moved, he groaned and tried to catch his breath.

"What the hell happened?" he asked after a moment.

"There's been a leak," Teddy said.

"A leak? When a dam breaks it's not a leak. It's the end. What do you think the chances are that Holmes will get a fair shake in court now?"

The answer was none. The jury pool had been poisoned. If it went to court, the Veggie Butcher was dead.

Teddy glanced at the morphine again, doubting Barnett was in any condition to handle an update on the case. He gave him one anyway, briefing him on what had happened since he was run over by the car. Barnett seemed particulary shaken by the fact that the district attorney had widened the scope of the investigation to include ten more missing women. Still, Teddy noted the glimmer of hope in the man's eyes when he mentioned that Nash thought Holmes was innocent. The hope faded just as quickly, however, as Teddy brought up their theory that they were looking for an artist. When Teddy was finished, Barnett picked up his copy of the *Daily News* and rested it on his lap.

"This is exactly what I'd been hoping to avoid, Teddy."

"Nash seems to think we're making progress."

Barnett sighed and shook his head. "You still don't have any evidence," he said. "You're still counting on best guesses and a theory that sounds like it's built on hope. Holmes is an artist, but maybe he's not the artist you're looking for. Rosemary Gibb is missing, and may or may not be a victim of the same man you don't have any proof even exists."

Barnett may have been mainlining morphine, but it hadn't impaired his judgment after all.

"Let me ask you a question," Barnett said. "Imagine we're in trial and you're not a member of the defense. Instead, you're sitting with the jury on this one."

Teddy nodded, ready to listen.

"The prosecution presents its case," Barnett said. "A young woman is brutally murdered. A man is seen running from her house. The cops find the murder weapon in the man's car. DNA links the man to the murder weapon, and the weapon to the victim. But the DNA also links the man to another murder that occurred some time ago, and there are ten more missing women who look just like the first two victims. Bloody clothes are found in the man's trash. The man's an oddball from the word go. Everyone in the jury can see it with their own eyes, including you. Even better, the oddball freely admits being at the crime scene but can't remember what happened. The prosecution fills in the blanks with photographs of the victims, a shot of the accused with blood all over his face, fingerprints found on the corpse, and charts of the DNA results proving their match is a statistical lock. You with me so far?"

Teddy nodded hesitantly. He knew where Barnett was headed. He'd been down the same road himself.

"So now it's the defense's turn," Barnett said. "Remember, you're still a member of the jury. You don't live in a vacuum, so you're aware of the case before trial. The Veggie Butcher case. You remember reading about the murders because the Veggie Butcher is a cannibal and eats people. You saw the stories on TV, but you haven't made up your mind yet because you're either dead from the neck up or a damn good liar. The defense steps up to the plate. The defense says the Veggie Butcher couldn't have done it because he takes care of this little neighbor girl. The Veggie Butcher couldn't have done it because serial killers aren't known to run away from crime scenes. While the defense agrees that the man responsible for these gruesome murders is an artist, it couldn't be the Veggie Butcher because he paints landscapes. The defense shows you a novel about the life of Michelangelo. They even read a passage from the book. And guess what—the defense has something more up their sleeve. There's another victim out there. Lucky thirteen. Another girl who looks something like the others and disappeared after the Veggie Butcher's arrest. This proves, of course, that the Veggie Butcher couldn't be the real murderer. Although he's odd looking, he isn't really a cannibal. He may have been a butcher, but all that's behind him now. The defense shows you a copy of this newspaper, points to the front page, and raises a question. How could the Veggie Butcher be the one when he doesn't even eat meat?''

It was a performance Teddy knew he would never forget. A summation of the facts and arguments so complete and concise, nothing had been left out. Barnett sank back into the bed and groaned. It had cost him considerable physical effort, but he'd made his point and lived up to his reputation as a master at the end game during trial. They'd spent a lot of time on the big ride to nowhere.

''Send me a copy of the profile,'' Barnett whispered after he caught his breath. ''Have someone drive it out tonight when you're through.''

When Teddy tried to speak, Barnett waved him off and closed his eyes saying he needed to get some rest. It looked as if his mental anguish was even greater than the pain emanating from his broken legs. Teddy slid the chair away from the bed and left the room.

Thirty-eight

He checked the time. When he punched Nash's office number into his cell phone and reached his assistant, Gail Emerson, he told her that he had two stops to make but would be in as scheduled following lunch.

It would be a morning of putting out fires—suppressing his anger. If he couldn't dowse the flames and kill them, at least he would confront them.

Teddy forced the issue with the warden at Curran-Fromhold. Holmes had been quoted in the *Daily News*. Someone had gotten to him at the prison, and Teddy demanded an explanation and a look at his client's cell. The warden protested. Teddy struck the visitor's list with a closed fist. No one from the paper had made a trip out to the prison. No one other than Teddy had signed in. The warden finally agreed, calling the request unusual and escorting Teddy up to the quarantine pod in building B himself.

Teddy had expected to find the inmates locked in rows of cells behind steel bars. As he entered the pod, he was surprised to see this wasn't the case. It was a large, open room that reminded him of a cafeteria in a high school. Twenty or so modern tables with stools were set into the floor. A short set of steps led down to a sitting area where a TV hung from the ceiling. Beyond the chairs were a row of ten steel doors. Each cell door was painted a bright yellow and included a small window. Teddy noted a stairway off to the side leading up to an open level above and another set of ten yellow doors.

Two guards sat at a table within the pod by the entrance. As Teddy followed the warden over and checked in, he looked for Holmes among the fifteen inmates milling about. His client didn't appear to be in the pod. When he heard the sound of a basketball, he turned to his right and saw two inmates shooting hoops on the other side of a glass wall. Holmes wasn't with them either.

Well aware that the inmates were keeping an eye on him, Teddy followed one of the guards down the steps to a cell in the far corner by an open shower stall. The guard pointed at the yellow door, saying it wasn't locked and that Holmes rarely came out of his cell or mixed with the others.

Teddy glanced at the inmates and saw the uneasy looks on their faces as he reached for the door handle. The leak at the DA's office was in play even here. Holmes was no longer a common murderer. He was the Veggie Butcher now.

Teddy swung the door open and found Holmes sitting on the floor with a piece of charcoal and a sketchbook. Holmes seemed more than a little edgy by the interruption.

"If I need help," Teddy said to the guard, "I'll scream." Then he gave the man a hard look and slammed the door closed.

Holmes dropped his piece of charcoal on the floor. The cell was the size of a closet, and without bars, the space felt particularly confining. Two beds were bolted into the wall one on top of another. There was just enough room left in the cell to fit a stainless steel bench and a john. Although there was a narrow window over the beds, the glass was frosted and didn't offer a view.

Teddy noticed the newspapers spread out on the top bunk—each paper folded to the crossword puzzle. Holmes had filled the words in using a crayon. On top was today's copy of the *Daily News*.

"You like crossword puzzles, Holmes?"

Holmes nodded, but didn't say anything. His eyes were bloodshot, his face wasted as if he'd been driving all night without rest or stopping for gas.

"Well, at least you don't have a cellmate," Teddy said, glancing at the john and taking a seat on the bench.

"I read the paper," Holmes said. "They're saying I did things."

"That's why I'm here. Who have you been talking to?"

Holmes looked through the window at the guard staring at them from the other side of the door.

"Not him," he said in a voice that wouldn't carry. "There's others who come in at night. They're taunting me."

"With what?"

"Steaks," Holmes said. "And real coffee."

Teddy didn't understand and gave him a look.

"The prison only serves turkey," Holmes said. "You know how you feel after Thanksgiving dinner?"

"Sleepy," Teddy said.

"It's the tryptophan in the meat. Turkey's cheap and has lots of tryptophan. It works like a natural tranquilizer. That's all they serve here. Three meals a day. And nothing with any caffeine."

"So at night," Teddy said, "they bring in the steaks and real coffee."

Holmes nodded. "When I told them I'm a vegetarian, they laughed and called me names."

"That won't happen again, I promise you. But you need to do me a favor, Holmes. Don't talk to the guards. Don't say anything at all, no matter what, okay? And watch who you're with. You don't know who's who in here."

Holmes nodded as if a child.

"May I look at your sketchbook?" Teddy asked.

"Why?"

"Because I need to."

Holmes seemed reluctant, but finally passed the sketch-book over. Teddy flipped through the pages until he reached the beginning, carefully examining each drawing. After a moment, he realized Holmes was recreating the view from the sun porch at his apartment in the city. His art studio. He could see the park outside, figures moving down the sidewalks like shadows.

"Have you ever done any portraits?" Teddy asked.

"I've tried, but they don't come out right."

"You still having nightmares?"

"Only when I sleep," Holmes said.

Teddy caught a faint smile on his client's face. The first he'd ever seen. His sense of humor was subtle, but there. Teddy handed the sketchbook back.

"What about your memory of the day Darlene Lewis died?"

Holmes's face went blank again. "That's the nightmare. The day she died."

"What about before this, Holmes? Before Darlene was murdered. How's your memory? Are there any other blank spots?"

Holmes thought it over as if he hadn't considered it before. After a moment, he shook his head at the discovery.

"Tell me about that day," Teddy said.

"No," Holmes said.

"How bad can it be if you don't remember what happened?"

"I remember touching her," Holmes said. "Doing things to her with my hands."

"What's her face look like in the dream?"

Holmes lowered his eyes to the floor and shook his head. "Her eyes are bulging," he whispered after a moment. "She's dead."

Thirty-nine

Teddy stood on the sidewalk beside his car, smoking his first cigarette of the day and keeping an eye on the building. His fuse was burning. Once he saw Carolyn Powell, he was afraid he might explode.

He crossed the street, ditching the smoke and entering the building lobby. Security in the district attorney's office was tight. Three male receptionists worked the desk behind bulletproof glass. They looked like ex-cops, real bruisers. Beside the desk on the left were the metal detectors. You couldn't pass without going through.

He pulled his cell phone out and entered her number. When her assistant picked up, he gave her his name and told her he was in the lobby. A moment later, Powell came on and said she'd be right down.

Benches were set up like church pews off to the side. Teddy took a seat and waited, unable to appreciate the ornate wood paneling or moldings that lined the walls of the old building. There had been a leak and it came from this office. Although Teddy had let Barnett make his point from his hospital bed without a response, the evidence seemed less important than what he was packing in his gut. District

Attorney Alan Andrews had the wrong man. And now Holmes was tarnished beyond resurrection, his ability to defend himself ruined.

Powell entered the lobby carrying a file folder. When she spotted him, she passed through the security gate and walked over.

"You want to come up?" she asked, handing him the file.

"I don't have time."

"It's the toxicology report," she said. "Let's go in here."

He followed her into the empty press room and watched her close the door without switching on the lights. She looked upset as she crossed to the window. It read like guilt.

"We didn't leak the story, Teddy."

"If it wasn't you, who else is there?"

"We're trying to figure that out," she said. "We've been working on it all morning."

"Let me give you a hint. His name's Alan Andrews and he's a politician. Now you can stop wasting your time and get back to work on making the biggest mistake of your life."

She took the blow and looked disappointed. Teddy didn't move.

"We're back to this," she said after a moment.

"Not Andrews himself. He's smarter than that. You know who's working the case better than I do. You'll have to figure out who's talking yourself. Maybe it's his scary cop friend, Michael Jackson. By the way, Jackson drinks from a flask. Not the one I saw the night Barnett was run over. He's got another one now."

She gave him a look and sat down. "Do you know what you're saying?"

"I know what it looks like, Carolyn."

She turned to the window without responding.

"It was in the papers before the Lewis murder," he said. "An overzealous prosecutor with political ambition screws up and needs a big case to get himself out of a deep hole. That's the context. The specifics get better. The lead defense attorney is in a hospital bed and may not walk again. Details of the crime scene have been leaked to the papers killing the jury pool. Prison guards working the night shift are taunting the accused and trying to get him to talk.''

She was staring at him, her eyes burning in the dim light and measuring his anger. ''The evidence against Holmes is overwhelming. What you're implying is ridiculous. You're spending too much time with Nash.''

She stood up and turned to the door, reaching for the handle. She'd written him off and was ready to leave. Teddy pushed the door closed and could feel her breath on his face.

''What about Rosemary Gibb?'' he said.

''Refresh my memory.''

She didn't know who Rosemary was. He tried to get a grip on himself.

''You said you spoke with Ferarro in missing persons,'' he said. ''There's another girl and I can't even get a look at the missing persons report.''

She flashed a reluctant smile, remembering. The kind of smile that said Rosemary hadn't made the cut. Even worse, it seemed clear that she'd written off Teddy's motives as some sort of cheap defense tactic. Teddy felt his pulse smack the ceiling and steadied himself against the door.

''You said at breakfast the other day that you regretted what happened between us,'' he said in a low voice. ''I'm sorry we did it, too.''

She was staring at him. She was dressed in a turquoise suit that brought out the color of her eyes. Teddy ignored what he felt for her. He tried to, anyway, and moved on.

''You're dangerous, Carolyn. You're just like Andrews. Maybe you're in it with him. Is that what happened? Were you keeping me busy that night? Did we get drunk and fuck so the hatchet man could get a clean shot at Barnett on his own?''

She seemed stunned. Her eyes suddenly looked glassy. What he was saying was outrageous, even vicious. Still, he needed to break the flow. One way or the other, he needed to change things.

"You really fooled me, you know it?" he said. "I thought it was more than that. I haven't been able to get you out of my mind since it happened. But you're playing on another level. You're in another league. You and the city's next mayor. You don't give a fuck about anybody just as long as you chalk up another conviction. Another win for the record books. You want it so bad you're blind to what's really going on. You can play follow-the-leader all you want. But keep your guards away from my client. We'll deal with the leak next time we're before a judge."

She didn't say anything. She didn't move. Teddy opened the door, leaving her in the empty press room where the lights were out.

Forty

Her tits were too big. Eddie checked his canvas, then peered back at Rosemary slumped in the chair before him in his basement studio. The light was right, the sun hitting the greenhouse and feeding the room with a soft, steady haze that glowed. It was her body that was wrong. She didn't match the others. She seemed too voluptuous. Even with her eyes closed, she radiated too much beauty, too much life.

He looked back at her and wondered if she might not be moving. She'd been sleeping for the past three hours—in a stupor since they'd become friends and partied on the *Love Drug*.

Eddie moved in for a closer look. He couldn't really tell. Maybe she was moving, but maybe she wasn't. When his eyes fell across her naked body, his dick got hard again and he swore. It was a pitfall that went with the job. A wrong turn up a dead-end alley if he wanted to become famous.

Work before pleasure. It's a lost secret, son.

He stepped back behind the large canvas, deciding he wouldn't look at her again for the rest of the day. Not until he could tell if she was moving or not. Not until he backed out of the wrong alley. He dabbed his brush in the paint, swirling it through a blend of deep reds. He'd spend the afternoon working on the background. The buildings and lights along the streets that were in his head.

The doorbell rang.

Eddie flinched, his brush driving across the canvas and ruining an entire section of the large work.

The bell rang again. His jaw muscles tightened as he heard it vibrate through the house. He wanted to scream. Instead, he wiped the brushstroke away with a rag and assessed the damage to his masterpiece. It would take him all night to fix. It might take him longer if Rosemary didn't wake up and start cooperating.

Someone began pounding on the front door. Eddie threw the rag down.

"Sit still," he ordered Rosemary.

Then he hurried up the steps, too upset to worry if the neighbors were eavesdropping on his mind or not. He entered the kitchen and saw a figure through the living room window. It was Mrs. Yap, staring back at him and beaming. Her needless visit had almost ruined his life's work.

He tried to control his anger. Faking a loose smile, he crossed the room, switched the lock, and popped open the door.

"I was worried about you," his landlady said. "I stopped by the other day, but you didn't answer. May I come in?"

He nodded as if he had a choice, stepping aside as Mrs. Yap entered.

"I hope I'm not disturbing you," she went on. "I was afraid I might have to use my key or call the police. You don't look so good."

The chattering had started. Her peppy energy only seemed to turn his anger into rage. He followed her into the kitchen, watching her grab the teapot as if she owned it and fill the vessel with tap water. As she rambled on, she noticed the curtains were drawn and pulled them open.

Eddie squinted as the light struck his face. He looked through the window at the house on the corner. There was a man on the roof, adjusting the fake satellite dish pointed at him. Their listening device was down, the monitor on their computer blank. The watchers had no idea what he was thinking.

Eddie was free. At least for now he was.

He looked back at Mrs. Yap. She had the drawer open, admiring his Sterling silver flatware. She was dressed in bright colors—the mouth below her beaklike nose prattling in overdrive. Soon the babbling turned into chortling, the woman transforming into a bird before his eyes.

It wasn't the drug after all, he thought. It was his vision. His strength.

He drew the curtain. When he saw the giant canary turn from the stove, he noticed he was trembling. Still, he moved toward the bird without hesitation. It was pecking at him with its beak, flailing its wings in the air. It seemed so close. So fucking real.

Eddie lunged at the animal, biting its beak off and spitting it on the floor.

The canary did a stutter step and looked overwhelmed and defenseless. Blood spewed all over its nape and chin, staining the brightly colored feathers on its chest. The bird's eyes widened and the pecking stopped. It flapped its wings again. When the bird tried to fly away, Eddie grabbed a butcher's knife off the counter and plunged it into the animal's back. Over and over again until the pesky thing stopped jittering and fell on the living room floor.

Forty-one

Teddy ran up the stairs to Nash's office, sensing that something had happened. It felt like a cold draft, working its way inside him until it blew against his core.

When he entered the office, Nash wasn't there. Instead, he found someone he didn't know seated at the jury table with the murder book and a copy of their initial profile. The man looked at him and smiled. Teddy guessed he was about fifty. His light brown hair was streaked with gray, his dark eyes sparkling with amusement.

"You must be Teddy," the man said, offering his hand as he acknowledged Nash's absence. "He's giving an exam. He'll be back in a few minutes. I've spent the morning reading through all this and trying to catch up."

The man introduced himself as Dr. Stanley Westbrook, a criminal psychiatrist from the FBI's Behavioral Science section who'd made the trip up from Washington via the Metroliner as a favor to his friend. He said he'd been a student of criminal behavior for most of his career, and worked with Nash many times in the past. When he mentioned some of the cases he'd been associated with over the last ten years, Teddy recognized most of them and knew Westbrook was real.

A copy of the *Daily News* was set on the table. As Teddy glanced at it, he tried to find some assurance in the psychiatrist's presence, but couldn't. It felt like they were moving too slowly. As if their feet were anchored in piles of dry sand.

"There's been a leak," he said.

"Nash told me about it," Westbrook said, glancing at the newspaper. "He admires you, by the way. He trusts you. He wishes you'd been his student and thinks we should hire you."

Taking a seat at the jury table, Teddy handed over the medical examiner's report Powell had given him. As Westbrook opened the file and scanned through the autopsy results, Teddy couldn't help but think about what he'd said to Powell just a half hour ago. Even though a life was at stake, he'd been out of line and didn't feel very proud.

Westbrook thumbed through the report until he reached the toxicology results and shook his head. Teddy noted the coffee cup on the table set beside an ashtray.

"This is troubling," the psychiatrist said, still eyeing the report.

The door opened and Nash walked in, carrying a sheaf of papers and dumping them on his desk. "Sorry I'm late," he said. "You two have had a chance to meet?"

Westbrook looked up from the report and nodded.

"Good," Nash said, opening a fresh cigar and joining them at the table. "So where do we stand?"

"I think you're correct," Westbrook said. "You're looking for a man in his twenties or thirties with a history of serious mental illness. He was abused as a child, or suffered some great emotional crisis as a young boy. If we could look back at his childhood, I'm certain we'd find numerous cases of animal abuse as well."

"What are the chances that he's an artist?" Teddy asked. "Even an attorney? Have you thought about the tattoos, or is it a stretch?"

"I don't think it's a stretch at all."

The crime scene at the Lewis house flashed before Teddy's eyes before the psychiatrist could say anything more. The sitting room on the other side of the hall with the magnificent paintings by Seurat, Gauguin, and Cezanne hanging on the walls. He hadn't thought of it before. He'd seen it, but its meaning hadn't registered.

"A chair was turned toward the paintings," Teddy said. "Someone had moved the chair to look at the art. At the time, I thought it was the owner."

Nash and Westbrook traded looks and nodded as if the insight impressed them. For Teddy, this new observation read like everything else. It wasn't evidence of anything. But it was another sign.

Westbrook lit a cigarette and looked at him. "Nash told me your theory, and I agree. Darlene was rejected because of the marks on her skin. Since there's a good chance you're dealing with an artist, there's a certain appreciation for purity going on here. Valerie Kram is a different story. She spent time with the killer. She modeled for him. When she was used up, he threw her away. But remember, Valerie Kram was part of his work by then, something akin to sacred, so she was placed in the water where he found her and cleansed."

"What about Holmes?" Nash asked.

"Based on your profile, I'd say he's outside the model or field of inquiry. Of course I've never spoken with the man and there's always the chance that I'm wrong. What interests me most is the condition of the body found in the river."

"The cut down the middle of her chest," Teddy said.

The psychiatrist nodded and turned to Nash. "Teddy brought the toxicology report with him," he said. "Cutting the victim open could have more meaning than it seems. The medical examiner found drugs in her system. It's a safe bet they're in his system as well. You're looking for a user and your profile should be amended to reflect that. Valerie

Kram may have died from strangulation. But she was on the verge of overdosing on Ecstasy as well.''

This was new. Teddy hadn't looked at the toxicology report Powell had given him earlier. He was too upset with her, too upset with himself for treating her the way he did, and he'd been running late. But Teddy knew something about Ecstasy. It was pretty much the drug of choice with his classmates in school. He'd used it a handful of times himself, but stopped when he woke up one morning overwrought with depression. He knew the drug's effects, though. He knew its power and what a single dose could do.

''He's using Ecstasy as a way of controlling his victims,'' Teddy said. ''He's using the drug to soften them up.''

Westbrook glanced at Nash again, then turned back. ''But Ecstasy has a nasty side effect, Teddy. Particularly in high doses. Beyond what chronic use can do to the brain, the drug causes a marked increase in body temperature. In an overdose like this, Valerie Kram was literally cooking from the inside out.''

''Then this could be another explanation for dumping her body in water,'' Nash said.

Westbrook sat back in his chair. ''And for cutting her open. Steam would have been venting from her body. Her internal organs would've felt hot to the touch. Don't forget the sexual implications of the knife.''

Teddy grimaced as the horror settled in. The sickness. The idea that the murders were a result of the killer's twisted sexual fantasy.

As Westbrook showed Nash the toxicology report and discussed the results, Teddy looked up at the photographs tacked to the wall—the girls' faces watching them from the other side. They seemed so familiar, so innocent. He noted the time and began to feel anxious again. He turned back to the psychiatrist.

''Tell us who we're looking for,'' he said. ''Give us your best guess.''

Westbrook lowered the toxicology report and folded his

hands on the jury table. "You're looking for a mad-dog killer," the psychiatrist said. "A real motherfucker with delusions of grandeur. Someone whose paranoia is off the charts. Someone who suffers from hallucinations, not necessarily from the drugs he's taking, but because of his illness and the way he was mistreated as a child. If you were ever to meet this individual, you'd know instantly that something was wrong. If you were ever to meet this individual, I'd make sure you knew how to handle a gun. You're not looking for a human being, Teddy. He's past that now. You're looking for an animal."

This time it was Nash and Teddy who traded looks. Ominous and sobering looks. The situation appeared so grim, Teddy could taste it in his mouth.

Forty-two

Eddie Trisco peeked through the curtain, wondering if it was safe to go outside. The sun had set an hour ago, yet the windows in the corner house remained dark. He checked the roofline and saw the satellite dish pointed toward him. He couldn't tell if the strange device was working or not, but the man he'd seen making repairs this morning was long gone. So were the cars parked along the street. Maybe this was the break he'd been waiting for. Maybe they were between shifts.

He turned away from the window, staring at Mrs. Yap's body on the living room floor as he considered his options. He needed to get rid of her car. He could deal with her body later. Still, he didn't want to leave Rosemary alone.

He went downstairs and found her sleeping in the chair before the easel. He checked the clasps on the handcuffs and ankle irons—the chains running through the arms and legs of the chair. She'd been sleeping for most of the day. He didn't want her to wake up like this. She might be hungry or need to use the bathroom.

The decisions in an artist's life could be so hard.

He opened the bottom drawer in the cabinet, pulled a

blanket out, and draped it over her. Then he turned his back on her and marched upstairs.

Although the lights were out, he could tell that Mrs. Yap had lost her feathers. She wasn't a bird anymore. She wasn't peppy. He stepped over the body and opened the closet by the front door. Pulling on a hooded ski jacket, he wrapped a scarf around his neck and grabbed his gloves. Then he picked up her purse and went through it in the darkness. This was her fault, he reminded himself. She'd stuck her nose in his business and almost ruined his life's work. What did she expect?

He found the keys to her new Mercedes and dropped the purse on the floor. Cracking the front door open, he checked the street. Christmas lights adorned most of the houses in the neighborhood. All except his and that house on the corner where the watchers lived.

The coast looked clear.

Eddie slipped out of the house, pulling the door shut and locking it with a key. But as he hurried toward Mrs. Yap's Mercedes, he heard something in the air. A chopper in the black sky. Ignoring the arctic breeze, he bolted for the car with the key ready, then yanked the door open and jumped inside.

It was *them*. He could see the searchlight panning over the houses on the next street. They were getting their bearings. They were working their way toward his house. He'd better hurry.

He looked at the dashboard, getting a feel for the controls. The car started on the second try. Backing out the drive, he pulled down the street at an easy, *I'm not the one you're looking for* pace. When he reached the stop sign, he ignored the corner house and waited for a Ford Explorer to pass. It was another woman on a cell phone. Eddie made a right, heading for the city and thinking all Explorers came equipped with women jabbering on cell phones. It was so ugly. So telling.

He glanced out the window, digging into a bag of chocolate chip morsels. The chopper was behind him now, the

sound of its rotors fading in the distance. There wasn't time
to make an airport run, he decided. Dumping the car in long-
term parking would mean having to take the bus back to
the airport, then a train into the city. He knew from experience that the process took hours.

He yawned and smacked his lips as the chocolate chips
melted in his mouth. He hadn't slept for two days. The
thought of sipping a delicious caffe latte crossed his mind.
He wondered if the window table might be open at Benny's
Cafe Blue. Maybe he'd cruise by.

Forty-three

Teddy met the messenger on the street outside Nash's office, handed him a copy of the profile sealed in an envelope, and told the driver Barnett was in room 314 at Bryn Mawr Hospital. As he watched the messenger take off for the suburbs, Teddy got in his car and drove back into Center City.

Although Nash had invited him to dinner with Dr. West-brook at his club, Teddy declined. It had been a long day trying to plug the leak. All he wanted to do was check in at the office and head home. Maybe give Barnett a call and see how he was doing. Teddy had written a note to Barnett and placed it in the envelope with the profile, wishing him well and giving him the news Teddy had been hoping for. The FBI was *in*. By tomorrow morning, agents would be meeting with District Attorney Alan Andrews and ADA Carolyn Powell for a full review of the Holmes case. Teddy wondered how Powell would handle it. Whether she'd become defensive with the agents and take Andrews's side, or consider the possibility that maybe she was seeing things wrong.

He stepped off the elevator, opening the lobby door with

a key. The lights were down. The receptionist was no longer there to give him a dirty look, nor was Larry Stokes. It looked as if most of the attorneys had gone home for the day as well. When he walked into his office, he found Jill at the computer studying for her bar exams.

"There's someone here to see you," she said with a look.

"Who?"

The look didn't go away. "The assistant district attorney," she said.

"Where?"

"Conference room three. She's been here for an hour. She wouldn't wait in the main conference room because the windows face the lobby."

Teddy rushed down the hall to the other side of the building. Powell was sitting in a chair with her back to the door. As he entered the room, she turned. He noticed the file on the table and looked at her face. The distance was gone.

"What is it, Carolyn? What are you doing here?"

"I've brought you a gift," she said, sliding the file across the table. "You can't keep it, but you can read it if you like and take notes."

Teddy opened the file. It was a copy of the missing persons report on Rosemary Gibb. He looked at her and sat down. When they met earlier in the day, he was in the heat of it and said a lot of things he didn't mean to say or even think were true. His accusations had been outlandish and rude. Now she had come to him with Detective Ferarro's file on Rosemary.

"I'm sorry for the things I said to you," he whispered.

"Apology accepted," she said. "But we still can't find the leak, Teddy. It didn't come from the roundhouse. You're not gonna like hearing this, but I don't think it came from Andrews either."

"Then why are you doing this?" he said, deciding to let it pass for now.

"You've got Detective Ferarro worried, and he's a smart man. The evidence is on our side, but I can't take the chance that we've overlooked something. Ferarro went back to the gym. According to the report, that's the last place anyone remembered seeing Rosemary Gibb.''

"You just used the past tense. What's changed?"

"There's a café across the street. Ferarro went back and interviewed the employees for a second time this afternoon. The manager thinks she came in that night, but isn't sure."

Teddy thought it over. "How about a pick-me-up?" he said.

She smiled. She hadn't looked at him like this for days.

"It's just a few blocks from here off Walnut Street," she said. "You can check the report out while we walk."

Forty-four

Teddy spotted the place on the other side of the street half a block down.

Benny's Cafe Blue occupied the first floor of an old brick building. An awning stretched across the front, but was rolled up for winter. He could imagine five or six tables lining the sidewalk in warmer weather, and wondered why he hadn't frequented the café himself.

As they crossed at the corner, Powell gave him a nudge and he turned. A young woman was walking away from her car parked in the alley beside the building. She had a gym bag slung over her shoulder, and was obviously heading for the club across the street. Teddy noted Powell's eyes on the girl. Her grimace. As they passed, they looked down the alley. It was dark. Narrow. The perfect dead end.

The café was slow. It was only seven-thirty, but they were between rush hours. The manager, Harris Carmichael, said their timing was good and offered them free cups of the house blend. He'd join them at a table when their drinks were ready.

Teddy chose the table in the corner. As he sat down with Powell, he passed the file over. The missing persons report on Rosemary Gibb amounted to fifteen sheets of paper and even fewer leads. Ferarro had left out personal details when they met at his office yesterday, but nothing relevant to the case. The detective had been straight with Teddy and told him everything he knew.

Teddy turned to the window and looked outside. He could see the gym across the street. The girl he'd just seen in the alley was entering the floor and mounting a stationary bike. It was a close-up view. The distance between them no more than twenty-five yards. He felt a chill as he watched the girl working out, but thought it might be from the walk over.

The manager arrived with their coffees. As he set them down on the table, he gave Teddy a strange look and cocked his head.

"Is something wrong?" Teddy asked.

Carmichael paused. He wasn't much older than Teddy and about the same size, though he had a paunch growing beneath his apron. He scratched his curly black hair.

"I don't know," he said. "Seeing you sitting here like this. I was making your drinks and watching you. I remember a guy sitting in the same seat. He's been in here before. He orders a caffe latte and sits in this seat nursing it for as long as he can. Most people sit where she is when they're alone so they can people-watch. But not this guy. He always sits with his back to the room and stares out the window."

Teddy glanced outside, watching the girl ride her bicycle to nowhere. The chill hadn't come from the cold air.

"What about the night Rosemary came in?" Powell asked.

"The trouble is she came in lots of nights," Carmichael said. "That's what I told the detective this afternoon. It's hard to remember which night you're talking about. They're all pretty much the same around here."

"It would be the last one," Teddy said. "The last night you saw her."

Carmichael sat down, his eyes flicking back and forth as he tried to remember. After a moment, something happened and his eyes shot straight ahead.

"He was here that night," he blurted out. "The last night I saw her, he was here. I remember now because he switched seats. I looked over and saw him staring out the window. When I looked back, he was facing the other way."

"What does he look like?" Powell asked.

"About thirty," Carmichael said. "Light brown hair, almost shoulder length. The kind that goes blond in the summer. I remember his hands. There was paint on them."

"House paint or bright colors?" Teddy asked.

"Bright colors."

He's a painter, Teddy thought to himself. They were on the right track.

"What about his face?" Carolyn said. "Who's he look like?"

Carmichael thought it over and shook his head.

"Tall or short?" she said.

"Normal," Carmichael said. "Thin, maybe even wiry like he's in good shape. He's got blue eyes, sort of piercing. He's the nervous type. Kind of out of it and a little strange. But what I remember most about him are his teeth."

"What about them?" Teddy asked.

"He's got bad teeth. He doesn't need braces. That's not the problem. His teeth look like they're rotting."

It clicked in Teddy's head. The man was an artist and a drug user.

"One more thing," Carmichael said after a moment. "The last night I saw Rosemary. I think he followed her out the door."

It hung there. When someone walked out of the café, they turned to the entrance like they could see into the past. The man with bad teeth following Rosemary out the door.

Forty-five

They were sitting at his table. They were looking through the window at the gym, putting it together and talking about him.

Two plus two equals four. Eddie's the one who followed Rosemary out the door.

He felt the chill of a cold hand grabbing him by the back of the neck. It was the proverbial cold hand. The one he felt when he knew he was in deep trouble.

He started shivering. He looked up the street at the gym, then turned to the storefront directly before him and pretended to window-shop. Reaching into his pocket, he pulled a Milky Way bar out and tore open the wrapper. As he popped the candy into his mouth, he read the words *Fun Size* printed on the front and back of the wrapper. This usually triggered a smile, but not tonight.

Eddie pulled the scarf over his mouth and stepped closer to the window, peering at them in the café from the corner of his eye. He could see them drinking coffee and going over it again with the manager—the guy who always gave him funny looks when he ordered his usual caffe latte, the guy who liked to flirt with Rosemary. Eddie had seen the woman with blond hair in the papers. She was a prosecutor working the Darlene Lewis murder case. He didn't recognize the man seated across from her, but he seemed young and eager and too intense. Eddie had never liked people who were eager. Mrs. Yap had been eager, and look where it got her.

Two young women and a man passed him on the sidewalk. They were wearing expensive clothing, walking arm in arm, and giggling at him. Obviously, they had stopped off for drinks after work and were popped. Snarling at them as they vanished around the corner, Eddie turned back to the café.

The manager was saying something, and the other guy was writing it down. They were getting up, moving to the door, the manager waving at them. As the door opened, Eddie heard the manager say, "If I remember anything else, I'll let you know. If he comes in again, I'll call the cops."

The man started up the street with the blonde. They were getting away and they had something.

His eyes moved back to the café. The manager was behind the counter, flirting with a female employee as he wiped the counter with a towel.

Eddie turned away and started up the sidewalk, deciding he'd follow the two of them until he could figure out what he was supposed to do. He dug his heels into the pavement, hurrying his step until he was right behind them. He liked the woman's hair and face. As he eyed her figure beneath her coat, he realized he liked that, too. But the man was another story. He had a cell phone to his ear, ignoring the woman and jabbering into his phone on a public street.

They stopped at the corner, waiting for the traffic to pass. Eddie was with them, part of the crowd and playing it casual. Close enough to smell the rich scent of her skin. The man closed his phone and slipped it into his pocket, glancing back at the café and then right at Eddie. Their eyes met. Eddie looked away, adjusting the scarf over his mouth. When the traffic cleared, the man turned back to the blonde and they crossed the street.

Strike three, Eddie thought, keeping close like a shadow and imagining himself a ghost.

"It was Jill," he overheard the man saying to the woman. "Andrews called and says he wants a meeting first thing in the morning. It sounds like something's up."

The woman shrugged as if she didn't know anything about it. But Eddie knew who Andrews was. The district attorney had gotten more coverage in the papers than she had.

He kept his eyes on them as he followed from three feet back. There was something about the guy he didn't trust. Something about him he didn't like. A certain darkness in his eyes. A strong chin and prominent cheekbones. It was the look of someone who had taken a hit in life and was ready for the next one. The look of someone who might turn on him, reprimand him, tell him that he was no good.

Eddie couldn't keep his eyes off him. The more he looked at the man, the more frightened he became. The more he hated him.

They were walking down Seventeenth Street. Then without warning, the man swung a door open and followed the blonde into the ground floor at Liberty Place. The first two floors of One Liberty Place were something like a high-end mall. Eddie followed them in, slowing down his pace and thinking they might be getting something to eat. When he saw them pass through the doors into the building lobby and walk toward the elevators, he realized he was wrong. The man didn't work for the district attorney. He wasn't a cop or even an art critic with an eye in the center of his forehead.

Eddie watched them through the glass, turning away as they stepped into the elevator. He heard the doors close and entered the lobby. The elevator was rising up into the towers above. He could see the numbers over the doors clicking by one after the next. When the elevator stopped on the seventeenth floor, he crossed the lobby and checked the building directory. The sixteenth and seventeenth floors were occupied by Barnett & Stokes. He knew the law firm. He'd read about them in the papers. The man he'd just seen was a defense attorney representing that stupid mailman, Oscar Holmes. So why was he on such good terms with one of the prosecutors?

Eddie didn't know what to do. The manager at the café had obviously recognized him and said something. He could feel his life slipping away. Fame and fortune burning to the ground.

He heard someone shout at him and looked up. It was a guard, staring at him from behind the front desk.

"Can I help you, pal?" the man said.

From the tone of the guard's voice, Eddie could tell the man didn't really want to help him. He looked up and saw the cameras. The moment was being recorded on TV.

"I was looking for a company," Eddie said. "It looks like they've moved."

"Then maybe you should, too."

The guard jerked his hand up and pointed at the door. Eddie took the hint and exited the building. As he walked up the street, he dug his fingers into his pockets fishing for another Milky Way bar or even some leftover chocolate chip morsels. There weren't any left. When he felt his pocketknife, he wrapped his hand around it and realized he was heading back to the café. He smiled beneath his scarf as he thought about the manager flirting with his female employees, even Rosemary. It was a vicious smile. The hidden smile of the world's next genius. Eddie finally knew what he was supposed to do.

Forty-six

Eddie walked into the 7-Eleven on the corner, perusing the aisles for just the right item. Something that would make the act stand out and give it panache. He was an artist. It was the only way he knew.

His eyes stopped on the tubes of Crazy Glue hanging from a rack between the Frito Corn Chips and Ramsey rubber display. An idea formed as he put the two items together in his head. A montage of sorts.

This was it, he decided. Crazy Glue.

He crossed the aisle to the register, and the man behind the counter rang up the order. As Eddie dug into his pocket for his wallet, he noticed the Tootsie Pops stuffed into a jar beside a cigarette display. Even better, they weren't out of grape pops. Eddie had read somewhere that grapes were good for the cardiovascular system. He tried to eat at least one grape-flavored Tootsie Pop a day, but they were hard to find. The word must have gotten out, he figured. He sifted through the bowl and bought all ten pops, stuffing them into his pocket with the Crazy Glue. Then he legged it out of the store to the Honda Accord parked on the far side of the empty lot.

The café manager was waiting for him in the backseat, bound and gagged and looking as if he'd just woken. Eddie could hear him whimpering, trying to talk through the gag and making animal noises. His eyes were the size of silver dollars and particularly expressive, Eddie thought. Like the kind you see drawn in cartoons or the funny papers.

"We'll discuss it later," he said to the man.

Eddie pulled out of the lot. They needed a place to talk. A place to take a high-level meeting with some degree of privacy.

As he turned down Spruce Street, he remembered a park by the river at the very end and checked the clock on the dashboard. It was after midnight, the temperature well below freezing. Not many people would be sitting on the benches enjoying the view of the South Street bridge.

He made a left on Twenty-fifth Street, pulled over, and killed the lights. Then he sat back, letting his eyes adjust to the darkness and unwrapping his first grape Tootsie Pop in three days. The candy would've tasted better if he'd had a little peace and quiet. The grunts and groans coming from the backseat were hard to ignore. So was the smell inside the café manager's car. At first he thought it was stale coffee. But when he turned and saw the man staring at him from the backseat, he realized it was urine. The idiot manager had wet his pants.

Eddie checked the windows. No one was in the park or on the street. When he glanced about at the cars, every one of them appeared empty. This end of the city looked as if it were asleep for the night and safely tucked away in dreamland.

He got out and opened the back door. Yanking the man out of the car, he pushed him into the park. The man stumbled toward a bench, slipping and sliding across the snow.

"Have a seat," Eddie said, pushing him down.

The man stared back at him, tugging on the belt holding his arms in place behind him.

"We're gonna have a little chat," Eddie said. "Then we're gonna have some fun. You're doing the talking. When you're done, I'll decide on the fun. Do you understand what I'm saying?''

The man nodded, shivering in his bones.

''I want to know what you said to them. I want to know what's going on. You ready?''

The man nodded again, eager to please. Eddie removed the gag.

''Please don't do this. Please don't do this.''

The guy was crying. Eddie checked the park. They were alone.

''Stop whining, and tell me what you said to them.''

''I'll tell you everything. Anything. Just leave me alone.''

''Start talking,'' Eddie said, bearing his rotten teeth.

And the man did. He told him everything from a worm's point of view. His name was Harris Carmichael. He'd singled Eddie out and given them an accurate description. They knew he had Rosemary and they were looking for him. Searching him out. Eddie wondered if Carmichael wasn't lying at times, or even using amateur psychology. Carmichael said they didn't know his name, but it was only a matter of time. He thought Eddie should leave him and the girl alone. If he had any brains, it was time to run.

Eddie thought it over, sorting through the man's message to the gist of the deal. But when he looked back, it was too late. Carmichael was snorting like a cornered bull, driving his head into Eddie's stomach and knocking him down.

The blow felt as if he'd been hit by a freight train, and Eddie almost swallowed the Tootsie Pop. As he lay in the snow, the thought of accidently choking to death on his favorite candy brought on the rage. He struggled to catch his breath, watching the café manager scurry into the night with his arms bound behind his back.

Eddie took a deep breath and sprang to his feet. He was fast and agile, and he grabbed Carmichael by the back of his neck and yanked him down on the ground. The man started screaming, yelping. Eddie pushed his face into the snow, holding him down with the weight of his body as he opened the tube of Crazy Glue and pierced the top with the sharp end of the cap. When Carmichael came up for air, Eddie squirted the glue into both nostrils and pinched the man's nose.

Carmichael didn't know what was happening at first. He seemed confused, even stunned by Eddie's creativity. He shook his head back and forth, broke out in a heavy sweat, even shit his fucking pants. As he turned back, he flashed a hard look into Eddie's eyes as if he'd just met a fortune-teller and his fate seemed to dawn on him. Eddie emptied the rest of tube all over Carmichael's lips and pressed them together. Ten seconds passed, then twenty and thirty until he finally let go.

It's what you did to talkers, Eddie thought. You closed their mouths and let go.

Carmichael appeared panic-stricken. Eddie unwrapped the belt, releasing the man's hands and watching him squirm in the snow. He was twisting and turning at Eddie's feet, pulling at his mouth and struggling to rip it open. He was staring at Eddie with those big, cartoon eyes of his. They looked so swollen they might pop or even explode right out of his head. But in the end, his lips were sealed. When Carmichael's face turned blue and he finally stopped moving, Eddie couldn't help but think of a balloon. He opened his pocket-knife, knelt down, and got started. It was a small knife, but it would have to do.

Forty-seven

It had been a strange request. . . .

Worried about Barnett's condition, Teddy had called him last night at the hospital to see how he was making out. Barnett thanked him for the call, but kept it short saying that the pain was getting to him and he still felt like shit. After making a few more calls over a couple of beers, Teddy grabbed a third bottle and went upstairs, checking his voice mail before he closed out the night. Among the list of messages was one left by Alan Andrews himself. The district attorney wanted a meeting in the morning just as Jill said he did. Teddy's first thought had been that the FBI was off to an early start. Rather than wait until morning, agents had approached Andrews the moment Dr. Westbrook called to brief them on the case. But Andrews didn't want to meet at his office. Instead, he'd given Teddy another address. The Museum of Art, he said. Nine sharp.

Teddy entered the Conservation Department, spotting Andrews and Powell with a group of men and women from the museum. The room had the look and feel of a modern laboratory. As he approached them, he noticed several canvases leaning against the wall and recognized them.

They were the work of Oscar Holmes. The paintings Teddy had seen in his client's apartment with Detective Jackson standing over his shoulder. Obviously, Jackson had reported Teddy's interest in the paintings to his boss when he reached his favorite watering hole.

Andrews smiled like a snake and shook Teddy's hand. He had a twinkle in his eye. Powell stood beside him and seemed unusually subdued. Something had happened and Teddy could hear the telltale rattle. Andrews was ready to strike.

"Thanks for fitting us into your busy schedule," Andrews said. "You're five minutes late."

Teddy ignored the hit. Then Andrews introduced him to the curator of the Modern Contemporary Department, two conservators, and the conservation photographer. From the looks on their faces, it was clear to Teddy that he was the odd man out. Everyone there knew something he didn't.

He glanced about the lab, taking in the room in quick bites. He noticed one of Holmes's paintings on an easel set before a high-resolution video camera. Behind Andrews he saw a long row of light tables covered with sheets of X-ray film.

"Why don't we get started," Andrews said to the curator.

They were standing beside a computer. One of the conservators sat down at the keyboard and clicked open a window. As everyone moved in for a closer look at the monitor, the curator filled them in on what they had done over the last two days.

"X rays were taken of each of the paintings and scanned into the computer," she said. "What you're looking at is a negative image of the surface of the canvas."

Teddy studied the black-and-white image on the monitor, realizing it was the same painting he'd seen on the easel. A peaceful landscape. A view of rolling hills with the shadows of a man and woman stretching over a field.

"But there's an image underneath," the curator said.

As if on cue, the conservator at the keyboard clicked an option on the menu. Teddy watched as the peaceful landscape began to fade and a second image gradually appeared. In spite of the curator's gentle voice and easy manner, Teddy felt a whip of fear snap against his spine right between the shoulder blades. It was a nude. A young woman with blond hair who looked as if she were being consumed by her emotions. There was a sadness to the work. An oppressive stillness.

Teddy didn't recognize the model's face. As he thought about the missing persons bulletins tacked to the wall in Nash's office, he noticed a resemblance but wrote it off as a coincidence and matter of style.

"Let's see another," Andrews said.

Teddy eyed the district attorney, then looked back at the monitor. The snake was still rattling its tail. It hadn't struck yet.

A second black-and-white image appeared on the screen. Within a few moments, another pastoral setting gave way to a second nude. Teddy noted the blond hair, the common bone structure, and realized it was the same model. She was wilted on the floor, the melancholy as overwhelming as the first painting they'd seen. But the work was also beautiful, like the warmth of a fire burning under the mantel on a string of rainy-day afternoons.

"I believe there's a third," Andrews said. "This one in particular caught my eye."

Teddy winced at the district attorney's smooth delivery. Andrews was enjoying the moment, his slickness coming off like grease. Teddy tried to get a grip on himself, but it didn't work. As an image of a slow-moving river painted in moonlight began to fade, he recognized the face, the body, even the tattoos rising to the surface.

It was another nude. But this time he knew the model. It was Darlene Lewis.

Teddy staggered back as if he'd been hit, and everyone turned. He looked away, moved to the light tables, took in the sheets of X-ray film as he caught his breath. He tried to remember what Holmes said the first night they met. Darlene

Lewis used to let him look at her. But it hadn't been about sex. Holmes had been studying her body for his painting.

"I'd like to thank you," Andrews said in a quiet voice.

Teddy could feel the district attorney standing right behind him now. He held a file in his hand. He opened it and tossed it on the light table.

"I spoke with your client last night," Andrews said. "He confessed to the murders of Darlene Lewis, Valerie Kram, and ten other women. This is a copy of his statement. You'll notice his signature on page ten."

Teddy felt the snake's teeth pierce his skin, the venom freely entering his bloodstream. "You can't talk to Holmes without permission from his attorney," he said. "You broke the law, Andrews. This paper isn't worth shit."

"But I did have permission from his attorney," Andrews said. "Not you, Teddy Mack. Holmes's lead attorney. Barnett offered his advice and consent. He listened to the confession over the telephone."

It felt like a knockout punch. As if he'd been tossed from a moving car and dragged over the concrete at high speed. Teddy paged through Holmes's statement, unable to read it. When he turned the statement over, he froze. On the bottom of the file was a copy of their profile. The profile he'd sent to Barnett in his hospital room. Teddy's note to the man was still attached.

"Apparently you thought the killer was an artist," Andrews said. "Thanks for making my case."

"He's an artist, Andrews. He's just not this artist. You've bungled another one. You've got the wrong man."

The district attorney chuckled. "You're young, Teddy Mack. You've got a lot to learn. Better luck next time. Barnett needs verification that the X rays exist. Next time you talk to him, tell him what you've seen."

Teddy felt the poison enter his heart and shoot through his body. He flashed a hard look at Andrews, hoping he had enough inner strength not to strike the man. The district attorney couldn't hold his gaze and stepped back. Teddy shook his head, still stunned. He thought of Holmes's fragile mental state and knew his client would've agreed to anything if he was told it might stop his nightmares. He thought of Barnett selling them out and betraying them in order to make the deal. When he glanced at Powell, he saw her wipe something away from beneath her eye and turn away.

Forty-eight

Teddy sat in the museum coffee shop, mulling over the aftermath of the explosion and filled with self-doubt. Andrews had a complete case now. He had the physical evidence linking Holmes to two murders. A witness who saw Holmes running away from the Lewis house. A painting of Darlene Lewis in the nude. And now he had a confession. Alan Andrews was a slime bag, but he had everything he needed to put Holmes away for the rest of the man's life.

Barnett's betrayal was a different story. Teddy still couldn't believe what Barnett had done. He thought he knew the man. He thought he'd been a good judge of character his entire life. Yet there it was in Holmes's statement. Teddy looked away from the file Andrews had given him, wondering what kind of man would sell out his own brother-in-law. A member of his family who needed him.

He felt sick.

Powell entered the coffee shop and gazed at him from the doorway. After a moment, she stepped up to the counter, ordered a cup of decaf, and sat down on the other side of the table.

"You okay?" she asked.

Teddy nodded even though he wasn't. He wasn't sure who was worse, Andrews or Barnett.

"I didn't know about this, Teddy. Not until this morning. Alan wanted to keep it a surprise."

He gave her a look. He believed her.

Still, the implications of the deal between Andrews and Barnett stabbed at his soul. The confession meant that the FBI would be out before they even got in. He could see Rosemary Gibb modeling for the painter with bad teeth who liked to order caffe lattes. The girl trying to hold on with no one looking for her. Time running out, and Rosemary not making it. The killer having his way with her, doing things to her with the knife, her lifeless body submerged in water when he was through.

"What about the manager at the coffee house?" he said. "He wasn't describing Holmes."

"No, he wasn't," she said. "But Holmes was in prison when Rosemary turned up missing."

"Did you mention it to Andrews?"

She nodded. "He doesn't think they're related. People turn up missing every day. Besides, the confession changes everything."

Teddy lowered his eyes.

"I know it's hard," she said. "You gave it a good shot. I've gotta get back to the office. But think it over, Teddy. The evidence is overwhelming. Read your client's statement. I'll give you a call this afternoon. Maybe we can meet somewhere and talk."

She hadn't touched her coffee. She started to get up, then sat down again.

"I did a little checking on my own," she said. "The night Barnett was run over, Andrews attended a fund-raiser."

Teddy came up for air. "What about Michael Jackson?"

"He went with him," she said. "He likes free food."

Forty-nine

Teddy pushed the doctor out of the room, slammed the door shut, and flipped the lock. When he heard the doctor start pounding with his fists from the other side, he ignored it and turned to face Barnett. The window curtains were drawn, and Barnett was still confined to his bed in the darkness. He looked frightened, but he couldn't move—his legs held together by that array of metal pins and hardware.

Teddy knew he should have gone straight to Nash and told him about Holmes's confession. But Barnett had acted something like a father toward him ever since Teddy joined the firm. A mentor. Barnett had taken a special interest in his career, guiding him through his introduction to the legal profession. Teddy had trusted the man and admired him and made the mistake of emulating him. Now he was nowhere.

The banging stopped, followed by shouting from the hallway. Teddy moved to the window, jerking the curtain open and flooding the room with light.

"What are you gonna do?" Barnett said, shaking.

Teddy looked at the IVs in the man's arm. He felt like pulling them out, watching Barnett squirm his way into the void where he belonged. He glanced at the chair, but didn't sit down. For a moment he thought about his college loans, but only long enough to count up his debt. One hundred and ninety thousand dollars. Teddy didn't care anymore.

"I closed the deal," Barnett managed. "The death penalty's off the table. Holmes will get the care he needs. He'll live, for Christ's sake."

"Stop pretending that this is about helping Holmes," Teddy said. "This is about you. It's always been about you."

"What are you talking about?"

"Your little secret," Teddy said. "Your brother-in-law. The minute the story showed up in the papers, you folded. You don't even care if he's innocent or not. All you care about is you."

"Keep your voice down."

"Are you afraid they'll hear me? They already know. Everybody does. The Veggie Butcher and Jim Barnett are brothers."

Barnett cringed. "Who the hell do you think you're talking to?"

"I came here to ask you the same question. Who the hell do you think you are?"

"My name's Jim Barnett," he said through clinched teeth. "And I've got a reputation to uphold."

"You sure do. That's why you sold Holmes out from the beginning. You were embarrassed. You made the deal thinking you might contain the secret. Holmes never had a chance. Not with a brother like you."

"Stop calling him my brother," Barnett shouted. "He's always been strange. He's an oddball. He's a freak."

Teddy gave Barnett a long look, deciding he'd let what was just said pass for now. "How did you convince Andrews to make the deal?" he asked.

"It was easy. They did the X rays yesterday. When Andrews told me what they found underneath the paintings, I told him about the profile you and Nash put together. I think it caught Andrews by surprise. He seemed shocked by it and wanted to see it. He said he thought he needed a confession. We worked the deal out in five minutes. Holmes confessed in less than two.''

"Thanks for letting me know.''

Barnett looked away and seemed to shrink. "That was Andrews's idea,'' he said after a moment. "I needed to know that what he told me about the paintings was true.''

Teddy grimaced, burying the scope of the betrayal as deep as it would go. "So now you're saved,'' he said. "You can host another treasure hunt and gloat over your picture in the society pages. If I were you I'd hire someone who knows how to handle the press. They'll need to turn you into a victim. Tell the whole story from your point of view. You can handle the interviews from here. A picture of Jim Barnett in his hospital bed should go a long way. Holmes hurt everyone. Even you.''

"Larry Stokes already has someone in mind,'' Barnett said. "You should know better than me why I did everything I could to keep the story from getting out. Look what happened to you after your father's arrest.''

It hung there. Teddy standing motionless.

"That's right,'' Barnett said. "I know all about your goddamn father. That's why I asked you to help me with Holmes. You're a loser, Teddy. You don't get it. Wake up and smell the roses. Your father's arrest for murder ruined you and the reputation of your family. No matter what the truth was, is, or will be, you will always be Teddy Mack, the son of the architect on the Main Line who murdered his business partner. I asked for your help not because I thought you might bring something to the case. How could you at your age? I asked for your help because I thought you'd toe the line just like every other asshole who's running from the truth. But you didn't. You couldn't. Everything you did made things worse. Now get out and toe the line.''

The door burst open. Teddy was lunging for the bed when two security guards grabbed him from behind and tackled him down to the floor.

Fifty

The aftermath. The done deal. It had been so ugly.

Teddy sat at the jury table and stared at the pictures of the missing look-alikes tacked to the wall. They seemed so far away. The confession changed things. Whether it was true or not, Holmes's statement and signature on the document had a certain weight about it.

"Would you like a cup of coffee?" Nash asked from his desk.

"I'm okay."

"What about something stronger?"

Teddy shook his head, then turned to the door as Gail Emerson, Nash's assistant, entered the room with a cup of coffee. Her eyes were puffy and she appeared as upset as they were. She set the cup on the table before Teddy, wouldn't take no for an answer, and gave Nash a worried look as she left the room. Teddy liked Gail, and sipped the coffee. It tasted fresh and hot, and he appreciated the kind gesture.

Nash cleared his throat. "Barnett shouldn't have said those things to you, Teddy. I'm sorry. Did he fire you?"

"I don't know yet. He's still bedridden. They'll need

someone to do the paperwork and sit at the table with Holmes. I'm not sure anyone at the firm really wants their picture taken beside a serial killer.''

Nash flashed a warm smile. ''I'd say you're right about that.''

''What about Rosemary?'' Teddy asked.

''As far as I'm concerned, nothing's changed. We already knew something was going on between Holmes and Darlene Lewis. Now we know what it was. The confession, based on the man's state of mind, isn't even worth reading. But we're alone. Westbrook called when the bureau got the news from the DA's office. He's upset. He said he'll do anything he can to help, but it will have to remain unofficial now.''

''We know the profile's accurate,'' Teddy said. ''From what the manager at the café told us, this guy with bad teeth followed Rosemary out the door the night she disappeared. Her gym bag wasn't found in her apartment. We know she never made it home.''

Nash got up from his desk and sat down with Teddy at the jury table. He'd been collecting press clippings on Alan Andrews since he began researching the DA's past. He laid several of them out on the table, one beside the next, then bummed a cigarette from Teddy's pack. He'd never done that before.

''What do you think of this?'' Nash asked. ''What's your opinion?''

Teddy counted six clippings. He scanned the copy long enough to get the gist.

''Andrews was an overzealous prosecutor,'' he said. ''Judges complained, but he ran a hard race and became the district attorney. He wasn't liked much. Still, the office generated a lot of prosecutions and crime was down.''

''What else?''

Teddy thought it over. ''It looks like the press tolerated him. Judges were relieved he wouldn't be appearing in court as often, if ever, as long as he held the office.''

''Then what?''

''You hit Andrews for sending the wrong man to his

death," Teddy said. "All his faults were in the papers again. But it didn't last because Holmes was arrested that very day. People got scared. The city was being terrorized by a maniac. As far as they were concerned, Alan Andrews saved them and any mistakes he made in his past were forgiven. So what if the wrong man got the needle. That's the way people think. The guy was probably a lowlife and deserved to die for something else he'd done."

Nash gazed at Andrews's clippings, his eyes more dilated than usual, more sad. "You have to admit that it's remarkable though. His resurrection, I mean. I thought he'd be booted out of office when my workshop made its findings public. Now it looks like he'll be rewarded. He'll become the city's next mayor; then who knows? Maybe even governor. Whether you like him or not, he's a survivor. You have to give him credit for that."

"What about your workshop next semester? What about the other cases you're working on?"

"They're old," Nash said, lowering his voice. "Evidence is scarce. In some cases contaminated or even destroyed. Money's an issue as well." He blew smoke toward the window, watching the sunlight give the cloud form. "It's an uphill battle," he said. "It'll take time."

Nash became silent. Teddy watched him smoke the cigarette for a moment, then grabbed his briefcase and stood.

"There's just one thing I don't understand," Teddy said before leaving.

Nash looked at him without saying anything. He seemed tired. Like Teddy, he needed a break.

"I was thinking about it on the drive in from the hospital," Teddy said. "I know why my boss wanted to make the deal. All he cares about are his own press clippings and what his neighbors think. I even understand why the district attorney thinks Holmes is guilty. If I were Andrews, I might think it, too. Let's face it, Andrews still has the facts on his side. The case is so strong, I have doubts about what we're doing every day. But look at these clippings. Just these few clippings tell a different story, and I don't get it."

"What part of the story don't you understand?"

"Why Andrews made the deal," Teddy said.

A moment passed. Nash had a faraway look going in his eyes, as if Teddy had found another fault line in the rocks. A crack in the mountain no one else had seen.

"Why stop the headlines?" Teddy said, pointing at them on the table. "Why make a deal that would end this, especially when everyone on the street wants Holmes dead? If he'd refused to plea the case, the trial and headlines would've lasted until his election. Now they're gonna go away. Every blood-and-guts idiot in the city is gonna be pissed off at him. It's not in Andrews's interest to make this deal. It doesn't make sense."

Nash took a second cigarette and handed over the pack, appearing stunned.

"No, it doesn't," was all he could say.

Fifty-one

He knew the word was out the moment he entered the lobby. He knew it wasn't good. Jill filled him in as soon as he reached his office.

Teddy's stay at the firm was finished.

He'd be kept on to see Holmes through the process, just as he thought, because no one else wanted to be associated with a serial killer. No one in the firm wanted their picture taken beside the Veggie Butcher. Once Holmes pled guilty and received his sentence of life without parole, Teddy would receive his notice. Jill had gotten the news from Barnett's assistant, Jackie, who'd overheard Larry Stokes on the phone. Stokes had already written the termination notice and would keep it in his desk until Holmes was admitted into a psychiatric facility for the criminally insane. According to Jackie, Stokes told Barnett that he never liked Teddy and was secretly glad to see him go. She couldn't hear the entire conversation, but thought it had something to do with Teddy's father and the reputation of his family.

Teddy sat down at his desk. Brooke Jones passed the door

without looking inside, but he caught the faint smile branded
on her profile.

He opened his briefcase, found the aspirin, and chugged
two pills down with bottled water. As he sat back, he went
over the events of the day in his head. He remembered the
way it had ended at the art museum this morning with
Andrews on his back. He'd been too upset to really notice
what was going on at the time. Andrews had just nailed
Teddy, yet the man couldn't keep eye contact. Andrews had
looked away like maybe he was nervous. Like something
else was on his mind.

Why did he do the deal? It didn't make sense.

Andrews should have insisted on a trial. Fought for it
until the bitter end. Instead, Barnett had said it was easy.
The district attorney agreed almost immediately. The entire
conversation only lasted five minutes.

Why?

Barnett read the profile and initiated the call. Andrews
spoke first and told Barnett about the nudes that Holmes
had painted over that included Darlene Lewis. Then Barnett
brought up the profile Teddy and Nash had created and said
that they were looking for an artist. A painter or sculptor.

Teddy wondered if it wasn't the profile. But what? There
had to be a reason why Andrews would risk taking heat
from the public to do the deal.

He looked at Jill, staring back at him from the computer.

"You think you could do me a favor?" he said.

"Sure."

"Pull up Andrews's past cases for the last ten years. Sort
them by verdict and print them out. All I need is the list
and a summary. But do a second printing and sort them by
the crime. Is that doable?"

"It's easy," she said.

Her eyes flashed toward the door. Larry Stokes entered
the room without noticing her. His face was shut down, his
appearance as lifelike as a body in an open casket.

"I'd like to have a word with you," he said quietly. "In
my office."

Teddy shot Jill a look and followed the man out of the room. They walked down the hall to the other side of the floor without exchanging a single word. When they reached his office, Stokes stepped aside and let Teddy enter first. Teddy didn't notice the older man sitting on the couch until the door closed.

"Have a seat," Stokes said, pointing to the chair before his desk.

Stokes hadn't bothered to introduce Teddy to the man on the couch. Teddy did as he was told and took the chair. There was a mirror behind the desk, and he could see the man staring at his back. The man knew who Teddy was. He was sure of it. Yet Stokes had no intention of introducing them.

Stokes leaned across his desk, folding his hands. "Your future at the firm of Barnett and Stokes is in jeopardy," he said. "How you conduct yourself over the next few weeks will determine your fate. Is that clear, young man?"

Teddy knew his future had already been determined, his fate sealed. It was in an envelope in Stokes's desk awaiting delivery. He checked the mirror and saw the strange man staring at his back. The man looked like he was in his sixties. His hair was almost white. His face narrow. His eyes an arctic blue. Teddy wondered if he was one of Stokes's buddies from the club. Some idiot rich guy with good breeding who wanted to witness this moment for laughs.

"Is that clear?" Stokes repeated.

"Perfectly," Teddy said.

"In return for your good behavior, no charges will be filed against you for attempting to assault Jim Barnett at the hospital this morning. You have my word."

Stokes was a stupid man. Teddy could see it in his eyes. His capped teeth, and the gold ring. The seal from a yacht club on his blue blazer. And his threat didn't sting because Teddy already knew it was a lie. He was immune.

"I believe Jim mentioned something to you about toeing the line," Stokes said after a moment. "That's what we do here. We do what we're told. We do it with sincerity and in good conscience. We do what we believe is right. We carry a certain standard at this firm and . . .''

Teddy stopped listening to the bullshit. It was the man's stump speech. The one he used with new clients. When he thought Stokes was finished, he got up and left the room.

Fifty-two

He found Jill in his office by the printer. She'd pulled the district attorney's cases for the past ten years. There were hundreds, thousands—the printer spewing out so much paper, all he could think about were dead trees.

"What did Stokes say?" Jill asked.

Teddy shrugged. "I'm toast, but I'm not supposed to know it yet. He gave me a pep talk."

He sat down at the computer, checking the list on the monitor. They'd made a mistake. Because Andrews was the district attorney, the search parameters were including every case the office had handled since the election.

"We need to stop this thing," he said.

Jill leaned over his shoulder, grabbed the mouse, and hit CANCEL. When the printer continued eating up trees, she shut the machines down to clear the memory and rebooted.

"What's wrong?" she said.

"I want to narrow the search down to cases Andrews handled on his own as a prosecutor."

"What are you looking for?"

"Beats me," he said. "All I know is we don't have time to look through this much paper."

They switched places. Jill changed the search parameters. Within a few minutes the printer was spitting out more paper again. There were two hundred and thirty-seven cases. It still seemed overwhelming, but Teddy grabbed the printout, sat at his desk, and got started. He had two copies of the list. The first was sorted by verdict, the second by crime.

Teddy started with the second list, weeding out the misdemeanors and concentrating on felonies. There were only seventy-five. When he cross-checked them by verdict, three stood out. Each case occurred within the first two years of Andrews's promotion to homicide in the district attorney's office. Each case was a loss.

The first involved a man accused of murdering his wife. She'd been shot once in the chest. Medics couldn't revive her, and she was pronounced dead at the scene of the crime. The man claimed it was an accident. While cleaning a gun, his wife stepped through the doorway just as the weapon fired. Although he said he didn't know the weapon was loaded, he was a gun collector and should have. Andrews figured he was lying and prosecuted the case based on interviews with neighbors who heard the couple arguing earlier in the day. The medical examiner agreed. The woman's death only required a single bullet because it was a bull's-eye aimed directly at her heart. But Andrews was a young assistant district attorney at the time. He lacked experience in jury selection. He loaded the box with women, thinking they would sympathize with the victim. What he didn't count on was the defendant. He was a lady's man. Smooth, handsome, even sympathetic. What Andrews didn't realize was that every woman in the jury had fallen for the guy. They couldn't keep their eyes off him. When the man took the witness chair and spoke in his own defense, he worked the women in the jury like Gato Barbieri making it with a saxophone. He spoke of his love for his wife, his devotion, how much he missed her. Wiping tears from his eyes, he said his life was ruined and didn't care what happened to him now. The jury bought it, and found the man not guilty. Once he was free and clear, Andrews learned that the man

had been having an affair for six months with a younger
woman who lived down the street. She'd moved in the day
after his release from prison.

The second case involved an armed robbery at a conve-
nience store that ended in homicide. Although the incident
occurred after midnight, three people witnessed the shooting.
A young man wearing a ski mask walked up to the counter
with his gun drawn. Pocketing the cash from the register,
he shot the clerk four times before he fled. As he ran across
the parking lot, he pulled the mask off and three people got
a good look at his face. The murder was even recorded
on videotape from a camera mounted behind the counter.
Andrews thought the case was a slam dunk. He figured he
couldn't lose, but eventually did. The defendant was a gang
member. The names of the witnesses, a matter of record
due to their testimony at the preliminary hearing. Fear and
intimidation flourished. One by one, the witnesses backed
out. And the tape was inconclusive. Because of the ski mask
and poor video quality, identifying the murderer proved
impossible. Andrews took the loss, and another murderer
was set free.

But it was the third case that must have really gotten to
the man. As Teddy read the summary, he wondered how
Andrews managed his climb to the top.

It was a brutal case, though much less clear than the
others. A teenager stood accused of shooting his girlfriend
when he learned she was pregnant. The gun was never
found. The crime occurred in an alley off the street at night.
Andrews had an eyewitness who saw them standing beneath
a streetlight. A middle-aged woman who heard a gunshot
and ran into the boy as he tried to flee. Another sure thing.
Another case a young Alan Andrews thought he couldn't
lose. Even better, the boy couldn't afford to defend himself.
Instead, an attorney had been appointed by the court.
Andrews had learned his lesson by now, stacking the jury
with men who were either grandfathers or fathers of young
girls. The defense claimed the boy was innocent. The girl
had been shot by someone else no one had seen. The police

couldn't produce the murder weapon and gunshot residue wasn't found on the boy's hands. Andrews countered that the boy ran away, ditching the weapon with plenty of time to wash his hands. The defense said the boy ran to get help and introduced testimony from a series of character witnesses. From all accounts, the boy loved the girl and planned to marry her. He'd attended the girl's pregnancy exam with her doctor, but couldn't be with her for the results. A friend of the boy testified that they'd talked it over. The boy was hoping she was pregnant and wanted more than one because he'd grown up an only child.

But Andrews had his eyewitness. His sure thing. The middle-aged woman took the stand. She'd heard the shot and seen the boy's face. She claimed he practically ran into her.

When Andrews was through, the defense attorney spent an hour going over the details in cross-examination. How sure she was and why. Then he spent another hour drilling her on the boy's physical description. His face. What color his eyes were, their shape and size. And what about his nose, his mouth and hair? The defense attorney was blocking the witness's view of the defendant. Every time she tried to peek around him, he'd step in her way. The attorney said he wanted to know what the defendant looked like on the night of the murder. Not now.

What Andrews didn't know, nor anyone else, was that the defense attorney had hired an artist to sit in the courtroom. A young woman who taught at the College of Art. She was sketching the face based on the witness's description. When the testimony seemed complete, the defense attorney showed the picture to the witness and asked if this was the man who fled the crime scene. The woman said yes. She was emphatic about it. That picture was him. Then the attorney passed the drawing to the jury for a look. It wasn't the defendant at all. The likeness wasn't even close.

Teddy's eyes rose above the summary, searching out the defense attorney's name. It was a man he'd never heard of, and this surprised him. His work was impressive and stood out.

Teddy set the stack of summaries down. Disappointed that he hadn't found anything relevant to the Holmes case, he let his mind wander. Three trials. Three losses. Andrews had licked his wounds after that and turned his life around. Become more shrewd and found a way to win. Still, there had to be something. A reason why Andrews wanted to plea the Holmes case away. Andrews needed to get something in return for the deal. There had to be some kind of trade-off.

Teddy looked at Jill, typing something into the computer.

"What are you doing?" he asked.

"I found a Web site that publishes political contributions," she said. "Andrews already has a lot of money in his war chest. The election's more than a year off."

"You mean the names are there? The contributors?"

Jill nodded.

"Read them off," he said. "All I need are last names."

Teddy grabbed the printout. As Jill read the names aloud, he searched through Andrews's cases. There were more than three hundred contributors, and it took time to page through the sheets of paper. But after an hour, he'd found a match. It was the only one. A case that Andrews had handled a year before he ran for district attorney. It wasn't a felony case. Not even a misdemeanor. It was a case in which Andrews had decided not to prosecute. Instead, the accused was sent to a psychiatric facility for treatment. His name was Edward Trisco III.

Teddy glanced at the summary. Apparently, Edward was an aspiring artist with a drug problem.

Fifty-three

He bolted up Seventeenth Street, zigzagging his way to Benny's Cafe Blue at a full run. He had a photograph in his pocket of Edward Trisco III printed off the Internet. There had been a lot of pictures of Edward Trisco. More than they needed.

The Trisco family was a brand name.

They owned several technology companies and had a major interest in one of the state's largest banks. Their political influence was substantial. Once Jill had a name, she typed it into the search window on the election Web site. The list that appeared was up to date and included every contribution the family had made over the past three presidential campaigns. Most of their individual contributions went to conservative candidates running for every type of office in every state in the nation. But the big money, some checks written for a million dollars or more, went directly to the national committee in Washington.

When Jill isolated their contributions to Alan Andrews, Teddy realized what a fool he'd been. Andrews hadn't sent Edward Trisco to a psychiatric facility because the boy needed help and it may or may not have been the right thing to do.

It had been a pass.

Andrews received his first political contribution from the family two days after Edward's arrest. A check in the amount of two hundred and fifty thousand dollars followed one week later. It was made out to the state party. Teddy knew all about soft money. Frank Miles, a media consultant from Washington, had been a guest lecturer on campus last year. The quarter million would have been laundered through the system. Once the money disappeared, it would have made a surprise return in the form of TV ads against Andrews's opponent.

But this wasn't about money. This was about Edward Trisco III. An aspiring artist who'd kidnapped a model. The model managed to escape and was unharmed. She hadn't pressed charges. When Teddy finished reading the stories that appeared in the newspapers, it felt like lightning shooting through his veins.

He saw the café ahead. In spite of the traffic, he charged across the street and ripped open the door. As he hurried to the counter, he looked for the manager, Harris Carmichael, but didn't see him. A young woman he recognized from last night stood behind the counter. Her hair was black and appeared dyed, the color of her eyes lost behind a pair of blue-tinted glasses set in heavy black frames.

"Where's Harris?" Teddy said.

She gave him a look and appeared frightened. Harris Carmichael must have filled her in after Teddy and Powell left last night.

"We don't know," she said, glancing at the kid mixing coffees on the far side of the counter. "He hasn't shown up yet."

"What time does he usually come in?"

"He opens the place," she said. "Melvin called me this morning. I came down with the keys as soon as I could."

"Did you try calling him?" Teddy asked.

"Nonstop," she said. "No answer."

Teddy could feel the pinpricks moving up his neck and through his scalp. He pulled the photo out of his pocket and unfolded it.

''I need to know if you've ever seen this man before,'' he said.

She looked at the photograph of Edward Trisco III. She was staring at Trisco's face, trying to remember. Teddy slid the paper across the counter and she leaned closer.

''He looks familiar,'' she said. ''But people come in every day. He's not a regular.''

Teddy knew it would be tough. If what Harris Carmichael had said was true, Trisco sat at the corner table with his back to the room so that he could watch Rosemary Gibb work out at her club across the street.

''Do you remember serving anyone here that seemed strange?'' Teddy said.

''We get a lot of those.''

''What about bad teeth?''

Her eyes pitched back to the photo and something clicked. Dread washed over her face.

''He comes in at night,'' she said. ''He smells like paint.''

''Where does he sit?''

The rush of adrenaline hit Teddy between the eyes as she pointed at the table by the window.

''There,'' she said. ''With his back turned.''

Fifty-four

The hills were snow covered and blushed out in a deep red from the afternoon sun sinking below the horizon. Splotches of purple marked the shadows. As Teddy gazed out the window from the passenger seat in Nash's Lexus, the landscape appeared in a deep sleep and heavily bruised.

They were making the drive out to the Haverhills Psychiatric Facility. The institution was located about five miles south of Bryn Mawr Hospital in the suburbs. Teddy turned away from the sight of new homes under construction. The fields were gone. The woods. And he didn't want to think about his father right now. Instead, he watched Nash launch the car through the winding two-lane road at high speed. The engine made a rushing sound. It felt as if they were burning jet fuel.

Teddy had called Powell on his way over to Nash's office. He didn't tell her about identifying Edward Trisco at the café. He felt uneasy about it, but he didn't tell her. The DA's office still had Holmes's confession. As far as they were concerned, Holmes was the one. And Teddy felt he needed a better understanding of just what Alan Andrews had done before he said anything to her. He kept the conversation short, telling her that Harris Carmichael was missing. Still, he'd gotten the reaction he'd been hoping for. Powell wouldn't be waiting the usual forty-eight hours to see if the man turned up. The search for Carmichael would begin immediately.

Nash pulled into the entrance and gave the guard at the booth their names. As the cast-iron gate opened, they started up the long drive. Teddy looked at the buildings set on top of the hill in the day's last light. Although it was a modern facility, the institution had been operating for over a hundred years. And the main building, now relegated to administration offices, looked as if it had been around for even longer. There was a spooky feel to the place. At first he thought it might be because the Haverhills Psychiatric Facility was a madhouse for the criminally insane and looked the part. But it was more than that. Trisco had stayed here. Like tracking an animal in the field, they had their first sighting and were in the hunt.

Nash parked before the main building and they walked toward the entrance. The air was ice-cold, their breath venting from their bodies in quick puffs. Nash pointed to a wing of the hospital that looked as if it was new. Not the building itself, but the words blasted into the concrete along the side. The wing had been dedicated to the Trisco family.

"Now we know how he got out," Nash said with his brow raised.

Teddy took it in stride, and they entered the lobby. In spite of the hour, a receptionist sat behind the front desk. He was a middle-aged man wearing a flannel shirt and wool vest. The glint in his eye appeared just off center. Teddy wondered if he wasn't a patient.

"We're here to see Doctor Gleason," Nash said. "He's expecting us."

The man flashed a big grin like he was off his rocker, then looked up the psychiatrist's extension on a piece of paper that was laminated in a plastic cover. Within five minutes they were in the doctor's office with the door closed.

Dr. Gleason looked to be about forty. He was a thin-boned man with blond, wavy hair and a mustache. Although he wore glasses, Teddy thought his clear brown eyes looked wounded. They shook hands and greeted each other. As they sat down, Teddy spotted Trisco's medical records on the psychiatrist's desk. Gleason was a colleague of Westbrook, and had worked with the FBI in the past. Nash was about to take advantage of that friendship. But there were political issues to consider, particularly in light of the new wing financed by the Trisco family.

"I'm talking to you, but I'm really not," Gleason said. "If I'm ever asked, I'll deny it. At least until you've got something more concrete. Westbrook said you'd play ball."

"We understand your position completely," Nash said. "And we're more than grateful for your help."

Gleason appeared satisfied and obviously wanted to do whatever he could. He picked up Trisco's medical records, opening the file on his lap.

"Edward Trisco walked through the front door five years ago thinking he was J. Edgar Hoover and asking where the ladies' room was. He entered our drug treatment program immediately. He had the usual problems that go with drug abuse. Paranoia. Depression. After six weeks, he was clean but his symptoms remained. I began to wonder if his problems weren't more than drugs, but I couldn't be sure."

"What was he using?" Nash asked.

"Edward liked everything. He wasn't a casual user, and his brain damage was measurable. That's what made it difficult to sort out. I kept hoping he'd bounce back, but the paranoia remained."

"When was he released?" Teddy asked.

"Two years after his admission. The depression eased some. His mood swings evened out. The chief administrator concluded his behavior was caused by drug abuse and signed his release without my consent. According to the hospital, he was better now and fit to live in the world again."

"What were your conclusions?" Nash asked.

Gleason thought it over. "Where did you park?" he asked after a moment.

"Out front," Nash said.

"Then you saw the new wing. It opened last year."

Gleason didn't need to flesh out the details. They'd known it before they even walked in. Edward Trisco had received another pass. First from Andrews, then from the institution's chief administrator.

"Edward's problems had nothing to do with drugs," Gleason said. "He used the drugs to forget what happened in his childhood. I never found out exactly what his problems were. Just as I was beginning to get somewhere, the paperwork went through and he was released."

"What about the woman he kidnapped?" Teddy asked. "Did he ever talk about her?"

Gleason winced. "That's even more troubling," he said. "He was arrested on charges of kidnapping and sexual assault. Then what happened became less clear. Drugs were found in the girl's system as well. Maybe he kidnapped her, but maybe they'd met at a party and it didn't work out. That was the story anyway. But I've spent many hours in therapy with Edward Trisco. He told me himself that he held her against her will and raped her. His parents gave the girl a lot of money. In return, she didn't press charges and refused to testify. She didn't talk."

"Was there any remorse?" Nash asked.

Gleason shook his head. "He was cocky about it. He knew his parents would bail him out. I guess they'd done it before. Because the charges were dropped, there was no need to appear before a judge in order to win his release."

"When he wasn't in therapy, did he socialize with the others?" Nash asked.

"No. He was a loner. He spent a lot of time reading."

"About what?"

"Artists mostly."

"Anyone in particular?"

Gleason passed the file over to Nash, pointing to his notes and fidgeting in his seat. No question about it, the psychiatrist was deeply concerned about his role in the payoff that led to Trisco's release.

"I think it's right there," he said.

Teddy leaned in for a closer look, searching out the notation the psychiatrist had jotted down in his file so many years ago. When he read the name, he turned to Nash and kept quiet as the horror took root and forged ahead. Their eyes met.

Edward Trisco had been reading about Michelangelo. He'd found the dead room.

Fifty-five

He felt the ping in his dick and gave it a hard squeeze. He needed to take a leak real bad.

Eddie Trisco backed into the alley just off Sixteenth Street, killed the lights, and looked at the entrance to the parking garage at One Liberty Place through the stream of cars and people moving up and down the sidewalks. It was just after midnight. He'd spent most of the day in the car, but it couldn't be helped. This morning he'd woken to a series of warning sirens in his head, whipped up another scenario in first-draft form, and spent the early afternoon keeping an eye on Benny's Cafe Blue just in case.

His dedication paid off.

At half past three he'd seen the kid run into the place, show that ugly woman behind the counter a picture of someone, then shoot out the door like a human cannonball in a circus act. It was the same kid he'd seen in the café last night with the woman from the district attorney's office. The attorney he'd followed to One Liberty Place. The DA had arrested that stupid mailman, yet the kid with gusto was still nosing around. Still asking questions and trying to fuck up his life.

But Eddie had his name. His number.

The manager at the café had told him all he needed to know the previous night. On his knees and shaking before he shit his pants. Harris Carmichael had been a real talker. Spilled it out in the snow as Eddie filled in the dots and thought about what to do. It hadn't required a knife. Carmichael had died like a talker with his lips sealed. The Crazy Glue had been a nice touch. But when it was over, Eddie used a knife anyway. He couldn't help himself. He was mad at it. He hated it. Over and over again he went at the thing until he spotted the first two wharf rats moving in from the river and his mind cleared.

Teddy Mack. He knew his name and had his number.

He'd followed him from the café back to his office this afternoon. Watched him change cars just off Penn campus like he knew what he was doing and knew just where to go. And it seemed as though he really did. Eddie followed the Lexus out to the fun house on the hill in the suburbs. The place where they locked the doors at night and let you scream. After about an hour, the Lexus shot down the hill and through the gate, speeding back to town.

Eddie kept up with the bright white car as if it were a warning beacon that might lead to his salvation. He caught a glimpse of the kid with gusto entering an office back on campus and found a place to park. Time ticked by. Hours spent looking in the second-floor window from his car. Men in dark suits arrived. With short-cropped hair and narrow ties, he knew they were Feds the moment he set his eyes on them. He could see them in the windows, scurrying like ants. Eddie knew that he'd been made. They were on the phones, writing things down. It looked as if they might work through the night. Then, just twenty minutes ago as he was about to drive off, he spotted the kid with gusto getting into his Corolla and tailed him back to his office in Center City.

Eddie followed the building's long lines up into the black sky.

There hadn't been time to find a bathroom, and Eddie hoped he wouldn't wet his pants. He was in his own car and didn't want to soil the leather upholstery. He dug his teeth into his lower lip and tried to concentrate. He wasn't a loser like Harris Carmichael had been, he decided. He could hold it until dawn if he had to, just as his mother had taught him when he wet her bed as a child.

He gave it another hard squeeze the way she had done, and turned to the people passing his windshield. He'd been avoiding eye contact, but needed a distraction. They weren't watching him. They were leering at him.

Eddie tried not to scream, but couldn't help a short outburst or two. When the eyes turned away and hurried off, he shivered in the cold night air and hit the door locks. Then he turned up the heat and checked his watch again. Two minutes had passed. It was okay, he told himself. He knew he could wait the guy out because he had to.

Headlights struck the windshield, filling the car with light.

He turned back to the building and saw the Corolla spring from the garage and pull onto the street. He caught a glimpse of the face. The one with gusto. He slid the shift into drive, let two cars pass, and eased his shiny black BMW forward. He was finally moving again. One of the watchers instead of the watched.

Eddie followed the taillights down JKF Boulevard. As the Corolla hit a red light at Thirtieth Street Station, he watched the car skid on a patch of ice. The Corolla slid forward and almost plowed into the flow of traffic circling the train station. Why was the kid with gusto driving such a piece-of-shit car? How smart could he really be?

He heard cars blasting their horns as the Corolla finally stopped. Eddie slowed down, keeping his distance and timing it perfectly. When the light turned green, he sped up and followed the Corolla down the ramp onto the expressway.

Teddy Mack lived in the suburbs. The ass-wipe attorney who couldn't afford a decent car was driving west toward the Main Line.

Eddie eased his foot off the gas and settled into his seat, always keeping a car or two between them. He hadn't been seen the entire day. He was following an idiot. He and Teddy Mack were finally driving home.

The traffic thinned out as they reached King of Prussia, then broke down all together as they exited off Route 202. Eddie backed off, watching the Corolla start up the hill on Devon State Road. He knew the area well. As they crossed Lancaster Pike, he pulled the scarf over his mouth and moved closer just for kicks. A mile or so later, the Corolla slowed down and turned into a driveway. Eddie noted the house and continued down the road. At the stop sign, he made a right onto Sanctuary Road and pulled over.

His dick hurt so badly he thought it might pop off like a cork. He leaped out of the car, yanking at his zipper and knowing he couldn't make it beneath the trees. Instead of writing his name in the snow, he aimed at one spot as he thought a stray dog might do. Craning his neck back and forth, he kept an eye on the road, searching for headlights from approaching cars. There weren't any and he smiled. Then he zipped up and sighed with relief. It was a quiet winter night, and they were home.

Eddie leaned across the driver's seat and opened the glove box. The knife he would be using tonight was one of his favorites. A professional eight-inch carving knife purchased at Williams-Sonoma. Made of high-carbon stainless steel, the imported blade was well balanced, its edge particularly keen. Eddie wrapped the knife in the kitchen towel he'd brought and carefully slipped it into his jacket pocket. Locking up the car and engaging the alarm, he turned the corner and made the short walk up Waterloo Road.

He had a song in his heart and felt like whistling. But as his eyes adjusted to the darkness, he saw someone at the top of the hill and ducked into the bushes. He waited, listened, pulled himself together. After a moment, he took a peek.

It was the face with gusto, standing at the end of the driveway.

The kid was smoking a cigarette and staring at the housing development on the other side of the road. He was thinking something over and it seemed as if it might just take forever. Eddie wondered if the kid had figured out that he was followed. But he wasn't looking down the street. He was staring at the houses. When he finished the cigarette, he flicked it at them like he wished they might burn down and walked away.

The gesture threw Eddie off because he liked it. He wished they'd burn down, too. He got to his feet, brushing the snow off his pants and moving quickly up the street. He saw the kid walk down the driveway and vanish behind the house. He heard a door open and close, followed by silence.

Eddie let the stillness settle in. He noticed the snow falling from the sky, light and gay, the kid through the window pouring a drink in the kitchen. When he scanned the property, he spotted a barn in the backyard. The lights were on and the scent of oak was in the cold air. Someone was in the barn and had a fire going. It looked warm and inviting.

He stepped back and took the place in again. Something about the property seemed idyllic. It made him nervous. It stole his strength and made him feel small. Even weird. Why was he spending his life all alone?

After a moment, he noticed a fence along the property line, hidden behind a hedge that was kept trimmed. Eddie entered the yard, slowly working his way toward the barn. He spotted a grove of rhododendrons and stepped inside the canopy. Moving quietly, he kept away from the light and gazed through the window.

A woman was painting.

He could see her working the brush on the canvas. He locked up and choked.

She looked like an angel. She was the most beautiful woman he had ever seen. She looked gentle. Caring. Nurturing. A certain glow lingered in her eyes, and he wondered if she was even real. He began to feel dizzy, staring at her and wanting her. As his eyes drifted away from her face, he noticed the paintings on the wall. Her work. He recognized two canvases. He'd seen them in a show last fall—

through the window from the street because he'd been too afraid to walk in.

A noise from the house snatched up his dream.

The back door opened and closed.

As he shrank away from the window, his eyes flicked across the yard. It was Teddy Mack, trudging through the snow toward the barn. But the kid wasn't heading down the path for the door. He was taking the same route Eddie had. Through the shadows along the fence.

Eddie slithered out of the bushes and around a tree. The kid was tracking him. Hunting him. He pulled the knife out, unwrapping the sharp blade and stuffing the towel in his pocket again. He wasn't sure what to do. He could still see the angel. It looked as if she had wings. He clenched his teeth and pain shot through his head. Averting his eyes, he raised the knife and inched his way back around the trunk of the tree.

Eddie couldn't believe what he was seeing. The kid had slipped into the grove of rhododendrons just as he had. He was sipping his drink and staring at the angel through the window. Eddie lifted the scarf over his mouth and quieted his breath. He was standing less than six feet away, pretending to be a tree. He could see the kid's face. The gusto had been painted over with a heavy brush. Only sadness remained.

Fifty-six

Teddy caught a glimpse of the metallic flash from the corner of his eye. The knife was moving toward him in an arcing motion from just behind his right shoulder. He let go of his drink and locked both hands around the man's bony wrist. It was a gut shot, coming at him hard. Instead of pushing the blade away, he concentrated on steering the knife wayward.

The tip tore through his jacket, then plunged into something soft and stayed there. Blood splattered all over the snow, and he tumbled onto the ground. In a split second he assessed the damage. He felt no pain and knew that he hadn't been stabbed. When he looked at the man squirming beneath him, he saw the blade of the knife stuck deep into his right thigh. Maybe even all the way through. He caught the rotten teeth and heard the man cackling. Saw the madness smoldering in his eyes like coals glowing at the end of a house fire. It was *him,* and Teddy did a double take.

It was the face Holmes had described in his dreams.

Not a woman or a man, but a pale and lifeless ghost. Chasing him and laughing at him. Pushing his hands and face into Darlene Lewis's body to leave fingerprints and lip prints and a trail of evidence the police could find.

Teddy threw a shaky punch, aiming at those teeth. When he missed, he threw another and hit the mark.

Trisco's eyes lit up and he groaned. He wrenched the knife out of his leg and kicked his feet in the air. For some reason he was wearing socks over his shoes, and Teddy stared at them half a moment too long. He took a hard shot to the head, paused as he heard the barn door opening, and watched Trisco flee across the yard.

He jumped to his feet, shouting at his mother as he raced toward the house. "Get back inside and lock the door."

Trisco vanished around the corner, heading for the driveway. Teddy ripped open the back door and bolted upstairs. His father's shotgun was hanging on his bedroom wall. He grabbed the gun, switched the safety off, leaped down the front stairs. As he rushed onto the front porch, he spotted Trisco legging his way down Waterloo Road.

Teddy sprinted across the driveway into the neighbor's yard, vaulting over the fence and tearing through the bushes. He could see Trisco on the other side of the trees, hobbling toward a black BMW. He could feel his heart beating as he gripped the gun and dug in his heels. He hit the trees and burst onto the street. The driver's-side door slammed shut and the engine turned over.

Teddy raised the shotgun and pulled the trigger.

The gun rocked back into his shoulder and the muzzle flashed, waking up the dead of night with the sound of burning gunpowder. Teddy's eyes skipped through the flash to the rear window, watching it shatter into a thousand pieces. Shards of glass sprayed through the car all over the front seat and dash, and he heard Trisco groan.

The BMW whined back at him like a wounded animal, its wheels churning up snow as it strained to pull forward and escape. Teddy fired a second blast from twenty-five yards off. He heard the sound of buckshot piercing sheet metal, but the car hurtled down the road at high speed. Trisco switched his headlights on. A quarter mile down, the lights blinked in the darkness. When they blinked a second time, Teddy wondered if it wasn't a message from Trisco that he was okay.

There wasn't enough time to come forward and explain to the local police that he'd just been attacked by a mad-dog serial killer. He'd seen the neighbor's windows light up as he ran back toward the house. He guessed they'd call 911.

Because the shots had come from Sanctuary Road, the cops would focus their attention on the pine forest and the last open field across the street. Deer roamed freely here. Over the past few years, the herd had become quite large. Poachers were known to hunt in state parks at night. It wasn't too big of a stretch to think someone had taken an illegal shot at a buck and raced off. The whining sound of Trisco's BMW stealing into the night might even help sell the story if the cops bothered to stop by and ask. Teddy didn't think they would.

He tapped on the barn door. When it opened, he saw the look on his mother's face and knew nothing would fly but the truth. Her eyes were roving over his body and torn jacket, instinctively checking his arms and legs and counting the number of fingers on his hands.

"I'm in trouble," he said. "The man we're looking for has found me."

"Are you hurt?"

He shook his head. "But it isn't safe here. You need to pack a bag and go over to Quint's. I need to get downtown."

She looked at the shotgun, but didn't say anything. She'd heard her son fire the weapon. The smell of gunpowder lingered in the air.

"We need to hurry," he said.

She gave him a nervous look but understood. "I'll call Quint right away."

He stepped back from the door to let her pass, then followed her down the path to the house. He could see her wheels turning. He could tell she was dredging up the past and trying to make sense out of what happened tonight without enough details to fill it all in. As they reached the kitchen door, he grabbed the handle and opened it for her.

"When Dad went to prison," he said, "how did you know he didn't do it?"

She turned back, confused. "Why would you ask that now?"

"Could you see it in his face, Mom? His eyes?"

"No," she said in a quiet voice. "Your father couldn't hide his emotions very well. He looked guilty because he felt guilty. That was the problem."

"You mean the police found out how much cash the company had and assumed he did it."

She nodded. "Your father thought he should've seen it coming and blamed himself for the murder."

"If he looked guilty, then how did you know he wasn't?"

She thought it over. "I just *did,*" she said after a moment. "When he died and his accountant came forward admitting what he'd done, I wasn't surprised. Your father and I thought it was him all along."

"What about the prosecutor? Did you tell him?"

"He was young and wouldn't listen. He was trying to make a name for himself. Your father was a trophy."

Her gaze fell away and she stepped inside. When she went upstairs to pack, Teddy checked the lock on the front door, peering through the glass to the street. He didn't see any sign of the cops, and didn't think Trisco would be back until he could deal with his wound. Heading up to his room, he returned the shotgun to its rack and grabbed a flashlight. Then he hurried down the hall, looking in on his mother before he went downstairs. She was sitting on the bed, speaking with Quint on the phone. Thank God for Quint.

"I'll be in the backyard," he whispered.

She nodded. She was upset, worried about him, unable to hide it.

Teddy checked the flashlight for power as he rushed down the steps to the kitchen and grabbed a handful of plastic bags from the drawer. Once outside, he crossed the yard to the fence and panned the light across the ground. Trisco had been wearing socks over his shoes. It seemed so strange at first. But as Teddy examined the footprints in the snow, he knew why. The indentations were soft and round without any definition. There was something diabolically ingenious about it. Teddy shook his head, following the tracks toward the barn until he reached the grove of rhododendrons by the window.

He lowered the light to the ground. There wasn't as much blood as he remembered. Trisco might be in pain right now, but wasn't mortally wounded. The thought crossed Teddy's mind that he was about to interfere with a crime scene. That he should return to the house and call 911 immediately, even Nash. But then the downward cycle would begin all over again, he thought. The local cops would listen to his story and have evidence to gather whether they believed him or not. Rumors would follow, history unearthed. The house would be a crime house again, irrevocably linked to murder. People would drive by and point, just as they had when his father was arrested. Some would get out of their cars and have their pictures taken in front of the house. If his mother was in the yard, they might even ask her to pose with them. It had happened before. Not to his mother, but to him just after his father's death. A middle-aged couple had parked across the street and wanted to take a picture while he raked leaves in the front yard. They were strangers, but seemed friendly. Teddy wasn't sure if he was supposed to know them or not. He was just a boy at the time, trying to sort his way through the confusion. They wanted a picture of him standing before the house and he agreed. When he told his mother about it, she called them ghouls and started to cry.

Not this time.

Teddy knelt down and scooped the bloodstained snow into the bag. As he stood up, he spotted the glass he'd dropped before the struggle. A candy wrapper lay beside it in the snow. He moved toward it, carefully eyeing the wrapper without touching it. Flipping it over with a stick, he read the label. It was the wrapper from a grape-flavored Tootsie Pop. It looked like something was smeared on it and he moved closer. When it registered that he was staring at cum, he flinched. He looked at the window, playing the scene back in his head. Trisco had been spying on his mother with his dick out. The sick motherfucker had been jerking off.

He shuddered, fighting off the urge to vomit. After he caught his breath, he flicked the wrapper inside a second plastic bag with the stick. Holding the bag to the light, he pressed the seal and double-checked its grip. Then he glanced back at the house and saw his mother in the kitchen ready to go. She looked so innocent. Almost like an angel. He knew she hadn't asked for this.

As he stood up and crossed the lawn with two samples of the serial killer's DNA, he thought about firing the shotgun. The feel of the kick, and the roaring sound it made. He could see the window exploding into the car. The wheels gripping the asphalt beneath the snow. The license plate fading into the gloom. The plate was issued in Pennsylvania. Teddy had always been good at remembering numbers. This was one he wouldn't need to write down, D07-636.

Fifty-seven

Teddy stood over the jury table, cupping his hands around the coffee mug and soaking in its warmth. Nash was at his desk, on the phone with an agent from the FBI's field office in Center City. He'd given the agent Trisco's license plate number and was trying to explain why Teddy collected blood and semen samples on his own and fucked up the crime scene. It didn't sound as if it was going very well. Nash sipped his drink undaunted. Not his usual coffee, but a glass of Skyy vodka poured over ice.

Teddy shuddered. He could still hear Trisco laughing. Still see him in the snow giggling with the knife spiked through his leg like a lightning rod . . .

His decision to touch the evidence had been made in the heat of the moment after firing a gun at another human being. He'd been worried about his mother, his own family, and their past.

He shook it off. What mattered was that he and Nash weren't alone anymore. They were working with the FBI again, and had been the minute they returned from their meeting with Trisco's psychiatrist that afternoon. They'd called Nash's friend in Washington and given Dr. Westbrook a full report. The field office had been mobilized, and the FBI would be running their own stealth investigation in spite of Holmes's bogus confession to the district attorney.

Teddy looked at the stack of faxes on the jury table that had been coming in from the field office all night. Before his arrest five years ago, Edward Trisco III had been a promising artist of some talent. His name was mentioned in several art journals, and the reviews in most cases were better than good. But as his insanity burgeoned, Trisco seemed to lose his edge. His last one-man show had been a disaster, and the articles began to dwindle off. When he kidnapped the model, they stopped all together and his career was over.

A copy of the model's initial statement was here. The one she made before Trisco's parents choked her with fistfuls of cash. Teddy picked it up and began reading. When Trisco wasn't painting the girl, he kept her in his bedroom closet, bound and gagged. He'd broken three of her fingers and managed to sprain her wrist. Bite marks were visible on her body and photographed by a police photographer after her escape. As Teddy studied the photos, it didn't seem as if she and Trisco met at a party, got high, and had a falling-out.

He turned away and glanced out the window. The streets were empty, the hour late. He couldn't shake the image of Trisco's face. The one haunting Holmes in his dreams. There was something familiar about it. He'd seen him before, but couldn't remember where. That off-center look in his eyes. His madness in full bloom. Teddy couldn't believe that Andrews hadn't seen some trace of his insanity five years ago. Even if Andrews were blind, Teddy wondered how he could give Trisco a pass after reading the victim's statement. And what about Trisco's family? What were they saying to Andrews as they handed him a check written in blood for his campaign?

Edward's a good boy at heart. He had a crush on the girl. He didn't mean to sprain her wrist, break her fingers, and bite her. He would've untied her and let her go. Edward's a good boy and would have let her go. . . .

Nash hung up the phone and sipped his drink. He looked pale and subdued, more worried than Teddy had ever seen.

"They want the DNA," he said.

"Are they pissed?"

"They want it. Let's leave it at that. Two agents in plain-clothes are going out to your house. They'll take a look and keep an eye on things."

"What about the license plate?"

"They're working on it," Nash said. "But the results are in from earlier this evening and they aren't good. They've run Trisco through their computers in Washington. They've checked telephone records and looked for a street address. Trisco doesn't have a bank account or a single credit card issued in his name. He lives without health insurance or even an auto policy. According to the IRS, he hasn't filed a tax return in five years. After his release from Haverhills, Edward Trisco dropped off the map."

"What did they say?"

"That he fits the profile. And he's living under another name."

Teddy felt the push of anger rising up his throat. If Andrews had done his job five years ago, none of this would be happening. When Teddy noticed that his hand was shaking, he hid it behind him as he leaned against the wall. He thought about Trisco wearing socks over his shoes in order to mask his footprints in the snow. Trisco's brain damage might be measurable, but on what scale? Teddy guessed that the license plate number he'd seen on the back of his car was nothing more than another dead end.

"What about the hospitals?" he said. "He's wounded."

"Every agent is on the street."

There was a videotape on the desk, something Dr. West-brook had sent them from Washington. As Nash slipped the tape into the VCR and hit PLAY, Teddy leaned against the jury table and looked at the image fading up on the screen.

A twenty-year-old boy was on a stretcher, overdosing on Ecstasy outside a nightclub. Nash appeared deeply troubled as he watched, and for good reason. The boy's body shuddered, then buckled like a fish pulled from the cool sea and thrown down on a hot frying pan. Twisting from side to side, he arched his back, fell down, and bounced up again in a tortured flexing motion he couldn't control. Instead of quietly passing away, the kid was making an extended run into the black.

"He's burning up from the inside out as if someone cooked him in a microwave," Nash said in a somber voice. "He never made it to the hospital, Teddy. Eight hours after his death, his body temperature was still over a hundred and six degrees."

Teddy turned away, unable to watch. After a while, he heard Nash click the TV off, the sound of ice clinking as he picked up his glass.

"Why do you think Trisco stepped out into the open tonight?" Nash asked.

It was the right question. The one that changed everything.

Teddy started pacing in frustration. "He knows we're on to him."

"I agree," he said. "But I find it troubling. Particularly when you consider what's in one of those plastic bags."

Teddy followed Nash's eyes to the semen sample on the jury table. He knew where Nash was headed. The thought had crossed his mind as well—the possibility that Trisco was tiring of Rosemary after only five days.

"We need more help, don't we?" Teddy said.

"I think so, too."

"But what about Andrews?"

Nash lowered his drink and pushed it aside. "I wasn't suggesting that we turn to the district attorney," he said. "I had ADA Powell in mind. I think you'll find she's ready to listen to you now."

Their eyes met. As Teddy grabbed his jacket and pulled his arms through the sleeves, he couldn't help but agree.

Fifty-eight

It was three-thirty in the morning. Teddy threw his brief-case into the car, got the engine started and the heat on. He didn't have Powell's home number, but knew she carried a cell. If she didn't answer, he had her address.

He flipped the phone open and noticed that it was switched off. When he turned it on, he saw the message icon blinking on the screen and entered his code. There was only one call, but it had been left by Powell at ten-thirty that night. After initiating the search for Harris Carmichael, the missing persons unit found out that Teddy had returned to Benny's Cafe Blue with a photograph of someonc. Powell wanted the name and sounded angry.

That makes two of us, Teddy thought.

He punched her number into the phone. Powell picked up after five rings, sounding tired.

"We need to talk," he said.

"Yes, we do."

"I met the man who followed Rosemary out of the café."

"Where?" she asked, her voice picking up speed.

"My house," he said. "He knows where I live."

A moment passed. A long silence followed by the sound

of a police siren in the background, and Teddy wondered if she slept with the windows open even in winter.

"Where are you?" she asked.

"In the city. Outside Nash's office."

"I'm working, Teddy. I'm not at home."

He lit a cigarette, the faint image of Powell in bed tumbling down the empty street with a gust of wind.

"Is Andrews with you?"

"No," she said. "I'm with Detectives Vega and Ellwood. We found Harris Carmichael."

"What's he saying?"

"Not much."

It hung there. Teddy cracked the window open, realizing Carmichael was dead. Nash had been right. Powell would finally be ready to listen.

"Where are you?" he asked.

"The west end of Spruce Street. There's a park by the river."

"I'll be there in five minutes."

He slipped the phone into his pocket, accelerating through the intersection in spite of the red light. Edward Trisco had murdered Harris Carmichael. He must have seen them together the other night at the café. They were sitting at the table by the window. The same table Trisco used to sit at and watch Rosemary work out. An image surfaced, along with a shiver, and Teddy suddenly remembered where he'd seen Trisco before. On the street as he and Powell left the café. When they stopped at the corner, Trisco had been standing just a few feet behind them. He had a scarf over his mouth, but the zombie look in his eyes was the same. Trisco had followed them to his office that night and found out who he was.

Teddy grimaced as he thought about the violation, Trisco's invasion of his property and life. The idea that like Carmichael, Teddy or even his mother could have been the next milestone in the misinvestigation of Darlene Lewis's murder, tagged and bagged and shipped off to the morgue. When he met with Powell, he'd have to control his impatience, reel his anger back a couple of notches, find a way to seize his composure and hold on.

He looked at the speedometer and eased off the gas, keeping an eye out for ice patches and listening to the rock salt beat against the underside of his car. As he made a right onto Spruce Street, he saw the lights three blocks off. Police cars, crime scene techs, the medical examiner's van. Finding a place to park would be impossible. When he reached a break in the cars and spotted a fire hydrant, he pulled over, grabbed his briefcase, and started hustling toward them on foot.

The press had been pushed up Twenty-fifth Street, the park surrounded by bright yellow crime scene tape. Teddy could see Powell standing with Detectives Vega and Ellwood, watching the medical examiner bag the body. As Teddy dipped beneath the tape and a cop protested, Powell looked up and gave the okay. She was wearing a ski parka over a black skirt and tights. Her blond hair and blue-gray eyes were bright and shiny and more vivid than the moon. But the expression on her face matched the detectives'. It wasn't easy. Just grim and hard.

Teddy's eyes drifted down to the body bag, already set on the gurney. Vega yanked the zipper open and stretched the plastic apart. When Ellwood hit the corpse with a high-powered flashlight, Teddy tried not to flinch.

Harris Carmichael had been mutilated. Puncture wounds littered every inch of his frozen body. His eyes were open but milky, and looked as if they'd popped out of his head. His mouth and nostrils were pressed shut and unnaturally crooked.

"What's wrong with his mouth and nose?" Teddy said.

"They're glued shut," Vega said. "The rest was just for kicks."

"Who found the body?"

"A neighborhood dog," Powell said. "Carmichael was buried in the snow. Now let's talk."

He followed them to an unmarked car idling by the curb. Vega and Powell took the front seat with plenty of attitude.

Teddy climbed in back with Ellwood, opened his briefcase, and pulled out the photograph Jill had printed off the Internet.

"His name's Edward Trisco, and he comes from money. He's got a history with the district attorney. The Holmes confession and the evidence you collected at Darlene Lewis's house is bullshit. Trisco's the one you're looking for."

They traded glances, which Teddy expected but ignored.

"There's blood on your jacket," Ellwood said, eyeing him carefully.

The detective switched on his flashlight, following the splatter down the front of Teddy's coat until he reached the tear just above the pocket. He poked his finger through the hole, examining the shape of the cut while Powell and Vega watched. The material was slashed open and shredded. Trisco's knife had been sharp.

For the next half hour, Teddy told them everything he knew about Edward Trisco III. Seeing him on the street the night he and Powell spoke with Carmichael at the café. The assistant manager's positive ID of his photograph. Trisco's history with the model five years ago, along with an off-the-record summary of what Teddy and Nash had learned from his psychiatrist. Vega spent most of the time drinking coffee from a Styrofoam cup and shaking his head. Ellwood remained silent, leaning against the door for distance and studying Teddy's demeanor. Powell wanted to see evidence of the money Andrews had received from the Trisco family. When he showed her the papers and pointed out the dates, her eyes sharpened and she passed them over to Ellwood, who switched his flashlight back on.

It was the first time Teddy had gone through the case from beginning to end. Vega and Ellwood were particularly interested in Holmes's nightmares. Both detectives had been present when Holmes confessed to Andrews, and heard Holmes talk about his dreams in detail. What Teddy had just told them did not discount the physical evidence against Holmes, or even his confession that he murdered Darlene Lewis, Valerie Kram, and ten others. But Teddy could see the troubled look on their faces, the disappointment and worry. There was the chance that they'd made a mistake, the veil suddenly lifted. Everyone knew that with enough work, confessions could be made to happen whether they were true or not. Teddy felt certain that at the very least, he had their attention. When he was through, he dug back into his briefcase and handed Vega the death threat he'd received in the mail, sealed in a plastic bag.

The medical examiner tapped on the driver's-side window. Vega turned and lowered the glass.

"Some asshole's got a camera on the roof," the ME said. "I wanna get the body out of here. You got a problem with that?"

They looked out the windshield, scanning the rooflines and spotting the video camera on top of a town house on the corner. One of the local TV stations must have paid off the owner in spite of the hour. The camera operator had a bird's-eye view of the entire crime scene.

Vega nodded at the ME, then raised the window slightly and lit a cigarette. He leaned against the door, examining the letter and envelope Teddy had received from Colt 45 on Somebody Street. After a moment, he passed it over to Powell without showing any emotion. He was mulling it all over, the glint in his eyes moving like the runner lights on a plane sweeping across a midnight sky.

Teddy's cell phone rang. It was Nash, calling from his office with news from the FBI. When Teddy hung up, he pushed his briefcase aside and sat back in the seat.

"The plate on Trisco's car was stolen from the long-term parking lot at the airport."

"So what else is new?" Ellwood said.

Teddy shot a look at Powell and held it.

"The car they found parked beside it," he said. "It belongs to Rosemary Gibb."

Fifty-nine

As they swept up the long drive, the Trisco estate came into view through the leafless oak and maple trees. It was a large Tudor-styled mansion in Radnor, just a few miles from Teddy's house, and he remembered reading about the place in the magazine section of the Sunday *Inquirer* as a boy. It was more of a building than a house, set on fifty acres of undeveloped land in the woods. In spite of all the cars parked before the entrance, the place looked closed.

It was six-thirty in the morning. Vega had picked the time wanting to cause as much disruption as he could. Ellwood had stayed behind at the crime scene, asking for the keys to Teddy's car. The detective wanted to shepherd the evidence back to the lab at the roundhouse, coordinate their effort to find Trisco with the FBI, and review the evidence against Holmes in light of Teddy's story. Everything would be done on the QT, and Vega agreed. Apparently both detectives had a thing for Andrews that began with their inherent distrust of Michael Jackson, the detective assigned to the DA's office. Still, they were a long way off from reaching a conclusion on Alan Andrews, or even thinking about their approach to the problem if what Teddy said was true.

Teddy wasn't angry that the detectives or even Powell hadn't bought his story at face value. They were acting on hunches, but grounded in the methodical world of what they could see and touch with their own eyes and hands. And the situation was delicate. Tedious. Edward Trisco had attacked Teddy and was the prime suspect in the disappearance of Rosemary Gibb and the tortured murder of Harris Carmichael. Although there was good reason to believe Trisco was involved in the murders of Darlene Lewis and the others, Teddy hadn't given them anything tangible to work with. There wasn't a hard link, a piece of physical evidence, threading its way between Trisco and the serial murders. Not yet anyway.

Still, there was a certain thrill to the investigation now. And Teddy had to admit that he was surprised by their reaction to his story and how far he'd gotten. Even when he recounted firing the shotgun into Trisco's car at point-blank range, they seemed more excited than fazed.

"That was close" was all Vega said. "He went at you with the knife. I might've done the same fucking thing."

Powell was speechless and just looked at him with those eyes of hers.

They parked beside a Mercedes and got out of the car. Teddy followed Vega and Powell up the steps, leaving his ripped-up jacket behind. The feel of the place and deep sound of the bell reminded him of an old black-and-white film from the 1930s. A place entrenched in the past. When Trisco's mother answered the door herself, the whole thing seemed too up-close, even strange. He knew it was Trisco's mother. In spite of the gray hair, there was a harshness to her face that she'd passed on to her son. The same hollow eyes.

Vega flipped open his badge. "Mrs. Trisco?"

She was staring at it. She was stunned, but trying not to show it.

"Yes," she said with hesitation.

"We're investigating a missing persons case. We're hoping you might be able to help. We're trying to locate your son.''

''Do you have a warrant?'' she asked Vega as if offering him more tea.

Vega smiled politely. ''No, ma'am, I don't. But I can get one if you like in about half an hour. Unfortunately, my cell phone's dead. I'll have to call it in over the radio. Every newsroom in the city will be listening.''

Her eyes flipped up from the badge and stayed on his face. After a while, she looked at Powell, then settled on Teddy.

''Who are these nice people?'' she asked Vega.

''Attorneys. Carolyn Powell from the district attorney's office, and Teddy Mack.''

She looked them over, considering her options. Then she swung the door open and let them in.

It wasn't a house or a building. It was a museum. Mrs. Trisco showed them down the long hall, pressing forward in short, choppy steps as if marching in a military parade behind a tank. Her posture was agonizingly perfect, her back as stiff and straight as a flagpole. Teddy glanced at the rooms they were passing—the staircase, the ornate moldings he knew were hand-carved, the oriental carpets lining the floors, the furniture that must have been in the family's possession for more than a hundred years, the art collection from the nineteenth century, mostly religious and each painting worth more than he could hope to earn in his entire career. The place was dark, the smell of fresh wax in the air. Small lamps lit the way. When he saw the array of Sterling silver pieces filling out the shadows, his eyes rolled over the room searching for a collection of antique shot glasses like the one he'd found the night Barnett had been run over. He didn't see any, but gave Powell a nudge. She took the silver in and nodded.

They finally reached the end of the hall and stepped into a large sitting room off the rear terrace of the house. It was brighter here, the furniture more modern. Windows lined the wall from floor to ceiling in one-foot squares set in iron frames. French doors with polished brass handles led outside, and Teddy could see an Olympic-sized swimming pool beyond the stone wall of the terrace just this side of the tennis courts. Mrs. Trisco asked them to sit down, then excused herself. It was more of an order than a request. She wouldn't speak to them without her husband, she said. Vega nodded, flashed an affable smile at her, and didn't seem to mind. When she left the room, the detective raised his brow and grimaced.

But they didn't sit down.

The stern-looking woman was demonstrating her knowledge in her very being, Teddy figured. No one would act this way if they were ignorant of the situation. She knew exactly why they were here.

A door was cracked open beside the fireplace. Teddy watched Vega give it a slight push with his elbow and moved closer. The room gave way to a short set of steps leading down to an outside door on the back of the house. Boxes were stacked along the wall. Through the window they could see a van parked in the driveway. A man got behind the wheel and drove off. Teddy looked at the floor, noting it was wet from melting snow.

"It's a little early for deliveries," Powell said.

Vega nodded. "Maybe they're carting the stuff away," he said. "Maybe we're interrupting something."

They traded looks. As Vega closed the door, Teddy noticed a picture on the mantel. It was a photograph of Edward as a young boy sitting on the lawn with his dog. The dog was a mutt and wore a plaster cast on its front leg. Little Edward spawned an off-balance smile and must have been ten years old at the time. He wore shorts and sneakers and a polo shirt. He looked angry and vicious, even then.

Twenty minutes passed before they heard footsteps in the hall. When they entered, Teddy looked at Trisco's father and knew his termination notice from the firm of Barnett & Stokes was in the mail. It was the same man he'd seen in Larry Stokes's office. The old man who sat on the couch behind his back and listened to Stokes deliver his bullshit lecture on toeing the company line. Obviously, Teddy hadn't followed instructions. Trisco's father either knew Stokes or threw business his way in order to have some degree of influence over him. From the grim expression on the old man's face, Teddy suspected the latter. The man had the look of a reptile.

But there was a younger man with them as well. One with bigger teeth whom Teddy guessed would be doing all the talking. He wore an expensive suit, appeared meticulously groomed, and approached Vega with an outstretched hand and well-practiced smile. He introduced himself as Rick Colestone. The Triscos had waited the twenty minutes out until one of their lawyers arrived.

"The Triscos haven't heard from their son for several years," Colestone said matter-of-factly. "They're deeply concerned about his whereabouts and will do anything in their power to help."

That's why they called you, Teddy thought. Because of their great concern and power and willingness to help. He looked at the Triscos, saw their wooden faces, and noticed no one was making a move to sit down. Colestone's job was to deliver his prepared statement, and get them out of the house as pleasantly as he could.

Vega narrowed his eyes and appeared undaunted. "We have reason to believe Edward may have information that would shed some light on a missing persons investigation."

"But you're from homicide," Colestone said. "You're the lead investigator in the Holmes murder case. What's your interest in a missing person?"

"The witness who saw Edward leave with the girl used to manage a café. Now he's in the morgue."

If the goal was to shake up Trisco's parents, Vega succeeded. Teddy watched them take the jolt, and noticed beads of sweat forming along the attorney's hairline. Vega had played it perfectly. He'd given them the big picture without saying it. They were looking for Edward because he was a suspect in the murders of twelve women. Harris Carmichael made it thirteen. Rosemary Gibb, they hoped, would still be alive when they found her. It had to remain unsaid. Because of the district attorney, because of Holmes's confession, Vega had to stir things up carefully. Paint the context in a light wash with watercolors, rather than define it in oils. He was a pro.

"If you're referring to Edward's medical history," Colestone said, "or anything he might have done in the past, let me tell you that the boy was released from the Haverhills facility with a clean bill of health."

"So I've heard," Vega said. "I haven't had a chance to pay them a visit, but I understand the Trisco family is responsible for funding the hospital's new wing and it's open now."

Colestone blinked, then caught himself. Obviously, his clients had failed to give him a full briefing.

"The Trisco family has interests in many charitable endeavors," the attorney said. "Now I think it's time for you good people to leave."

They started for the door. Teddy caught Trisco's father staring at him.

"What happened to the dog?" Teddy said.

The old man's eyes widened a little. He appeared confused by the question and very irritated. Teddy smiled and pointed at the photograph in the Sterling silver frame on the mantel. When the man saw it, his withered cheeks twitched.

"The dog's got a broken leg," Teddy said. "What happened to him?"

"He died," the old man said through his teeth.

Teddy ignored the man's fury. He knew his job was lost the moment they walked in. Had the old man asked for Stokes's phone number, he would've given it to him.

"How did he die?" Teddy asked.

The old man showed his fangs. "Someone fed him rat poison," he said.

Sixty

Eddie jabbed the hypodermic needle into his thigh, let out a moan, then pushed the morphine into his leg. The right side of his body was throbbing from head to toe. He checked his watch, calculating that it would take ten to twenty minutes before the pain slipped away.

As he got up off the seat of the john, his image raked across the bathroom mirror and he set the needle down. His face looked like an etching in cuts and scratches. When the kid with gusto fired the shotgun into the car, glass sprayed forward and bounced off the windshield into his face. He'd had enough sense to cover his eyes. He hadn't been blinded. Still, the experience and pain that went with it was harrowing enough to spawn a series of nightmares. Last night he dreamed he was a beekeeper without a mask. As he collected honey from the nest on orders from his mother, the bees swarmed his face and began stinging him. There were hundreds of them. Thousands of them, clinging to his face in a mask three inches thick. He woke up in a cold sweat, gasping for air and swatting at the insects until he remembered the shattered glass. It was the shards of glass that had disfigured him. The kid with gusto who had transformed his appearance and made him stand out.

He stepped into the bedroom and opened the closet door. As he got dressed, he could hear Rosemary start up again from the basement. He thought she might be hungry. But maybe it was more than that. Since he'd seen the angel painting in the barn, he hadn't been able to look at Rosemary or get any work done. There was the chance he'd made a horrible mistake with his painting, wasted the entire fucking year on the wrong fucking face. How could he break through and become famous when he'd painted the wrong type of woman? Rosemary wasn't an angel. None of them had been. Eddie shook it off. He'd deal with it when the pain went away. Try to look at his painting from a fresh perspective and decide if his life was ruined or not.

He walked downstairs into the kitchen, opened the door to the pantry, and reached for another can of Chef Boyardee ravioli. Then he descended the stairs into the basement, entering the workroom and listening to his model rant and rave. He unlocked the bathroom door and switched on the light. She was sprawled out on the concrete floor, staring back at him with wild eyes. The housedress he'd given her was partially open and made her look like a whore. She was beginning to smell and needed a shower as well.

"Here," he said, offering her the ravioli.

"I'm tired of eating out of cans," she said. "I hate ravioli."

Eddie looked at the two cans on the floor and realized she hadn't finished either one of them.

"People are starving, you know. When someone offers you food, you should be more grateful and not waste it."

"Fuck you," she said. "And fuck your stupid painting."

She stood up on her bare feet. She was grinding her teeth and moving closer with her hands behind her back. Eddie had lost count and didn't see it coming. A third can of Chef Boyardee beef ravioli flying through the air. Rosemary swung it forward and crashed it over his forehead. The blow knocked him against the doorjamb. He felt her pushing him aside, and saw her streak by and bolt out the door.

She wasn't an angel. She was an ungrateful bitch.

He tried to shake the dizziness away and sprinted forward, catching up with her on the stairs. He was right behind her, grabbing at the dress with his fingers and pawing at her legs. Rosemary burst into the kitchen, swung the door back and forth, banging him on the head. Then she yelped and fled away. Eddie chased her into the living room, pulling her off the front door as she fumbled with the locks. She was squirming in his arms, twisting out of his hands, driving her elbows into his stomach, and searching for his balls. When she pulled away and raced up the steps to the second floor, Eddie decided he'd had it. He climbed the stairs, slower this time because of the pain in his leg. The wound had opened again. He could see the bloodstain blooming all over his clean pants. And then he heard her shriek.

He followed the sound up to the attic, felt the cold air tumbling down at him as he hobbled up the narrow steps.

Rosemary had found Mrs. Yap.

Curiously, his landlady's frozen body was no longer in the trunk. The lid was open and she'd managed to crawl halfway out. Eddie had taken her for dead two hours before he dragged her upstairs.

The windows were open, keeping the room chilled down like a walk-in freezer. Rosemary had stopped screaming. She was staring at the corpse in disbelief and trying to catch her breath. Mrs. Yap appeared more than cold. Ice crystals had formed around her mouth and eyes, and it didn't look as if she'd found any peace on her journey to the other side.

Eddie helped Rosemary up and led her downstairs. Closing the door behind them, he tried to think about what to do. She didn't pull away. Not even once. Instead, she held herself in her arms and quietly wept. It occurred to him that this might be the right time for another trip on the love train. Rosemary looked like she needed it. And Eddie thought he could probably use the break, too.

As they entered the kitchen, he sat her down at the table

and opened the drawer for his stash. He shook two pills out and dumped them into the mortar, then thought it over and added two more. Working the pestle into the marble cup, he pulverized the pills until they were a fine dust. Every so often, he turned back to check on Rosemary. She wasn't even watching. Her eyes were pinned to the ground and looked dull.

He opened the refrigerator and found the orange juice. But as he reached into the cabinet for two glasses, he lost his balance and grabbed hold of the counter. Something was happening deep inside him. It felt like a slow wave rolling through his head. Maybe even an earthquake. After a moment, Eddie realized it was the morphine. The wave seemed to pass, along with the pain, and he stared at the *Love Drug* in his mortar. Mixing medications might not be a good idea, he decided. Rosemary would have to make the trip on her own.

He emptied the ground-up pills into a single glass, filled it with orange juice, and gave the mix a good stir. Then he handed to her.

Rosemary's eyes rose from the floor.

"Drink it," he said. "You'll feel better. Then I'll fix you something to eat."

"You're really ugly, you know that."

Eddie smiled, feeling the wounds on his face and thinking himself a phantom.

Then she took the glass, finishing it off in three quick gulps. Rosemary must have been thirsty. Twenty minutes later, she smiled. It was the first smile he'd seen from her in two days.

Sixty-one

Vega pulled into the lot at the roundhouse, cruising past the row of black-and-whites until they found Teddy's beat-up Corolla. Ellwood must have been waiting for them outside the lobby. Before Vega could get the keys out of the ignition, his partner snapped open the back door and slid in beside Teddy with his fuse burning.

"What took you so long?" Ellwood asked.

"They said they didn't know where their son was," Vega said. "We had to wait for their attorney to show up before they could tell us how much they wanted to help."

Ellwood glanced at Powell, then back to his partner. "Andrews is protecting them. They've got him in their pocket."

Vega turned, but didn't say anything.

"He's at their house," Ellwood said. "They must've called him as soon as you left."

"How do you know that?" Teddy asked.

"He checked a car out on his own. A car without a driver. But the fool wrote down the address when he left the office and logged out."

Powell turned away. Teddy could tell she'd been hoping

it might not be true. After all, she'd worked with Andrews and had known him for a long time. The truth had to be rippling through her memory of the man—who she thought he'd been and what he really was.

Ellwood must have noticed Powell as well and lowered his voice. "We'll have a warrant to search their house within the hour. Phone records. Wiretaps. The whole thing."

"How?" Vega asked.

"Trisco's hair," Ellwood said. "They took a sample after his arrest five years ago. A strand was found in the glue around Carmichael's mouth. Looks like we've got a match. Trisco did Carmichael." He glanced outside as the windows began to fog, then leaned forward, no longer able to restrain himself. "And we've got fingerprints," he said. "Five years ago they took his fingerprints, and a partial's turned up."

"Where?" Powell asked. "Teddy's letter?"

Ellwood shook his head and his jaw tightened, his emotions jammed up into his face as he turned to his partner. "Darlene Lewis's house."

It hung there. It felt as if they were sitting in a vacuum. As if the air in the car had been sucked out onto the street and run over by a passing bus.

"Not enough to hold up in court," Ellwood said to his partner. "But shit, Dennis, the motherfucker was there."

"Where was the print found?" Vega asked.

"In the den across the hall from the living room. Three paintings hang on the wall. Trisco touched one of the frames."

It settled in hard and fast. Teddy remembered entering the room and seeing the chair turned toward the wall. His hunch had proved out. Trisco had cut away Darlene's tattoos and was waiting for her to bleed to death. He'd been sitting in the chair viewing the paintings when Holmes showed up with the mail.

It felt like vindication. It wasn't a theory anymore. A best guess made after a series of long steps. Edward Trisco had murdered Darlene Lewis. And his client, Oscar Holmes, the odd-looking man who thrashed at his chains during the preliminary arraignment and was known all over the city as the Veggie Butcher, was innocent.

No one said anything. Vega lit a cigarette, cracked the window, and gazed at police headquarters through the cloudy windshield for at least five minutes. The evidence had told one story, then discounted it and told another. . . .

After a while, Ellwood handed Teddy his keys and they got out of the car. Teddy offered to drive Powell to her office. Vega and Ellwood looked pumped, even angry, and hurried across the lot to the building en route to another, more careful review of the evidence and working with the FBI to find Trisco and Rosemary.

On the drive uptown, Powell remained quiet as Teddy called Nash at his office and filled him in. It was hard to think, everything going by so fast. When Nash heard the news, he couldn't seem to find his voice right away. After he did, he sounded delighted but still overwhelmed. Holmes was truly innocent and would be a free man. Every once in a while Teddy would look over at Powell. She was slumped in the seat—staring out the windshield with a blank expression on her face—going over something in her head, or maybe just stuck in neutral. When he saw her building a few blocks up the street, he ended the call with Nash and made a left into a parking structure so that she wouldn't be seen getting out of his car. He found a place to park, deciding he'd stop for coffee and get something to eat after he dropped her off. But as he reached for the door handle, Powell didn't move.

"I can see why Nash has taken you under his wing," she whispered after a moment.

She was still staring out the windshield with her hands in her jacket pockets. Beyond the concrete barrier was a view of South Philadelphia. In a way, it felt as if they were parked on a hill overlooking the city. He could see the Walt Whitman Bridge, jets lined up in a row dipping into their final turn as they approached the airport.

"Your instincts, Teddy. You found the mistake and figured it out."

"You have, too," he said.

She gave him a look, then turned back to the view. He tried not to think of her as a woman. Tried not to acknowledge the smell of her hair. Her skin. He looked at her face, her gorgeous profile. Tried not to feel the sting of her gentleness and overwhelming beauty. Her legs were spread apart. His eyes ran down her black tights to her shoes. It was good to be alive, he thought.

"I want to apologize," she said.

"For what?"

"For not believing you."

"It doesn't matter," he said. "We're in this together now."

Her eyes sharpened. "When we met for breakfast and you told me someone hit you over the head, no matter how outrageous your claims, I should've listened. You could have been killed last night."

His mind wasn't on Trisco, and he couldn't take it anymore. Couldn't reel it all back in. He kissed her.

She opened her mouth, kissing him back softly. He sensed a light smile in the kiss, felt her hands moving from her pockets, touching him and pulling him closer.

"It was that shot glass," she whispered.

"The one with ships and whales."

"Your story sounded so preposterous, Teddy."

"I know it did," he said.

They laughed and held each other, eye to eye. When her cell phone rang, he gave her a kiss and a look and leaned back in his seat. Powell dug into her pocket for the phone and flipped it open. Once she heard the caller's voice, she pulled the phone away from her ear and turned up the volume so Teddy could listen as well.

It was Andrews, driving back to town from the Trisco estate and in a foul mood.

"How dare you redirect an investigation without my knowledge!" he said, spitting the words into the phone.

"I don't know what you're talking about," she said.

"You and Vega and that asshole kid went out to the

Triscos this morning. You told them you were investigating a new missing persons case, but implied that their son was involved in something different. Something more."

"But he is," she said. "Edward Trisco is wanted for the murder of Harris Carmichael."

The phone went dead, followed by digital breakup as Andrews began screaming. Teddy noted that she didn't mention the young women or the link pointing to Trisco as the serial killer. But in the end, Andrews was a step ahead.

"Do you really think that I'm that stupid?" Andrews shouted over the phone. "I know exactly what you're doing. And believe me, you're gonna pay for it. I'll be in my office in twenty minutes. You better be there, too."

Andrews fumbled with his phone, swearing in the background before he could find the right button and end the call. With any luck, he'd veer off the road and slam into a telephone pole.

Teddy entered the Wawa minimarket, poured a large cup of coffee, grabbed a poppy-seed bagel with lox-flavored cream cheese, and moved to the counter. Oscar Holmes's picture was on the front page of both papers, but the *Daily News* said it best. Stamped over Holmes's face in four-inch-high text were the words VEGGIE BUTCHER SAYS, "I CONFESS!"

Teddy picked up copies of both papers, asked the woman behind the register for a pack of Marlboro reds, and walked out.

JKF Plaza was less than a block away from the district attorney's office. It was another unusually warm day for December. He'd told Powell he would wait for her there until things shook out.

He crossed the street, found a seat with a view of the building, and sat down. Tearing into the pack of cigarettes, he lit one and took a sip of coffee. He'd been up for more than twenty-four hours and was beginning to feel punchy. Fighting off a yawn, he checked his watch and figured that

Andrews should've arrived by now. As he scanned the street and looked at the skyline, his eyes fell on a high-rise building a block south from where he'd parked. He knew that the Trisco Corporation owned the building, that they were the sole occupants and had commissioned the structure to be their flagship and national headquarters. The architecture seemed to fit its owners like a glove. The building was nondescript. Another boring flattop with mirrored glass.

Teddy turned away, sipping his coffee and letting his mind wander as he looked at the newspapers on the bench. The district attorney was in a bad place. Every good word written about the man over the last week would come back as a nail in his political coffin. He'd made another mistake. Arrested the wrong man after reassuring the public that they were safe. No one would forgive him this time. No one would forget.

His cell phone rang. As he flipped it open, he heard Powell's voice.

"I've been transferred out of homicide," she said.

"Where?"

"The juvenile division. Habitual offenders. . . ."

It sounded like a move to Siberia. Andrews had struck back and knocked her all the way down the food chain. Teddy wasn't sure if he felt guilty, or just inept.

"It's not your fault, Teddy."

"Did you tell him about the fingerprint?"

"Yes," she said.

"How did he react?"

"It didn't seem to faze him. He took it in stride."

"You wanna meet somewhere?" he asked.

"He only gave me an hour to move my office," she said. "After that I think I'd rather go home, take a shower, and change. We were up all night, remember?"

"Yeah," he said. "What about Vega and Ellwood?"

"They're looking for Rosemary, and Trisco's the one. Nothing's changed. They're working it hard."

"I'll call you back this afternoon," he said. "Maybe I'll have better news."

He slipped the phone into his pocket. As he gazed at the building, he noticed a man staring at him from the corner. It was Alan Andrews, striding toward him like he knew who Teddy had been talking to. He'd seen him on the phone. Seen him sitting on a bench in December across from his office. Teddy set his coffee down and stood up as the district attorney moved closer. The man stopped just short of his face. To Teddy's surprise, he didn't appear anxious or even angry. Instead, Alan Andrews was relaxed, his voice eerily smooth.

"Do you really think you're ready for the big leagues, Teddy Mack?"

Teddy didn't say anything, and took a step back.

"I didn't think so," Andrews said, sizing him up. "I just got off the phone with a partner at your firm. It's official. You've cashed your last paycheck. Your career's over. You've been fired."

Teddy took it in and buried it. Andrews gave him a long look, then turned away and started off as if pleased.

"At least it won't be in the papers, Andrews."

The man turned back. "What did you say?"

"I wasn't fired in public," Teddy said. "When they get through with you, I don't think it'll be so easy."

Andrews smiled and took a step closer. "You really think so?"

Teddy nodded.

"What do you think they're gonna do to me?" Andrews said. "What's your best guess? I'll tell you what they're gonna do. They're gonna make me mayor. That's how it's written. That's how it ends."

Teddy found Andrews's confidence astounding, his armor impenetrable, if not bizarre. "Can I ask you a question?"

"Sure," Andrews said.

"How much money have you raised so far?"

"For mayor?"

Teddy nodded.

"It's only an exploratory committee," Andrews said. "I

haven't announced my candidacy yet. If I did, I'd have to give up my job.''

"But how much have you got socked away in your war chest?''

Andrews shrugged as he thought it over. "More than anyone else, times five or six.''

"Then why do you need the Triscos' money? How do you expect to get away with it?''

"Get away with what?''

"Protecting him. A serial killer.''

"But I'm not protecting anyone,'' Andrews said with an odd glint in his eyes. "The man who murdered Darlene Lewis is awaiting trial in a city jail.''

Teddy walked down the sidewalk, heading for the parking garage and wondering how Andrews could maintain his composure given what had happened and the things all of them knew. The man's cavalier attitude was unnerving. Either Andrews was in shock and had lost his ability to reason, or he was two steps ahead of everyone else and had found a way out. Like Nash had said, Andrews was a survivor.

As Teddy crossed the street and started down the next block, he pretended he was Alan Andrews and tried to imagine what the way out might look like. Andrews had the evidence against Holmes, but Trisco's fingerprint on the painting would seem to discount it.

What would the way out look like? What would the results be if Andrews got his wish?

Teddy thought it over. Holmes would take the fall and be found guilty for the murders, no question about that. And Edward Trisco III would be spirited off to a psychiatric facility as he had before, so that the killings would stop. Only this time Trisco's exile would be unofficial. It would last the duration of his life with his parent's blessings and a guarantee that they wouldn't buy his way out.

But what about Harris Carmichael, the manager at the

café? How would Andrews explain away his murder? Holmes was already in prison and wouldn't be available to take the fall. Trisco's hair had been found in the glue around Carmichael's mouth, the lab reporting a match. Vega and Ellwood were beating down the evidence trail. How could Andrews cover it up?

It didn't make sense, Teddy realized. There was something missing from the puzzle. A piece they hadn't considered or seen or imagined.

Something caught his eye and he turned to the storefront on his left. When he looked through the window, he realized it was the lobby to the Trisco building and stopped in his tracks. There was a model on display, some sort of building project. The sign read MARSH CREEK ESTATES.

Teddy entered the lobby, avoiding the guards behind the front desk and trying to hide the fact that he needed a shave. As he approached the model, he read the words TRISCO LAND CORPORATION and picked up a pamphlet. He'd known about the Triscos' holdings in technology and banking. That's how they made their fortune. But he hadn't been aware of their interest in real estate.

Apparently the corporation owned 2,500 acres of open countryside thirty-five miles west of the city. The property bordered Marsh Creek State Park and included the north side of the lake. According to the pamphlet, the Trisco Land Corporation wanted to develop the property and had already presented their plan to the county. The hills would be bull-dozed down and carried off to make room for an eighteen-hole golf course and hotel along the shoreline. Luxury homes and condominiums would rim the country club for miles. The land just north of the turnpike would be relegated for the construction of yet another shopping mall. From the way the presentation was worded in the pamphlet, it sounded like the project was about to be green-lighted.

Teddy flipped the page over and saw a photograph of the lake. The water looked choppy and people were sailing. Teddy had never been to Marsh Creek before, and the size of the lake took him by surprise. Beside the text was a small graphic that included a map of the area.

He looked back at the model, comparing it with the map. When he noticed a building structure on a lane just off Lakeview Road, his eyes widened and he caught his breath.

The Triscos owned a summer home. If the model was accurate, the place sat right on the water.

"May I help you?" someone said.

Teddy looked up and saw two guards standing on the other side of the model. It took a moment to register, but the man standing behind them was Edward Trisco's father and his fangs were out.

Sixty-two

Eddie heard something hit the concrete floor and peeked around his canvas as he tightened the straps on the gas mask over his head.

It was Rosemary. She'd fallen on her face, hit her chin, and wasn't moving. Her eyes were cracked open, and she was drooling. It looked as if she might have chipped a tooth. With her smile gone, she reminded him of a stupid whore girl again.

Rosemary had been a complete failure. Obviously, she was no longer up to the job of modeling for an artist. She couldn't even sit in a chair. The truth was that she hadn't worked out from the beginning. Her attitude was all wrong. Rosemary never understood her contribution to the larger cause. What was life in the face of great art?

Eddie ignored the interruption and returned to his canvas. He'd been experimenting with various shellacs, and thought he'd finally found one that would do. The problem had always been with the finish. The shellac was only being used in the background, and he didn't want it to stand out. As he brushed in a thin first coat, he listened to the rhythm of his breathing through the gas mask. It was even and steady, just like his hand. After an hour or so, he lowered the brush and took a step back.

The work was coming together, he decided. It hadn't been a waste of time after all. He could feel the excitement in his chest as he took another step back, then another. The painting's perspective was changing. He liked the way the shellac drew out the color of the oils and gave the work added depth.

The eyeholes in the gas mask began to cloud over. Listening to his breath, he realized he was hyperventilating. He sat down and peered at the painting through the mask. He couldn't take his eyes off it. His work even looked good in a fog. After a few moments, he got a grip on himself and noticed a gurgling sound coming from somewhere in the room.

It was his model, Rosemary—interfering again.

He rose from the chair and strode around the large canvas. Was he Napoleon or Michelangelo? He couldn't really tell. All he knew was that the bitch had thrown up the meal he'd given her, all over the fucking floor.

He rolled her over with his foot as if he'd come upon a casualty from a great war that couldn't be helped. Her eyes were open but lost somewhere in the battle. Sweat streamed from her body as if she'd been caught in the rain. He felt her forehead. She was warm, but not piping hot.

It was time, he decided. Time to prepare for another visit into the past. Time for Rosemary to make her final contribution to the cause.

He grabbed her by the arms and dragged her out of the studio. Clearing his sketches off the worktable, he laid out a plastic drop cloth he'd purchased by the case from the paint department at Walmart, then lifted her body up and set it down. She buckled a moment involuntarily, but appeared to settle. One by one, he secured her wrists and ankles to the legs of the table with rags. Her eyes remained open and Eddie wondered if she was watching him. He wondered if somehow she *knew* what happened in the dead room.

He felt her forehead again. Her cheeks. She was starting to cook. In another hour or so she'd be ready. Almost done.

Sixty-three

A wave of panic crashed over the car as Teddy paid the toll and started down Route 100 toward the park. That feeling was back in his gut. The one that told him something horrible was about to happen or already had. He couldn't stop moving. He couldn't shake it off.

He saw the turn ahead and made a left onto Lakeview Road. When he spotted the private drive, he pulled over and glanced at the street sign. Then he took another look at the map in the pamphlet he'd pocketed before he was thrown out of the Trisco building. Shoreside Lane had to be it. He could see the frozen lake stretching over the land at the bottom of the hill. A large house and barn were nestled in the trees halfway down. Idling along the street, he reached a break in the curb and stopped. The driveway to the house was snow covered. All except for a double set of tire tracks.

He lit a cigarette, got out of the car, and examined the tracks closely. They looked fresh, but were melting in the afternoon sun. A car had entered the property at some point during the day and left, he figured. No one else had used the road since the last storm several days ago.

That left Trisco out. He wasn't living here.

Teddy took a deep breath and tried to relax as the realization settled in. He hadn't expected to find Trisco here. Every sign pointed to the madman living in the city. Teddy had made the forty-minute drive because he sensed there was something missing and he needed to be sure. At least that's what he kept telling himself. But as he gazed at the house in the distance, he knew it was more than that. It was all about the lake. The water. Finding Valerie Kram's corpse in the river at the boathouse. The ominous feeling he got when he looked at the map in the pamphlet and learned that the Triscos had a place on the shoreline.

He climbed back into the Corolla. Turning into driveway, he eased the car down the hill following the tire tracks from the car before him. Although the snow was eight to ten inches deep, he could see the gravel beneath the tracks and had plenty of traction.

The house began to come into view through the trees. It was a farmhouse, not much different from his own. The driveway appeared to lead to a parking area around back. As he cleared the house and didn't see any cars, he caught his breath again and pulled to a stop.

The view through the windshield was magnificent, the sprawl of the lake at the bottom of the steep hill inspiring. Several fishing tents were set up on the ice, and he saw a man with rod and reel crossing the lake on foot to the other side. Houses dotted the woods in the distance, built along the road to the park a half mile down. Teddy followed the fisherman's progress on the other side of the lake until he got into a pickup truck and drove off in apparent silence, the sound of the engine too far away to reach him.

Teddy got out of the Corolla and glanced at the Triscos' house, guessing it was built in the 1820s. Although the walls were whitewashed stone, modifications had been made to the back within the last twenty years or so to take advantage of the open views. Clearly, money wasn't an issue in the renovation, and the building wasn't exactly a farmhouse anymore.

He crossed the drive, noting the tire tracks melting in the

snow from the car that had come and gone earlier in the day. It looked as if the driver pulled into the parking area, then backed up to the porch. He could see footprints on the path, the snow packed down as if someone had made more than one trip into the house.

He checked the door and found it locked. Then he stepped over to the window, got rid of his smoke, and cupped his hands. It was a living room. Light and airy and about as far from the Trisco museum in Radnor as a trip across the universe. He looked for any indication that someone might be living here. An open book or newspaper, a pair of shoes left by a chair, or even a bowl of fresh fruit. The sun was streaking into the room from a window to the left. He followed the shaft of light to a side table and noted the layer of dust. Someone may have dropped something off today, but no one had spent any time here for months.

He stepped off the porch, gazing at the hills rolling toward the horizon and trying to imagine a country club and hotel set on the landscape after it had been shaved down and carted off. There was a place for everything, he figured. This just wasn't it.

He trudged through the snow over to the barn. The doors were locked with a chain, but the building was old and weathered and pleasingly dilapidated. Prying the barn doors apart, he squeezed through the opening and slipped inside. It was colder in here, the space filled with speckled light. A breeze whistled through the rafters. He shook the snow off his shoes, padding the leather soles dry so that he wouldn't slip as he eyed a late-model Ford Explorer. The car was clean, but dusty. No chemical residue from winter driving could be seen on any of the fenders. He opened the door and noted the interior light. Checking the glove box, he found nothing. Then he saw a copy of *Time* magazine on the floor behind the driver's seat. He reached around and grabbed it, his eyes moving directly to the nameplate. MR. AND MRS. EDWARD TRISCO, JR. He checked the date. September 6 was more than three months ago.

Teddy threw the magazine back into the car and shut the

door. As he moved deeper into the barn, he noticed a small boat on a trailer beside a stack of cinder blocks and gardening supplies. A tractor used for cutting field grass down in the fall was parked off to the side. He thought he heard something and turned. That's when he noticed the door to a small room behind his back.

A bird flew out of the doorway, landed on a rafter, and began cooing at him from above. A mourning dove that appeared melancholy and alone. Teddy tried to get a grip on his nerves and stepped toward the door. The room beyond was dark, and he entered the space slowly, carefully. A lightbulb hung from the ceiling. He saw the switch on the wall and turned the light on.

The room seemed harmless enough. Fishing rods were tacked to the wall, along with coils of nylon rope. A toolbox sat on a workbench before a window that had been boarded shut. In the corner he noticed a large wooden bin that had probably been used to store feed at some point when the farm was more active. Teddy lifted the heavy lid up and back and leaned it against the wall, then looked inside. On the right was a pile of fishing nets. On the left, a wetsuit lay over a pair of goggles, fins, and air tanks. Teddy thought about his run-ins with Mr. and Mrs. Edward Trisco, Jr. They didn't strike him as having any interest in scuba diving . . . .

It was all about the lake, he reminded himself.

He closed the lid and exited the room, pried the barn doors apart, and slid out into the light of day. The rope, the cinder blocks, even the diving equipment—everything Trisco needed to make people disappear was here. Teddy's eyes flicked over the lake and zeroed in on his car as he walked through the wet snow. Checking the time, he thought he'd better head back into town.

The Corolla sprang to life on the first try and he pulled out his cell phone, searching for Powell's number on the phone log. As he pressed the clutch down and shifted into reverse, his foot slipped off the pedal. The car snapped into gear and stalled, then began rolling forward.

Teddy felt his pulse quicken as he looked through the

windshield at the hill. He threw the phone onto the passenger seat and jammed his foot on the brakes. The car slowed some. But then the brake pedal gave way, sinking into the floor as if it was broken. He turned the key, heard the engine fire up, and eased the clutch back. The car shook and vibrated, vaulting over the rough ground and skiing toward the lake at high speed. He checked the rearview mirror, the barn fading in the distance, then checked the mirror again trying to decipher what he was seeing through the jumbled blur. There was a man hiding behind the house dressed in dark clothing. A figure. A shadow. Someone watching him tumble down the hill into oblivion.

He tightened his grip on the wheel, the lake rushing toward him as he instinctively jammed his foot into the place where the brake pedal should be. There was a boat launch at the bottom of the hill. The car leaped into the air, then bounced on the ice and slid forward across the lake. Water sprayed up over the windshield and he thought about the warm sun. But only briefly as he heard a loud snap.

The ice broke open and collapsed under the car.

He looked back at the house, heard the splash, and felt the terror swell through his chest. The car was rocking back and forth, and he flinched as that first sensation of ice-cold water bit through his shoes into his feet. His eyes flipped down to the base of the door and caught the water gushing in. The engine was dead, the electric windows useless. He looked back at the hood, eyes wide open, as it dipped below the ice. Water sprayed out the air vents, around the seams of the doors and windows.

Teddy grabbed the door handle, ripping at it and driving his shoulder into it, but the door wouldn't open. The ice on the surface began fading away, the weight of the motor pitching the car down at an angle. Staring out the windshield, he tried to think, tried to stop shaking and not panic.

What lay on the bottom of the lake didn't seem real at first. He spotted a chimney, then a roofline, then two more houses eerily set on the other side of an underwater street. It suddenly occurred to him that he wasn't hallucinating or on a passage through hell. The lake was man-made. The valley had been flooded as a result of a dam many years ago.

His eyes shot down to his legs, checking the water level in the car and how much air he had left. The water was rising over his knees, coming on fast. He looked back out the windshield. As the car drifted by the first house, Teddy eyed the buildings covered in bright green algae. The walls were made of brick and stone and hadn't collapsed. A thick layer of mud had taken over much the street. Debris had punched through most of the windows and he craned his neck to watch a school of fish swim inside.

That's when he spotted the faces, staring back at him. He shuddered, his nerves unraveling. There were faces in the windows. Hideous faces cloaked in fishing nets, and anchored into the rooms with rope and cinder blocks. In spite of the cold water, many of the forms were bloated and hairless. Others looked as if they'd become part of the food chain a long time ago. Still, Teddy recognized two of the women from the pictures he'd seen on Nash's wall. They were keeping an eye on him. Watching his entrance to their hidden piece of the underworld.

The car suddenly rolled over, and he screamed. Gallons of water from the floor followed the course of the roll, washing over the interior door panel and splashing him over the head. Everything was upside down now. He felt the car bounce off something, then come to a rest on the bottom.

The water was rising up his chest, so cold it burned. He couldn't get enough air, couldn't move his lungs. When he kicked at the windows, nothing happened.

He pawed at the door again as the water line reached his neck. Stabbed at the handle with his fingers, but couldn't find it. He took a breath and went under, opened his eyes and let the icy pain shoot through them to the back of his head. The door handle was where the floor should be. He grabbed it, yanked at it, kicked the door with his knee, but still couldn't make it budge. He surfaced and let out a scary gasp. Six inches of air. Six inches to death.

He'd seen someone hiding behind the fucking house.

He looked up and spotted the trunk latch on the floor over his head. He gave it a hard pull and thought he'd heard something click. Stepping across the ceiling toward the back, he plunged his hands deeper into the water and flung the rear seat out of the way. Inching his feet back, he tried to beat the confusion and keep in mind that everything was upside down. As his shoes slipped on the metal lid of the trunk, he felt it sway open. Then he did a gut check and took a last breath.

Sixty-four

He was getting too old for this shit. His back ached, his knees hurt, and his toes were so cold he thought they might be frostbit.

Michael Jackson hated the fucking snow. When he retired, he figured he'd point his DeVille south, load the CD player with the *Best of Frank*, and hit I-95 South until he ran out of road. Miami Beach, baby. Maybe even Cuba if they ever worked all the bullshit out.

He stepped away from the house and wiggled his feet in his shoes. How could he lounge on the beach if some asshole doctor chopped off his frozen toes? Chicks noticed that kind of thing. They'd turn away as if he were used goods. His eight-inch cannon might never see the light of day.

He lit a cigarette and started to cough, then spat on the snow-covered driveway. Wiping the brake fluid off his switchblade, he closed the knife and returned it to his pocket. He'd cut the brake line while the kid was in the barn, then found a hiding place on the other side of the house so that he could keep an eye on things. It seemed like the way to go. The Corolla looked like a real junker, and the bald tires jumped out at him. If anybody checked, the whole thing would look like an accident.

Jackson doubted anyone would look into it though. And if they did, not very closely. This was the sticks. The hinterland. He'd heard inbreeding was big out here. Rumors of farmers who went out to the barn at night to spend *quality time* with their sheep. He guessed the rumors might be true when he tailed Teddy Mack out here from the city and saw mile after mile of fast-food joints along the road. Not a decent restaurant. Not even a bar that looked like it knew how to make a mixed drink.

Jesus Christ, he thought, Einstein lived in Jersey. This one was a no-sweat deal.

He walked down the drive, eyeing the lake. He hadn't really expected the car to break through the ice. The goal had been to follow the kid and keep him busy for an hour or two. When the car started down the hill, Jackson peeked around the corner and tried not to laugh. As the thing bounced onto the lake and skidded across the ice, he couldn't hold it in anymore. It looked like he'd come through in spades. Teddy Mack would be stranded out here with the sheep fuckers all night long. He'd get out of his car, walk across the ice, and try to call a taxi with that cell phone of his.

But then he heard the sound of the first crack snap against the side of the house. The ice opened up, the lake swallowing the car in one big gulp. Jackson's jaw dropped. He'd watched the whole thing go down. The car still had forward momentum as it slipped beneath the ice. He guessed the Corolla would end up somewhere near the middle of the lake.

It was a solemn moment, even though Jackson had been through it before. As the chunks of broken ice settled in the water, he glanced at his Rolex and noted the time. A minute passed without any sign of Teddy Mack. Then another. After five minutes, Jackson turned around and started up the hill to the road. He said a blessing for the kid and crossed himself as he kicked the snow out of his shoes and spat. Climbing into the DeVille, he got the heat going, flipped on the CD player, and cruised back into town. His memories of Teddy Mack would be fond, he decided. He really didn't have anything against the kid. What happened was just a matter of the way things went down.

Sixty-five

The biting pain from the cold water ate through every pore in his body. Backing out of the trunk, Teddy followed the course of his feet until they landed in the muddy bottom and stuck. He looked past the houses, the faces—Trisco's secret playground—trying to get his bearings. Overhead, the ice-covered lake sparkled—all lit up from the sun. He spun around, unable to find the spot where his car had broken through. But he saw a shadow in the light, a dark circle or square, and remembered the fishing tents set up on the ice.

Teddy pushed down on the lake bottom, thrusting his body upward. Wriggling through the water, he thrashed at it with his arms and legs as if the dead bodies were chasing him and pulling him down. The weight of his clothing felt like an anchor, the pain in his chest as if his lungs were made of lead. He was in the tunnel, squirming toward the darkness and running out of air. He thought about drowning. He was scared shitless his body might override his brain in the confusion and make the mistake of trying to draw in air. He knew that's the way it would happen. Sucking in water instead of air.

He sank his teeth into his lips, rising closer and still closer.

The shadow darkened, then went black. He reached toward it with an open hand, felt a paper-thin layer of ice break over his head and wake him up as it vanished.

His body heaved, then bobbed to the surface. He seized hold of the ice, fighting off tears and gasping for air. He was inside one of the tents, huffing on the fresh air in the darkness. His eyes glanced off a five-gallon bucket set beside a couple of canvas chairs. Stabbing at the ice with his finger-nails, he clawed his way out of the hole and just lay there. He was panting like an animal, whimpering and shivering in the cold air. He stared at the hole in the ice for a long time. The water glowed like a lit window in the middle of the night.

He pulled himself together and managed to get to his feet, then found the opening in the nylon tent and staggered outside. His shoes were long gone. Ignoring the feel of his socks on the ice, he kept his eyes on the shoreline and moved toward it as if a monk in prayer, one brittle step at a time. He thought someone was walking with him as he reached the boat launch and started up the hill. Powell maybe. Kissing him and hugging him and keeping him warm as he listened to her breath wisping in his ear.

His eyes were fixed on the brake fluid, following its trail through the snow. When the second set of footprints registered, he filed it away and rose up the porch steps until he stood before the window like a zombie. He threw his elbow into the glass, reached inside for the lock, and hoisted the frame up and out of the way. Then he plunged through the hole, pivoting his stiff legs around the shattered glass on the floor and moving deeper into the house.

The rooms felt warm and toasty. When he spotted the thermostat on the wall, he became worried because it was only forty-five degrees. He turned the dial up to ninety, heard the furnace in the basement fire up, and searched for the stairs. He couldn't find them. Room after room of closed doors led in a circle until he found himself in an entryway off the kitchen and stopped.

The boxes were stacked against the wall, and he wondered

which house he was in. They looked like the same cartons he'd seen with Powell and Vega at the Trisco's estate in Radnor. He counted fifteen of them. He ripped one open, then another. Most of the boxes contained men's clothing. Others were packed with pictures still in their frames and odd bric-a-brac. When he found the photograph of Edward with his wounded dog, the picture he'd seen on the mantel, Teddy understood what was going on.

Trisco's parents were getting rid of the evidence. But not from the crimes. Not the kidnappings or even the murders. They were trying to hide their relationship to their own son.

He shivered as he took it in.

After a moment, he reached inside the box for the last of the photographs. He couldn't place it at first, his mind still icy and dull. It was a young woman with blond hair. A photograph taken a long time ago. Still, the face seemed so familiar to him. He stared at it and forced himself to think. Her mouth was shaped something like Valerie Kram's. Her eyes reminded him of the picture he'd seen of Rosemary Gibb. . . .

He dumped the photograph into the box, grabbed an armful of dry clothing off the floor, and stepped into the den. Emptying his pockets onto the desk, he ripped off his wet clothes and sorted through the pile. The pair of jeans he found were tight, but they fit. As he slipped a T-shirt over his head and found a sweater, he couldn't help thinking that he was getting into the killer's clothes.

He shook it off, his eyes on the phone. Above the number pad were the names of people the Triscos frequently called. Beside the names were twelve buttons that activated the number programmed into the phone. What struck Teddy was button number three. The entry was blank. Leaning closer, he noticed a faint impression of someone's name that had been erased.

He glanced into the entryway and thought about the Triscos' attempt at boxing up memories of their only son. Then he picked up the handset and hit the third button. The number flashed up on the display as the phone started dialing.

He recognized the exchange from his days as a student at Penn. It was west Philadelphia, a depressed part of town.

As he listened to the phone ringing through the handset, Teddy opened the top desk drawer, found a pad of paper, and grabbed a pen. He wrote the number down and thought it over. How many people could the Triscos know living in that part of the city?

Only one.

Sixty-six

The fucking phone wouldn't stop ringing. . . .

Eddie looked at Rosemary stretched out on the table and couldn't believe the lousy timing. Her engines were just heating up. But the phone rang past the usual eight and just kept going.

He couldn't take it anymore.

He ran upstairs into the kitchen, grabbed the handset, and slammed it back down again. Reveling in the silence, he parted the curtains and peered through the window toward the house on the corner. A man dressed like a plumber was getting out of a van and starting up the drive reviewing his clipboard.

The man was a good actor, but not good enough. Eddie knew it was *them*. It had to be them, and they were destroying the moment.

The phone started ringing again.

Eddie screamed at the house through the window, then caught himself as the satellite dish on the roof caught his eye. It looked bigger than usual. Different. The eavesdropping device was pointed straight at him.

He shuddered. He couldn't take the chance that his Fed

neighbors were watching their monitor and knew what was going on inside his head right now. Turning away from the window, he spotted his Walkman by the sink and slipped the headphones over his ears. As he rolled the FM tuner back and forth, he searched for the country station but couldn't find it. He took a deep breath, switching over to the TV band and settling for a rebroadcast of *The Lawrence Welk Show* on public television. Lawrence Welk would have to do.

He dialed the volume up until the sound of the phone became negligible, then headed upstairs to prepare for Rosemary's final contribution to world history and the arts. Turning on the shower, he waited for the hot water and got out of his shirt. Inside the bedroom closet he pulled his robe off the hanger and laid it out on the bed with care. Then he kicked off his shoes, unbuttoned his pants, and sat down at the end of the bed.

The headphones had slipped out of position. Eddie pushed them over his ears and listened. It was a recording from a live broadcast at the Champagne Theatre in Branson, Missouri. All five living Champagne Ladies were there, and Welk promised that the Hotsy Totsy Boys would be singing a special tribute to Dixieland music later in the show.

Eddie smiled. Pure heaven waited in the wings.

He glanced at the clock radio on the side table, then removed the bandage from his leg and examined the wound. The cut was scabbing over and appeared to be healing. When he touched it with his finger, it stung a little but the morphine was still in play. He wouldn't need to see a doctor, he thought. All in all, he was glad he only carried a sharp blade.

Sixty-seven

Teddy listened to the ring over the speakerphone as he searched the place. He hadn't found Trisco's address in the city, but the keys to the Explorer were in his pocket and he had a pair of boots on. Even better, he'd stumbled onto a locked cabinet built into the bookshelves by the fireplace in the den. He'd broken through the wood with the letter opener and pried the door away from its hinges. Eddie, Jr., the killer's old man, liked to hunt pheasants and grouse. Inside the cabinet, Teddy had found an assortment of guns.

He pressed the speakerphone button down and the room quieted. Then he picked up the handset and called Nash. No answer. He would've liked to call Powell, but he couldn't remember her number and his cell phone had drowned along with his car. As a last resort, he punched in his own number at the office. Jill picked up in a panic.

"Where are you?" she said.

"What's happened?"

"I need to close the door," she said.

Teddy grimaced, but waited, listening to dead air. After a moment, Jill picked up the phone again.

"The letter's sitting on your desk," she said. "You've been fired. Stokes had the locks changed an hour ago. We're not supposed to talk to you."

Old news. Still, Teddy wondered why his termination notice was on his desk if he couldn't get into the office to read it. Stokes was an obvious genius, he figured, and had his own way of doing things.

"I need you to do me a favor, Jill."

"Anything."

"Find Carolyn Powell. If not Powell, then Detectives Vega or Ellwood in homicide. You're only to speak to them or Nash. No one else no matter what."

"Right," she said.

He gave her Trisco's phone number in the city and asked her to repeat it once she'd copied it down.

"Give them the number," he said. "And tell them that's where he is. My cell phone's dead. I'll check back with you in half an hour."

He hung up, pressed the speakerphone button down, and punched Trisco's number in again. He'd let it ring forever, he decided. Maybe it would drive Trisco all the way over the edge and he'd do himself in.

Teddy sprang from the desk, crossing the room for another look at the gun collection. He spotted a twelve-gauge shotgun he recognized and pulled it out of the case. It was a Winchester Model 12 pump gun. Boxes of shells were in the drawer. As he tore into the box, he noticed they weren't light field loads like the rounds he kept in his own gun. Instead, they were three-and-a-half-inch magnums. The full monty.

He pressed three shells through the ejection port into the magazine, then noticed someone had removed the plug. Probably Edward. After loading two more shells, he pumped the slide and heard a round enter the chamber. Then he added a last shell to the magazine, making it a hot six.

He grabbed the box of shells and bolted into the entryway. When he spotted a closet, he ripped the door open. He was hoping he might find something warm to wear, but the long raincoat would have to do. He got it on, emptied the box of shells into the pocket, and hustled to the door.

He was ready, he decided. If not ready, at least he was armed.

Sixty-eight

He didn't have a key to the lock and chain around the barn doors. He didn't need it. He gave the engine a heavy shot of gasoline and broke through, ignoring the sound of the barn doors crashing behind him and tearing across the lawn until he reached the private drive that led to Lakeview Road.

Once he hit the four-lanes, he brought the car up to eighty-five miles an hour and started weaving his way into the city. A speed trap would've been a blessing, but unfortunately, he didn't see a cop the whole way. As he vaulted up the exit ramp and swung around Thirtieth Street Station, he made a right onto Market. He'd had time to think as he drove. Trisco was used to the good life. There were neighborhoods on the other side of campus. Large homes from the past that were being refurbished after decades of white flight. He wondered if Eddie wasn't playing a part in the gentrification of the neighborhood. It seemed to make sense that Trisco would seek out a place where he wouldn't stand out and felt like home. Beyond comfort, the size of the houses would offer some degree of privacy as well.

He spotted a 7-Eleven on the corner and pulled in. There

were three pay phones by the doors. Two of the handsets had been cut away from the phones, but the third one looked as if it still worked.

He counted his change. Most of it was in the lake. Opening his wallet, he punched in his office number, then the number printed on his phone card. As he waited, he noticed the cashier staring at him through the window. At first he thought it was because gentrification hadn't reached this part of the neighborhood yet. When he caught his reflection in the glass, saw the black circles beneath his eyes and his wasted face, he realized it had nothing to do with the neighborhood and turned away as Jill finally picked up the phone.

"Did you reach them?" he said.

"Just a few minutes ago," she said.

"Where are they coming from?"

"The Triscos' house in Radnor."

Teddy thought it over. The search warrants must have come through.

"What about Nash?" he said.

"His assistant said she'd give him the message. I've got the address, Teddy. But I think you'll be disappointed."

"Why?"

"The house is owned by a woman, Diana Yap. She runs a small realty agency, specializing in rentals. No one can seem to find her, but the man in the office told me the house is leased to someone by the name of Evan Train. He's never heard of Eddie Trisco. He told me Evan Train has lived in the house for years."

"What's the address?"

She read it to him and he wrote it down. Then he jumped into the car, rumbling down the street and wishing he'd had time to buy a pack of dry cigarettes. He wanted one, needed one. But he was close. Just five blocks away.

No one was there. . . .

Teddy pulled over and checked the address, then cracked the window open and listened for sirens. The city remained quiet, even still. Dusk was settling in—the Christmas lights strung about the neighborhood popping on as if the holiday spirit was in the air.

He grimaced, turned back to the house, saw a car hidden beneath a canvas tarp in the driveway as he chewed it over. After a moment, he grabbed the pump gun and got out. He couldn't wait any longer. Couldn't take the chance. It was about the girl, he told himself.

He crossed the street, shielding the Winchester beneath the long raincoat. As he approached the car in the drive, he spotted a woman pushing a stroller along the sidewalk two doors down. Teddy lifted the tarp, his eyes taking in the holes in the sheet metal, the smashed rear window. Then he noticed the sound of a telephone, ringing endlessly from inside the house. This was the place. The one with the shot-up BMW in the drive.

He stepped up onto the porch and checked the mailbox, but couldn't find a name. Just the initials E.T. printed in gold. Eddie Trisco. Evan Train. The extraterrestrial head case who'd landed from some black hole on the other side of Mars.

The woman passed the house with her stroller. She glanced at Teddy and seemed nervous.

"Where do you live?" he asked, following her eyes to the gun.

Her face locked up, and she wouldn't answer.

"You need to go home," he said. "Check your doors and call the police."

She hurried down the sidewalk. As she passed out of view, Teddy noticed the house on the corner with the satellite dish on the roof. The bricks had been remortared and new windows installed. It looked like the family was living in the home despite the renovations. A little boy, maybe six years old, stood before a window on the first floor looking outside. After a moment, his father joined him. Teddy knew they were too far away to see the gun, yet they were staring. Maybe keeping an eye on Trisco's house was just part of their routine. Maybe E.T. didn't exactly blend.

Teddy turned back to the house. When he tried the door, the knob turned but the dead bolt was locked. He moved to the window and looked inside. He could see the entryway rug pushed against the wall and half turned over. What looked like a rag at first glance had been tossed on the floor. As he mulled it over, Teddy realized it wasn't a rag at all. He was looking at the signs left behind from a struggle. The rag was a piece of someone's dress.

Rosemary's dress.

He slammed the butt of the shotgun into the window, numb to the sound and feel of shattering glass, and climbed in. His eyes ate through the room in edgy gulps. As he walked through the dining room and kitchen and found a den, he tried to ignore the ringing phone. Still, the first floor was clear.

He raised the pump gun and headed upstairs. He went through every room in the dim light until he found Eddie's bedroom at the end of the hall. A lamp was on. He could see a towel thrown on the bed beside the extraterrestrial's clothing. Teddy moved into the room, lowering a hand to the towel as he eyed the closet. The cloth was damp. Eddie had recently showered and changed. Curiously, the windows had been covered with sheets of aluminum foil.

He shrugged it off and stepped into the bathroom, noting the water drops on the shower curtain. There was a hypodermic needle by the sink and an IV bag filled with an amber liquid that looked as if it had been stolen from a hospital room. He read the label.

Morphine.

He backed out of the room into the hall. Moving down to the landing, he spotted a door with an unusually heavy latch. And then the phone stopped ringing. A wave of fear blew through his body as he listened to the silence. It was an oppressive silence, the kind with voices in it that chanted *turn back*.

Teddy swung the door open, revealing a narrow set of steps ascending to an attic. Leading with the pump gun, he flipped the light switch, listened a moment, and started upstairs. The steps creaked, but he kept moving. He checked behind his back, to the left and right. Nothing except for the body of a woman stretched out on the floor.

Another corpse. Another victim. This one frozen all the way through.

He turned the body over with his foot and examined the face long enough to realize it wasn't Rosemary Gibb. When he noticed the windows were open, he walked over for a lungful of fresh air. The house was clear. Yet someone had picked up the phone and hung it up again. He looked outside, then down at the backyard. There was a greenhouse attached to the house. Another floor.

He raced for the stairs, legging it down to the first floor as quietly as he could manage. He went through the rooms again, checking every door until he found the one in the kitchen.

He swung it open and peered into the basement. The lights were on, but he still couldn't hear anything. Not even a distant siren from outside. His hands were trembling. He wiped the sweat from his brow. Then he planted his foot on the first step and started down.

Although the stone walls remained unfinished, the basement had been subdivided into a maze of various rooms. Teddy found himself standing in a narrow hallway, the doors at each end closed. He could smell mold, the scent of paints and chemical solvents wafting in the air. For a moment, it crossed his mind that he might be in the waiting room outside another version of hell.

He moved toward the door closest to the base of the stairs, thinking it would lead to the greenhouse and a possible exit to the yard out back if something went wrong. Then he turned the handle, cracked the door open, and paused. When he didn't hear anyone react, he pushed the door open and entered. He could see the greenhouse on the other side of the room. A chair and easel. He was standing in Trisco's studio.

He crossed the room to the easel, glancing at the chair and noting the chains and handcuffs. The canvas was large, five feet by six, maybe even bigger. As his view cleared the back of the painting, he spotted the French doors opening to the backyard. Then he turned around for a quick look at the painting and stopped dead. . . .

It was a cityscape. A young woman with blond hair stood on the corner at night waiting on a red light as men in suits openly stared at her naked body and pawed at her breasts with their hands. As Teddy looked at her face, it dawned on him that her features were a composite of the faces tacked on Nash's wall before the jury table. The eyes were used from one victim, the chin from another, with Trisco's memory of his mother as a young woman the standard everyone had been judged by.

Eddie was painting his mother, then killing her over and over again.

But it was the background that left Teddy dead inside. He took a step closer, eyeing the buildings carefully as the horror reached out with a cold finger and pushed his soul closer to the grave. The buildings were littered with graffiti, but hadn't been painted with a brush. Teddy let out a deep groan as he stared at them and realized exactly what Trisco had done. He recognized the graffiti, even though he'd never seen the images sprayed on a single wall in the city. They weren't drawn in paint, but had been inked in by another hand.

Teddy knew he was staring at the very thing that made the void black. He was staring at Darlene Lewis's tattoos . . . .

The buildings were made of human skin, stretched across the canvas and sealed with a thin coat of varnish or shellac. He felt his stomach turn, thought he might be sick, and stepped back. He needed distance. The canvas was huge, and there were a lot of buildings with graffiti filling out the background. More tattoos and skin than Darlene could have provided. As he thought it over, Teddy realized there had to be another list of victims no one was aware of. A list of women whose faces didn't match, only their skin.

Someone moaned.

Teddy heard it and flinched. He looked about the room and noticed all the doors feeding into the hellish maze.

He heard it again, trying to get a grip on himself. The sound was coming from the door to his right. He inched over, listening through the wood. It was a woman.

Teddy raised the pump gun and gave the door a push.

He saw Rosemary stretched out on a worktable. When she lifted her head, her eyes rolled back, then forward again, passing over him without seeing him. He scanned the rest of the room, didn't see anyone else, then rushed to her side. It didn't take much to realize that she was overdosing on something. She was sweating profusely, her skin hot to the touch. Even worse, tremors rocked through her body as she tugged at the rags holding her down. She was in a continual state of involuntary motion. Teddy watched her try to get up, hit the limit of her restraints, and fall back, then try to get up again. Rosemary was on automatic pilot. She couldn't stop moving. She was circling the drain.

Someone walked across the living room floor. Teddy froze, listening to the footsteps overhead. Trisco. When he heard them start downstairs, he looked at Rosemary. All he could think about was the videotape he'd seen in Nash's office. The kid overdosing on the sidewalk outside a night-club, bucking like a fish until he was dead. He needed to do something, but what? He needed to do it now.

He checked the door, ripping the rags away from her wrists and ankles. Then he picked her up in his arms, grabbed the Winchester, and burst into the studio. In spite of the dress she was wearing, he could feel the burn of her body as he pulled her closer. Kneeing open the French doors, he stepped out into the cold night air. Then he set the gun against the doorjamb and lowered her into the snow. She seemed to be looking at him now. Staring at him. Trying to communicate without words or even reason.

He dug his hands into the snow, pushing the stuff over her body as quickly as he could. One armful after the next until he sensed something behind his back. A shadow in the gloom. Someone's presence. He stopped and turned.

Edward Trisco was standing in the doorway watching him. His eyes were the color of morphine—the same shade of amber Teddy had seen in the IV bag upstairs. There was a glow about them that flared up, then appeared to die out in the smoke of his ravaged face. He wore a short robe and a new pair of Nikes. His body was thin, his muscles still well defined.

Trisco took a step closer, passing the pump gun leaning against the doorjamb without noticing it. Teddy's heart skipped a beat. If Trisco spotted the gun, he'd snatch it up with one sweep of his hand. The safety was off, a round in the chamber, the weapon ready to rock and roll.

"Help me," Teddy said. "She's dying."

Trisco took it in, surprised by the request and gliding his hand over the hundreds of cuts and scratches etched into his face. Then he spawned his rotten teeth and smiled. Teddy had to admit that asking for the madman's help was ridiculous. But it had given him a chance to adjust his legs. If he needed to, he was ready to spring.

The sound of a door opening and closing came from somewhere in the basement. Trisco had heard it, but didn't move, his eyes locked on Teddy's.

Teddy struggled to hold the glance, searching the perimeter of his vision for the madman's other hand. Although he couldn't look directly at it, he didn't think Trisco was armed. A muscle in Trisco's neck rose and began twitching. After a moment, Trisco backed into the house and vanished, so smooth on his feet he might have had wings.

Teddy shuddered, hyperventilating. He looked down at Rosemary's face and caught her staring at him. As he smoothed his hand over her forehead and hair, he noticed that she'd stopped fidgeting. He dug his arms into the snow, raking the flakes over her until her body was entirely covered. And then he heard the sound of a gunshot.

Teddy grabbed the pump gun and ran back into the basement. The sound had been muffled, and he guessed it had come from one of the rooms behind the closed doors at the other end of the studio. Bolting past the greenhouse, Teddy kicked the door open and raised the gun. As he found his mark, saw it standing before him, he felt the blood in his veins heat up and boil over.

It was the district attorney.

It was Alan Andrews, in the room and crouching over Trisco's body. He held a semiautomatic in his right hand, pressing the weapon into Trisco's head as if he wanted to take another shot but had just been interrupted by a witness. Trisco had been hit in the mouth. He was pawing at the wound, gasping for air, unable to swallow the blood gushing out as he lay on the floor.

Teddy stared at the missing piece to the puzzle and shuddered. Andrews wasn't protecting Trisco and didn't have plans to ship his mistake off to an insane asylum. Andrews had come to get rid of it. He'd seen his way out. Murder Eddie Trisco and prosecute Oscar Holmes for the crimes in spite of his innocence. Teddy took the jolt, his mind racing. The district attorney had read their profile and knew they were looking for an artist. But he'd also known about Trisco. That's the only possible explanation for why he made the deal with Barnett so quickly. Andrews wanted to rush Holmes through and win a conviction. He'd known about Trisco since he read the profile. Andrews was on his own, trying to keep everything secret.

"You knew," Teddy said.

"Lower the gun," Andrews shouted.

There was a gas mask on the floor. Trisco reached for it and was trying to place it over his face.

"You *knew*," Teddy repeated.

"Lower the fucking gun, kid."

Teddy shook his head. Andrews glanced at him, then turned back to Trisco. He kicked the gas mask away, wiped his forehead, and seemed overwrought.

"You think I did this?" Andrews shouted. "I just got here. It's an obvious suicide."

"Bullshit."

Teddy flicked his eyes around the room. He saw the open door directly behind Andrews. To the right was a passageway leading to the stairs. On the other side of the hall was an open door to the room he'd found Rosemary in. The dead room.

"Lower the fucking gun," Andrews spat through his teeth.

Teddy shook his head again. Andrews was staring at him now, mulling it over with a crazed expression on his face. He knew the way it looked. The way it really was. After a moment, he raised the semiautomatic and pointed it at Teddy.

The man had come to murder Eddie Trisco.

In the end it was his only way out. His misguided attempt to save face, continue his career and become the city's next mayor. Teddy adjusted his grip on the pump gun. The dots were finally connected, the picture drawn.

Andrews fired the gun.

The piece of shit actually did it, bolting for the door and slamming it behind him. Teddy felt the round crease his shoulder. Blood splattered onto his cheek and something shattered behind him. He swung the Winchester toward the door and pulled the trigger. The sound of the three-and-a-half-inch magnum was deafening and shook the house. The door broke away from the hinges and blew back into the room. He could see Andrews scrambling through a second doorway and trying to get away.

Teddy pumped the slide and pulled the trigger. The round exploded through the room and he heard Andrews scream.

He pumped the slide again, stepped over the broken door, and stopped, listening to the spent rounds dissipate into silence as he peered into the second room. The lights were out. Teddy noted a door cracked open at the other end of the room and took a moment to let his eyes adjust to the darkness. The furnace began to appear in the shadows. Tools leaning against the wall. A bin used for storing coal a long time ago. He didn't see Andrews and started across the room.

Three steps in was all it took before he heard the sirens approaching the house. Then something brushed against the ceiling and he felt Andrews drop onto his shoulders from above. The shotgun fired and he crashed to the floor with Andrews on top of him. He saw the district attorney's pistol slide across the concrete. The man was like a live wire, clawing at his face and neck and reaching for the gun. Teddy tried to pull Andrews's hand away, but his arm was pinned down and felt heavy from the wound. Andrews inched forward and stretched out.

Then someone else entered the room and stopped in the darkness. Michael Jackson, Teddy thought. Maybe even Trisco. It was over. The police wouldn't make it in time.

Andrews wrapped his hand around the gun. The figure moved closer, his face grazing a shaft of light. Teddy spotted the color of his eyes as they glistened and cut through the darkness like headlights.

Cat's eyes. Cobalt blue and heavily dilated.

Nash grabbed a shovel and swung it down with his teeth clinched. The blow was devastating, the steel shovel pinging like a tuning fork as it smashed against bone and crushed it. Andrews took the hit on his forehead and dropped onto the concrete floor like a dead soldier. People were rushing down the stairs and shouting, everything moving in a blur. The gun fell away from Andrews's hand and he wasn't moving. Yet Nash stepped on the district attorney's hand and raised the shovel in the air, giving Andrews a second hard whack over the head just to make sure. Then the lights switched on, and Teddy saw Powell's face. She was running toward him and bending down. Vega and Ellwood were right behind her. Their eyes seemed fixed on his left shoulder.

Sixty-nine

The veil had been ripped away from Andrews's face. In spite of his pleas to the contrary, everyone knew who he was and what he'd done. How deep and far he'd slid into the cosmic hole to nowhere.

Teddy lay on the gurney, watching Powell and Nash approach Trisco's skin painting as a medic worked on his shoulder and two others dug Rosemary out of the snow. He saw their eyes drifting across the canvas, then stop, their faces flushing with dread. The bar had been reset, and he could tell that's what was on their minds. Trisco had advanced the cause of the unthinkable. Pushed it another mile or two down the road. And Powell and Nash were seeing it for the first time. Feeling the challenge. Wondering what came next.

Nash glanced at him a moment as if he'd aged some, then turned back to the canvas.

Teddy could hear Vega and Ellwood in the next room, directing a small army of crime scene techs. Glancing over his shoulder, he saw the medical examiner bagging up Edward Trisco's remains. Trisco's eyes were still open and he held the gas mask in his hand. But there was something odd about his face Teddy couldn't put his finger on. Maybe it was the lighting, but Trisco reminded him of a caricature of a human being and didn't appear real. Like a broken toy lying on the floor without batteries.

The medic asked Teddy to face forward and he did. The wound didn't hurt. The bullet had grazed his shoulder. Although he'd lost enough blood to weaken him, he'd been more than lucky. Vega had emptied the clip in Andrews's gun. The rounds were hollow points. If the bullet had been another inch lower, it would have ripped out his chest.

Teddy glanced over at the district attorney. He was sitting on the floor with his wrists cuffed behind his back. The buckshot peppered through his backside wasn't deemed serious by the medics, and could wait until later. But his eyes were still dulled from the concussion. Underneath his blank face, Teddy could tell that the man was seething.

Andrews maintained it had been a case of suicide. He'd heard the shot, followed the sound into the room, and found Trisco on the floor. He spotted the gun right away and picked it up because Edward wasn't dead and still appeared dangerous. That's when Teddy entered the room with the shotgun, Andrews said. Teddy wouldn't lower the gun. Fearing for his life, Andrews fired a shot in self-defense and fled. The serial numbers had been filed off the gun, so there was no way to determine who owned it. Andrews's story had a certain ring to it until Ellwood walked outside and searched the district attorney's car. A box of ammunition was found in the glove box. Hollow points. After that, Andrews requested an attorney and quieted down.

The basement windows lit up. Teddy guessed that they were camera lights and the press had arrived. Andrews must have noticed as well because he was staring outside and suddenly looked frightened.

After a few minutes, Vega and Ellwood entered the room, trading glances. Teddy realized they'd been waiting for the press to arrive before taking Andrews outside to their car. They wanted it on videotape. They wanted the image on the TV news. Andrews would be ruined in a single, decisive blow. He would be humiliated in public for all to see, and resee. Teddy had no doubt that the video clip would be played over and over again for months.

"You can't do this," Andrews shouted as they approached him.

"Sure we can," Vega said. "Let's go."

"But they're out there with their cameras."

Ellwood smiled. "Yeah," he said. "You're gonna be a movie star."

Andrews yelped as they grabbed him by the shoulders. His faced reddened and he began sputtering out words and making grunting noises. He was fighting them off as best he could, shrinking away from them with his hands bound. When he refused to walk or even stand, neither one of the detectives had much patience. Instead, they muscled him up off the floor and led him away. Once they reached the stairs, Andrews began whining.

Teddy wondered if the prosecutor who took his father away ever faced the music. He needed to see this, he decided. Pulling the medic's hand away from his shoulder, he eased himself off the gurney and followed the detectives upstairs. Then he crossed the living room to the window and gazed outside.

It was more than a local party—the number of cameras waiting for the district attorney too many to count. A black-and-white idled directly before the house with its lights flashing. The car looked as if it had just been washed and waxed for the occasion. Teddy noticed the crime scene tape had been brought in so no one would miss the shot.

Ellwood opened the front door and glanced at his partner. As they started outside, the video cameras zoomed in for their close-ups and the strobe lights started flashing. The barrage of light was so fast and heavy, everything fixed to the ground appeared to be shaking. Andrews tried to lower his head, but it didn't work. Vega and Ellwood had him by the shoulders and it looked as if his neck was stuck.

When they reached the car, the detectives hesitated before opening the rear door and turning their suspect over to a stern-looking man with a mustache dressed in plainclothes. A new wave of fear exploded over Andrews's face. Vega pulled a card from his pocket. Microphones popped out of the crowd. They were reading him his rights in front of everyone, Teddy realized. Slowly, and in a voice loud enough that everybody could hear. As Andrews listened, his eyes went dead and bottomed out like an empty sky after a shooting star. He'd been made. Snuffed out as he crashed into the atmosphere. All burned up like a small rock that didn't have enough stuff to reach the ground.

Seventy

Teddy gazed at the IV bag slung over a stand on wheels, noting the amber color of the morphine. His eyes drifted with the tube down to the needle in his arm. The pain in his shoulder must have been caught in traffic, he figured. It never made it to Trisco's house. Instead, the pain was waiting for him when he reached the hospital and his adrenaline ran out. It struck with a vengeance, enveloping his arm and shooting through his chest and back in waves. When the doctor ordered morphine, Teddy had mixed feelings about it until the needle pierced his skin and the drug eventually chased the agony away.

He didn't mind the hospital room that much. He found the din of city street noise filtering through the window somehow reassuring. Even soothing. Outside his room he could see a cop sitting in a chair reading a magazine. It wasn't really necessary. The cop was here to run interference. But no one really thought a reporter could get past the team of cops downstairs.

Detectives Vega and Ellwood had stopped by a few hours ago and taken his statement with a small tape recorder laid on the bed. Teddy went through what he'd said to them, hoping he hadn't left anything out. He'd told them about finding the bodies in the lake, and how he figured out where Eddie lived. He said he couldn't wait for them to show up because of Rosemary. He had the gun, knew how to use it, and made the decision to go in. Both detectives agreed that while it was crazy and he could have been killed, in an emergency the situation defines the rules and they probably would've done the same thing. As they were leaving, Teddy asked them what they were going to do with Alan Andrews. Ellwood's face lit up. Vega just smiled.

Teddy glanced at the clock on the wall and fought back a yawn. It was after midnight, and he was having difficulty staying awake. Fearing that he might close his eyes, he cast his legs over the side of the bed. The images he'd confronted over the last week were still so vivid. Darlene Lewis's body stretched out on a dining room table. The faces staring out at him from the houses at the bottom of the lake. Trisco's skin painting.

As he lowered his bare feet to the chilly linoleum floor, he realized there had been a scent to the painting. The same one he'd noticed at the morgue. It was the smell of death, leeching through the shellac. He could smell it now. See it as clearly as if he were still standing in the maniac's studio. He didn't want to dream about it. Didn't want to be alone with it in the dark.

Nash walked into the room.

"I need to get out of here," Teddy said.

"Then let's go."

Teddy tightened his robe. Grabbing the IV rack, he rolled it through the doorway into the hall. The cop looked up from his magazine.

"We'll be down there," Teddy said, pointing toward the intensive care unit.

The cop seemed annoyed, but nodded. Then Teddy led Nash down the hall.

"I've already checked," Nash said. "She's still in critical condition, but expected to pull through. Packing her in ice was the deciding factor. According to the doctor, you saved Rosemary's life.''

Teddy spotted the exit and pushed the door open. Cold air swept past them as they stepped outside. There was an ashtray on the landing. Teddy pushed the IV rack over, reached into his pocket for the pack of cigarettes the ambulance driver had given him, and lit up.

''What did the doctor say about me?''

Nash grinned at the sight of him smoking with an IV in his arm. ''Your situation's hopeless,'' he said.

They traded warm smiles. Nash bummed one from the pack. As Teddy held the flame to the end of the cigarette, he gazed at the man's eyes. They looked so gentle, even sad.

''Westbrook's called three times from Washington,'' Nash said. ''It sounds like they're gonna make you an offer.''

Teddy drew on the cigarette. He didn't have any interest in working for the FBI.

''What about the skin?'' he said.

They were sixteen floors up. Nash turned to the view of the city and leaned against the rail.

''They found a collection of tattoos in his freezer. They were wrapped in plastic and packed in Tupperware.''

''Any idea how many other victims there might be?''

Nash shook his head slowly. ''Not yet,'' he whispered.

Teddy looked down at the sidewalk. A woman was getting into a car with a man dressed like Santa Claus. They were giggling and kissing each other, in the peace of their own world and headed home.

''When do you think Andrews knew it was Trisco?'' Teddy said after a moment.

Nash shrugged. ''My guess is that the day you found Valerie Kram in the river will be the day prosecutors use as their starting point. She was a student at the College of Art. Knowing what Andrews knew about Trisco should've triggered something in his head.''

''How could he expect to get away with it?''

''You tell me,'' Nash said.

Teddy had been wrestling with the question since he opened the door and saw the district attorney standing over Trisco with the gun. After killing Trisco, Andrews would've had to murder Rosemary and dump her corpse in order to keep his mistake a secret. He obviously didn't know that the remaining bodies were hidden in the lake, and if they were ever found, that they would point back to Trisco in a heartbeat.

"His world was unraveling," Teddy said. "He was desperate. He wasn't thinking clearly. What's ahead will be a circus."

"I expect so," Nash said. "A district attorney charged with the murder of a serial killer. I'm not sure that's ever happened before. But I guess in this world there's a first time for everything."

A moment passed with Teddy thinking about his role in the trial as the prosecutor's chief witness.

"Did you talk to Powell?" Nash asked.

Teddy nodded.

"When will Holmes be released?"

"Tomorrow afternoon," Teddy said. "I'm driving him home."

Nash turned back to the view. Then he flicked his cigarette over the rail, watching it land on the sidewalk sixteen floors below.

Seventy-one

Teddy spotted the news vans as he turned onto Lakeview Road. He'd borrowed an old Ford wagon from his mother's friend, Quint Adler. In spite of his wealth, Quint drove old cars. This was something Teddy had always liked about the man, perhaps because it reminded him of his father. Quint didn't feel the need to wear who he was on his sleeve. In fact, both men pretty much hid their identities from the world.

He found a place to park, but kept the engine running as he listened to an update on KYW news radio. The shock waves from what the *Daily News* and *Inquirer* tagged as the *E.T. Killings* this morning were eating through the city, blistering people's nerves and torturing their faith. A photograph of the skin painting appeared in both papers beside head shots of Holmes and Trisco, and another of the district attorney as Vega read him his rights. On the other side of the page was a picture of Teddy and Nash, walking out of the house with Rosemary Gibb on the gurney. A graphic was included, detailing the contributions Andrews had taken from the Trisco family.

The two reporters interviewed on the radio said they

smelled blood in the water and worked through the night. What Teddy and Jill had found on the Internet had only been the beginning. Apparently, more than fifty percent of the contributions made to the district attorney's campaign were from employees at the Triscos' various corporations. Several people came forward, confirming what everyone guessed. They'd been forced to write checks to Andrews and were later reimbursed by the corporation in the form of a matching bonus. Details would be published in tomorrow's papers. Eddie, Jr., and his stone-faced wife didn't have time to mourn the death of their infamous son. They were in a legal jam of their own now. Together with Andrews, they'd become the world's next three lepers in a city that didn't really want any.

Teddy switched the radio off, reaching across with his right hand to open the driver's-side door. As he moved, a stabbing pain bit into his shoulder, then relaxed its jaws. He got out of the car, lit a cigarette like a real user, and started for the press line. The two cops working behind the crime scene tape saw him approach and helped him through. Reporters were shouting questions, photographers snapping up pictures and asking him to smile.

He started down the drive, not sure how to handle the press. They needed the story, and he had one to tell. He just wanted a little time to sort things through. Trisco was dead, and Andrews locked up. In spite of this, it didn't feel like it was over. They were still mopping things up. Each new discovery left a bad taste in his mouth, opening memories of his childhood like clams thrown down on a hot grill.

He saw Powell in the distance, standing on the boat launch with a group of men. One of the beneficiaries of last night had been Powell's immediate resurrection in the district attorney's office. She was clearly in charge. As Teddy passed the house, he spotted three vans from the medical examiner's office backed up to the barn like dump trucks waiting for their payload from hell. Crime scene techs were walking in and out of the house and barn. A photographer with spiked hair was getting shots of the brake fluid in the snow, while two techs waited off to the side with their evidence bags ready to go.

He turned back to the lake, following the crime scene tape to the bottom of the hill. The ice had been cut away from the shoreline with chainsaws, and divers were braving the frigid water in their wet suits. The operation was a joint effort among city, local, and state police departments. Teddy looked about for Vega and Ellwood but didn't see them. Of the men standing with Powell, Teddy recognized only two. They'd met the other night in Nash's office. Both men worked out of the FBI's field office in the city. The investigation was running down a single track now.

The agents nodded. The others gazed at him with a certain reach in their eyes. Everyone knew who he was.

Powell turned and gave him a look. She was bundled up in that ski parka, wearing jeans and a pair of leather boots. He knew she'd missed another night's sleep. Still, her blue-gray eyes were bright and steady and he noticed the hint of a sleepy smile buried in her will. Powell looked good—anytime, anywhere, no matter what.

"They let you out," she said.

Teddy nodded. "I don't see Vega or Ellwood."

"Our warrants came through. Vega's over at Andrews's house. We've got another team going through the Trisco's estate in Radnor. Ellwood's in the water with the camera. He dives."

Teddy followed her eyes to a small TV lying in the snow. He hadn't noticed it because the monitor was wrapped in a blue canvas tote case with a hood shading the screen from the stark, winter sun. The monitor was attached to a video recorder. A yellow cable ran from the back of the recorder into the water.

He knelt down with Powell and the others, gazing at what looked like a blank screen. His first thought was that he wished it had been just a bad dream. But as he glanced at the lake, he saw the indentation in the ice where his car broke through. His pulse quickened some and he turned back to the monitor sensing movement on the screen. Ellwood panned the camera through the murky water, and the houses at the bottom began to take on definition. When the faces appeared in the windows, the models Trisco had used for his painting, the camera shook and Teddy noticed that no one on the dock was talking anymore. Other divers swam in and out of the shot, waving the fish away from the nets as they cut the corpses loose and began towing them back to shore. But the bodies weren't just in the windows. Several women had been strapped down to chairs. Others were in the kitchens tied down to stoves, or lying out in bathtubs. Trisco had done more than merely dump his victims here. He'd populated the underwater setting, positioning the corpses as if they were dolls. Teddy imagined Trisco visiting his playground, swimming through the rooms as often as he could.

"How many are there?" Teddy said to Powell.

"Twenty-three," she said with a look. "So far."

Teddy did the math. Darlene Lewis had been the twelfth murder, Harris Carmichael number thirteen. The previous eleven murders could be isolated from the list of missing persons because they shared a similar appearance. Trisco had chosen them as models because they looked like variations of his mother. But Eddie was also collecting tattoos and harvesting skin for his painting. Physical appearance wouldn't have been a consideration with the second group. No trend would have been detected. Trisco could have hung out at any tattoo parlor, strip club, or in Darlene Lewis's case, found her with a computer on the Web.

"Most tattoo artists keep records of their work," Powell said. "Once we've had another look at missing persons, I think we'll have a better idea of who they are. Maybe even a list of names."

"What about Valerie Kram?" he said. "Why do you think he dumped her in the river instead of here?"

"We're working on a time line," she said. "The lake would freeze before the river. She hadn't been in the water very long. Either he had a problem with ice, or he just got lazy and didn't want to drive this far."

Teddy turned back to the monitor and saw a diver swim into the shot and wave Ellwood forward. The nets vanished and his car appeared in the middle of what used to be a street. Teddy grimaced as he stared at the screen. The Corolla was lying upside down beside a streetlight and a stop sign. The trunk was open. Pointing at the tires, the diver grabbed a hose and waved Ellwood closer. Then he made a slicing gesture as if he held a knife in his hand. It was the brake line. Someone had slashed it with a knife.

Teddy had seen enough and stood up. Powell followed him off the boat launch into the yard, her eyes on him.

"Vega called an hour ago," she said in a voice that wouldn't carry. "He's found something at Andrews's place."

"The shot glass?"

She shook her head. "Papers. Records of payments in a notebook."

"To who?"

"Michael Jackson," she said. "The payments weren't big, but they go way back and it adds up."

Teddy took the news in without saying anything. He was still thinking about Valerie Kram's body in the river at the boathouse. The woman who called him and led him there. Dawn Bingle.

"Jackson's not the only name on the list," Powell said. "There's another."

It hung there. Dark and heavy like the sight of his car turned over on the lake bottom.

"Is it a woman?"

Powell nodded.

"Would I know her?"

"I don't think so," she said. "But my guess is that Nash would. She works in the lab. She's a forensic scientist. Her name's Vera Handover."

Something about the glint in Powell's eyes told him all he needed to know. The five cases Nash had been working on when they first met. Each one of them was a death penalty case in which the district attorney may have gotten it wrong.

He remembered Nash telling him about the lack of evidence. In some cases, it had been mishandled. In others, the evidence was lost or destroyed.

"Do you think she's the one who called me?" Teddy asked.

"She's already in custody. You'll have to come in and listen to her voice."

Teddy glanced at the lake and saw Ellwood emerge from the water with his camera. His dark cheeks had a blue tint to them. In spite of the cold, he looked all wound up from what he'd just seen. Teddy turned back to Powell.

"You realize what's happening," he said. "Andrews is gonna take the heat for everything Trisco did."

Powell nodded. "I'd say he's gonna need a good attorney."

Teddy gave her a look and realized she wasn't really thinking about Andrews's attorney. Something in her face had changed. The warmth was gone, and Teddy figured that she had the brass ring on her mind. The *needle*. After she got through with Andrews, he probably wouldn't need a lawyer anymore.

Seventy-two

The steel door clanged shut behind them, and Oscar Holmes, formerly known as the Veggie Butcher, trudged into the prison lobby wearing his own clothes and clutching his sketches, along with several magazines and a stack of mail, close to his chest. His dead eyes flirted with the walls, then zeroed in on the entrance and parking lot outside. His ruined face remained blank, his emotions still in a trancelike sleep. What he'd seen and chosen to forget remained out of reach.

Teddy pushed the door open and they stepped outside. The sun had vanished. Oceans of dark gray clouds were tumbling in from the southwest. As he watched Holmes lumber across the parking lot in silence, he knew Nash had been right. Oscar Holmes wasn't ready for the world just yet.

Teddy pointed to the Ford wagon and they climbed in. Holmes's oversize figure dwarfed the car and the man slid the seat back without a word. Pulling out of the lot, Teddy noticed Holmes staring at the press lined up behind the guard shack outside the gate. Holmes didn't even blink as the strobe lights started flashing. Instead, he turned in the seat, keeping an eye on them and watching the Curran-Fromhold Correctional Facility fade into the background.

Teddy made a left onto the entrance ramp and brought the car up to speed as he eased into heavy traffic on I-95. He wouldn't be driving Holmes to his apartment. Arrangements had been made with his neighbor, the young mother who lived across the hall and stood by Holmes with her daughter from the beginning. They would be spending the holidays at her parents' home in Cape May at the shore. In a week or so, with a little luck, the press might take a step back and give Holmes the breathing room he needed.

At least it sounded good on paper. . . .

Teddy glanced over at the man, still holding his possessions tight to his chest with his large hands. Tears were streaming down the man's cheeks as he stared out the windshield.

"I don't want to see my sister," he whispered. "Don't want to see Barnett either."

"You don't have to, Holmes. You can do anything you want. You're free."

"But they've been calling."

Holmes wiped his cheeks and turned away. Teddy followed his gaze to Holmesburg Prison in the distance. Black smoke could be seen rising from one of the chimneys. Unwilling to face his own demons, Teddy tightened his grip on the wheel and looked away.

"And then there's this," Holmes said.

Teddy felt an envelope drop onto his lap but didn't pick it up. Exiting off the interstate, he wound through a construction zone until he reached Third Street, and found a place to park beneath the Benjamin Franklin Bridge. Holmes's neighbor hadn't arrived yet. He left the motor running, easing the heat back as he opened the envelope and withdrew the letter. Noting yesterday's date at the top, he started reading. It was a business offer, and a large sum of money was on the table. Someone wanted to open a chain of restaurants in the city using Holmes's nickname as the *Veggie Butcher*.

When Teddy glanced over at Holmes, the man actually smiled at the irony.

"I'm gonna need someone to oversee my affairs," Holmes said.

"I'll do whatever you want."

Holmes glanced at the business offer. "I don't want to do that."

Teddy nodded, slipping the letter into his jacket pocket and reaching into the backseat for a paper bag. He handed it to Holmes, who seemed surprised. After a moment, Holmes lowered his sketches and magazines and dug into the package. Teddy had stopped by an art supply house on his way to the prison and bought a variety of paints and brushes. Holmes stared at the gift and appeared overwhelmed.

"Darlene Lewis modeled for you, didn't she?" Teddy said.

Holmes remained quiet, flicking his thumb over a brush.

"I saw your paintings," Teddy said. "The X rays. You knew about the tattoos. Why didn't you say anything?"

"I used to take my time sorting the mail and peeking in the front window. Darlene thought I was looking at her, and sometimes I was. Who wouldn't? Most of the time I was just looking at what they had hanging on the walls."

"But she modeled for you, right?"

"No," he said slowly. "She didn't believe I painted. She teased me about it and called me a fool."

"Then how did you know about the tattoos?"

"On the computer. She told me where the pictures were."

"Why did you end up painting over them?" Teddy asked.

"They didn't come out right. They looked so sad."

Holmes turned away, his eyes lighting up as he noticed a metallic-blue Honda Civic pulling up to a parking meter across the street. Teddy recognized the young girl in the backseat as Holmes's neighbor and looked at the woman behind the wheel. The gray sky was reflecting off the glass and blocking most of his view, but he caught the blond hair, her high cheekbones, a hint of blue in her eyes lost in the clouds. She looked young, gentle, somehow familiar. After a moment, it dawned on Teddy that she had modeled for Holmes as well. The first two paintings Andrews had shown him at the art museum had been of her. Only now, all the melancholy was gone.

Holmes gathered his sketches and paints and opened the door.

"Do you remember what happened?" Teddy said. "Is the day Darlene Lewis died any clearer?"

Holmes shook his head and lowered his voice. "Just his face. The one in the paper. It's the same face I see in my dreams. He's holding a knife and slicing open my hands."

Holmes shivered and gave him a look. The story was rising to the surface in bits and pieces, Teddy thought, like an airline that had broken up and plummeted into the sea.

"You've got my address and phone number at the house, right?"

Holmes nodded.

"What about your medications?"

Holmes tapped his jacket pocket and nodded again. They shook hands. Then he swung the door shut with his knee and crossed the street. Teddy watched him climb into the Civic, hugging the woman and her daughter and kissing them. When they finally drove off, the girl glanced back at Teddy through the rear window, flashed a smile, and waved.

Teddy pushed open the door and found Nash's assistant, Gail Emerson, working at her desk. The door to Nash's office was closed, but voices could be heard from the other side. Gail checked the wall clock and smiled.

"He's in a meeting," she said. "It'll probably go for the rest of the afternoon. Maybe into the night."

"Who's he with?"

"The district attorney's office and three students from the workshop. They're going over their work from last semester."

The five death penalty cases Andrews had been involved

in. The district attorney's office had put the investigation on the fast track.

"Is Carolyn Powell in there?"

Gail shook her head. "It's only a briefing. They want to know what we have."

She gave him a knowing look and smiled again like they had the goods.

"Do you think he'd mind if I went in?"

"I don't think you should, Teddy. But I'll let him know that you stopped by."

Teddy took the hint and walked out. As he stepped into the cold air and started down the sidewalk to his car, he was struck by a feeling of loneliness. He was out of the loop. His role had played out and given way to a kind of emptiness he hadn't experienced since his years as a teenager. He thought a beer might help. Maybe after two or three the pain in his shoulder might fade into the background as well.

Seventy-three

He looked at the note left by his mother on the kitchen counter by the coffeepot. Apparently there had been a lot of calls to the house last night. So many that she decided to switch call-forwarding on and send them directly to his cell phone, not knowing that it was at the bottom of the lake.

As he poured a cup of coffee, Teddy checked the drive and noticed his mother's car was gone. It was after nine and he'd managed to sleep in.

He sat down at the table and picked up the phone, dialing his cell number. Then he punched in his pass code and waited for the digital voice to count his messages and retrieve them. There were fifty-seven. Apparently, the digital voice didn't know that the phone had drowned either.

Teddy leaned back and grabbed the pad and pen off the counter, sipping hot coffee and paging through the messages without listening to them for more than a second or two. Most of the calls were from people he didn't know. Reporters wanting information and requesting interviews. Jill had called from the office and left two messages, once yesterday afternoon, and another this morning. Barnett had even called, announcing his release from the hospital. His voice had a certain perk to it. A fake vitality Teddy found so irritating, he skipped to the next message. But it was the last call that really shook him up. He peered through the steam in his watch, ignoring traces of the lake trapped inside the lens, and realized the message had been left just twenty minutes ago.

Alan Andrews had called. He wanted to meet as soon as possible and said they needed to talk. He was being held at Curran-Fromhold, and guessed that Teddy knew where the prison was.

Teddy thought it over as he gazed through the doorway at the greenhouse his father had built. The additions to the house had been made with precision and remained seamless. His father had been in his prime when he'd been knocked down by a man like Alan Andrews.

He lifted the handset and punched in the direct number to his desk at the office. To his surprise, the line hadn't been changed and Jill picked up after the first ring.

"What's going on?" he asked.

"They've spent the morning tearing apart your office," she said.

"What are they looking for?"

"Your termination notice. First Stokes, then Barnett on crutches. They're looking for the envelope. Stokes put it on your desk and now it's gone. They seem upset. Even frantic."

Teddy detected a certain joy in her voice, but couldn't keep up with her.

"Start at the beginning, Jill."

"Have you seen the papers this morning?"

"No. Not yet."

"You're on the front page," she said. "The story's coming out. They're saying you solved the crime. You saved the girl's life. You're the reason the E.T. Killer is dead, and an innocent man was set free."

"Who's they?"

"Nash, Caroyln Powell, the police, and the FBI—everyone."

Teddy took another sip of coffee without saying anything.

"Barnett and Stokes are looking for the termination notice because they want to tear it up. It makes them look bad that they fired you. Don't you see, Teddy? You and Holmes are famous now."

He thought about the business proposition offered to Holmes. A chain of restaurants opening around town called the Veggie Butcher. The circus was under way, American ingenuity afoot.

"I haven't been in," he said. "I don't have the letter."

"Of course you don't. Stokes changed the locks. Now he's had them changed back again so you won't notice."

He shook his head. Stokes defied explanation.

"Then where's the notice?" he asked.

"In my purse," she said. "I picked it up for you the day Stokes put it on your desk."

He smiled as he listened to her laugh. She'd spent the past few hours watching Barnett and Stokes squirm and probably savored every minute of it. Barnett and Stokes deserved to squirm and more. Much more. And Jill was a good friend.

"I'll see you in an hour," he said.

He crossed the garage and stepped into the elevator, carrying two boxes he'd picked up at the liquor store on his way into town. The law firm occupied the sixteenth and seventeenth floors. He could probably empty his desk and make it out the door before Barnett and Stokes received word that he was even in the building by simply entering the office on the lower level and using the stairs within the firm to avoid passing the receptionist's desk. That was if he cared. But he really didn't.

The elevator stopped at the lobby and a woman entered. He knew her to be a seasoned attorney and partner at another firm on the fourteenth floor. In the past she had never spoken to him. Today she said hello, and even smiled as she got off. The doors closed again, the elevator starting up.

He could feel his heart beating in his chest and became angry at himself as he acknowledged his nervousness. He couldn't work for a man like Barnett. No matter what his financial situation, or the hardships he might face, he couldn't do it.

The elevator opened, and he breezed through the lobby ignoring the people staring at him. From the corner of his eye, he caught the receptionist reaching for her phone.

He legged it down the hallway and into his office, lowering the boxes to his desk. Jill turned from the computer, got up, and gave him a long hug. He felt her lips press against his cheek, then move to his neck, burrowing in. He tightened his grip, holding her in his arms.

"I was so worried about you," she whispered.

"It's over, Jill. It's done."

She pulled away and looked at the boxes. "You're leaving," she said.

He nodded without saying anything, then moved around to his desk. He started with the top drawer, jerking it out and off the rollers and dumping the contents into the first box. As he pushed the drawer back into the desk and yanked out the second, he sensed someone in the doorway and looked up.

Jim Barnett was standing in the hall, dressed in one of his hand-tailored suits from Milan and leaning on two aluminum crutches, his legs now set in plaster casts. He looked pathetic. And Teddy knew that he was using it, milking it, but that it wouldn't work.

Teddy dumped the contents of the second drawer into the box and grabbed the third.

"You're being overly dramatic," Barnett said. "If you want a raise, it's done. If this is because of what I said about your father, then I apologize. I said things I didn't mean."

Teddy dumped the third drawer into the box and reached for another. "Who said anything about money?"

"I mention it because I know you need it. We all do. Some more than others."

Barnett hobbled into the office, irritated when he noticed Jill in the room and realized they weren't alone. Teddy moved on to the next drawer. Unfortunately, nothing Barnett could say would change what the man had done. On the upside, until ten days ago Barnett had treated Teddy like a son. There was something to be said for what he'd suffered after being run over by his car as well. But in the end, Barnett had betrayed his own brother-in-law, selling him out to the district attorney in order to hide their relationship. He'd betrayed Teddy, making the deal with Andrews in secret and allowing Holmes to confess to a crime he'd only witnessed. As Teddy thought it over, he realized the position Barnett was in. Holmes had been innocent. Barnett had sold out a member of his own family in order to maintain his social standing. When the story appeared in the papers, no amount of work by a PR firm could balance the scale. Barnett would be dropped from consideration in *Philadelphia Magazine*'s *Power 100* issue. He'd be bounced off the list. Cast to the side as nothing more than an overeager worm.

"For the sake of your career," Barnett said, "I think you should take some time off and think this through."

Their eyes met. Teddy noticed the man was sweating.

"Whose career are we really talking about?" he said. "And I was fired, remember? I didn't toe the line. You said it yourself, and Stokes did, too. That's what we do here. We toe the line. Somewhere over the last week I realized I'm no good at that."

Teddy finished with the desk and moved to the credenza, closing up photos and collecting bric-a-brac for the second box.

"You weren't fired. Stokes doesn't have the authority. He's old and made a mistake. He was only thinking about the firm."

Teddy shrugged. He closed the second box and lifted it onto the first, thinking about his afternoon meeting with the devil. In an hour, he would be sitting in a visiting room with Alan Andrews. As he stepped around the desk, he glanced at Jill and nodded.

Barnett grimaced. "I'd have to accept your resignation and I won't. You're not thinking clearly. You're out of your mind."

"That makes two of us," Teddy said, passing the man on crutches and leaving him behind.

Seventy-four

Teddy heard the chains beating against the linoleum floor and turned to look through the window into the hall from visiting room two. Alan Andrews, the district attorney, stepped into the room dressed in an orange jumpsuit like any other member of the population at Curran-Fromhold. Only this one remained handcuffed, his ankles bound in leg irons. Two guards escorted Andrews to a chair and helped him sit down at the table across from Teddy, then left the room without closing the door.

They were waiting in the hall, staying close. They looked nervous.

Teddy picked up on the sound of people jeering and looked through the glass at the inmates with their families staring at Andrews outside the booths in the main visiting room. Some appeared angry, others astonished. When he turned back to Andrews, he realized the man's attitude had been confiscated along with his street clothes. He was fidgeting in the seat. His left eye twitched. It had only taken two days in prison to beat the devil down.

"I didn't shoot Eddie Trisco," Andrews whispered in a

shaky voice. "I need your help. You were there. I need people to understand what really happened."

Teddy didn't have any sympathy for Alan Andrews. His decision to meet with him was a result of the emptiness he'd been feeling deep inside himself ever since the night Trisco was found and killed. It was entirely a matter of confronting his own demons. First with Barnett and now with the district attorney. Andrews was the kind of prosecutor who had taken his father away from him so many years ago. Teddy had come here today because he wanted to look the man in the eye. See him behind bars. Gain some degree of resolution, even if it was only secondhand and he'd never had the chance to meet the man who virtually sent his father to his death in a prison cell.

"I know the way it looks," Andrews said. "But I didn't do it."

"How do you think it looks?" Teddy asked.

"Like I'm worse than Eddie Trisco. Like I was in it with him. They think I murdered Trisco to cover it up."

"Trisco was sick," Teddy said. "He couldn't help what he was, but you could. You had a choice."

"I didn't shoot him," Andrews said. "I didn't go there to shoot him."

"When did you know it was him?"

"I didn't. Jesus Christ, kid. When I read the profile and realized you guys were looking for an artist, it scared the shit out of me. I hadn't thought about Eddie Trisco for five years, and I was out on a limb with Holmes."

"How could you have forgotten about Trisco when you were taking payoffs from his parents?"

"Stop calling them payoffs. They were legitimate political contributions. I'd helped them with their son. Five years ago Eddie was just another kid wacked out on drugs. He didn't really hurt the girl, and I didn't think the prison system would do him or anyone else any good. He belonged in a medical setting. A hospital where he could receive treatment. I didn't have any contact with his parents. Their first contribution to my campaign was *after* I made my decision about Eddie. Not before.''

Teddy folded his arms over his chest, ignoring the pain in his shoulder from the gun Andrews had fired at him. ''When did you know it was Trisco?'' he repeated.

''When I read the profile. I could feel that something was wrong. But the evidence kept pointing at Holmes. We knew he was a painter as well, and your profile didn't exactly rule Holmes out. When Jackson met you at his apartment the second time, all you wanted to do is see the paintings. I thought it deserved a closer look and had them moved to the art museum. The X rays seemed to point back at Holmes. When I spoke with Barnett, I agreed to plea the case. But only if Holmes confessed so that I could be sure.''

''Why plea the case? It never made sense that you didn't want to take it to trial.''

''Barnett wouldn't let me speak with Holmes unless we had a deal. I had to give to get. That's the way the world works.''

He was dancing around the issue. He'd need a better answer before his trial.

''When you met with Holmes,'' Teddy said, ''I'm surprised you didn't sense that something was wrong with the man. It seemed obvious to me the moment I met him.''

''Holmes wasn't coerced. I didn't grill him, kid. The confession came quick, like what he'd done had been eating at him and he wanted to spit it out.''

''If you were so sure that it was Holmes, then why did you start looking for Eddie Trisco? And why did you do it in secret?''

''What choice did you give me? You went out to their house, intimating that their son was involved. They called me when you left. I needed to find him to make sure. I needed to see him and talk to him before I could straighten it all out.''

Teddy narrowed his eyes. ''By demoting Carolyn Powell, you mean.''

Andrews didn't respond, his hands trembling.

"You're bullshitting me, Andrews. But it sounds good. With a little polish, maybe it'll work for a jury."

"I have a friend in the lab," he whispered. "When the manager at the café was found, she told me what was going on. A hair sample matched Trisco to the body. His fingerprints were found, a partial anyway, on the frame of a painting at Darlene Lewis's house."

"It would seem that was the time to come forward," Teddy said.

"But I'd fucked the thing up. I couldn't admit it was true. I knew what it looked like when you opened the door."

"But it is the truth, Andrews. It really is. You knew it was Trisco and you didn't say anything. Instead, you tracked him down and murdered him. What do you want to happen? What do you think should happen? People think you're worse than Trisco because you are."

"You're not hearing me, kid. I didn't shoot Eddie Trisco. The basement was like a maze. I heard the shot and opened the door. The gun was on the floor and he was still alive. At the time I thought I'd walked in on a suicide. But now I'm not so sure. Someone else could've been there. Someone else could've fired the gun."

He was reaching at straws. Still playing Teddy for a fool. And he couldn't explain why he'd pointed the gun at him and fired, then hid in a room and attacked him. Or even how the box of hollow-point shells ended up in the glove box of his car. As Teddy mulled it over, he realized that Andrews couldn't explain anything at all. He'd say and do anything to save his skin. His record over the years proved as much.

"Think it over," he said to Andrews as he stood up. "How many people's lives have you wasted and ruined? And for what? Just so that you could climb onto the pile and stand on top."

Teddy walked out of the visiting room. Glancing at his watch, he noticed the date. Even though it was Christmas Eve, he couldn't turn the other cheek or dig any compassion out of an empty hole. He couldn't help it. He hoped the motherfucker would burn.

Seventy-five

Teddy could see the judge pounding his gavel on the bench, the jury pronouncing their verdict, the turmoil that followed in the press, six years of appeals in a case too bizarre not to be real . . . District Attorney Alan Andrews had been convicted of the murder of Edward Trisco III, a serial killer who authorities estimated had tortured and brutally murdered more than two dozen people.

It defied the imagination. Ate at a person's soul, leaving the gristle behind. At a certain point, Andrews withdrew from the courts and finally gave up.

Teddy glanced at Nash sitting beside the pilot, then gazed out the window at the ground, watching the world sweep by in the darkness. They were making the short flight from West Chester to State College. Teddy had made arrangements for the twin-engine plane. Once they landed, a car and driver would be waiting to take them to the execution complex at Rockview prison. Alan Andrews was due to make his exit by lethal injection in less than two hours and they were running late.

It had been a tumultuous six years. . . .

Andrews had also been convicted for two separate

attempts on Teddy's life. When Detective Michael Jackson was confronted with both the payments he'd received from Andrews and his shoe prints found in the snow out at the lake, he copped a deal and admitted cutting the brake lines on Teddy's car. He'd been following orders from Andrews, he said. Although Andrews denied it, and there were suspicions Jackson might be lying to save his own skin, the detective had enough experience in court to appear like a reliable witness and sell his side of the story to the jury. When confronted with hitting Teddy over the head and running Barnett over with his car, Jackson swore he knew nothing about it, took a lie detector test, and passed.

On the second count, not even Andrews denied that he'd pointed a gun at Teddy and fired. His fingerprints were found on the weapon. Gunshot residue had been detected on his right hand. His story that he considered Teddy frightening, that Teddy was armed with a shotgun and wouldn't put the weapon down, that under the circumstances he'd panicked—just didn't gel.

Unlike Michael Jackson, the forensic scientist working in the police lab, Vera Handover, wasn't offered a deal at all. Although Teddy was disappointed that Handover's voice didn't match his memory of Dawn Bingle's, and how he was led to the boathouse remained in question to this day, the investigators didn't need her to talk in order to figure out exactly what she'd done. Nash and his students participating in his legal workshop pointed the way with their research. What they couldn't resolve, Detective Jackson did as part of his agreement. The forensic scientist had taken payments from Andrews that had been recorded in the notebook found in his town house. In return for those payments she'd manufactured evidence and given false testimony in some of his most high-profile cases. She'd acted as part of the team responsible for sending a total of six innocent men to their deaths. In her defense, she said that she thought they were guilty, and at the time, thought she'd been doing the right thing by putting them away. The money amounted to gifts and bonuses from Andrews for a job well done. She hadn't lied in court, she said. Her opinions, particularly in fingerprint analysis, were open to interpretation and she'd done the best she could. As the investigation against her deepened, twelve more bogus cases turned up. Nine men and three women were pulled off death row and set free, while Vera Handover went to jail.

Alan Andrews was about to be executed for a single murder. But everyone knew his death was a result of his professional life in toto. The decisions he'd made along the way. His knack for setting aside the truth in favor of a winning record. Terrorizing a city so that he could score points and look like a hero.

The plane landed smoothly, the drive to Rockview taking less than twenty minutes. Teddy spotted the line of protestors waving hand-painted signs in the air and chanting outside the prison walls. As the driver pulled through the gate, Teddy's eyes stopped on a strange-looking man who stood off to the side. He was holding a flashlight to his Bible and reading the words aloud to anyone who might be listening. It didn't appear that anyone was.

The car pulled to a stop and they got out, following their escort toward the execution complex. As they climbed the steps, Teddy noticed that Nash was walking with a slight limp. When he asked about it, Nash told him he'd slipped on the floor at his gym.

"It's nothing, Teddy. Nothing that won't heal with a little time."

Their escort showed them into the building. After they checked in, they were taken down the hall to the witness room on the first floor. As they entered, only a few seats remained. Although the seats were together, they were in the front row, and Teddy hesitated a moment before following Nash down the aisle and taking his seat.

The witness room was fairly small. Enough seats to keep twenty-five people on edge for the rest of their lives. He turned and looked at the faces. Some he recognized as members of Andrews's family. His mother and sister sitting beside their spiritual advisor. Andrews had never married

and wasn't leaving any children behind. Others he'd seen
in the paper from the families of Andrews's victims. Wives
mostly, who claimed on the news on a nightly basis that
they needed to see the man die just the way their husbands
did. The rest of the audience was filled out with official
witnesses and reporters. The young woman dressed in an
Armani suit with big hair was a new face on one of the
local TV stations. She'd replaced the woman before her who
wore the same clothing, even the same hair, but refused to
get a face-lift when she began to look experienced and
slightly middle aged. As Teddy looked at the young replace-
ment, he noticed her eyes were a little wider than usual
tonight. Maybe she'd stepped into more than she could handle. Maybe life was more important than reading what she
was told to read before the cameras just for the money.

He turned back in his seat and peered through the windows
into the dead room. He was calling it the dead room, even
though Nash had told him more than once that it was still
called an execution chamber. As his eyes roamed back and
forth, it felt more like a stage. More like an operating room
with its tiled walls than a room that had been renovated and
might once have housed a gas chamber or an electric chair.
In fact, Teddy had read somewhere over the past few weeks
that the execution complex at Rockview had once been a
field hospital.

He looked back through the bulletproof glass. A single
chair was bolted into the floor, its design much like that of
an airline seat reserved for first class. An electrical cord ran
from a control box attached to the chair and was plugged
into the wall. Teddy had expected to see a simple gurney.
Instead, someone had built the padded chair specifically for
the purpose of killing people. It looked cold and sterile and
ultramodern—perhaps the work of Frank Lloyd Wright's
ghost. Beside a door on the far wall, a small shelf had been
bolted into the tiles just large enough to hold a desk phone.

Why a desk phone? Why not a simple phone mounted to
the wall?

A man entered the room. An older man dressed like a

surgeon who might even double as a medical examiner. A face mask hung about his neck and he carried a pair of latex gloves. He stepped up to the chair, his eyes avoiding the twenty-five faces staring at him through the windows along the near wall. Then he pressed a button on the console. The chair tilted back and flattened into a lounge. When he pressed a second button, the curtains behind the windows closed.

"They're bringing Andrews out," Nash whispered. "It'll only be a few minutes now."

Teddy shivered in his seat, wondering if he could remain in the audience and watch the man die. He dug his hand into his pocket, pulling a small photograph out. It was a picture of his father. He'd taken it himself with a 35mm camera as they walked through the open field across the street from the house, rooting out pheasants hidden in the tall grass and watching the birds take flight. He looked into his father's eyes and stroked his face with his finger. This is how he remembered him. Wearing a leather jacket with the collar turned up. The carefree smile on his face with the afternoon sun whisking through his windblown hair.

Teddy had found some degree of closure over the past six years. On a weekend during Andrews's first trial, he'd removed the accordion file from his mother's closet and taken it into his bedroom. He'd always known she kept a record of what happened to his father, saved the stories that appeared in the newspapers, but he could never look at them before. As he read about his father's arrest and eventual death in prison, questions remained. He sought out the prosecutor, an ADA named Stephen Faulk, but couldn't find him. From what he'd read, his mother had been right. Faulk was young and trying to make a name for himself in Chester County. Teddy's father had been a man of good reputation and looked like a big prize. When Teddy asked her about it, she said that the prosecutor died a long time ago. He saw the look in her eyes, the hurt flaring up again, and didn't want to press her for details unless he had to.

And so he began searching out what happened to Stephen Faulk on his own. He started with the local police department, but no one could tell him any more than what his mother had. Faces changed with the passage of time, and those who remained didn't appear very interested or talkative. This surprised Teddy. For almost half his life, every time he'd seen a cop pass the house, he thought the story was the only thing on their minds. After several weeks of getting nowhere, Teddy went to the library and spent a day going through microfilm archives from the *Daily Local News*, a newspaper based in the county. His mother had stopped saving press clippings on the day of his father's death. But it was the next two weeks that told the story. Faulk had pressed the detectives working the case for an arrest. He held press conferences on a daily basis, and used every opportunity to try the case in the papers before a court date was even set. It was obvious to Teddy that Faulk had a chip on his shoulder, and one reporter described his voice as shrill. But after his father died, everything changed. The accountant came forward, overcome with guilt, admitting that he was the real murderer, not Teddy's father. Faulk actually tried to discount the confession, but local and county detectives took issue with the prosecutor and fought back. The controversy went on for a week or so, spilling into the press until the county decided they'd had enough and fired the man. Three days after that, Faulk's body was found behind the wheel of his car with the garage door closed and the engine running. The piece of shit took the easy way out and ate the pipe.

Teddy's nightmares seemed to vanish after he found out what happened. He threw himself into his career, looking after Oscar Holmes's interests, but spending most of his time in the courtroom as a criminal defense attorney. Small cases at first, with Nash guiding him through the process. As his experience grew, his practice began to flourish. Oftentimes Nash would take a day off from teaching to sit in the courtroom and watch. After each trial, particularly in the beginning, Nash would offer his detailed critique over a pot of hot coffee in the office. When Teddy began to hit his stride a year or so ago, they switched to good wines and broadened the discussion.

As he gazed at the photograph, he wished his father were here to see how things turned out. He wished his father could see that he was on his own and doing okay. He was managing his debt, living in an apartment in the woods in Radnor on County Line Road—a large house built well over a hundred years ago that had been cut into apartments, couldn't pass the zoning laws, but no one in the neighborhood talked about. His mother seemed to have come into her own as well. She and Quint had someone new to paint with. A new friend in Oscar Holmes. Oftentimes when Teddy stopped by for a visit, he'd find them in the studio painting together. Holmes had married his neighbor and adopted her daughter. Although he was managing to make a small living from his artwork, he remained psychologically damaged from his ordeals with Alan Andrews and Eddie Trisco. Even worse, people still pointed at him on the street at times and called him the Veggie Butcher. Teddy's mother was perhaps the only person on earth who understood what he was going through, and his frequent visits to the house seemed to help both of them.

The curtain opened to the dead room.

Teddy closed his hand around the photograph and slipped it into his pocket. As he looked at Andrews through the window, he realized his seat was too close. Less than three feet away.

Andrews had lost weight since the last time he saw him, and his skin was considerably more pale. He was strapped down to the chair, but seemed to be resting comfortably beneath a sheet. The doctor was wearing eye protection now, and the face mask was drawn tight over his mouth. The two appeared to be speaking as the doctor rolled the electrocardiogram closer and checked the wires attached to Andrews's chest.

Teddy's eyes flicked down to Andrews's arms. A single

IV was attached to each just above his wrists. Curiously, the plastic tubes connected to the needles snaked around the chair into a small opening on the far wall. Above the opening was another window, but the curtains remained drawn.

The lights dimmed in the witness room. Teddy's focus shifted to the reflections on the glass. He could see the people sitting behind him, their faces taut and still. Some were wiping their eyes with handkerchiefs. Others looked defiant. A woman in the back row, perhaps the reporter, started coughing and couldn't seem to stop.

He checked his watch. Six fifty-eight P.M. A man in a uniform who Teddy guessed was the warden entered the dead room and stood by the telephone. It seemed like a formality because everyone knew that the governor had presidential aspirations. Executions were an image consultant's dream and an important step if you were going to make a run as president of the free world. Odds were that the governor wouldn't be making any calls from his mansion in Harrisburg tonight.

Teddy's eyes drifted to the left and he noticed another window. Another witness room. He saw Detectives Vega and Ellwood behind the glass, along with District Attorney Carolyn Powell. She seemed edgy and vulnerable, but most of all, she looked tired. Teddy hadn't seen her for a couple of years. Their relationship hadn't survived his decision to practice criminal law as a defense attorney, or her promotion and election to the new job. For Carolyn, the prosecution of Andrews seemed to draw her into a cocoon and tighten her up. For Teddy, the trial had been a release. They still checked in with each other every couple of months or so, but never mentioned getting together for another round of martinis. It had become his drink of choice now. And he hadn't ordered one in six years without thinking of her or remembering that night they spent together.

A light mounted on the far wall started blinking, and the speakers on the wall were switched on.

The warden glanced at the doctor, then asked Andrews if he would like to make a statement. Andrews declined with a simple shake of the head. As the two men left the room and the door closed, Andrews settled in beneath his restraints and took a deep breath. He was alone. Ready for the deepest of sleeps to begin.

Then the curtain opened in the window on the far wall, revealing three men wearing black hoods. As Teddy noticed them, he tried to remind himself that he was living in a civilized world. Still, the image of their eyes peering out from beneath their hoods in the anteroom behind Andrews was horrifying. He knew what they were doing. He was well aware of the process. The execution team comprised three prison employees. Two would be feeding Andrews a drug cocktail that would lead to an overdose and wash away the spark of life. The third would be feeding a dummy bag with the lethal brew. In the end, no one would be certain exactly who wiped out Andrews's life.

Teddy thought he knew when the sodium Pentothal hit the man's arm and made the big push. Andrews was fighting the anesthetic, but at fifty times the dosage in a normal operation, his eyes finally wavered and became lazy. Drifting across the ceiling, they floated down the wall until they passed over the window and penetrated the glass. He was searching out the faces in the audience, moving from one to the next in the dim light. He was lingering on some and passing over others until his eyes found Teddy in the front row and slid to a sleepy stop.

Teddy flinched. A wave of fear buzz-touched his spine, rattling across the back of his neck. The seconds ticked by in shivers. Almost a full minute. Andrews was staring at him. Giving him a last look before he let go and said good-bye to the witness who did him in. The expression on his face wasn't hard, but unexpectedly gentle and relaxed. It seemed to last forever, and in a sense, it was.

When his eyes finally smoked out like a candle, Teddy thought he was dead and checked the monitor. To his surprise, Andrews's heart continued beating. It took ten minutes for the pancuronium bromide to paralyze his diaphragm and collapse his lungs. A few minutes more before the potassium chloride reached his heart and pulled the last switch. Then the glint in his eyes shifted and faded and rolled off to the side, becoming lost in the distance of forever.

The chaos was over. The battle lost. The decision final.

After a moment, the doctor entered the room and walked over to the chair without glancing at Andrews's corpse or the faces staring at him through the window. Teddy watched his hand drop to the console. When he pressed the button, the curtain closed.

Seventy-six

In spite of its length, most of the trip back to Philadelphia was spent in silence. As they drove from the airport into the city in Nash's new Jaguar, Teddy noticed the crowds on the sidewalks and wondered what was going on at midnight. Then Nash pointed at a man on the corner waving a sign. ALAN ANDREWS IS DEAD. They were partying. Celebrating. Dancing in the streets.

Ding, dong, the witch is dead.

Teddy looked away, trying to keep his mind busy until they reached Nash's office. There was the promise of a glass of wine. Teddy expected it would take more than one glass to settle his nerves.

Nash pulled into his space in the lot behind the building. As they climbed the stairs and entered the office, Nash switched on the lights and headed straight for the cabinet beside his desk. His limp was less noticeable, but still there.

"I don't think champagne's necessarily appropriate tonight. Let's see what we've got."

Nash searched through the bottles until he found one to his liking. Then he pulled two glasses out of the cabinet and fished through a drawer for the corkscrew. Teddy moved to the jury table, lit a cigarette, and sat down. He'd quit smoking a few years ago, but bought a pack for the night.

"I've got something I think might cheer you up," Nash said.

"If it's the wine, I'm ready."

Nash laughed. "It's old. Let's hope it hasn't turned. But I wasn't thinking about the wine."

He pulled the cork and carried the glasses over, filling each glass to the brim as he often did if they were drinking alone. Teddy tapped Nash's glass with his own and took a first sip. The wine tasted clean and rich, and he glanced at the label as he swallowed another large mouthful. It was a Chateau La Mission Haut Brion that had been bottled nineteen years ago.

His eyes moved to the window behind Nash's desk. He could see the E.T. House lit up in the distance. The house had been given the name and title by the curious, who still drove by for a look at the place on weekends. Nash followed his gaze and smiled at the irony of Trisco living within view of the office, his own desk, and the window that often served as a looking-glass.

"I have something I want to show you," he said.

Nash opened the doors to the library, and Teddy followed him inside. At the other end of the main aisle a new set of double doors had been installed. Nash sipped his wine and opened them. What had always been a storage room was now a second office as large as Nash's and completely refinished. Teddy glanced at the desk and table, the view of the E.T. House outside this window as well.

"We have another case, Teddy. Something fascinating. It involves traveling to Dallas, Washington, maybe even L.A. It will require a great deal of investigation. I think it's something we can both sink our teeth into."

Teddy finished off his glass, overwhelmed by the prospect of sharing offices with Nash. He realized that his mentor had been guiding him to this point in his life. That his friend thought he was ready to make an important leap. The next big step. When he noticed that Nash's glass was empty as well, he smiled and told him he'd get the bottle and his cigarettes so that they could celebrate.

Teddy bolted through the library into Nash's office. His new partner's office. As he rushed over to the jury table, his foot knocked over a walking stick leaning against one of the chairs and he watched it skid across the hardwood floor. He set his glass on the table and reached for the cane, hoping he hadn't broken the thing and worried about his friend's limp. When the metal tip dropped away from the shaft, he picked it up feeling guilty and gave it a quick glance.

His chest tightened. Everything stopped.

Teddy stared at the tip of the cane in the palm of his hand for a long time. It was made of Sterling silver. He noted the etchings and recognized the tall ships and whales. The last time he'd set his eyes on it, he'd thought he was looking at an antique shot glass. But it had been dark that night. Blood was strewn all over the snow.

"It was my father's," Nash said in a quiet voice from behind his back. "I probably should've gotten rid of the thing, but it had sentimental value and time had passed. With the understanding you've gained over the years, I wonder if it's relevant at all."

Teddy was afraid to turn around. He gritted his teeth and imagined himself fleeing across the ocean's surface, the backs of sharks his only footing. He looked at the lithograph on the wall—the empty prison cell—pulling himself together as he turned to face his new partner. His mentor and friend.

Nash stood in the doorway, studying him with a faint grin on his face and those dilated eyes of his.

"You're upset," Nash said, glancing at the cane in Teddy's hand. "Maybe we should talk it over."

Nash crossed the room, taking the cane away from him and leaning it against the far wall. His movements were casual, even graceful as he refilled each glass. Teddy stood motionless, keeping his eyes on Nash as he finally slid a chair away from the jury table and sat down.

"You ran over Barnett," Teddy heard himself saying in a hollow voice.

"He's a pimp, Teddy. He wanted Holmes to plead guilty to a crime he hadn't even committed. Come on. You've thought about this yourself a hundred times. I find your attitude astonishing."

"I didn't try to kill him," Teddy whispered.

"I didn't either, but other people's lives were at stake. All I wanted to do is get the fool out of the way so that we could get started. He slipped on the ice. He got hurt, but survived. In the end it all worked out. Holmes is free and Rosemary Gibb's alive and well."

Teddy shuddered, playing back Barnett's *accident* in his head and realizing for the first time that what Andrews had told him in prison was probably true. Someone else had shot Eddie Trisco.

Nash set the wine bottle down. "If this is about me giving you that whack over the head, then please accept my apology. At the time, it couldn't be helped."

Teddy wasn't thinking about being beaten unconscious. "I met Andrews in prison," he said. "He told me that he thought someone else could've been in the house the night Trisco was killed."

"You mean murdered, don't you, Teddy? Alan Andrews was executed tonight for the murder of Edward Trisco the Third."

Nash seemed amused. He took another sip of wine and lit a cigarette from Teddy's pack. Teddy ignored the smirk, forcing himself to keep going.

"I met him two days after it happened," Teddy said. "Andrews told me that he heard the shot and found Trisco on the floor when he entered the room. Someone else put the gun to Trisco's head and pulled the trigger. Someone else planted the box of hollow-point shells in Andrews's car."

"Given what we know, Teddy, I'd say that's entirely possible. I believe the defense attorney at his trial raised the same point. No one paid much attention to him though. Not after your testimony as an eyewitness.''

It hung there. Teddy's role as the prosecution's eyewitness.

"That person is *you*," Teddy managed.

Nash seemed delighted by the news, casually wiping a fallen ash from his sleeve. It took Teddy's breath away.

"You set Andrews up from the beginning. Ever since I met you.''

"I don't hate the man," Nash said in an even voice. "I loathe him. And I guess after what happened tonight I should get used to speaking about him in the past tense. When we left the prison this evening, the man looked quite dead. The world is a better place without Alan Andrews. I've been following his career for a long time. Long before you and I ever met. Why do you suppose he was the subject of my legal workshop? I never hid my distaste for Andrews. I did everything I could to make it public.''

"But he died tonight for something he didn't do. . . .''

"Oh, really? After all that's happened, is that what you really think?'' Nash tapped the ashtray with his cigarette and briefly watched the head burn. "You might have a hard time convincing the families of his victims, Teddy. They died for something they didn't do as well. Something they never even asked for. What happened tonight seems more poetic than what you're suggesting. Andrews got what he gave out. Nothing more and nothing less would really do.''

"What about the missing women? The murders? The bodies? That fake call from Dawn Bingle wanting to meet me at the boathouse?''

Nash stopped to consider the sudden barrage of questions. "You're thinking I used you," he said after a moment.

Teddy nodded without saying anything. As he played it all back in his head, it seemed so clear now.

"It wasn't planned, Teddy. Much of it happened as we went along. After you've had a chance to think it over, I'm sure you'll agree that it was the only way. I found Valerie Kram's body quite innocently a few days before Darlene

Lewis's murder while on a walk along the bike path by the river. There's a bench on the other side of the boathouse I like to use. I saw her in the ice as I sat down."

"Why didn't you call it in?"

"She was frozen in the ice. She wasn't going anywhere. And it would've been a distraction. I was thinking about the work my students had done. I didn't come forward because I didn't want it to interfere with the findings we were about to make public regarding the district attorney. It would have confused the issue if I'd called the police and used my name. But with the Lewis murder and Holmes's arrest, everything changed. I was hoping someone at the club might find the girl's body, but a day passed and no one did. Then you showed up at my office. You were following Barnett's lead, ready to send Holmes off to prison for the rest of his life without even questioning what happened. I thought you needed a wake-up call. I asked a friend, and she was only too happy to oblige."

"You say it wasn't planned, but you knew about the body at the boathouse. You must have known it was a serial killing."

"I suspected it when Darlene Lewis was murdered," Nash said. "I was struck by their likeness, but wasn't sure."

"When you printed the bulletins on the missing girls, when you laid the flyers out on this table, it was a charade for my benefit. You already knew."

Nash shrugged. "I wasn't sure," he repeated. "Not until then."

"When did you know it was Trisco?" Teddy said.

"The same time you did. Actually a little later. You solved the riddle, Teddy, not me. When you told me that it was Trisco, that's when I knew. You've got talent. An authentic gift. Instincts and an imagination most attorneys would die for. Let's leave it at that."

Teddy became silent, trying to slow his mind down. He was rushing over the details and missing them. He remembered the press leak detailing what the authorities thought Holmes had done to Darlene Lewis at the time of her murder.

Teddy had always blamed Andrews for the leak, but now he realized it had come from Nash. The city was up in arms over the brutality of the girl's death. Leaking the details stirred the pot, pushing Andrews further out on the limb with his case against Holmes. Nash had pushed Andrews to the point of no return because he thought Holmes was innocent and knew how the district attorney would react. Nash had had the man cornered. But still it wasn't enough and the district attorney could have slipped through.

Teddy remembered what Andrews had told him in prison. After reading their profile, Andrews had been stunned. He had the evidence against Holmes, but wasn't certain. He'd gone to Trisco's house trying to verify his mistake, gone in secret because he'd been afraid to admit that he had the wrong man. In the end, Nash pulled the trigger and killed Trisco because he knew it would change everything. Nash knew what it would look like before anyone else did.

"I'm surprised at you, Teddy. Maybe a better word would be concerned. You don't seem to understand that society has great difficulty in dealing with a man like Alan Andrews. The powers that be can barely handle someone as obvious as Eddie Trisco. How could anyone become that ill without someone noticing and doing something about it? But the former district attorney, the late Alan Andrews, is an entirely different matter. There are lots of Alan Andrewses in the world, more than you think. People who will destroy evidence, suppress it, or even make it up in order to win their verdict because in their head they *know*. Or what about the prosecutor who makes an honest mistake, but doesn't have the strength or integrity or conscience to correct it? Society doesn't punish people like this because it doesn't want to admit that they even exist. I can assure you that what I may or may not have done would've been performed only as a last resort. What Alan Andrews did is far worse than what Eddie Trisco did because of his intent. Had Andrews been on top of things when Trisco was first arrested, not one woman would've been murdered. The idea of watching society reward the man by making him mayor of the city—

well, thank goodness neither one of us has to sit on the sidelines and watch that. You should know all this better than most. You've had a firsthand view. Your experience with your father. His arrest and untimely death.''

It was the way he said it that shook Teddy to the bone. Mentioning his father so easily and the way he spoke about Andrews's demise as if he suffered no guilt or regret. Nash had acted as judge and jury, sentencing Andrews to death as if it were a calling from a higher order. And while much of what Nash was saying seemed familiar to Teddy, even true in the cosmic sense, the implications of his behavior were impossible to deal with.

Teddy's eyes rose from the floor. Nash was looking him over carefully.

''What's happened since we met was never about catching a serial killer like Eddie Trisco,'' Nash said after a long moment. ''Or even about hunting down a district attorney who lost his way and put innocent people to their deaths. It was about us, Teddy. I came back for you. I came back to help you get past your father, shed your demons, and show you the way out.''

Teddy steadied himself against the wall, riding on the train through the tunnel into the black.

''What way is that?'' he asked.

''When you walked into my office with the Holmes case, I knew who you were. And it was obvious that you were still running. Your father was falsely accused of murdering his business partner. Your father was murdered in his cell as he awaited trial. Your father's murder changed a lot of people's lives in this city. Not just yours.''

Teddy wiped his eyes, no longer trying to hide the fact that his hands were shaking. ''What do you know about my father? Who are you talking about? Whose life was changed?''

''Mine,'' Nash said. He stubbed the cigarette out, then leaned back in the chair and gave Teddy a hard look. ''You see, I was responsible for his death.''

Teddy's mind blurred and almost faded. ''The prosecutor's name was Stephen Faulk,'' he said. ''The man's dead. He committed suicide.''

''I was an ADA at the time,'' Nash said, gazing into the past. ''It was Faulk's case, but he was young and didn't make the decision on his own. He came to me with what he had. I reviewed the case with the district attorney, but still had a lot to learn. I didn't see it and made a mistake. When the county jail was faced with overcrowding, I made arrangements with the city and had your father transferred to Holmesburg Prison. Don't you see? I'm the one who put him in that cell.''

It hit like napalm, the flames stretching out in a fiery wash that clung to Teddy's flesh and burned his soul.

''That mistake changed everything for me,'' Nash whispered. ''Words can't describe how sorry I am. I've spent my entire life trying to right that wrong. And now we're together, and I'm hoping you won't burn down. You won't be a victim of your past. Instead, I'm hoping you'll learn from it, Teddy, fight back and join the cause. We've got work to do. Enough to keep us going for a long time.''

Nash eased Teddy's wineglass across the table as an offering to their partnership. Teddy spotted his cigarettes beside the glass. They seemed so far away. He wasn't sure he could move, really. He wasn't sure he could reach them . . . .